To Liz,
Best Wishes,

Sleeping Dogs

Chris Simms

CHRIS SIMMS

Copyright © 2014 Chris Simms

The right of Chris Simms to be identified as the author of this work has been asserted by him in accordance with the Copyright, Designs and Patents Act 1988.

All rights reserved.

ISBN-10: 1503365050
ISBN-13: 978-1503365056

DEDICATION

In fond memory of Courcey and Nanna: two special people from an incredible place.

'The name drifts across the mind like cloud shadows on a mountainside.'
Tim Robinson, *Connemara*

PART I

CHAPTER 1

Trees stood gnarled and naked beneath a dead winter sky. Everything was still: mist hanging motionless above grass made white by the cold. Jon Spicer looked around for his Boxer dog, Punch. The animal's nose was low to the ground, legs moving fast as it sped along the zigzagging trail of a rabbit long gone.

Trying to keep up was his six-year-old daughter, Holly. Her bright red wellies made it difficult to cope with the sudden changes of direction and with each turn she let out a breathless giggle, the sound contrasting sharply with the park's subdued air.

'So, could it have been him?' asked Alice, her voice low.

His eyes went to his wife and he let his gaze linger on the smoothness of her skin. She was wearing a knitted beret, the wool dyed with a rich mix of russet and maroon. The colours seemed to emphasise the blondness of her hair, fine strands of it hanging over the raised collar of her quilted coat.

It was lucky, he reflected, that she had chosen such a loose-fitting style; the swell of her stomach was now plain to see beneath it. Another two months and their second child would be born. Before he could reply, she glanced up at a point somewhere near his ear.

'Here,' she frowned, 'your scarf is all twisted at the back.' Twirling a finger, she indicated that she wanted him to turn round. He did as she asked, bending his knees to make it easier for her to reach up. Fingers probed at the back of his neck.

'Cow!' he gasped, straightening as a fragment of ice slipped down his back to lodge in the waistband of his boxer shorts.

She let out a cackle of laughter and he span around, tugging at the back of his trousers. 'No!' His eyes widened as he felt it slide lower. 'It's in with the crown jewels!'

Half-doubled with laughter, she started backing away.

He kicked a foot about and, finally, the freezing shard fell out the leg of his trousers. 'Where did you get that?' he giggled, raising his arms and closing in on her.

'Pregnant woman! Pregnant woman!' she gasped, directing a finger at her stomach. 'You can't get me!'

He dropped his hands, the questioning look still on his face.

Wiping a tear from her eye, she pointed to the group of trees they'd just emerged from. 'The frozen puddle back there.'

Holly called across, a confused smile on her face. 'What are you doing?'

'Just putting a spring in your daddy's step,' Alice replied, tugging on Jon's sleeve. Their daughter looked at them for a moment longer before turning away. They resumed their slow walk.

'Had it really gone right inside your grundies?' Alice smiled.

'Yes,' he said through gritted teeth. 'Touching my plums, it was.'

She giggled. 'Well, that'll teach you for getting me up the duff again.' A hand touched her bump as she let out an amused sigh. 'Where were we? Oh yeah,' her voice dropped, 'you weren't sure if it was your grandad or not.'

He felt his smile fade. 'I'm pretty certain it was him,' he replied, relieved the dank conditions meant the sound of his voice couldn't carry. 'But there's only that one photo in mum's house – taken God knows when, where he's tucked away in the background. He must be knocking on ninety, now.'

Alice linked a gloved hand through the crook of his elbow. 'Was the person like you? I mean in size. In that photo he looks pretty big.'

Jon thought about his own height. Six feet four and now knocking on sixteen stone; still mostly muscle. He knew about his great-grandfather, Padraig. The giant navvy who, back in the early 1900s, had gathered enough money through bare-knuckle fighting to get his family out of the Manchester slum known as Little Ireland.

How, he reflected, did the man he thought was his grandfather compare? 'He was tall,' Jon stated. 'And heavily built, once. You could tell that from the size of his hands.' He lifted his own thick fingers, most of which bore nicks and scars. The legacy of a lifetime spent playing rugby. Stamps from the opposing team's boots. He examined the old wound running across one thumb – caused when a punch he'd thrown had caught on the other player's tooth. 'Called me a wee fucker, he did.'

'You what?' Alice's voice was incredulous.

Jon chuckled. 'He was just sitting there in a porch-type thing, staring out across the bay. Making the most of his view while it lasts.' He looked off to the side, checking for Holly and Punch. 'Someone's building a dirty great house on the plot of land directly in front of his bungalow. Once it goes up, he won't be able to see anything at all.'

'Why did he swear at you?'

'I was standing there – a stranger wearing trousers and a ski jacket. I think he mistook me for the site manager or something.'

'Obviously not happy with it being built, then.'

'Neither would you be, Ali. The thing will dominate everything.' A snapshot of the tiny fishing village appeared in his head: a row of pastel-coloured buildings overlooking a quiet bay lanced by a short stone pier. Feeling cold air on his neck, he tucked his scarf back into the collar of his coat. They were now on Heaton Moor golf course, following the footpath that clung to its outer edge. Away to their left loomed the faint form of Mauldeth Hall, a phantom in the haze. Holly was jogging towards them, cheeks flushed. 'So,' he continued more quickly. 'How do you reckon I should mention it to mum? She might hit the roof I've been out there or she might be relieved to know he's still alive.'

'I don't know,' Alice murmured. Then, more quickly; 'But, tread carefully, Jon, whatever you do.' She turned to Holly. 'Hi gorgeous, you OK?'

'Can I have a sweetie now? You said once we got to the golf course.'

'I did,' Alice replied, reaching into her pocket for the mini-pack of Jelly Babies. Bribes given at set intervals to lure their daughter along.

As Holly peered into the bag, trying to decide which colour to choose, Jon's mind went to the reason he'd made the trip over to Ireland in the first place. His wayward younger brother, Dave, had been murdered a few years before. During what turned out to be the last years of his life, he'd formed a relationship with a troubled young woman called Zoë. The two of them had made a home of sorts and she'd given birth to a boy who they'd named Jake.

But Zoë had always found it hard to care properly for her son, and, unable to cope with the news of Dave's death, she'd simply abandoned the boy and disappeared. Jon's parents had taken guardianship of Jake, the youngster seeming to act as some kind of substitute for their murdered son.

For the next four years they'd heard nothing from Zoë.

Then, in the summer, a postcard arrived. On it, she'd written that she was travelling over to Ireland to find a friend who also used to sleep rough on the streets of Manchester. The friend's name was Siobhain. Zoë had heard she was now living in Clifden, a small town that, like Roundstone, was in Connemara.

A few weeks after that another postcard had arrived, this one sent from the city of Galway. The image on the front was of a narrow cobbled lane, both sides lined with cafés and bars. Zoë had written that Galway was great – she was hanging round the city for a while to earn money by working in a pub, then she was getting a bus out to Clifden where she'd start trying to find Siobhain. The postcard had ended with a few kisses for Jake, crammed in the corner almost as an afterthought.

And that had been all they knew about Zoë's whereabouts until the call from a few nights before. It was almost midnight when the phone had started to ring. A woman with an Irish accent was on the other end of the line. Quickly explaining that her name was Siobhain, she pleaded that Jon come to Clifden straight away. Zoë was out of her depth with some very nasty people. He had to get her out of there, fast.

His mind snapped back to the present and he glanced about. His wife was now a few metres ahead of him. 'Alice, where's Holly?'

She paused and looked around. A small frown appeared on her face. 'I think she ran off after Punch. Over there.'

Jon looked to his left, feeling the familiar tickle of unease whenever he lost sight of his daughter in a public place. On the other side of the fairway was a tight screen of laurel bushes. Beyond that was the golf course's clubhouse. Sure enough, a twin trail of pawprints and footprints led across the silvery grass and through a narrow gap in the hedge. 'Probably helping Punch find his tennis ball – it got lost somewhere over there yesterday.'

Cupping his hands round his mouth, Jon set off towards the far end of the bushes. 'Holly! Where are you? Punch! Here, boy!'

He stared at the mass of green leaves, waiting for the pair of them to reappear. Aside from a couple of golfers ambling towards the nearby green, nothing moved. Jon was about to call again when a terrified scream pierced the air. His heart jolted in his chest. Holly! The noise came again, this time even higher. He broke into a run.

Further down the fairway, the two golfers had stopped to stare beyond the laurel screen. Then one clapped both hands to the top of his head. A gesture of impending disaster.

'What?' Jon shouted in their direction, still running.

The other golfer simply shook his head in horror.

His daughter's scream abruptly died away and he rounded the far end of the bushes. What he saw caused him to falter, then stop.

A grassy area stretched away before rising steeply to the perimeter of the clubhouse car park. Holly was motionless, half-way across, standing with her back to him. Closing slowly in on her was a dog like no other Jon had ever seen.

My God, he thought, it's massive. Bigger than my girl. Its muzzle was black, the dark fur spreading up to encompass deeply-set amber eyes. Two cropped ears looked like a pair of sharp horns. Teeth bared, it edged nearer to Holly like a leopard about to strike. Jon looked wildly about for its owner, for anyone. There was no one to call it off.

Holly's hands were clamped over her ears and he knew that her eyes would be tightly shut: her standard response to anything scary. As Jon gauged distances a sickening realisation hit home. I'm too far away to stop this. He started forward, waving his arms and yelling in desperation. 'Get away from her! Get away!'

Eyes not leaving Holly, the beast flattened its ears and sank down on its haunches.

SLEEPING DOGS

'No!' Jon bellowed. 'No!'

From the direction of the clubhouse, a bolt of brown entered the edge of Jon's vision. Punch. His pet's paws made a rapid drumming sound as it hurtled straight at the other dog. The thing's spadelike head swung round and it circled to calmly face the Boxer.

Punch streaked closer, seeming like a toy dog in comparison. Jon could only look on helplessly as, at the last moment, the other dog leapt forward. The two animals met in mid-air with a loud and meaty slap. Punch instantly went backwards and they transformed into a snarling blur of limbs and teeth.

The terrible sound broke the spell which had paralysed Holly and she looked over her shoulder. 'Daddy, Daddy, Daddy!'

He scooped her clear of the thrashing animals. 'You're OK.' Running back towards the laurels, Holly's red boots banged against his knees. Her arms grasped his neck tightly and she started sobbing in his ear.

The sound of fighting continued behind him as Alice appeared at the screen's end, one hand on her stomach, face full of fear. Eyes widening, she took in Jon and her daughter coming towards her. 'What...?' She looked beyond them and all colour vanished from her cheeks.

By the time Jon had covered the last of the ground, the snarling had been replaced by a series of yelps. 'Take her!' He extricated himself from his daughter's grip and thrust her towards Alice, now aware the noise had dropped to a desperate whining mixed with a deeper, throaty growl. The sound a dog made when its jaws had locked on another.

Alice clutched Holly to her chest and Jon turned. The beast had Punch pinned to the grass, mighty jaws clamped over his Boxer's throat as it shook its huge head back and forth. Jon saw Punch's hind paws weakly brushing at the creature's underside, more of a spasm than a kick. He was about to start running back when a whistle sounded.

The dog immediately released its grip. Its bloodied

muzzle came up and, with an agility that seemed impossible for something of its size, it bounded effortlessly away towards the car park.

Jon's eyes went back to Punch. Oh Jesus. His dog was lying on its side, head bent back, most of one ear missing. The coat around its head, neck and shoulders was torn open in several places, little curls of steam rising from the wounds.

One of the golfers appeared at the other end of the bushes, a mobile phone in his hand. 'My wife's a vet! She works close to here!'

The creature was now near the top of the incline. Parked with its rear bumper against the kerb was a dirty white van, back doors wide open. Inside the gloomy interior Jon could make out the silhouette of a man. He was kneeling down, slapping the metal side of the van in encouragement. From a distance of fifteen feet or so, the animal leapt up, sailing through the air to land inside the vehicle, paws thudding on what must have been a carpeted floor.

The man leaned forward, flicked a little salute in Jon's direction and started swinging both doors shut. 'Go!'

Jon registered the slightly squeaky pitch of his voice. I've heard that somewhere before.

Engine revving, fumes began to belch from the vehicle's exhaust. Jon ran to Punch and fell on his knees. His dog was still breathing but had now started to shiver violently. Shock, Jon thought. From the first-aid courses he'd done, he knew that – given enough blood loss – any mammal will go into shock. Soon after, the major organs would start shutting down. He whipped his coat off and tucked it round the animal. Blood was pumping out of a deep tear in Punch's throat. He pulled a handkerchief from his pocket and pressed against the wound. 'Punch, it's OK. You hear me? It's OK. I'm here.'

He could see no reaction and bent forward to look directly into Punch's big brown eye. Memories of getting the animal as a puppy from the rescue centre returned. The awkward way it had bounded about, paws too big for its legs, sheer joy propelling it round the house.

'Punch,' he whispered, voice hoarse. 'Punch. Come on, boy, please.' He touched his forehead against the top of the animal's head. 'Come on, Punch.'

The van's engine roared louder and Jon glanced up. A rag had been draped over the rear registration plate and he could only watch as the vehicle lurched across the car park, aiming for the narrow lane that led back to Mauldeth Road. 'Bastards,' he hissed. A thought occurred. Glancing over his shoulder, he calculated distances. A minute or so for them to drive back along the lane. If they turn right, there are temporary traffic lights on the first two side streets. That meant continuing along Mauldeth Road.

The golfer called out. 'She's on her way, mate!'

'How far away is she?' he shouted back.

'Literally two minutes' drive. The practice is on the corner of St Andrew's Road.'

Jon knew it. She really would be here in no time. He glanced over his shoulder once again. If I cut across to Errwood Road on the other side of the golf course, I might just intercept the van at the roundabout where it meets Mauldeth Road.

Alice appeared at his side, arm round Holly. He looked anxiously at his daughter. So small, so fragile, so close to being mauled by that... She looked at Punch and immediately burst into tears. The sound made something in his chest twist tighter.

I can't go, he thought. I can't leave them. But the image of the roundabout wouldn't budge from his head. What is it, he thought, a five-minute sprint? The vet won't be much longer. The sound of the van's engine still ringing in his ears, he looked down at Punch. If it hadn't been for you, Holly would be lying here now. My little girl. His jaw unclenched. 'Alice, keep this pressed against the wound.'

'What are you doing?' she asked, crouching down.

As soon as her hand was in the right place, he jumped to his feet. 'Going after them.'

He raced towards the green, breath pluming the air like smoke from a steam train. After crashing through the laurels, he took a diagonal towards the faint shadow of trees on the golf course's far side. A bunker came into view and he leapt across the expanse of sand, landing on the other side and stumbling slightly before regaining his stride.

The other side of the golf course was bordered by clusters of houses. Seconds later, he got to the trees, darting between their dark and shiny trunks. A five-foot-high garden fence blocked his way. He placed his hands on the top and jumped up, the toes of his walking boots banging loudly against the wood as his arms slowly straightened. He swung his legs over and dropped down onto a neat lawn. A large, detached house. A middle-aged woman was staring open-mouthed through her kitchen window. He ran to the side, but his way was barred by a heavy metal gate.

'Trevor!' The woman from inside. 'There's a man in our garden!'

He peered over the neighbour's fence. The passage running down the side of their house led directly out on to a close. He vaulted over, narrowly missing a large terracotta pot.

Out on the close, parked cars all over the place. He tried to jink between two, hip banging against a wing mirror. An alarm started to shriek as rushed towards Errwood Road. The roundabout was less than a hundred metres ahead. The number of vehicles queuing at it gave him hope. I might just have got here first. Please, he prayed. Please let them have turned this way out of the golf course. Leg muscles now burning, he kept his eyes on the left-hand side of the roundabout, the direction from which the van would be approaching.

Forty metres away. He could see the front of the queue

waiting to join from Mauldeth Road. Six vehicles back, a white van. Yes! The pain in his legs instantly vanished. Got you, you bastards. He was floating, balls of his feet barely connecting with the ground. He became aware of the muscles in his shoulders and upper arms. The sensation he always felt on the rugby pitch before smashing a member of the other team. Seeing only the driver's side window, he closed in on the vehicle.

The driver, drumming his fingers impatiently on the top of the steering wheel, glanced to his side. His eyes widened. Jon was now close enough to see the movement of the man's lips as he mouthed a single word. Fuck.

Immediately, the engine revved and the driver's hands started pulling at the wheel. The vehicle veered round the car in front, horn blaring as it moved quickly along the gap between the two lanes of traffic and out on to the roundabout itself.

Ten metres away. Jon watched as the van – rather than trying to negotiate the roundabout's curve – cut straight onto the circular patch of grass at its centre. Cars started slowing in confusion. He dodged into the path of a Volvo, one hand slamming on its bonnet as he jumped round its front end. Then he was on the grass, too. The van's tyres were spinning uselessly as he came up alongside the driver's door and reached for the handle. Locked. Shit.

Glaring through the glass, he could see the driver hunched over the wheel, cursing with frustration. From inside the van came the booming sound of the creature's barks. Keeping his grip on the door handle, Jon lifted his free hand and punched the window. Fire-like pain lanced his wrist. He swung at the glass again and felt something in his hand give.

Then the van's tyres bit and he was yanked forward. He desperately tried to keep hold of the door handle. The metal was too smooth and it started sliding from his grasp. Stumbling alongside the vehicle, he landed a last, futile slap on its side. A red smear of a palm-print was left on the damp metal. Punch's blood, he thought, toppling forward.

The corner of the van's rear bumper narrowly missed his head, and in the split second before the vehicle went beyond his grasp, he saw the dirty rag covering its registration plate. He lunged at the scrap of material, feeling cloth tear in his fingers as his face ploughed into the grass.

The van bumped onto tarmac once again, the dog inside going ballistic as the vehicle accelerated towards the main road which led out of the city.

Jon raised himself onto his elbows. The rag was flapping about, leaving the registration plate exposed. A series of numbers with a single letter in the middle. Irish. The vehicle was from Ireland. He closed his eyes. This was revenge, he realised. Revenge for what I did in Clifden.

CHAPTER 2

Four days earlier

Jon held the phone slightly away from his ear, toes flexing against the front hall carpet. 'Slow down, will you? I can't understand what you're saying.'

'I said my name is Siobhain. I knew Zoë from when I was in Manchester. We... we...'

Yeah, Jon thought, I know. You were homeless, like Zoë. Did you end up on the game, same as she did? Forced into working for that greasy pimp, Salvio? His mind jumped back to the incident in the half-derelict tower block. When Salvio had realised Jon wasn't a punter, it was too late for him to get away. 'She mentioned you in a couple of postcards she sent. You were both sleeping rough in Manchester.'

'That's right.'

Jon nodded. 'So where are you now?'

'It's a town called Clifden. Connemara?'

'I know it – at least I know where it is.' Somewhere near Roundstone, he thought, where Mum's side of the family were all originally from.

'Right. Well there's a nightclub here called Darragh's.

That's where you'll find her. You need to get her out of there.'

Jon heard a creak at the top of the stairs. He peered up between the spindles of the banister. Alice was bending forward, head cocked to one side. Who is it? she mouthed.

He held up a hand and shook his head to indicate it was no one she needed to worry about.

'Did you get that?' the voice at the other end of the line asked.

'I heard,' Jon replied. And I hear your southern Irish accent, too. Soft and lilting. God, he thought, how I love the way you lot speak.

'The owner is a right head-banger. She doesn't know the danger that she's in.'

Oh Zoë, Jon thought. Wherever you go, you end up in the shit. A shiver took him. No wonder. I'm stood here stark bollock-naked and it's freezing cold. He hooked his jacket off the end of the banister and shrugged it on. 'What kind of danger's that, then?'

'I can't go into it. Will you not come and get her?'

Jon took a deep breath in. 'How did you get my number?'

'She's talked about you. A lot. The time you dealt with Salvio for her. Did you really do those things to him? Snap his wrist and that?'

Jon said nothing for a moment. 'So what did you do, look me up in the phone book?'

'I did. On the internet, anyway. There aren't that many Spicers in Manchester. Zoë said you lived in a place called Heaton Moor.'

'I see.'

'Will you not come?'

Jon thought about how his mum and dad now looked after the boy left behind after their own son's death. The young lad had taken over their lives. The thought of returning from Ireland with Zoë in tow would hardly fill them with delight. Maybe she wouldn't be keen on seeing her son, he reasoned. After all, she hadn't exactly shown much interest in the last few years. 'What's the name of this club again?'

'Darragh's. There's only one nightclub in Clifden and that's it. I know this is weird me ringing like this but…'

Her voice had taken on a forlorn note. He sat down on the third step of the stairs and placed his elbows on his knees. 'Siobhain, I can't just drop everything and rush over there. I'm in the police – I've got cases to work.'

'It's Saturday tomorrow. You could be here and home again by Sunday, easy. Flights go from Manchester to Galway Airport all the time, so they do.'

He realised he was not due back on shift until the following Wednesday. And even then he was only in for the day before taking his family for a short break at Center Parcs. 'Say I came. Zoë's not going to just pack her bags and return to England with me. How long has she been living in Clifden for now? Almost six months?'

'She's desperate to get out, Jon. She's been sucked in, slowly and surely. She needs your help.'

Sucked in? Unease rippled through him. Sucked in to what? 'Who owns this club?'

'Darragh. Clifden is only small, but he's the biggest thing here. Outside this place, he'd be nothing. A thug, that's all he is. You'll be dealing with ten times worse than him every day in Manchester.'

'What's wrong with the local police?'

She didn't reply. That figures, Jon thought. Zoë's choices in life rarely meant going to the police was an option. 'Tell me what he's dragged her into.'

'Listen,' she whispered. 'I have to live here. I need to–'

'I'm not coming if you don't.'

She sighed. 'Smuggling stuff, mainly. Pirate DVDs. He's making her take a load up to Nutt's Corner market in Belfast. But if the boys running things up there get hold of her, they'll…I don't know what they'll do to her.'

Jon closed his eyes. 'Is she using?'

A slight pause. 'What do you mean?'

'Siobhain, don't piss me about here. She's used heroin in the past. Is she on it again?'

'I don't know.'

'Then how else has this Darragh bloke got a hold on her?'

'He's a powerful man. At least in these parts he is.'

Jon cursed under his breath then lifted his eyes, picturing his dead brother looking down. Feelings of guilt started to unfurl in his head, same as they always did. I wasn't there for you. When you needed me most, I wasn't there. Ah, Christ. He closed his eyes, but his younger brother's face was still there. Dave, if it weren't for the fact you loved this girl so much, I wouldn't be agreeing to this. 'So you reckon she'd be happy to come with me?'

'Yes.'

'But this Darragh bloke wouldn't be.'

'He wouldn't need to know. She could just pop out for a cigarette break – you'd be in your car waiting. She jumps in and you're away.'

You make it sound so easy, Jon thought. 'What about her stuff?'

'She hasn't got much. A small bag, she could have it with her.'

Jon tapped a finger on his knee. 'When is she making this delivery?'

'Sunday.'

'This Sunday?' There goes my weekend, he thought, standing up and padding into the front room. He turned the computer on in the far corner. 'What's your number, Siobhain? I might need to call you when I get there.'

'So you're coming?'

'I'm checking flights now. What's your number?'

'Listen, I can't get involved in this. I have to be careful – I said, I have to try and live– '

'I'll be discreet.'

'No. I'm out of this. Sorry.'

'Siobhain, I'll just use the last-number-called function. I'll keep the phone you're on ringing all night.'

'Go ahead. It's the public one outside the post office.' The line went dead.

Jon held the handset away from his ear. 'Great,' he sighed, pressing red and turning to the computer monitor. Using the forefinger of each hand he typed, 'cheap flights to Galway'.

He clicked on the site that topped the list and, as the page began to load, freeze-frame memories of when he'd got hold of Salvio started appearing in his head. Two of the man's teeth flying from his mouth, the bloke's choked pleading, Jon's hands as they'd struck him about the head, forcing him back. Then Salvio crashing down the concrete steps, his screams filling the stairwell.

CHAPTER 3

The port of Dublin drew closer. Jon leaned his elbows on the ferry's handrail. Cheap flights to Galway. He shook his head. Only if you're booking something for the following bloody decade.

The tone of the engine dropped as the vessel cut speed. Looking towards the port of Dublin itself, a chimney with faded red and white stripes at its top dominated the skyline. He breathed deeply. Alice hadn't been happy when he'd told her about Zoë's predicament.

The first thing that had shown on her face was alarm, followed quickly by a look of resignation. From across the breakfast table, Jon read her thoughts. Guilt panged him. She knows, he realised. She knows that I want to go over to Ireland. And only her refusal to give permission will stop me.

'You mean to go, don't you?' she'd asked in a neutral voice, a piece of toast half-raised.

He tried to read her expression, but she was keeping her face blank. 'What do you think I should do?'

'Does that matter? You decide on something, you go ahead and do it. Simple as that.'

He shook his head. 'That's not true.' Their recent near-divorce raised its ugly head. The reason she had kicked him out was largely due to his habit of going off and deserting her. 'I promised you, Ali. I'm never going to make those mistakes again.'

'So it's all on me now, is it?' Her smile was sad. 'You want to go, but not without my say-so. Thanks.'

'What do you mean?'

'If I say no, you'll mope around resenting it. And God forbid something bad happens to Zoë; then I'm responsible for that, too.'

He sat back. 'OK – I believe I should help her out. I won't deny that. She's family of sorts, Ali, whether we like it or not. She was my brother's partner and she's Jake's mum.'

'Jon.' Her voice was an urgent whisper. 'It was not your fault Dave died, OK? You have to stop blaming yourself. He didn't want your help – he only wanted your cash.'

'He was in trouble, Ali. And his own big brother...I should have done more.'

She let out a long sigh. 'We've been over this so many times. He chose to avoid you, your family, everyone from his old life. Anyway, Zoë...what about her own family? Why can't they drop everything and rush to her aid?'

He began to rotate his cup of coffee, eyes lowered. 'She has no family, Ali. She went into care when she was four.'

Alice's shoulders slumped forward. 'Christ.'

'I saw her file. She started absconding from her care home in her early teens – from there it was the usual path into drugs and prostitution. Until Dave came along and got her out of it.'

Alice put the piece of toast back on her plate and closed her eyes. After a few moments, she raised both hands and ran them down the sides of her face.

He took a sip of coffee, giving her more time.

Her hands dropped into her lap and she stared at the far wall, eyes unfocused. 'Say you go. What will you do when you find her?'

Wasn't that obvious? 'I'll get her out of there.'

'Yes,' she answered. 'And once you've done that?'

He paused before replying. That's a very good point, he realised. 'I don't know. Take her to…wherever she wants to go.'

'Jon, you just said – she's got nowhere else to go. In fact, take her away from this place in Ireland and she'll probably end up back in her old Manchester haunts. It's all she knows.'

'She wants to get out of there; Siobhain said so. I can't leave her swinging in the wind. There was an aunt mentioned in her social services file – Rochdale or somewhere. Maybe she could take her in.'

Alice seemed to slide an inch lower. 'This is…there's the potential for this to go really wrong.'

'Meaning?'

'She comes back to Manchester. What if she wants to see Jake?'

Jon shook his head. 'I can't see it. You want my opinion? It was Dave that wanted that kid, not her.'

Alice pursed her lips, looking unconvinced. 'What other choice is there? I always knew we hadn't seen the last of her. I just thought when she came back, it would be for her son. Not…not because of something like this. You'd better warn your parents.'

Holly wandered in from the telly room and climbed on to Jon's lap. He adjusted her weight. 'You are getting such a big girl,' he murmured into her ear. 'Daddy's legs are hardly strong enough.'

Unconcerned, she picked up a piece of toast and took a bite. Punch quietly uncurled himself from his basket in the corner and took up position by their feet, eyes glued to Holly's hand. She waved the crust back and forth, the dog's eyes tracking it like someone watching a tennis match.

'Don't tease him,' Jon said.

She pushed the rest of it into her mouth and wrinkled

her nose at Punch who took on a mournful expression.

'They always took him on knowing it would probably be a temporary thing,' Jon announced quietly.

'That was years ago,' Alice replied. 'A lot has happened since then. They've probably come to assume they've got him for good.'

Jon lifted his cup and took another sip, knowing his wife was right.

Holly looked round. 'When are we going to Center Parcs?'

He smoothed a hand over her straw-coloured hair. 'Not for a few more sleeps. Daddy's got to go away for a night or two, first. OK?'

'Where in Connemara?' his mother's voice was flat.

'Clifden?' Jon let the word hang a moment, eyes fixed on the side of her face. 'Not far from Roundstone, isn't it?'

She laid another child's T-shirt on the towel spread across the dining-room table, picked up the iron and began to run it over the garment. 'What's she doing there?'

He regarded the makeshift arrangement for a moment. Despite his many offers, she wasn't interested in having a proper ironing board; this was the way it had always been done in her family. Why spend money on an item that would only create clutter? 'Working in the town's one-and-only nightclub, apparently. She's got herself involved with a bad lot. I'm nipping over to get her out of there.'

She glanced at him. 'Why? Why has it got to be you?'

Jon shrugged. 'Mum, she's got no family of her own— ' He stopped as he saw her eyes lift to the other side of the room. Jake was sitting on the carpet in front of the television. A remote from the Wii Jon had bought him for his birthday was in his hand. Perched uncomfortably on a footstool next to him was Alan, Jon's father.

'Grandad, you missed the power pill!' There was a reediness to Jake's small voice. Jon gazed affectionately at the boy's wavy brown hair. Just like Dave's, he thought.

Jake's shoulders jerked as he carried out some kind of manoeuvre. So different, Jon reflected, to the emaciated little scrap I found in the flat in that tower block. On the TV screen, the dinosaur driving Jake's cart hit a ramp and the vehicle soared above the other competitors.

'Woo-hoo!' the boy cried excitedly.

He turned back to Mary. 'She won't be interested in having him back, Mum.'

She placed the iron upright on the towel, beckoning to Jon as she stepped through into the kitchen.

Jon followed her, bracing himself for what was coming.

When she spoke, her words were clipped. 'She's not having him back. I'll contest it if she tries. Involved with a bad lot. That's the story of her life, isn't it?'

If it is, Jon thought, would that include our kid, Dave? He resisted the temptation to ask. His younger brother may not have been a saint, but it was him who'd put a roof over Zoë's head.

'I bet she's still pressing muck into her veins,' Mary continued, arms crossed tight. 'I will not allow our grandson to be taken away by a junkie like her.'

'Mum, we don't know that. My guess is she'll go her own way the moment the ferry reaches Holyhead.'

She snorted, and before she could say what an unlikely prospect that was, he added, 'Besides, we all agreed that she'd reappear one day, didn't we?'

She nodded begrudgingly.

'And don't forget, no court will just release him into her care. They act in Jake's interests, not hers. Jake doesn't even know her.'

'I still don't see why you have to get involved. She doesn't deserve your help.'

'Mum, do you think I want to go over there?'

'Well, why are you, then?'

'You want to know why?' He stepped back to the doorway so he could see the little boy. 'What happens if, years down the line, Zoë gets in touch? Tells Jake about the time when she really needed help and I did nothing? What do I say to him when he asks me why that was? Why I didn't help his mum?' He turned to Mary. 'I couldn't look him in the face. It's hard enough as it is – knowing I wasn't there when his dad needed me.'

'Don't bring David into this,' Mary hissed.

Jon tried to swallow back his emotions. 'How can I not, Mum? He was struggling. I wasn't there and he ended up dead.'

Mary's eyes had closed and, when she spoke, her lips hardly moved. 'We all share the blame for David.'

He took a breath in, heart still racing. 'Anyway, Roundstone. Where the O'Coinnes are from, isn't it?'

As usual, reference to her side of the family was met with silence. Jon recalled the photographs he'd seen of the tiny fishing village on the wild and rugged Connemara coast. In the years following the Second World War, many members of the wider family had starting drifting back to the village – including Orla and Malachy, his grandparents. His own mother had been born in Roundstone but, at nineteen, was sent to live with a cousin whose family had remained in Manchester. It was there she studied for her nurse's qualifications.

Manchester, with its thriving Irish community, had appealed to her. After qualifying, she'd stayed and married Jon's father, Alan Spicer. But at some point around then, a rift had opened up between his mother and the rest of her family back in Roundstone. The few times Jon had tried to broach the subject, his mum had become tight-lipped and unwilling to elaborate. Over the years, he'd often wondered if it had anything to do with the fact his dad was a non-Catholic. Whatever the issue, discussing it was taboo.

He proceeded cautiously. 'Grandma and Grandad. It's where they live, isn't it?' He was beginning to wonder whether she'd heard him when her eyes opened and she spoke again.

'You know it is.'

'Well, it's been years. I was thinking, maybe I could use the opportunity to look them up. What do you think?'

She didn't respond. Once again, Jon wondered what had caused her to cut contact so decisively. 'Mum? I know it's awkward for you. But they're my grandparents. It's never really mattered before, but now I'm getting older and I've got a kid of my own, it's become important. They've got a great-granddaughter, Mum. I'd love them to see Holly.'

'No. It wouldn't be a good idea.'

'Are they still alive?'

'Did you hear me, Jon? It's not a good idea.' Her voice quivered.

'Why?'

'It's just isn't.'

'Why? I want you to tell me.'

'It's all too long ago to be dredged up,' she moved past him into the other room. 'Best left alone.'

He knew she wasn't going to budge. 'I've got some cash,' he announced quietly, trailing after her. 'Once we're off the ferry, I'll give it to Zoë. She'll be gone in a flash.'

The iron vented steam as Mary picked it up. 'Let's hope so, Jon. Because I don't want you bringing her to our door.'

The voice was distorted by the Tannoy. 'Will all owners of vehicles please return to their cars.' This ferry will be docking in ten minutes' time.'

Jon straightened up and turned round. Apart from a few smokers at the doors, he was the only person who'd been braving the icy wind out on deck.

After flashing his passport at an uninterested customs official, he joined a road that ran alongside a wide river. The Liffey, he thought, slightly disappointed at its dirty brown colour. This being the Emerald Isle, I expected it to be crystal clear.

SLEEPING DOGS

Once they were past the city's outskirts, the feeling of being in a different country immediately grew. The petrol stations were strange. Not Texaco, Shell or BP, like back in England. Maxoil or Petrogas, with little mini-marts attached with names like Fareplay or Supervalu.

After driving for a couple of hours, he pulled into one and headed into the adjoining shop looking for a hot-drinks machine. Packets of unfamiliar crisps caught his eye. Tayto. A laughing man with a potato-shaped head on the front. His gaze wandered over packs of biscuits he'd never seen before. Kimberley – a window in the wrapper revealing two spongy-looking cakes with a marshmallow centre. Slimming, Jon thought.

A menu behind the counter listed coffee, but there was no sign of any type of self-service machine. He approached the man sitting behind the till. 'Can I have a black coffee, please?'

'Sugar in that?' The soft accent seemed strange coming from such a large person.

'No thanks.'

The man flicked on a kettle and reached for a catering-sized tin of Mellow Bird's. Shit, Jon thought. That's not coffee. 'Could you make it strong, please?'

The man nodded, not turning round. 'Travelling much further then, are you?'

'Clifden.'

'Clifden?' The back of his head tilted as he regarded the ceiling. Seconds ticked by, and just as Jon thought he wasn't going to say anything else, the man announced, 'A few hours more, then.'

He reached the edge of Galway two hours later. A series of roundabouts skirted past retail parks and over a bridge to the N59. Beyond the small city, the landscape became more rugged. The road started to undulate, rising up past outcrops of rock topped by lonely pines. To his right was a river – its slow-moving water looking like it would be teeming with trout or salmon. This was more like the Ireland I imagined, he thought.

The road twisted and snaked as the hills on each side reared higher. He passed a green sign that read 'Welcome to Connemara'. Steep slopes were lined with pale grey scree, peaks straining at the sombre sky, the highermost ones encircled by wreaths of cloud. Now there were stretches of water to his left and right, the road wending its way between them. The hills seemed to be closing in and Jon had the sense he was approaching some kind of threshold. Radio reception kept fading in and out.

Then the hills were behind him and the terrain abruptly grew flat. Heathland sectioned by dry-stone walls. Jon examined their construction. Unlike the orderly arrangements of stone in the Peak District near Manchester, these walls comprised huge chunks of rough grey rock that seemed to have been piled randomly on top of each other. Whatever radio station he'd picked up in Galway was now completely lost. He pressed the scan button and eventually the static cleared to reveal a voice speaking a foreign language. He remembered something about Connemara being one of the last places where Irish was still spoken.

Dusk had fallen when he reached the outskirts of a small town. By the side of the road he spotted a large mound of dark lumps; dry mud or something similar. The houses lining the road became more dense and then the sign he was looking for appeared: 'Welcome to Clifden'. Here at last, he thought. Thank God. And all because of a phone call from someone I've never met. And I only have her word that getting Zoë out of here will be simple..

CHAPTER 4

The road straightened up and he followed it past a sign that read 'Garda'. The local nick, Jon thought, looking at the old-fashioned Victorian-style lamp in front of the police station. It contrasted sharply with the new building. A large radio mast was mounted at the far end of the roof.

He passed an Aldi supermarket before the road forked. He saw a shiny metal monument that looked like a plane's wing planted upright in the ground. The road took another right turn, this one much sharper. Jon realised he was approaching the junction he'd just negotiated: ahead was the straight stretch of road leading back to Galway. The centre of the town was a kind of market square, with an island of shops in its middle. He steered into one of the many spaces and turned his engine off. The dashboard clock read 7.27.

What had Siobhain said? Darragh's was Clifden's one-and-only nightclub. Surely it would be nearby. He climbed out of his Mondeo. To his left was a small shop. Derval Joyce's Books and Gifts. Shame it's not open, Jon thought. I could have got Holly a present. A little leprechaun or something. Maybe a woollen scarf for Alice. Next door was an estate agent's. Eamonn McDonal, Connemara

Properties. He peered through the glass at the illuminated board. Little white cottages overlooking craggy bays and deserted beaches. Four hundred and fifty thousand euros. Jon whistled to himself. And that's after the economy crashed.

An A-board outside a pub caught his eye. Homemade soup and a bread roll for three euros fifty. Not bad, he thought, crossing the road to examine various sheets of paper pinned to a noticeboard.

Vote Emma & Jon. All-Ireland Talent Show, RTE1.

Trad session for beginners. Dusty Banjo's, Thursday 8p.m.

Texas Hold'em Tournament, Mannion's Bar, Fri 9.30p.m.

Clifden Comhaltas, February Music Session.

Alongside the brightly-coloured pieces of paper was a newspaper snippet about an appeal for funds to replace the roof of Clifden's Gaelic football team clubhouse.

Looking around, he realised he still had to see another person. This was getting a little weird. He spotted the town's post office at the corner of the square, telephone mounted on the wall outside. He did a double-take. That's where Siobhain called me from. His eyes travelled to the left. A featureless building with grey stone cladding and double red doors. The silver lettering above them spelled a single word: Darragh's.

He approached the entrance. A little window was set into each door, the glass laced with wire in a spider's-web design. There was nothing to indicate when the place actually opened.

He looked away to the side. A large building with a pale green front was next door. Joyce's Hostel. Lot of Joyces in this town, he thought, debating what to do. Back to my car for a little sleep? I'm not tired, he decided. Hungry, maybe. But not tired. If I need some sleep, I'll get it on the ferry home.

He retraced his steps to the sign announcing soup and

a roll. Mannion's Bar. The place looked snug and warm, the flicker of a real fire inside. Pushing open the door, he found himself in a low-ceilinged room, walls adorned with black-and-white photos. A pungent aroma filled the air. The two middle-aged men at the bar and the lady behind it were all looking at him. He nodded. 'Evening.'

'Hello,' the barmaid smiled, accent just like Siobhain's.

'Are you still serving soup and rolls?'

The two men turned back to each other and resumed their conversation, words a jumble of strange sounds. Irish, Jon realised.

'We are,' she said. 'It's mushroom today.'

'One of those then, please.'

'Anything to drink?'

He regarded the taps. There was the Guinness. Ah, bollocks. I drive right across Ireland, it would be rude not to have one. 'Pint of Guinness.'

She produced a glass, placed it below the tap and flicked it down. 'British number plates.' She nodded toward the window. 'What brings you to Clifden?'

The two men's conversation paused. One turned his ear slightly. Something inside Jon suddenly urged caution. 'Just scouting for a holiday property – something on the coast.'

The barmaid raised her eyebrows. 'You'll find plenty of bargains, now times have taken a turn for the worse.'

From the corner of his eye, Jon saw the men exchange a glance. He made sure he didn't sound smug. 'Good news for me, I suppose.' The table by the wood-burning stove had a paper on it.

The barmaid tilted his glass as the pitch-dark ale filled to the top. 'There you are.'

'Cheers,' Jon answered, pointing a thumb at the wood-burner. 'I'll be over there.'

He sat down by the fire, noticing the basket next to it was full of the same dark blocks he'd seen piled at the side of the road as he'd entered Clifden. He realised they were dried-out chunks of peat, their ends bristling with the stems of plants that had died thousands of years before. Must be what the smell was. He took a sip of Guinness – as cool and silky as he'd hoped for. The flavour complemented the pub's smoky fragrance.

He slid the newspaper closer. *The Galway Advertiser*. The headline read 'Bishop Not For Turning'. Jon scanned the text. Something about the Bishop of Galway failing to apologise for the Church covering up years of abuse of minors. A spokesperson at Ireland's Rape Crisis Network had stated that the Church needed to stop presenting itself as a victim of circumstance.

Jon pushed the paper away in disgust, memories of what had happened to his own younger brother surfacing. It had been an assistant at Sunday school who'd abused Dave. Rather than share the secret, his younger brother had bottled it all up, his mood-swings becoming more severe, his behaviour wilder and wilder.

The Sunday-School lessons had finished when Dave reached eleven, but, by then, the damage had been done. Arrests for shoplifting and stealing cars had followed. Eventually, Jon's father had kicked Dave out of the family home. Jon stared down at his pint. Once his younger brother had started living on the streets, he'd never stood a chance. Contact became more erratic and, as he'd slid deeper into petty crime and drug use, he pushed all attempts at help away. Unless it was twenty-pound notes, Jon thought sadly. He'd always been happy to accept those.

Then, only a few years before, his body had been found. Hacked to pieces and dumped on a hilltop in the Peak District. Jon rotated his pint glass slowly round. His search for those responsible had eventually led him back to Manchester's city centre. The squalid flat Zoë was trapped in, Jake at death's door with a chest infection, the rickety cot and its single piss-stained sheet...

'Mushroom soup.'

Jon looked up, momentarily disoriented. 'Oh – cheers.'

She placed the bowl and side plate down and started making her way back to the bar.

'Excuse me. Do you know when that nightclub, Darragh's, opens?'

She turned. 'Well, usually around eleven.'

Ireland, Jon thought fondly. That's the most exact time I'm going to get. He looked at his meal. A spoon, but no knife or butter. Fair enough. He picked up the dense roll, tore it apart and started dropping pieces into the thick soup.

After reading the paper from cover to cover, he glanced at his watch. A quarter to nine. His glass was empty and he contemplated another. Better not, he concluded. A drink-driving charge in a foreign country would be a nightmare. He pictured the police station on the road leading out of town. May as well pop in, he decided. There's not much else to do.

Once he'd paid at the bar, he headed out onto the street. The police station's foyer was modern and spacious, with five-feet-high plants in the corners. Skirting round the empty seating area, he approached the front desk from where a young officer in uniform watched.

'Hello,' Jon said. 'Nice new station you have here.'

He regarded his surroundings. 'That it is. It was built for us last year.'

Jon waited for him to ask what his visit was about, but the man seemed content to say nothing, benign expression unbroken.

'I'm over from Manchester,' Jon said, extending a hand. 'Detective Inspector Spicer.'

'Oh,' the man nodded calmly as they shook. 'With the English police, are you?'

'That's right.'

He looked to his side where a door led into the back part of the station. 'Are you here to see someone?'

'No, no,' Jon held up a hand. 'I'm...' He wondered

what to say. Best play it straight, he decided. If anything does go wrong later, it won't help if I was lying in here. 'I've come over to collect a relative. She's been working in Darragh's.' He looked at the other man, searching for anything in his eyes. Nothing. 'But she's needs to head back to Britain now.'

'Only so many nights you can work before you miss seeing the day.'

'True,' Jon replied.

'Well, it's grand to have you here, Detective– '

'Jon.'

The man nodded. 'Patrick. Can I get you a tea or coffee, Jon?'

'I'd love one, if it's not any trouble.'

'Ah, sure it's not. What'll you have?'

'Black coffee, no sugar. Thanks.'

The man punched a code into the side door and stepped through. Jon glanced around the reception area. Rows of recessed halogen bulbs shone their beams down onto a pristine grey carpet. The blue seats looked like they were fresh out of their cellophane wrapping. Jon wondered if the place had been built with EU money. Ireland, he'd heard, had been awash with the stuff.

The door opened and the young officer stepped back through. 'Here you go, Jon.' He placed a mug down. 'It's a terrible business with this soldier, don't you think?'

Jon slid the cup across the counter. 'What's that?'

'The one who's been taken up in Belfast?'

He gave a brief shake of his head. 'I hadn't heard.'

'Oh.' The officer looked embarrassed at having raised the subject. 'He was returning to his barracks in the early hours. A taxi-driver saw him being bundled into the back of a van.'

Jon sighed. Every time the peace seemed to be properly establishing itself, something else happened. 'Anyone claimed responsibility?'

'Not yet. It'll be some offshoot of the IRA, keen to

show the world not everyone agrees with what's going on in Stormont.' He sat back. 'So, what's Manchester like, then? I have a niece studying there. She says it's a great craic.'

'Certainly plenty going on for students – and there are enough of them.' He leaned an elbow on the counter as the other man sat back in his seat. 'So what keeps you busy in these parts? The town seems so quiet.'

'Yes, this time of year it is. We got the odd thing – a lot of people live out on their own. Burglary is a bit of a problem. Folk who've got a few in them on a weekend – there's our share of that, too.'

'Booze-related crime?'

'Yes – drink-driving is the latest area we're to focus on.'

Jon was relieved he'd passed on a second pint. 'No problems with Darragh's? Clubs are a real flash-point for us over in Manchester.'

The officer seemed to be taking his time with an answer. 'Oh, Darragh's is no bother. Just dancing goes on in there.'

'Really?' Jon asked, thinking about Zoë. 'No issues with drugs?'

The officer looked at Jon for a second. 'We're not aware of any. Has your...what is she, again?'

Jon didn't want to say, my dead brother's partner. 'My niece.'

'Has your niece noticed anything?'

Was the other man was playing dumb? 'No.'

'I doubt most people round here would know an ecstasy tablet if it jumped up and bit them on the arse.'

'What's the owner like?'

'Darragh? He's sound. Puts a lot back into the town, so he does. Sponsored the Christmas lights this year. He always puts a hand in his pocket for local projects. We get the occasional complaint when the club closes. Mainly from folk staying in Joyce's next door.'

'What time's that?'

'At the chirp of the sparrow, sometimes.'

Jon lowered his head, unable to keep the smile from his face. At the chirp of the sparrow; it was an expression he'd only ever heard his mum use. Something she said she'd brought with her from Ireland.

They chatted for a while longer before the clock on the wall behind the desk caught Jon's eye. Just after ten. The club will be opening in less than an hour, he thought. 'Well,' he announced, sliding his empty mug across the counter. 'Thanks for the coffee.'

'My pleasure,' Patrick replied, getting to his feet.

Once they'd shaken hands, Jon wandered slowly back to his car. As he unlocked it and started climbing in, he glanced across the street to Mannion's Bar. The silhouettes of several more people were now inside, and from the tilt of the two men's heads sitting at the window, Jon knew he was being watched. An uneasy feeling nagged at him as he lowered the seat and settled back. 10.22 by the dashboard clock.

CHAPTER 5

Laughter brought him out of his slumber. Blinking, he looked around. The car windows were heavy with condensation. Beyond the misty layer, a group of girls were traipsing past, a bottle of something passing between them.

He looked at his watch. Twenty to twelve. I slept longer than I meant to. He wriggled his toes, realising they were frozen. 'Right,' he murmured, slapping his cheeks to drive the fugginess from his head. 'Find Zoë and get the hell out of here.'

He climbed out of the car and into the chill night air. Across the road, the lights were still on in Mannion's Bar. The pair who'd been watching him through the window were now gone. He walked back to the plane-wing monument and looked across to the entrance for Darragh's. The dull thump of bass carried from the building. One weaselly-looking bloke on the door and that was it. Thin black hair was plastered back on his head, both hands thrust into a leather jacket. He didn't look like much of a bouncer.

Jon approached him with a smile. 'Evening. Are there a few in?'

He looked Jon up and down before stepping to the side. 'Some. It'll pick up when the pubs shut.'

'Right.' Jon stepped through the doors. Red carpet and red walls. The music was louder. A lady of around forty was behind a little desk to his right.

'Five euro, please.'

Jon pulled out his money, found a five-euro note and handed it to her.

'And it's one euro if you want me to take your coat.'

He looked down at his ski jacket. I don't intend to be in here long, he thought. 'No, you're all right, cheers.'

She tore off a pink ticket from her roll and handed it to him. He felt its rough texture and a memory came back: going to the cinema with Dave on a Saturday morning. Orange Maids in the half-time interval. 'Thanks,' he replied, turning to the double doors in front and pushing them apart.

An empty dance floor dominated the middle of a large room, coloured spots of light gliding across it. On both sides were several seating areas, C-shaped settees with low tables for drinks. On the opposite side of the dance floor was a bar which ran across the entire far wall. Two men were behind it – one young and studenty, the other older with a bit of a double chin.

He walked to the edge of the dance floor and onto the orange carpet. The group of girls he'd seen earlier were in a booth, taking off their coats and scarves. Short skirts and shimmery tops. A couple flashed him looks and one of them whispered something to her mate, eyes staying on Jon.

At the bar, he pulled up a stool and plonked himself on it. There were two couples at the other end and a mixed group of seven in another of the booths on the far side of the dance floor. The music thudded on, some kind of Ibiza-style dance track.

'What are you having?'

He turned back to the bar where the younger bloke was

waiting. Jeans and a black shirt, the word Darragh's embroidered in yellow across the left breast. Jon scanned the fridges. 'Just a can of diet Coke, please.'

The man gave a single nod, as if to say, it's your choice. He plucked one from the nearest chiller, cracked it open, half-filled a glass with ice and placed them before Jon. 'Three euro, please.'

Ker-ching, Jon thought. Forgot what a rip-off night clubs are. He dropped the coins into the barman's hand. 'Is Zoë around?'

The guy stepped back to the till while looking over his shoulder. 'Who?'

'Zoë.'

He rang the order in and turned round. 'Zoë?'

'Yeah – she works here. British girl, Manchester accent. Stronger than mine.'

'Zoë?' the man repeated the name again, looking lost. 'Are you sure she works here?'

Jon felt a sinking feeling. 'This is the only nightclub here, isn't it?'

'It is. I've not heard of any Zoë, though.'

'Which nights do you work?'

'Any I can – I'm at the college down the road.'

'She's thin – about five foot six, or so. Dark brown hair, usually wears it long.' The man's face still looked blank and Jon began to get the impression that describing her was futile. 'She's got quite prominent incisors – they jut out. Make her look a bit like a vampire when she speaks.'

He shook his head. 'I've not heard of any British girl working here.' He called to the chubbier barman further along. 'Brendan? Your man here is looking for a Zoë. Does anyone by that name work here?'

His colleague studied Jon before shaking his head and resuming his conversation with the couple he'd just served.

'Nope, sorry,' the young man said. 'Unless you want me to ask Darragh – he's in his office out back.'

Jon glanced up at the two CCTV cameras trained on the bar. He's probably watching me right now, he thought. He decided to try another angle. 'Don't worry, it was Siobhain I was really after.'

'Siobhain?' The barman was now chuckling. 'Are you sure you're in the right town? This is Clifden.'

Jon felt a pang of irritation and tried to hide it behind a smile. 'She's not a barmaid here, either?'

'Afraid not.'

Jon sat back. This was bizarre. Even if Zoë was using another name, it didn't make sense. No British girl worked here. He thought of his phone in his pocket. I don't even have a number for Siobhain. This was a bloody joke. He sipped at his drink, wondering what to do. More people came in through the doors. The group of girls had started dancing. The one who'd whispered kept looking in his direction. Jon caught the barman's attention. 'Just nipping out to make a call.'

The barman nodded.

The bouncer and two lads were smoking cigarettes on the pavement outside. Jon caught the scent of tobacco and the old yearning immediately opened up. He walked a few metres down the street and took out his mobile. You're going to kill me for this, he thought, selecting his home number. His wife got to the phone on its fifth ring.

'Hello?' She sounded groggy.

'Hi babe, it's me. I'm really sorry to ring this late. Did I wake you?'

'Yes. What's going on?'

'Nothing. That's the problem. No one has heard of a Zoë or a Siobhain. Total blank. Siobhain hasn't called, has she?'

'No.'

'Shit. This better not turn out to be a waste of time. OK, sorry babe. I'll see you tomorrow.'

'Are you going to drive back now?'

'Probably. I'll just see if I can have a word with this

Darragh character.'

'Right.'

He cut the connection and walked back to the entrance, holding up his pink ticket out of politeness.

The bouncer nodded him in.

Back in the club, Jon walked over to the bar, giving the group of girls a wide birth. Signalling to the barman, he leaned across and pointed to the door in the corner. 'Can I have a word with Darragh, after all?'

'Two seconds.'

He disappeared, returning a minute later with a slightly-built man. Jon took a good look as he approached. He was wearing dark trousers and a fitted white shirt, open at the neck. Hair was cut short and carefully messed-up. The style reminded him of Rick's, the graduate he worked with back in Manchester. As he got closer, Jon could see he had very long eyelashes. The result was a slightly childish appearance.

'What's the problem here?' he announced a little impatiently. His voice was high, increasing the impression of immaturity. 'Joseph says you're looking for someone.'

'Are you Darragh?' Jon asked.

'I am.'

'Thanks for seeing me. It's a relative of mine. I was told she's working here, but she's needed back in England. A family matter. I've come to collect her.'

Keeping his elbows straight, he placed both hands on the edge of the bar and shook his head. 'There's no English girl works in this club.'

'She's called Zoë,' Jon persisted. 'Bit of a Manchester—'

'I know what you said she's called,' he cut in.

Why didn't you say so before, then? Jon thought. Instead of just referring to her as someone.

'But as I said,' he continued. 'No Zoë works here. Are you sure it's Clifden she's meant to be in?'

No, thought Jon. I picked this town at random from a map of Ireland and drove seven hours to get here. 'That's what I was told. Darragh's night club. In Clifden.'

He dropped his arms to his sides and shrugged. 'Well, I hate to say your journey's been wasted, but…'

Jon kept eye contact. The man was in no hurry to look away. Instead, he raised his eyebrows at Jon as if to say, what more do you want? Jon lowered his gaze. I don't reckon he's hiding anything. The guy seems genuinely clueless. Fucking Siobhain, what was she playing at? He placed a palm on the bar and gave it a gentle pat. 'Right. Looks like I've got a long drive back. Thanks for your help.'

'Drive safely.'

'Will do.' Jon slid his hand off the shiny surface and started walking for the door.

The girls were back in their booth and the one who'd been staring called out as Jon went past. 'Not going already, are you?' An impish smile was on her face.

'Afraid so,' Jon answered without breaking his stride. He pushed open the doors, anger sparking inside him. Something about Darragh didn't quite hang together. Jon replayed the man's comments, trying to put his finger on what it was. 'Night.' He stepped round the doorman and crossed the road, heading for the monument on the corner. What a twat I am, he thought. I should have known anything involving Zoë was never going to be what it seemed. What a waste of time and money.

He'd opened his car door and was about to get in when his phone started to ring. Examining the screen, he saw the word, home. 'Ali, are you OK?'

She sounded exasperated. 'That girl just rang. Siobhain.'

Jon stepped back from the car. 'What did she say?'

'That they're making the delivery first thing in the morning. They have Zoë loading boxes of DVDs into a lorry round the back of Darragh's. Listen, Jon, I think you should call the local police. I really don't like the sound of this.'

He was marching back to the corner. 'When was this?'

'I just hung up from her call.'

'Probably more horseshit. I'll take a quick look.'

'Why not ring the police?'

'I don't want to bother them about nothing – it'll only make me look a bigger fool.'

'Be careful, Jon. Please.'

'I will. I'll give you a buzz in the morning.'

'No. Ring me back. I can't sleep now, anyway.'

He snapped the phone shut and looked across to Darragh's. The doorman had his back to him, now chatting to a couple who'd popped out to share a cigarette. Jon looked along the terrace of buildings, seeing access to the rear was via a side-road.

That was the odd thing about Darragh, he realised. It's what he *didn't* say: there was no question about how I'd heard Zoë was working in his club. Surely you'd be interested to know how a misunderstanding like that could have occurred.

He skirted quickly across the road and down a slight incline, leaving the glow of streetlights behind him. Fifty metres away a white van stood in the glare of a single security light. It had a roll-up back and the chubby barman was reaching inside. The waistband of his boxers showed above his jeans as he pushed the object as far into the dark interior as he could.

Jon kept to the shadows, treading lightly to keep his presence a surprise. The barman rummaged around a bit more before straightening up with a crate of bottles in his hands. The rear door to the club was wide open, fire-exit sign visible on its inner side. The barman set off across the tarmac. The security light was directly above the doors, alongside a camera. Once the barman was back in the building, Jon bounded across and followed him inside. A narrow corridor, walls made of breeze blocks. A door at the end on the left-hand side. Jon closed in on the sound of the barman's voice.

'There're another five.'

'Will I carry on with this or do you want me to help?' A female voice with an Irish accent.

'No. You take care of those.' Darragh's squeaky voice this time.

Jon peeped through the doorway. The first thing that grabbed his eye was the dramatic painting on the far wall. A galleon being tossed against jagged rocks. Figures were just visible on the stricken vessel's deck and, along the shoreline just beyond, a series of flickering beacons provided the painting's only light. A plaque below it read, The Wrecking of the *Concepción*.

Below the painting, Darragh was sitting behind a large desk covered in piles of banknotes. Jon focused on them. Various denominations, all used notes. It's dirty, he thought. A couple of filing cabinets were against the wall beside him. Mounted on top of them were two monitors displaying images from both inside and outside the club. In the middle of the room a woman in her late twenties was kneeling before a large box. He recognised the picture of the jovial character with the potato-shaped head on its front. Tayto crisps. The barman placed the crate on to a stack of three others and turned round. He spotted Jon and started to frown. At the edge of his vision, Jon saw Darragh's head turn.

'What the fuck?' The nightclub owner took off the pair of designer glasses he'd been wearing and started getting to his feet.

Jon stepped fully into the room, seeing the girl's mouth drop open. He turned to Darragh. 'Where is she?'

'What?' He waved a hand at the barman. 'Get Conor in here. Now!'

Conor. Must be the bouncer, thought Jon, watching the other man hurry through the doorway on the other side of the room. He won't pose much of a problem. 'Let's avoid any trouble, Darragh. Let me take Zoë home.'

'You think you can march into the back of my club and tell me to avoid trouble? Fuck!'

Jon regarded him calmly. The bloke was easily wound-up, that was for sure. Pity it just made him look like a peevish eight-year-old. 'Where is she?'

'Who the fuck knows?' He kept behind his desk.

Jon turned to the girl. Bleached hair scraped back in a ponytail, bones of her face showing through. She looked no stranger to partying. 'Where is she?'

She looked across at Darragh.

'Say nothing, Hazel,' Darragh barked. 'I can't believe this. Jesus!'

Jon looked at the box she was next to. It hadn't been sealed fully shut. He leaned down, hooked his fingers inside the flaps and ripped them open. Bags of crisps. Jon delved through the layer, searching for the DVDs below. Crisps, nothing more.

Movement on the other side of the room. He raised his head to see the bouncer stepping through the door. Hey up, Jon thought, cavalry's arrived.

'Conor, get this prick out of here,' Darragh commanded.

Jon held up his hands. 'Conor, I'm leaving. I just need Zoë, then I'm out of here.'

The doorman shot a questioning glance at Darragh.

'Get him out!' Darragh yelled, eyes shifting to the money covering his desk.

The girl began to scrabble back as the doorman's nostrils flared. He started across the room, hands at his sides, palms showing. 'Come on, out.'

Jon saw his shoulders were hunched. I know what you're planning, he thought. Get in so close I won't know about your fist until it connects with the underside of my chin. He stepped back a pace. 'Conor, you don't need to–' The guy wasn't slowing down. Oh bollocks, this is not going to plan. Two more steps and he'll be able to swing for my face. He thought back to the man as he'd dragged on his cigarette outside the club. Right-handed. That's the fist he'll prefer.

'Time for you to go home,' the bouncer said, taking two more small steps. Jon saw his knees bend slightly and suddenly his right fist started to come up.

Jon parried the blow without any problem. 'Conor– ' The room jarred and, a nanosecond later, Jon registered an impact on his temple. Bastard was feinting with his right. Vision now full of stars, Jon just had time to dip his head, guessing the man would follow with his right. A fist glanced harmlessly off his skull. He shot a hand out, clamping his fingers on the man's throat to keep him at arm's length. 'Conor, for fuck's sake, you– '

He saw Conor's left swinging in again and had to reach out with his free hand to catch the man's wrist. Now eye-to-eye, he could see the bouncer wasn't going to stop. Jon yanked him forward and slammed his forehead into the other man's face. The guy dropped to his knees, eyes rolling up as a stream of blood started from each nostril.

Jon looked around. This is not good. 'Zoë! Can you hear me, Zoë!'

Darragh was staring at the bouncer who was now reaching a hand down to the floor. 'Don't get up, Conor,' Jon said. But the man had managed to raise one knee in readiness to stand. 'You're getting up,' Jon murmured resignedly. Careful to avoid the man's kidneys, Jon swung his shoe into the bouncer's stomach, knocking the breath out of him. He collapsed onto his side, mouth gaping.

Jon went past the cowering girl towards the far door, the barman shying from his approach. 'Zoë!' He stepped through. Two more doors in front. He pushed the right one open. A small toilet. He shoved against the left one and found himself behind the bar.

The student barman was looking at him, shock on his face. His eyes flicked to Jon's shoulder, widening slightly. Instinctively, Jon ducked as something heavy and hard thudded into the doorframe just above him. He span about to see Darragh raising a stubby little baseball bat. The nightclub owner jumped forward, swinging it again.

The confines of the bar hampered his movement and Jon stepped inside the arc of the impending blow, grabbed the man by his shirt and heaved him round. Darragh's feet left the floor and Jon brought him down on top of the bar, bottles and glasses flying. Pinning him there with one hand, Jon used his other to twist the bat from Darragh's grasp. He pressed the end of it against the man's nose. 'I should wrap this round your fucking head.'

'Get off,' Darragh snarled, veins in his neck bulging as he tried to struggle free.

Looking up, Jon saw the entire club staring at him. He shoved Darragh off the bar so he fell to the carpet at the edge of the dance floor. Turning round, he slipped back through the door through which he'd come.

The overweight barman was still rooted to the spot and the bouncer was now in a foetal position. I need to be out of here, Jon thought. I am seriously in the shit. How many people just witnessed that? Fuck!

'What have you done to Darragh? Did you hurt him?'

This from the scrawny girl, still on her knees, but now backed up against the wall.

Jon rounded on her. 'Zoë – is she here? Do you know her?'

She shook her head.

Jon's gaze stayed on her a moment longer. No time, he thought, to pump her for information. He crossed to the tape machine on the corner of Darragh's desk. Twin deck. 'Get some ice for his nose,' he ordered the girl, directing a nod at the bouncer. Then he slung the baseball bat into the corner, pressed the eject buttons, yanked the two cassettes out and jogged for the rear doors.

CHAPTER 6

Shoving his gear-stick across and down, Jon reversed out into the quiet street. Oh God, what the hell have I just done? He screwed his eyes shut for a second before putting his car in first and accelerating away.

The two security tapes were on the passenger seat beside him. Why, he asked himself, did you take them? Enough people saw what happened. You could be up for trespass, assault and theft. He thought about the twin streams of blood that had started to fall from the bouncer's nose. GBH, too. Shit!

He got to the junction for the main road. A few hundred metres ahead was the police station. No, Jon thought. Not that way. He signalled right, cut round a small island and headed back along the first part of the high street. I need to be out of this town. The road kinked right, leading back towards Darragh's. Jon braked. This was a nightmare. A narrower turn was to his left. He took it, vaguely registering a sign for Ballyconneely. Within minutes, he found himself negotiating a pot-holed route through dark countryside. Occasionally, he could sense yawning space off to his right. The sea, he realised. This road must be hugging the coast.

He drove for another half an hour and, as his adrenaline ebbed, fatigue kicked in. His head began to ache from where the bouncer had landed his blow. The road passed through a couple of small villages, traffic lights on green. A while further on, a small sign glowed briefly in his headlights. Parking. Let's stop there, he thought. Take a breather. He slowed looking for the side road. Another sign emerged from the darkness. Gorteen Beach.

He turned right onto a bumpy little track that sloped round into a small car-park. As he rolled slowly across the smooth surface, his headlights picked out a white structure on which was mounted an orange ring. Behind was a pale expanse of sand and beyond that, only blackness.

Knowing he was now out of sight of the road, he parked, turned his lights off and rested his forehead against the steering wheel. What are you doing? What possessed you to just barge into the back of the club like that? The phone call, he realised, that's what. Siobhain's message, saying Zoë was right there. But she wasn't. At least not by the time I turned up. Damn it, why did the bouncer have to launch himself at me like that? His temple was throbbing and he brushed his fingers across the skin. A nice lump was on its way up.

He leaned his head back and sighed. What a disaster. The sound of waves breaking gently on the nearby beach filled his car and the memory of Darragh pinned to the top of the bar materialised. Swinging at me like that. I didn't expect that from him. He thought about the piles of cash the man had been counting on his desk. Jon felt his eyes narrow. You know what? This might not be as bad as you think.

All I was to Darragh was some English nutter barging in and asking for Zoë. That's all he knows about me. Will he report the incident? If he does, it'll open him up to some very awkward questions. It's obvious the guy's into something very dodgy. Plus, there's the embarrassment of having some bloke stroll into his club, batter the bouncer, throw the owner across the bar and stroll back out again. Not something you'd want doing the rounds.

Jon sank down in his seat, feeling marginally better. There's a very good chance, he decided, this whole thing will be hushed up. He considered any other ways he'd left himself vulnerable. The drinkers in Mannion's bar. They'd clocked me parking. And the policeman at the station. Jon cursed. I gave him my name and where I worked. He shook his head. That was stupid, Spicer. Very stupid.

He reached for his mobile. What should I tell Alice? Your dickhead of a husband has just decked a couple of locals in Clifden. Oh yeah, and he stole the security tapes for the nightclub. But don't worry, there were a good twenty witnesses and the only person he gave his real identity to was a policeman. How's that for a night's work?

He accessed his text messaging service and started pressing keys.

No sign of Zoë. Have left Clifden, will get ferry in morning. Jon XXX

Hating himself for glossing over what had actually happened, he pressed send. I'll tell her everything when I get back, he told himself. No point in worrying her with details now.

He glanced at his watch. Twenty past one in the morning. All he could hear was the rhythmic sound of the ocean. It'll be light in another five hours, he thought, zipping his ski jacket up under his chin.

A seagull shrieked. Jon opened his eyes. Through a side window beaded with moisture on both sides, he could see the bird. It was perched on the life-ring stand, looking out to sea. Dawn was just breaking, everything cold and grey. A shiver went through him as he returned his seat to the upright position. So bloody cold. He rubbed his numb hands together, eyes feeling like they were full of grit. The two security tapes were on the seat beside him. Bollocks, he thought, I was hoping it was all a dream. The dashboard clock read ten past six. Feels like I've been asleep for twenty minutes. Three times he'd resorted to turning the engine on during the remainder of the night, welcoming the warm wash of air while knowing it was only a temporary respite.

He remembered peering from the window at one point to gaze in wonder at the night sky. Had the view been for real? He was used to skies dotted with a few dozen stars. Last night there'd been thousands.

He opened the driver's door and the seagull immediately took off. It banked away to the right, disappearing over a cluster of gravestones that clung to the slopes of a small hill. Silence. At the top of the grassy bank to his side, he could see a row of permanent caravans. All their curtains were open and none had lights on. Empty, Jon thought. Waiting for the holiday season. Inland, fields were lightly speckled with white cottages. Beyond, the terrain grew steeper, the rapidly-lightening sky dominated by a craggy brown peak.

He crossed to the waist-high wall on the other side of the car-park and surveyed the beach. A gentle curve of bleached sand, its inner side bordered by a sedge-covered dune. The strip of land stretched away to a grassy knoll about a kilometre out to sea. The ocean inching its way up the rocks at the bottom of the wall was as clear as spring water. A tiny crab emerged from beneath a shifting frond, edging its way cautiously along a barnacle-crusted ledge.

On a warm summer's day, Jon realised, this place would be absolutely idyllic.

Back at the car, his eyes went to the tapes on the passenger seat. I need to get shot of those, He took them out and shoved them to the bottom of the bin by the steps leading down to the beach.

After making sure they were concealed by a layer of litter, he returned to the vehicle and took the roadmap out of the glove compartment. I'm parked somewhere called Gorteen Beach. There was the city of Galway. To its west was a bulge of land fringed by a shattered coastline. The entire area was stamped with a single word: Connemara. He found Clifden and traced his finger along the minor road he'd taken the night before. When he found Gorteen Beach, his hand came to a sudden stop. My God, I'm about a mile away from Roundstone.

My grandparents, Malachy and Orla. I could try and find them. The significance of the little cemetery nearby hit him. It must be where the villagers were buried. The sun had now cleared a majestic line of peaks way off to the east. The cloudless sky was the palest shade of blue and the air had a crystalline quality about it. He followed a narrow footpath to the cemetery gate. The right-hand post was marked with a small plaque that simply read, In memory of the Deceased Infants.

Jon recalled his mother talking about the dilemma; those who died unbaptised were not allowed to be buried on consecrated ground. So mothers of stillborn children were forced to place the bodies of their dead babies just beyond the cemetery wall, the infants' souls sentenced to an eternity of exclusion. Jon looked sadly at the unmarked tussocks of grass. If there was ever a religious institution governed by unfeeling men, it was surely the Catholic church.

The iron gate creaked as he stepped into the windswept graveyard. Headstones had been erected wherever space allowed a grave to be dug: there were no rows or aisles. In fact, there seemed to be no order to the graves at all.

He meandered through the haphazard arrangement, noticing the same surnames again and again. Connelly. Folan. McDonagh. At the top of the hill he found the first headstone marked with O'Coinne, his mum's maiden name. The stone was old, inscription worn smooth by years of exposure to sun, wind and rain.

Kitty O'Coinne. Born 4th August, 1883. Died 15th June, 1949. R.I.P.

Jon frowned, wondering who she was. So much of my family I know nothing about. He searched the neighbouring headstones. Another old one; this time for Phelim O'Coinne. Died 1922. Another to the left was a lot newer. He saw the inscription and felt his shoulders droop.

O Lord have mercy on the soul of Orla O'Coinne. Born 18th September 1926. Died 11th January 2010. Aged 84 years.

My grandma's dead, Jon thought, crouching down. She died years ago. Did mum know? Surely she did. At the least, she'd have received a letter from one of her sisters or her brother. He pressed the tip of his thumb between his closed eyes. If she had been told her mother was dead, it had created no visible effect on her. What happened all those years ago? Something terrible.

He searched around for a headstone marked with Malachy O'Coinne but didn't find one. Could the old man still be alive? He turned to the horizon and took in the view. What a beautiful place to be buried.

A circular tablet of stone at the roadside let him know he was entering Roundstone itself. Parking in a marked area overlooking a sea wall, he got out of the car and glanced about. The village seemed to be little more than a short high street of pastel-coloured properties. A deserted-looking hotel was opposite him, followed by a small shop. Further down, he could see two hanging signs. One for a pub called King's, one for an art gallery. The first building on his side of the road seemed to be some kind of café. Jon realised he was starving. He approached the door, but the place was shut. The next building appeared to be a convenience store. Jon examined the single petrol pump set into the pavement before the open front door. The thing actually appears to be working. This place really is from another era.

Aware of the lump on the side of his head, he stepped into the shop a little self-consciously and nodded hello to the elderly woman behind the counter. A refrigerated section was off to his right. He plucked a pint of milk from the shelf along with a couple of pasties and a small block of cheese. Every item, he noticed, was priced with an individual sticky label. How long since I've seen them? He added a cellophane-wrapped sausage roll.

'Nice morning,' he smiled to the lady, adding a packet of mints to his pile.

She nodded pleasantly. 'It is, so.'

'Perhaps the last of winter is finally behind us.'

'Perhaps.' She didn't look convinced. 'That's nine euro sixty-five.'

He gave her a ten euro note. 'I see you've been having the same frosts we've had in England – you've got the potholes to prove it.'

'Oh, I don't know.' Her eyes twinkled. 'We have the pleasure of those whatever the weather.'

'Oh.' Jon grinned.

'So you are here on holiday?'

He hesitated. 'Kind of – looking about for a holiday home. Somewhere with a beach.'

She smoothed her apron with both hands. 'We get a few stragglers passing through this time of year.'

Stragglers, Jon smiled to himself. Like I'm trying to follow the summer herds, just a full six months behind. He wondered how to frame his next question and opted for simplicity. 'Do you know Malachy O'Coinne?'

'The O'Coinnes? I do.'

She said O'Coinnes, Jon thought. More than one.

'Turn your face to O'Dowd's. Go up the side street and you'll find Malachy's place at the top.' She pointed down the street to the pale blue pub sign on the other side. 'That way.'

Jon felt a tingle down his spine. 'Thanks. Is there a name or house number?'

She thought for a moment. 'I don't think so. It's the one with shells and things at the front.'

'OK.' He hurried back to his car, dumped everything but a pasty on the passenger seat and walked back past the shop. A tiny harbour opened up on his right, a palm tree growing at the top of the flagstone path leading up from the quay. Chewing his way through the stodgy pastry, he regarded the little jetty with its stacks of lobster pots and piles of nets. Two fishing boats were moored at the end, one blue, one red. The little roofs of the cabins were speckled with gull droppings. The bay beyond was like a millpond, orange buoys motionless on the calm surface.

He stuffed the last of the pasty into his mouth. That's my calories for the day, he thought, turning to O'Dowd's. The sign outside announced it was a seafood restaurant and bar. Black blinds bearing the Guinness logo had been lowered in each window. What a perfect place for a lock-in, he thought. The nearest police station must be Clifden – and that's miles away.

As he crossed the street, a mixture of apprehension and excitement was beginning to fill him. What am I going to do? Knock on his front door? Walk by? What do I say if he's actually there?

The side-road was a steep incline that soon made his thighs ache. The road ahead eventually merged into a lane which led directly for the craggy-topped hill he'd seen from Gorteen Beach. There were a couple of old-looking bungalows to the left of the road. Directly on the other side was what appeared to be the footings for a very large house. Piles of breeze blocks and bricks stood on pallets, alongside stacked sacks of cement mix. The driveway was yet to be laid and the area surrounding the foundations had been churned up by the thick tyres of a dumper truck parked alongside the pallets. What an eyesore, Jon thought.

He walked on, gaze shifting to the overgrown garden of the first bungalow. Shutters were closed over the windows and a For Sale sign had been bolted to the corner of the low building.

The next garden was tidier. Little stone rabbits dotted the lawn and seashells lined the pathway leading up to a large front porch. Jon stopped in his tracks. An elderly man was sitting in an armchair to the right of the open doors. Almost bald on top, he had a great bushy beard, in which patches of ginger still clung. He was wearing an old mustard-coloured cable-knit jumper, the cuffs of which were frayed. Impassively, he stared at Jon, looking for all the world like he had been sitting there through the night. Maybe longer.

Breaking eye contact, Jon continued walking. Sweat broke out in both armpits. Is it him? He had a beard in the old photo at Mum's, but not that long. It must be him. Seashells in the front garden, that's what the shopkeeper had said. He came to a halt, turning his back on the bungalow, sensing the old man's stare on him. Studying the footings of the building on the other side of the narrow road, he didn't know what to do. Should I say good morning? Ask if his name is Malachy O'Coinne?

A voice rang out behind him, hostility pitching the tone high. 'Will you not be getting on with it, you wee fucker?'

The Irish accent was so strong, Jon wasn't sure if he'd heard correctly. Slowly, he turned his head to look back at the bungalow. The old man was now standing, head leaning out the porch doorway, one hand waving at shoulder level.

'Go on with you, let's see if you can lift a fucking spade. It will not build itself.' With that, he opened the inner door and slammed it shut behind him.

Jon turned back to the building site. He thought I was the surveyor or something. Looking down at his clothes, he nodded. Fair assumption. What did he call me? A wee fucker. I'm six feet four. He grinned. I reckon that was my grandad.

He pondered the row of spectacular peaks on the horizon. The end one had been enveloped by low white cloud. He watched its soft edge sliding slowly across the neighbouring peak. A curtain, bringing an end to the show.

He'll lose this view, Jon realised. Once this house goes up, he won't be able to see a thing. How did a developer ever get permission to build a monstrosity like this? It was more like the ridiculous places Manchester's footballers built for themselves in the leafy villages that fringed the city.

He glanced again at the little bungalow. Do I try and introduce myself? The old man had vanished. He couldn't imagine walking up to the front door and knocking. You don't just appear like this, he thought. Not when, for some reason, your mum has avoided all contact with the person inside for over forty years. He turned back towards the high street.

Darragh de Avila pulled up at the ornately styled wrought-iron gates and pointed his remote. The motors in the carved stone posts begin to whir and the gates slowly parted. He drove his Audi along a drive that swept down towards a large lake. A little further along the shore was a sprawling neo-Gothic mansion with battlements, spires and a huge stained-glass window overlooking the main entrance.

He approached the garages and pulled up next to a Maserati Quattroporte. Dad's in, he thought to himself. No sign of Mum's Range Rover. With what I'm about to tell the old man, that's probably a good thing.

He climbed out of his vehicle and held a hand up to the pair of men pruning the bushes that bordered the enormous lawns. They'll already have radioed through to Dad that I'm here, he thought.

Gravel crunched under his feet as he made his way round to the studded timber door at the side of the residence. It led into a pantry area then through to the kitchen.

Gerrard de Avila was sitting at the breakfast bar, lining up documents in a smart leather briefcase. 'Son.' He nodded his bullet-like head. 'What brings you out here on a Sunday afternoon?'

Darragh took in the sheer bulk of his father with apprehension. 'Where's Mum?'

'Health spa, as usual,' Gerrard replied, attention back on his paperwork.

'Getting ready for a meeting, are you?'

'Something over in Dublin. Showing a few people round our property developments there. I'll let you know if the talks have any potential.'

Darragh leaned back against the granite work surface, gaze directed up at the ceiling's heavy beams. A spot light was shining down on his head and he shuffled sideways to escape its glare.

'Spit it out, son. You know I can't stand pansying around.'

His eyes dropped to the old man, who still seemed more interested in his documents. 'Er...there was an incident at the club last night.'

Gerrard was peering down his nose at a print out. 'Can I understand your bloody graphs? What sort of an incident?'

'A visitor.'

'Go on.'

'This fellow appeared in the office. Got in through the back doors as we were bringing in stock.'

The old man put the sheet down and turned his eyes to the younger man. 'He robbed our club? On his own? Who was this fucker?'

'It wasn't a...he didn't take any money.'

'What was he doing then?'

'Looking for a girl. Someone he thought worked at the club.' He cleared his throat.

'Try to be a man, for fuck's sake. Tell me what's going on.'

Darragh glanced back. He was now the focus of his father's piercing stare. 'This guy was big, Dad. A handful. I called Conor to get him out. They clash and Conor ends up on his back. He then starts banging around, shouting for this girl, throws me over the bar. By the time I got back into the office, he's gone.'

'But he took nothing?'

'Not nothing.'

'This a guessing game, son? What did he fucking take?'

'The security tapes for the nightclub.'

'What did he want with them?'

Darragh coughed again. 'When it was all kicking off, someone in the club must have called the Guards. Patrick was on duty, so he swings by. The guy who took the tapes? Turns out he's a peeler, Dad. From Manchester. Works for the Major Investigation Team there.'

Gerrard's barrel chest swelled as he drew in air. 'This was some kind of police operation? Why didn't Patrick give us warning?'

'The guy wasn't acting as a policeman, Dad. It was a personal matter. Nothing official about it — that's why he took the tapes, I reckon. Didn't want to leave any evidence of his visit.'

Gerrard placed both hands on his bulging thighs. 'Let me understand this. He takes it upon himself to force his way in looking for a girl. He doesn't find her?'

Darragh shook his head. 'Aside from Hazel, there's been no girl working behind the bar for months.'

The skin round Gerrard's eyes wrinkled. 'You're sure? Not someone Devlan might have…done anything to? Some lass passing through; no friends or family to speak of?'

'No. Besides, Devlan's been banging Hazel for ages.'

'And that stops him from going after other lasses? OK. So he knocks you and Conor about like you're kids and makes off with the tapes to cover his tracks. So why do you look fit to puke all over my floor?'

Darragh took his glasses off and pinched the bridge of his nose. 'Dad, it was the second Saturday of the month yesterday.' He looked nervously at his father. 'When I open the back of the club early and our people make their drop-offs? You said to always have the camera in the office recording.'

Gerrard kept looking at his son.

'The cash, Dad? Everything from the last few weeks. It was all on film being delivered. So is Patrick calling for his envelope. The guy from the council who sorts out our planning applications? Even Julian from Blackman and May's Galway office. He came by for his bloody slice. That tape is a snap-shot, Dad. Of our entire operation.'

When Gerrard spoke, his voice was quiet. 'This tan. What's his name?'

'Spicer. Jon Spicer.'

'Where is he now?'

'I don't know. Manchester, I suppose.'

'And you've heard nothing about the tapes yet?'

'No.'

The old man's gazed across the lake. 'That's something. If he took them to cover his tracks, maybe they've been slung already. We need to move carefully here, very carefully.'

'I phoned Devlan.'

Gerrard's head slowly turned. 'What?'

'I'm sorry, Dad. I wasn't thinking.'

'When did you call him?'

'Last night. Before I realised the tapes had gone.'

'You rang your brother?'

'None of us could believe what had just happened. I panicked; rang to say we'd been attacked. That I needed him and Sean back here.'

'Went through the roof, did he?'

'His phone was switched off.'

'It's always bloody switched off.'

'I left a message, mentioning it was a peeler from Manchester.'

Gerrard's voice dropped to a throaty growl. 'This is your brother who's currently somewhere over in England? Tell me you didn't give Devlan a name.'

'I can't quite remember.' Darragh screwed his eyes shut. 'I think I may have…yes. Yes, I did.'

'You cunt!' The old man roared. He slammed a fist down, causing his briefcase to jump. 'Stick to your fucking business plans and counting the fucking beans, do you hear? That's your involvement in this family's affairs!'

Darragh gave a miserable nod.

'Gave Devlan the peeler's name? Jesus, what were you thinking?' Gerrard climbed off his stool and started pacing the room. He whirled on Darragh and jabbed a meaty finger into his cowering son's face. 'Start praying. Start praying that mad fucker does nothing to make this any worse.'

CHAPTER 7

As the dirty white van roared away down Burnage Lane, scrap of material now flapping like a pennant behind it, Jon got to his knees. The single letter among the numbers of the vehicle's registration was a G. County Galway, he thought. That's where it's from. The vehicle's speed was still increasing and he knew it would be on the Kingsway in just a few second's time. Minutes after that, the flow of traffic on Manchester's ring road would have absorbed it.

He pummelled the grass with his fists, wincing as pain flared in the hand he'd used to punch the van's window. Traffic was tentatively beginning to move forward again.

A man in a builder's lorry poked his head from the cab. 'You OK, mate?'

Jon glanced up, nodding as he stood. 'Got a pen?' he asked, wiping a blade of grass from his lips as he started toward the driver.

'Course.' He reached for his dashboard and held a biro through the open window. 'Your van they nicked?'

Jotting down the vehicle's registration on the back of his hand, Jon shook his head wearily. 'I'm police.'

'Oh, right.'

The vehicle's heavy tyres began to roll. Jon turned in

the direction of the golf course and dread swamped his stomach. Punch could be dead. He stepped between the slow-moving cars and started to jog. What the hell was that thing? He could picture its powerful shoulders and neck, barrel chest and long tapered tail. The bristly coat was a mix of mustard and black, the lighter coloured bands brindled with darker streaks. A devil-creature. A fighting machine, pure and simple.

He thought about Holly. Would she realise, he wondered, how close she'd come to being attacked? She'd closed her eyes, I'm sure. And maybe, with her hands over her ears, she wouldn't have heard just how near it was.

The image of Punch being shaken about like a toy came back. Oh Punch. The sound of his Boxer's strangled yelps echoed in his head and he felt his pace increase.

He reached a sharp bend in the driveway and cut across the grass to approach the same line of laurel bushes he'd burst through fifteen minutes earlier.

This time, he slowed to a walk and stepped carefully round them. Alice was crouching down, arm around Holly whose shoulders were rocking with the strength of her sobs. The two golfers were at the edge of the car-park, arms moving as they described to several other people what had happened.

'It came from the nowhere.'

'Bounding down the slope, heading straight towards the little girl.'

'You're not serious?'

'I am – wasn't it, Aidan?'

'I don't know, I thought it was interested in the other dog.'

'Well, the Boxer dog charged at it. As far as I'm concerned, it saved that little girl.'

Jon felt a lump rise in his throat. Punch was no longer there. All he could see was his jacket lying next to a large patch of blood.

Alice looked up. 'Jon! Where did you go?'

He waved in the vague direction of the roundabout. 'Over there. Tried to catch the van.' He glanced at the patch of blood again.

Alice looked close to tears. 'He's at the vet's.'

His eyes went to Holly, who was staring at him, face all pasty. Her bottom lip buckled as another huge sob gripped her. Jon went down on one knee, pressing a palm against the side of her face. 'Holly, don't cry. The vet will fix Punch, you'll see. Let's go home, hey? We'll make hot chocolate and get warm.'

Alice straightened her daughter's collar. 'Holly? Would you like that?'

Jon watched as his daughter turned to the patch of blood. He glanced at it, too. There was a triangular flap of flesh in the grass. Punch's ear. He tried to block his daughter's view. This, he realised, will traumatise you for years. 'Come on darling, let's go.'

He retrieved his jacket, discreetly picking up the remains of the ear as he did so. To his dismay, he could see bloody little tufts littering the short grass. Clumps of Punch's fur. He dropped the piece of flesh into his pocket, moved back to Holly and took her free hand. Slowly, the three of them climbed the incline to the car park's perimeter.

As they got closer, the murmuring group of men fell silent.

'Any sign of the van?' someone asked.

Jon shook his head. 'Lost it at the roundabout.'

'Would you like to go into the club house?' another golfer asked. 'You can sit there. Call a taxi, perhaps.'

'Thanks, but no,' Jon replied. 'We only live a few minutes' walk away.'

The man who'd rung for the vet stepped forward. 'I've got a business card, here.' He held it up. 'For my wife's practice, where your dog is.'

'Thank you,' Jon answered, letting go of Holly's hand. 'I'll catch you up in a second,' he whispered to Alice.

Once the two of them were out of earshot, he turned to the man. 'Did you think that animal was about to attack my daughter?'

'I don't know,' he replied uncertainly. 'It was definitely interested – like it was stalking her - '

The other golfer butted in. 'It was going to attack something. Your dog defended the little girl.'

Jon took a quick breath in and forced the question from his lips. 'Was my dog still alive?'

The golfer looked uneasy. 'I think so. But…you know…it wasn't conscious.' He pointed at the card. 'If you call Valerie…'

'I will. How did she get Punch to her practice?'

'The boot of her car.'

'Really? I can pay for any cleaning - '

He raised a hand. 'She always has a blanket in the back. I wouldn't worry.'

'If you're sure.' Jon looked around. 'Have you ever seen that white van parked here before?'

'Never. It looked like it was here to carry out some kind of maintenance.'

Jon surveyed the watching group. 'Did anyone notice when it arrived? See the two men inside?'

Everyone shook their heads. A sprightly-looking man in a pale turquoise jumper and navy tie was striding over from the direction of the club house. 'Right, they're on their way.' He looked momentarily at the bloody grass then at Jon. 'Are you the animal's owner?'

'Yes.'

'Edwin Hughes. Club president.' He extended a hand and Jon wiped his own on his trousers before they shook. 'I've rung the police. They said a patrol car should be here presently.'

Right, Jon thought. Estimated arrival time, tomorrow. 'I'm an officer myself.'

'Ah.' Hughes' demeanour changed. 'Good show.' He gestured at the scene of the attack, 'That'll be of help, I imagine, with documenting the incident.'

Jon turned to the car park once again. 'I'm assuming that van wasn't authorised to be here?'

Hughes gave a shake of his head. 'We've no contractors booked in.'

Jon pondered the man's answer, his sense of alarm growing. Not only does it look like those bastards knew where I live, they had my routines, as well. Where I walk Punch everyday.

'What type of dog did you think it was?' The husband of the vet asked. 'Some kind of mastiff?'

'No,' his playing partner replied. 'Its face was Rottweiler, I'm sure. Plus, it was too squat to be a mastiff.'

'Rottweilers have black coats,' the first man retorted. 'That thing was covered in beige markings, plus its tail was long.'

'That just means it hadn't been docked. Anyway, part Rottweiler, I said. Crossed with one of those pit bulls, probably.'

No, thought Jon. Too long in the leg for that. Besides, it leapt into the back of that van from bloody miles off. No type of fighting dog I've ever seen is that agile.

He had the urge to have Alice and Holly in his sight. 'I've got to go. Thanks for your help.'

The club president shook his head. 'But aren't you going to wait for the patrol car?'

Jon started across the car park. 'No. I wouldn't bother waiting out here, either. They'll be ages yet. I'll ring in and speak to the officers later.'

'Well,' the president blustered. 'Can I give them your name?'

Jon thought about what had occurred in Clifden. If it's linked, I don't know what the hell I'm mixed up in. 'I can't give that information. Not at this stage of the investigation.'

The men looked nonplussed as he hurried off. Alice and Holly were making their way through a side gate on to

Sevenoaks Avenue, heads bowed, steps wooden. Keeping his distance, Jon pulled his phone from his jacket pocket and keyed in the number for the vet.

'Heaton Moor Veterinary Practice,' a young female announced.

Hello – can I speak to...' he glanced at the card, 'Valerie Ackford, please? It's the owner of the Boxer dog that's just been attacked on Heaton Moor golf course.'

'Oh, yes. She's in surgery with your dog at the moment –'

'Is he...' The words didn't want to come. 'Is he OK?'

'If you hang on, I'll pop my head in and find out.'

He heard the phone being put down. In the background came a low moaning yowl. The noise was repeated and Jon knew it must be a cat. He pictured the thing locked inside a carry-basket, staring out at the world with baleful eyes. Alice glanced over her shoulder and spotted him. He raised a hand and turned his head to show he was on the phone. She nodded and continued leading Holly along the pavement.

'Hello?' The female voice again.

Jon closed his eyes. She sounded subdued. He's dead. She's about to tell me my dog is dead. 'Yes?' The word cracked as it came out.

'He's extremely poorly. There's a faint heartbeat, but he's lost so much blood. Erm, given his state, Mrs Ackford wondered whether it might be kinder...whether you might consider –'

'No. I'll pay whatever, OK?' He thought about his bank account. Not a lot in there, as per usual. But there was the spending money they'd put aside for the coming stay at Center Parcs. And if they cancelled their fortnight in France that summer, they'd probably get most of the money back. 'Tell her money's not a problem. I'm taking my family home and then I'll come over with my chequebook, OK?'

***

Barking reverberated in the back of the van. It was a heavy, monotonous sound that caused the two men in the front to grimace.

Twisting in his seat, the passenger looked through the hatch. 'Fuck's sake, she's totally lost it!'

The shoulders of the man at the wheel stayed hunched. 'Bastard just came steaming down the road. This far from my face, he was. Punching at the glass.'

'Sean!' the passenger yelled. 'We need to get off this road. Find somewhere to calm her down.'

The lights ahead turned red and Sean had to stamp on the brakes. The barking intensified.

'Ah, Jesus, people are looking across.' The passenger sank lower in his seat, trying to cover the side of his face with a hand. 'They're all staring.'

'Where the fuck are we?' Sean murmured, glancing around. Shoppers were slowing, heads turning. 'Is that a sign, Devlan? Up ahead.'

Devlan nodded as the lights changed. 'Says the A34.'

'Shall I take it?'

'I don't know.'

'You said you knew where the motorway was!' He turned left and joined the two lanes of traffic. The barking was abruptly replaced by a low growl. 'What's she doing now?'

'Biting at the wheel arch.'

'She'll snap a fucking tooth. Shit.' Sean yanked the wheel and pulled into a lay-by. Cars flowed past. 'I'll try and settle her. You work out how we get on the motorway.' He jumped from the van only to reappear at the driver's door a second later. 'This is desperate.'

'What?' Devlan's fingers were pecking at his phone.

'Rag's not covering the registration plate. That peeler? I think he ripped it off.'

Devlan looked across. 'He saw our registration? That's a kick in the bollocks. We can't go on the motorway now. They have cameras over here recording every car. Ferry's out too.'

Sean climbed back in. 'We need to dump this van. It's the only way. If he's made the call, every patrol car in Manchester will be looking out for us.' His eyes went to the stream of vehicles going by.

'Then we torch it,' Devlan announced.

'And Queenie?' The barking began again. 'We can't be walking the streets with her. No way.'

'What do we do with her, then?'

'I don't fucking know!'

Jon pushed the cup of tea across the table as his wife stepped into the kitchen. 'How is she?'

Alice sat down with a sigh. 'She doesn't want to talk about it. She said she wanted to watch telly, so I put a DVD on for her.'

He watched his wife as she ran her fingers through her hair. Then she placed both hands on the table and looked directly at him. 'Those golfers, I could hear them talking. One of them thought that thing was about to go for Holly.'

Rage wanted to billow in Jon's chest. He had to suck in air before replying. 'I know.'

'What sort of an effect will this have had on her?' She blinked angrily. 'What is wrong with this country? I mean, why do people feel the need…'

He had to look down at the table. 'I think this is my fault.'

'What do you mean?'

He reached uneasily for his cup of tea. *What do I tell her? If my suspicions are correct, I've no idea what's happening.*

'Jon?'

He glanced back up. The sound of the man calling out to the driver of the van echoed in his head. High-pitched, with an Irish accent. It had sounded like Darragh. 'I'm not sure. I need to look into a few things.'

'What does that mean?'

He sat back, crossed his arms and tapped a finger against the bulge of one bicep, not knowing what to say.

'What's that on the back of your hand?'

He glanced down to see the registration of the van written there. 'It's…it's the number plate of the van.'

'That's not a British registration. Where's it from?'

His tongue slid across his lips. 'Ireland. It's Irish.'

Her eyes narrowed for a moment, then widened as she made the connection. 'You mean, this is to do with you going over – '

'I don't know. Not necessarily.' He could almost hear the cogs in her mind whirring. 'Ali, it could just be a – '

'They know where we live!' She stood. 'Oh my God, they know where we live.' Her eyes cut to the kitchen doorway. 'Holly.'

As she made for the door, Jon started to get up, one hand outstretched. 'Alice! They've gone. The van raced off heading for the…'

She hurried down the corridor and into the front room. Jon followed. She was standing over their daughter, looking anxiously towards the window. 'Are you OK, sweetie?'

Holly was staring up from her beanbag, face confused. 'What?'

Alice stepped round their daughter. 'I…I thought I heard you crying.' She checked the street outside then drew the curtains.

Sensing her mum's distress, Holly turned to Jon. He squatted down in front of her. 'It's fine. We just wanted to check you were fine.'

'Where did Punch go?'

He cleared some hair from in front of her eyes. 'He's at the vet's. A vet makes animals better and that's where Punch is.'

'And then they'll bring him home?'

'Yes. But not yet. He might have to stay a bit, like at a

hospital.'

'Can we visit him?'

In the periphery of his vision, he could see Alice move back to the doorway, fingers twisting together. 'Not yet. I'll pop round there soon. Perhaps we can bring him home tomorrow.'

'So he can come to Center Parcs with us?'

'I hope.'

'OK.' She turned back to the screen.

'Do you want a drink or anything?'

She shook her head, attention now on the film.

'OK. Mummy and me are just in the kitchen.'

They stepped out of the room and he started to shut the door.

'Leave it open,' Alice whispered, one hand fluttering.

'Alice,' he murmured, trailing behind her. 'We don't know for sure if this is connected to me going over there. And even if it was, they're gone. In fact, they couldn't get away fast enough. Come on, sit down. Please.'

'What happened in Clifden?' she whispered. 'You didn't tell me everything, did you?'

He brushed at an eyebrow, wanting to hide from her gaze once again. 'There was a bit of push-and-shove in the nightclub where Zoë was supposed to be working. The bouncer and the owner of the place.'

Alice sat. 'For God's sake, Jon, what did you do?'

'Me? I didn't do anything. The bouncer went for me. He ended up on his arse. Then the owner produced a baseball bat. I took it off him. Said something like he shouldn't wave things around he didn't know how to use.'

Alice bowed her head and Jon felt relieved to be free from her stare.

'What did you do to aggravate them?'

'I told you: I went in there asking for Zoë. Everyone blanked me. Then you got that other call from Siobhain to say Zoë was in the back office of the club.'

'Yes – you said you were going to the rear of the

building. Just to check.'

'I did.'

'And what was there?'

'A van. I presumed it was the one Siobhain said was being loaded with pirate DVDs.'

'Was it?'

'No. I checked on my way out. Just a delivery of drinks and crisps for the club.'

'And that's when they attacked you?'

Jon examined his tea. 'Not exactly.'

'Meaning?'

'I went into the back office. Of the nightclub.'

Anger had set her eyes ablaze. 'You did what?'

'I was trying to find Zoë. I went in and things...everything just escalated. There was no sign of Zoë or any DVDs so I got out as fast as I could.' Alice said nothing and he wondered if she was about to cry.

She raised her chin, face pale. 'They know where we live, Jon. Whoever they are, they've got our address.'

I know, he thought. They also have an idea of our routines. His mind ran back over the last few days. I got back from Dublin late on Sunday afternoon. Collected Punch from the Bramleys and took him for a walk. Next morning, I walked him again. Alice was over at her mum's with Holly. I spoke to Rick on the phone, telling him about Ireland. Walked Punch again at dusk, when he lost his tennis ball somewhere near the clubhouse. Went to bed feeling optimistic the police in Clifden hadn't been called by Darragh. That's three times I've walked Punch since getting home. 'It's not for certain there's any link.'

'Some bloody coincidence!'

He placed both palms flat on the table, lifting his fingers in appeal. 'I need to call in at the station and check a few things out.'

Shoulders still too high, she crossed her arms, wrists digging in under her breasts. He wanted to wrap his arms round her, tell her to relax, that there was nothing to worry about. But he knew that would be a lie.

'Let's say there is a connection,' she said in a small voice. 'How did they find out where we live?'

The prospect of the people in the van having that information made Jon want to hang his head. It was a policeman's worst nightmare. You went to work on the understanding the job didn't follow you home. All the scum, the low-lifes, the criminals – you visited their world. They didn't then turn up in yours. That was the deal. To have your home address out there, doing the rounds of the shitbags whose lives it was your duty to ruin…it didn't bear thinking about.

'Ali, there's no point in going down that route. It'll only make things worse.'

'I want to go down that route. How would they know our address?' A tremor of anger was now in her voice.

'OK,' he conceded. 'There are three possibilities, as I see it.'

She shot him a glance. You've considered this already.

'I spoke to a police officer in Clifden,' Jon rapidly continued. 'When I popped into the station to kill some time. I told him my surname and that I worked for the police in Manchester.' He held up a finger. 'That's one. Then there's my car. Plenty of people saw me driving around. All it took was to note down my registration.' A second finger went up. 'That's two.'

Alice was looking puzzled. 'Hang on. Both of those explanations would require co-operation from the police, wouldn't they? The officer you spoke to or someone with access to the computer system with all the car registrations on.'

'Could just be a contact at the DVLA.'

'But it suggests they're organised, Jon. Professional.'

He knew where she was heading. 'No, it doesn't. It could have just been a careless remark made by the officer in his local pub.'

'Which is hundreds of miles away in Ireland. Then days

later, that thing is let loose. Here, in Manchester. Pirate DVDs, dodgy nightclubs.' Her voice was starting to waver. 'I read the papers, Jon. You know as well as I do that organised crime in Ireland is linked to – '

'We are not being targeted by paramilitaries, Alice. Stop, OK? You're only going to terrify yourself.'

She took a deep breath. 'I should never have let you go over there.'

'If – and I say if – this is linked to Clifden, there's one other explanation.'

She raised her eyebrows.

'Siobhain. She found this phone number. She knows my name. She probably has our address, too.'

'Why would she ask you to help Zoë and then arrange for us to be attacked?'

Jon shrugged. 'Because I just buggered off? I don't know – but things don't add up with her. That's why I need to call in at the station.'

Alice looked horrified. 'Now?'

'It'll be fine. Whoever was in that van, believe me, they're long gone. Lock up after I go. I'll have my mobile with me and I'll also have a word with Simon from across the road. Ask him to keep an eye on the house. I'll be two hours, that's all.'

'OK,' she sighed, blinking a couple of times and uncrossing her arms. 'You're right.'

He gave a small smile. That was more like the Alice he loved. A thought sent his spirits plummeting. Punch. 'I'll go by the vet's, first.'

'Thank God he's alive,' she said. 'And thank God we've got this break in Center Parcs coming up. It'll take Holly's mind off what she saw and give Punch a chance to mend.'

Jon thought about the booking; they'd paid a premium for a lodge where dogs were permitted. There's no way she'll let me pull the plug on the trip now. He drained his cup of tea then placed the mug carefully on the table. 'I don't know what the vet's bill will be, Ali.'

'We've got insurance. You took out that policy – '

'It was years ago. I didn't renew it.'

Her face fell. 'Oh, Jon. The bill could be huge.'

'I'm sorry. We never made a claim – seemed like we were just throwing money away. When we started getting Holly's nursery bill, I let Punch's insurance lapse.' He watched her think things over.

'The balance for our summer holiday isn't due until next month,' she mused. 'If needs be, we could always forfeit the deposit and go camping in the Lakes, instead. I was a bit worried about driving all the way to the Alps with a newborn baby, anyway.'

Jon placed a palm over hers. 'Maybe it won't be that expensive.'

Alice gave him a look. 'Punch was protecting our daughter, Jon. I don't care about any bill.'

He wanted to kiss her.

'But I think we must go to Center Parcs,' she continued. 'Holly's been looking forward to it for weeks.'

He nodded. They were in agreement, forging a way forward. A team, working together again.

CHAPTER 8

A brass plate screwed to the bricks read 'Heaton Moor Veterinary Practice'. A short corridor ended at a waist-high door leading into a cramped office. To the right was a large waiting area. He glanced in and saw an elderly woman sitting in the far corner, a Highland terrier lying at her feet.

'Can I help you?'

He turned back to the office. A young lady in a white tunic was looking up at him. Uneasiness was playing at the edges of her eyes and he knew it was merely a reflection of the look on his face. He cleared his throat. 'I think I spoke to you a bit earlier. My Boxer dog, Punch, was attacked...I think your boss, is it? Mrs Ackford – '

'Yes, she brought him in.' She closed down the computer screen and stood up.

Jon searched her eyes for any hint of how Punch might be. 'Is he doing OK?'

Her eyes shifted momentarily to the side. 'Well, he needed a – '

At that moment there came the scrabble of claws in the corridor beyond the opposite side of the office. A Boxer dog appeared, straining at the leash. For a split-second, Jon thought it was Punch. But then he saw the large patch of white fur covering its chest. Another dog came round the corner, then a ruddy-faced woman with locks of thick ginger hair. Behind her was a slim woman in a medical gown.

The young lady in the office stepped back. 'Valerie – this is Punch's owner.' She glanced back. 'Sorry – what was your name?'

He thought about his reluctance to reveal his identity at the golf course. You can forget that now, he told himself. You're about to sign a cheque to pay for all this. 'Spicer. It's Jon Spicer.'

The vet spoke up. 'Mr Spicer, I'm Valerie Ackford.'

By now the two Boxers were in the office, both peering inquisitively about, squashed noses flaring at the wealth of strange smells. Their owner looked at Jon, sympathy making her eyebrows tilt.

Mrs Ackford squeezed past the two animals. 'These are Bertie and Bruno – they've just saved your dog's life.'

Jon looked from the dogs, to the owner, then back to the vet. 'Sorry?'

'Let's talk in the waiting room.'

Jon retreated, a flicker of hope in his head. Saved your dog's life. She definitely said that. He felt the tightness around his eyes easing.

Valerie stepped into the room and nodded at the old lady in the corner. 'Hello, Mrs Young. I'll see Flora in just a minute.'

The dog's owner smiled back. 'Thank you, dear.'

Valerie turned back to Jon. 'Now, Mr Spicer, your dog's not out of the woods yet. Not by any means.'

He felt the muzzle of one of the Boxers pressing against his thigh and glanced down. Big brown eyes stared up at him and he reached down to rub his fingers behind the dog's velvet ears. Punch is alive!

'Bertie and Bruno are two of my donor dogs.' Valerie continued. 'Pamela here kindly makes them available whenever we need blood.'

Jon glanced at the woman, trying to take all the information in. 'Thank you – but I'm not sure I follow…'

There was a half-smile on Pamela's face as Valerie spoke again. 'Punch had lost a lot of blood, Mr Spicer. He was – still is – in deep shock. His pack-cell volume was critically low. If Pamela wasn't able to bring Bertie and Bruno straight in, we would have lost him.'

A blood transfusion, Jon realised. The significance of the two Boxers before him sank in and he crouched down. Keeping his hand on the nearest dog, he reached out to cup the side of the second dog's face. Stumpy tails wagging wildly, they moved in to start licking at Jon's cheeks. He could have licked them right back. 'I don't know what to say,' he croaked, looking up at Pamela with tears in his eyes. 'Really, I don't know. Punch is like a member of…thank you so much.'

She smiled down at him, but he could still see a shadow of disquiet in her eyes. 'It's my pleasure. I can't bear the thought of any dog suffering. Now, I'd better get going. These two are due for some food.'

Jon stood, wanting to offer the lady something. Treats for the dogs. Money. But they were already pulling her towards the front door. A moment later she had it open and they vanished outside.

'Let's take you to see Punch,' Valerie said.

Jon followed her down the short corridor and through an open doorway. The far right-hand corner was taken up by a small inner room. Windows allowed him to see in. Its walls were lined with white tiles and a stainless-steel treatment table stood at its centre. The operating theatre.

He looked to his right and saw another treatment table. This one with a black plastic surface and a sink integrated into one end. It was covered with scraps of fur and droplets of blood.

'Sorry – there's been no time to tidy up,' Valerie announced. 'Punch is here.'

She pointed to Jon's right. He saw a bank of cages, each one with a metal clipboard hanging from its stainless-steel bars. The lowermost doors were the smallest, the upper ones twice their size. 'Punch is up here.'

Jon saw a drip-line going into one of the three cages forming the top row. Saliva suddenly filled his mouth. Swallowing it back, he stepped closer to look through the bars. A blue fluffy blanket lined the base of the cage. Punch was lying across it, eyes closed. The drip line was attached to the upper part of a foreleg. Large patches of fur around his throat and neck had been shaved off. Jon looked at the white flesh. Stitches lined the larger wounds. His dog's breathing was ragged and shallow and very fast.

This could have been a hospital, Jon said to himself. Me looking down on a bed. Holly lying there, bandages covering her face and neck...

'By the time I got him here, he'd gone into hypovolemic shock,' the vet said. 'As a result of inadequate blood volume. I've given him painkillers and antibiotics and all his wounds have been thoroughly flushed with saline.'

Jon wanted to open the cage door and rest his hand on Punch's head. 'What are all the little lumps?'

'Around his throat?'

Jon nodded.

'Puncture wounds. There's no need to stitch them; the tissue swells and closes them naturally. I just made sure they were as clean as possible. He lost an ear, too.'

Jon realised it was in his pocket. 'He's breathing so fast. Is he in pain?'

Valerie shook her head. 'No. He's still in deep shock, Mr Spicer. When he starts to come out, we can think about sedating him, if necessary. I'll need to look at his right front paw, too, at some point. There's crush damage to the bone.'

Jon noticed the leg was bandaged.

'Could I ask what sort of a dog carried out the attack?'

Jon peeled his eyes away from Punch. An image of the creature appeared in his head and he felt the corners of his mouth curl down. 'I don't know. I've never seen anything like it. I've been trying to think of a word and the best I can come up with is primitive.'

'Primitive?'

He shrugged. 'It had these markings like a tiger and there was a ferocity…it's hard to describe.'

She frowned. 'Was it a pit-bull type?'

'Kind of. But big, you know?' He held a hand to the top of his thigh. 'This kind of height.'

'A mastiff, then?'

'No, it was too agile. Its body was more like a heavily built Doberman's.'

'But it's head was brachycephalic?'

'Brachy – '

Her eyelids fluttered. 'Bulldog type? Square, wide muzzle, eyes set far apart?'

'Yes.'

She nodded. 'To inflict the damage it did, it had to be. Punch's foreleg looks like it's been in a vice. I'm also concerned about damage to his trachea – where the animal had hold of him.'

Jon turned back to Punch and sucked air in. He didn't dare look at the vet as he asked the question. 'He'll pull through this, won't he?'

From the corner of his eye, he saw her arms cross. 'I can't promise you that.'

His eyes were on Punch's partly open mouth. The gums – normally shiny and black – were a dry grey. 'But with the blood transfusion and everything…'

'He'll need to be monitored through the night and we'll assess him in the morning. If there are no further complications by then…'

'You can do that? Monitor him through the night?'

'A nurse sleeps over in the flat upstairs. She'll check every two hours and call me if there's a problem.'

Jon leaned close to the bars. 'Hang in there, boy. You hang in there. I'll be back soon.' He looked for any movement behind his dog's eyelids. There was none. 'OK,' he turned to Valerie. 'We need to talk money.'

She inclined her head. 'You have pet insurance?'

'I did, but not now.' He saw her face fall. Oh, shit. 'What sort of bill are we talking about?'

She blinked a couple of times. 'Treatment so far – including the transfusion – and monitoring for the next twenty-four hours? Well...it's going to be over one thousand two hundred pounds.'

Jon tried to keep the dismay from his face. The holiday in France wasn't happening. 'Fine. Do whatever you need.' He reached into his jacket. 'Is a cheque OK?'

She raised a hand. 'Let's settle up at the end. But Mr Spicer, you need to consider the possibility that Punch's condition might not improve. It could get worse. I've no idea if the damage to his trachea extends to his spine. You understand what I'm saying? We could reach the point where the fairest thing for Punch is...is to...'

Jon felt his head shaking. 'It won't come to that. It won't.'

She stared back at him with something like sorrow.

CHAPTER 9

Most officers in the incident room at Grey Mare Lane were doing paperwork or chatting as they waited for the next call to come in. In the centre of the room, three detectives were gathered round a desk with a newspaper in its middle.

'Makes you sick,' one announced, shaking his head.

'Where was he found?'

'Dumped in a supermarket car park. They reckon his body had been rolled out of a vehicle during the night. He'd been tortured.'

'What is it with Northern Ireland?' the third one demanded. 'We should just completely pull out. Let the Paddys rip each other to shreds – who gives a toss?'

Jon continued towards his desk. He'd rung Alice from outside the vet's and explained the situation with Punch. She didn't even bother to say that their holiday in France would need to be cancelled. Holly seemed fine, she'd replied to his question. Still watching telly.

Nodding hello to any fellow members of the Major Incident Team who caught his eye, Jon made his way across the room. The syndicate he was part of wasn't back on shift until the next morning, so the desks in his corner of the room were empty. He glanced at the side office belonging to his boss, DCI Christine Parks. There she was, typing away on her computer. He took in the black ringlets of hair dangling just above her collar. Thirty-nine years old and a DCI for the past three. Not bad going, he thought, especially considering she had managed it alongside starting a family.

As if sensing she was being watched, Parks glanced to her side. Hazel eyes immediately settled on Jon. He gestured to his desk, adopting an exasperated expression. With a knowing nod, she turned back to her own work.

As his computer booted up, Jon crossed to the brew table in the corner and flicked the kettle on. The lid to his syndicate's tin of coffee was off and he peered inside. Empty. Bollocks. He glanced about, wondering if the last of it had been thieved. Probably. He reached for the half-full jar of another syndicate and quickly spooned some into a clean cup before screwing the cap back on. As soon as the boiling water splashed in, he began to stir briskly, as if to remove the evidence of his pilfering.

Back at his terminal, he was about to access the Police National Computer when his fingers paused above the keyboard. From this point on, he knew all his activity on the system would leave a trail. And because it wasn't part of official police business, he was placing his career in serious jeopardy. He looked up at his screen, just able to make out the faint reflection of his face on its surface. Sod it. *I have no other choice.*

He went on to the vehicle database and, knowing the details of any officer who'd carried out a recent search on his own vehicle would be listed, typed in the registration of his Mondeo. The computer considered his request for a flash of the cursor then produced its result. No search had been carried out in the last six months. So, he thought, *that all but eliminates them tracing me through my vehicle.*

Tilting the back of his hand, he used his right forefinger to enter the van's registration. 93 G 48561. The result pinged up an instant later: no vehicle with that registration existed on the database.

'Maybe not on our system', Jon murmured to himself. He opened up Google, went into maps and entered his postcode. The road he lived on came up. Once he'd zoomed out a bit in order to reveal the nearby motorway system, he lifted the phone and called the intelligence bureau. The department served as a conduit for all information coming in and out of Greater Manchester Police. As the phone rang, he pictured Chester House, the massive headquarters building out near Old Trafford where the bureau was based. A man answered.

'Intelligence. Clive Knott speaking.'

Civilian member of staff, Jon thought. Will hopefully work in my favour. He opted for the informal approach. 'Hello there, Clive. DI Jon Spicer here.'

'Afternoon...Detective.'

'You guys busy today?'

'So so.'

'I've got an urgent one, here, I'm afraid. I need an ANPR search.'

'Nationwide?'

'No – here in Manchester.'

'That speeds things up.'

'Good.' Jon thought about the van. It had roared off in the direction of Kingsway. From there it would have accessed the M60 at junction 4. Automated Number Plate Recognition cameras, now mounted on gantries spanning the entire UK motorway network, would have first recorded the vehicle's presence there. Let's assume, he said to himself, they were fleeing back to Ireland. 'M60 at junction 4, then on to the M56 and into north Wales. After that, the A55 to the port at Holyhead.'

'Registration?'

Jon read it out.

'Irish?'

'Correct. Any idea how long the search will take?' He waited for the answer with eyes shut, listening to the sound of the other man typing.

'I had one the other day that only took fifteen minutes.'

Jon crossed his fingers. 'Cheers.' He looked at the phone on his desk. 'Can I give you my mobile, in case I'm in the field?'

'Yup. Have we got a FWIN for this?'

Force Wide Incident Number, Jon thought. Official justification for the search. Jesus, I hope this doesn't come back to bite me on the arse. He took a breath in. 'Being allocated now. As I said, this one is urgent.'

'OK. I've just put the request in. Let me know the FWIN when you've got it.'

'Will do.' After giving his mobile number, he hung up, wondering how he could access the Irish Police Force's vehicle database. Not easily, he concluded, going back to Google's homepage and typing in 'ferries to Ireland'.

The occupants of the van would be on some kind of listing somewhere. Only two companies operated the route: Stena Line and Irish Ferries. Bringing up the website for Stena Line, he sought out the number for their customer services department. A few minutes of easy-listening jazz played before a female voice came on the line.

After identifying himself and explaining the nature of his call, he was transferred. The phone was picked up after three rings.

'Hello, this is Gary Evans speaking.'

The guy seemed extremely young. Good news, thought Jon. He lowered his voice and injected it with urgency. 'Gary, DI Spicer here, Greater Manchester Police. I need you to run me a vehicle registration check, please.'

'Right...er, yes...I can do that.'

The other man was blustering and Jon pressed home his advantage. 'The last three days. Registration is 93 G 48561.'

He heard the sound of typing once again. 'What's it to do with?'

'Ongoing investigation. A fresh lead we need to follow up on straight away.'

'Right, of course. Let me see. Last three days, you said? Nothing's here.'

Jon frowned. Must have crossed with Irish Ferries, then. 'Nothing going either way?'

'No, I'm looking right now. Afraid not.'

'OK, Gary, thanks for your help.' Before the man could reply, he hung up and immediately called Irish Ferries.

This time he was put through to a woman who, when she introduced herself, sounded middle-aged. Her voice was calm and confident. Jon winced. This one might not be so easy. 'Hello, Mrs Houlcroft. DI Spicer here, Greater Manchester Police. I hope I haven't caught you at a bad moment?'

'No, it's fine, Detective. How may I help you?'

'I need to check your vehicle manifest, if I may. Crossings, say, three days either side of today's date.'

'Have you sent a DPA form across? Nothing's in my in-box.'

Jon pursed his lips. Data Protection Act. 'Sorry – it's all hands to the pumps on this one. Is there any chance you could run me a check now, and I'll make sure you receive the form as soon as I get a spare minute? It's really quite –'

She sighed. 'Just make sure it arrives today, Detective.'

As he read out the van's registration, he wondered how long he could stall her for when no DPA form showed up.

'Just checking now,' she stated. 'No, nothing.'

'Really? Nothing three days either side?'

'Correct.'

'Dublin across to Holyhead?'

'Dublin Holyhead.'

Hope caused his chin to lift. Maybe, he told himself, I've jumped to the wrong conclusion with all this. 'Thanks for your help.'

'No problem. And Detective, I suppose we can do without that DPA form, after all.'

'Much appreciated.' He replaced the receiver and stared at his monitor for a few seconds. *I need to know exactly who Darragh is.* He went back to Google's homepage, typed in, 'Darragh's nightclub, Clifden Galway' and hit return.

The search produced remarkably few results. A couple of mentions on official tourist sites for Connemara, comments in a handful of travel blogs, most by Americans. Something in Spanish, by a backpacker from the look of it. No site for the club itself.

He took out his mobile and scrolled down to M. There he was, under Maccer. They'd started out in uniform together before their career paths went separate ways. Maccer had worked in fraud for years before an off-the-record allegation of corruption he made about a well-known figure on Manchester City Council ended up in the papers. Maccer was forced to take early retirement at the ripe old age of forty-three. He now chased debts for a small firm of accountants. *When was it,* Jon wondered, *that we last spoke? Two years, maybe.*

'Spicer the Slicer, how you doing, mate?'

Jon felt himself smile. The nickname went back to when he'd captained Greater Manchester Police's rugby team. Some of the hits he'd put in on opposition players had earned him notoriety across the force. 'It's been a while since anyone called me that.'

'Not cut any more poor bastards in two recently?'

'Maccer? The only slicing I do nowadays is bread for my daughter's sandwiches.'

'Happens to us all, mate. How is the family?'

'Fine, thanks. Alice is due in two months with our second. Holly's six.'

His former colleague whistled. 'Time flies.'

'And you?'

'Yeah – Danny's five and Evie's three. Bloody handful, but doing well.'

'Good to hear. And how's life in the real world treating

you?'

'Not bad. The recession's made things busier, if anything.'

Jon could hear the man's forced cheer and he knew where it came from. Shoved out of the force so abruptly – losing the sense of cameraderie, the power that producing a police badge bestowed... 'I can imagine. Listen, mate, can you give me a few pointers? It's about looking into a potentially dodgy business – with two added complications.'

'OK. What are the complications?'

'First, the business is in Ireland.'

'Shouldn't be a problem.'

'Secondly, I need to do it off radar.'

'Ah. Does that mean totally off radar?'

'Far as possible.'

'Keeping completely out of police systems?'

'Until I have a clearer picture of the people I'm looking at.'

The other man chuckled. 'Care to tell me why there's a need for this approach?'

Jon checked no one was in earshot. 'Family walk in the local park. Some fucker let a fighting dog loose on Punch. He's barely alive.'

'Oh my God.'

'It might be linked to the owner of a particular nightclub in Ireland I had a run-in with.'

'This being the dodgy business you mentioned?'

'Yup.'

'And you need to keep it quiet from work?'

Jon thought about the summer before last. When his previous DCI, Mark Buchanon, had kicked him out of his syndicate, Christine Parks was the only other DCI in the Major Incident Team prepared to take him on. And now he was fucking things up again. 'That's right.'

'Christ, Jon, you want to be careful. Seen the reports about what happened to that squaddie? There are some seriously nasty operators over there.'

'Mate, you're talking Belfast, Northern Ireland. This is a rural town at the other end of the island. But I need some answers. If they found me in my local park, they know where I live.'

'Don't piss about – take it to your boss. You need police resources on your side. I'm serious.'

'I will – just once I know who this bastard is. What are my options?'

'What's the name of the person?'

'All I've got is Darragh.'

'Name of the business?'

'Darragh's nightclub.'

'Great,' he replied sarcastically. 'Not using police intelligence is going to severely limit you, especially if it's Ireland. Companies House is out – it's for UK-registered businesses only. Same problem for the Land Registry. Tax, too – Department of Work and Pensions is UK only. You've got a few options outside the government sector, but they'll cost you.'

Brilliant, Jon thought. More money I don't have. 'Those being?'

'Private business-information systems. I used to use Dun and Bradstreet, GMP had an account with them. I don't know what they charge.'

'Anything else?'

'You might get somewhere with a credit-reference agency. Experion or Equifax. Again, it'll cost you. Then there's your general open-source stuff.'

'Like?'

'The internet. Google the nightclub's name.'

'Have done. Fuck all.'

'Facebook – that stuff?'

'I can't see this guy being on them.'

'Then you need to use official channels, mate.'

'I know.' He glanced in the direction of his DCI's office. 'But the incident makes that awkward.'

'Incident? What happened over there? You decked somebody, didn't you?'

'Yeah, the nightclub owner. And the bouncer. And I stole the security tapes.'

He heard his colleague snort. 'Why aren't I surprised? Jon – take the hit, let your boss know what's going on.'

'I'm in the last-chance saloon here as it is.'

'Make it official and you can tap into the National Crime Agency. Those boys? They're akin to the Gestapo.'

Jon had heard more than one colleague describing the NCA's powers as draconian. 'How so, exactly?'

'In my day, it was known as SOCA, yeah? My biggest regret? Not getting in. What they're allowed to do is incredible.'

'Got any contacts there?'

'Mate – you know I didn't leave the job on particularly good terms with anyone. Apart from you.'

'Fair enough. Thanks anyway, Maccer, it's been useful.'

'My pleasure. Let me know what you find out – you've got me worried, now.'

'You and me, both.'

'We should go for a beer some time.'

'Yeah, it would be good to catch up.' He cut the call and rested his chin on the heel of his palm. What else? There had to be something. His eyes went to Parks's office. Do I just take all this to her now? No, he thought. Not until you're certain there's a link.

His mobile went and he snatched it up. Anonymous. Not Alice, at least, he thought, taking the call. 'DI Spicer.'

'Detective, it's Clive Knott from the Intelligence Bureau.'

'Wow – fast work, Clive. What have you got?'

'No vehicle with that registration's been on the M60 today.'

'Are you sure? Can we check the registration? Maybe we mixed it up.'

'93 G 48561.'

Jon raised his free hand and pressed his forehead against his knuckles. That means...what? The van was still in Manchester? 'Maybe it joined the M56 via minor roads. Can the M56 be checked?'

'It has been. I set the search parameters as the M60 and the entire M56. If you want to check Holyhead itself, we'll need to contact the port authority there. It's run by North Wales Police, I believe.'

Jon traced a fingertip across the scar that bisected his left eyebrow. No ferry booked over from Dublin, no return journey, either. Was the van – and its dog – over here all along? Why did it keep to local roads after attacking Punch? Did they know the area? Maybe the connection to Clifden didn't exist.

'Detective?'

Jon realised he was still on the phone. 'Sorry?'

'I said, do you want me to put a request into the port authority at Holyhead?'

'No – don't worry. Thanks.' He hung up and replaced his mobile next to the framed photo on his desk. The shot was of Holly with her arms round Punch. They were sitting beneath an oak tree on a carpet of autumnal leaves, diagonal beams of sunlight cutting through the branches above.

He swivelled in his seat and called across the room. 'Anyone worked any cases that involved dog-fighting?'

A thin man with greying hair got to his feet. Paul Evans, Jon thought. Been in the Major Incident Team longer than me. 'I had something last year. You want to get in touch with this guy at the RSPCA. Heads up a unit specifically for the problem.'

Jon's mind scanned back to recent news incidents. The little boy over in Liverpool mauled to death. The two guys and a woman caught organising fights in – where was it? Crumpsall? Chadderton? Somewhere beginning with a C. The young girl in north Manchester killed by the dog used to guard her uncle's pub. And those were just the cases that immediately sprang to mind. He rose to his feet and started across the room, notebook in hand. 'Do you have a name or number?'

'Hang on.' The other opened his bottom drawer.

Back at his desk, Jon contemplated the name he'd just been given. Nick Hutcher, Chief Inspector, Special Operations Unit, RSPCA Inspectorate.

Seeing the letters RSPCA made him think of Punch again. Fishing the vet's card from his pocket, he called the number. The same nurse answered the phone. 'Hello, it's Jon Spicer here. Just checking on Punch.'

'Oh, still out for the count. But that's nothing to worry about.'

He sent a silent thank-you to the ceiling. 'Right. Sorry – I didn't get your name.'

'It's Rebecca.'

'OK, Rebecca. Can I pop in to see him later?'

'We close at six. Visiting after that isn't permitted.'

He glanced at the clock on his screen. Half-two already. No wonder my stomach's rumbling. 'I'll try and make it over before then.' He keyed in his home number to let Alice know he wouldn't be much longer. She picked up almost immediately.

'Hi, babe, it's – '

'Jon! Where are you?'

He could tell she was moving quickly, voice clipped. Holly was shrieking in the background. He was vaguely aware of getting to his feet, phone pressed to his ear. 'What's going on?'

'Not sure – '

He heard the sound of a door opening and his daughter's cries of distress immediately got louder. 'There! It's there!'

Alice's voice. 'What sweetie? What's there?'

'At the window!' His daughter's words were a panic-stricken whine. 'The monster! It was at the window!'

Jon ran for the door.

CHAPTER 10

Engine howling, he tore along his street, scanning the front of his house as he drew closer. No sign of anything wrong. The car jerked as he mounted the pavement and came to an abrupt halt.

Telly-room curtains still drawn. How could she have seen anything at the window? He ran up the garden path. His key turned but the front door refused to open. Someone had drawn the bolt across. Oh Jesus. Heart beating even faster, he hammered three times. 'Alice!'

Movement from beyond the frosted glass and he heard her voice. 'Sorry, forgot I'd done that.' The bolt slid back and the door opened.

'Is everything all right?' he asked breathlessly, eyes cutting to the corridor beyond.

Her face looked tired and drawn and he could see a damp patch on her beige top. 'It's OK,' she said quietly, stepping back to let him in. 'She fell asleep on her beanbag. It was all a dream.'

'Oh.' His arms dropped to his sides. Is this how it will be from now on? A never-ending threat lurking in our lives? He closed the door behind him. 'You OK?'

'I think so. She's in there. I couldn't phone you; she

was clinging to me so tight.'

He looked into the front room. Holly was half-lying on her beanbag, hair ruffled, cheeks damp. 'Hi sweetie – did you have a bad dream?'

She looked to the windows. 'I saw that big dog looking at me.'

He knelt down and pulled her close. 'That big dog's gone. It's not ever coming back.'

She didn't respond.

'Holly? Did you hear me? Daddy called his friends at work. They chased the van with the dog in far, far away.' A mental image of the M60 materialised. Why hadn't the van gone on to the motorway? Where had the bloody thing gone? 'OK, Holly? The dog isn't coming back.'

'Are you sure?'

He shot a glance to Alice. She was waiting for an answer, too.

'Yes,' he replied. 'The person driving the van knows we'll be watching out for him. Daddy wrote down the van's number plate – and our special cameras will spot the van if it comes anywhere near here. So they won't ever dare – otherwise they'll be locked up in prison.'

'Really?' She angled her body so she could look up at him. 'They will?'

He nodded, wishing things were that easy.

'What about the big dog?'

It'll be given an injection, he wanted to say. And its body thrown into an incinerator. 'They'll keep it in a special place for nasty dogs. In a huge cage where it can't hurt anything else.' He felt her body sink back against him and he stroked her hair for a few seconds.

'Like a zoo?'

'Yeah, I suppose so.'

'When will Punch be home?'

'Soon, sweetie. Maybe tomorrow, if we're lucky.'

'So we can all go to Center Parcs?'

'Exactly – though Punch won't be doing much running

around. You can be his nurse, if you want?'

She nodded enthusiastically. 'He can have some of my purple medicine.'

Calpol, Jon thought. Holly revered the fruit-flavoured syrup. 'That's very kind of you.' He was surprised to hear her let out a giggle. 'What?'

'Your tummy just did a big grumble.'

He realised her ear was pressed against his stomach. 'That's because Daddy hasn't had his lunch.'

Alice uncrossed her arms. 'Holly? Are you hungry, too?'

She lifted her head. 'Can I have tomato soup?'

It was late afternoon before Jon got an opportunity to call the RSPCA officer.

The man who answered the phone had a gravelly voice, as if he'd just woken up.

'Hello. My name's Jon Spicer. I'm a Detective Inspector with Greater Manchester Police. Is this Nick Hutcher?'

'That's me.'

Now Jon could discern a hint of cockney in his voice. Probably about fifty, he guessed, maybe a bit younger.

'What can I do for you, Jon?'

'I gather you head up the dog-fighting unit at the RSPCA?'

'Well, it's a special operations unit. Plainclothes intelligence gathering of commercial cruelty.'

'Including dog-fighting?'

'Anything where someone's making money from the activity. Dog-fighting's my thing.'

'I was hoping you could help me, if you've got a few minutes?'

'Yup. I've got a meeting in quarter of an hour. Where did you say you were calling from?'

'Manchester.'

'That's what my meetings about. We've got word

there's an away kennels currently up there.'

Jon straightened slightly. 'Away kennels: what's that?'

'Like a visiting team. In dog-fighting you have kennels. Fuck all to do with kennels, really. It's the name the group or person gives themselves. So you've got the – I don't know – Waterloo Kennels were down in Portsmouth. But the guy who was behind that is now dead. Marshall Kennels, Middlesbrough.'

'And Manchester?'

'There's been a few around the North-West. Chad's. We're prosecuting them at the moment.'

'That was the name of the owner?'

'No – the kennels was a farm near Chadderton.'

Jon clicked his fingers. That case I was trying to recall earlier on. 'There was a woman – and two blokes.'

'That's it.'

Jon could tell the man was smiling.

'Clare Paul,' he continued with pride in his voice. 'Nearly broke my nose in the custody suite. We'd taken them to the local nick.'

'Where she punched you?'

'Oh yeah.' The man didn't seem in the least bothered; the opposite, in fact. I'm liking you already, Jon thought. 'No shy flower, then?'

Hutcher laughed, a sound like sandpaper scraping across brick. 'You wouldn't mess. It was when she asked what we were going to do with her dogs. You're ready for the blokes going ballistic when they hear they'll be destroyed. Wasn't ready for her haymaker, though.'

Jon leaned back. 'How long have you been doing this, Nick?'

'Twenty-odd years.'

'So what's this Manchester incident?'

'Intelligence is sketchy. A fight, that's for sure; but we might have missed it already. I'm travelling up this evening. We're hoping to know more by the time I arrive.'

Jon ran a thumb along the stubble on his jaw. 'Do you

know much about the scene in Ireland?'

'Only that it's bigger than over here. Pit bulls aren't illegal, for starters. Not being part of Britain, the Dangerous Dogs Act doesn't apply over there. What you find is a lot of dogs being fought in this country were originally bred in Ireland, then brought across to be fought in this country.'

'Smuggled?'

'No need. Just take them across the border into Northern Ireland – there are no controls – and catch a ferry from there. Give it some pills to calm it down and if anyone asks, it's a Staffy-Labrador cross. Something like that. It's not hard to fake a certificate.'

Jon thought about the white van. I was searching the wrong route. Should have been crossings from Belfast, not Dublin. 'Is there big money in it?'

'Not as much as the papers would have you believe. A puppy with a ROM that states it's from a Champion or Grand Champion may go for a few grand.'

'Now you've lost me again. ROM being?'

'Register of Merit. If a dog wins three fights, it's a Champion, five and it's a Grand Champion. Course, most don't last that long.'

'The dogs have fighting pedigrees? This is more organised than I imagined.'

'Oh yeah – it's meticulous. You should see the paperwork we seize. But it's not really the money that drives these people; it's their egos. The kudos of having trained up a winning dog.'

Jon's mind drifted back to the van. 'So, a lot of the breeders are based in Ireland.'

'And plenty of fights. Although it's also big in Belfast, too. Republican kennels versus loyalist kennels. They'll stop fighting each other to watch dogs doing it.'

Jon sat forward. 'You're saying it's got paramilitary links?'

'More organised crime. It's the world these type of

people move in, Jon. England, Ireland: they're just gangsters – dealing in drugs and all the usual stuff. We raid a fight here, it's often also being used to trade drugs or stolen goods. When we go in, it's alongside a lot of you guys. Mob-handed, like. Listen, I'm going to be late for this meeting. What was this incident?'

'It was an attack in a local park.'

'Dog on human?'

Jon found himself wanting to come clean. Caution held him back. 'No. Another dog. There was a young girl in the vicinity, though. The violent dog was a really strange breed. Not a pit bull.'

'Maybe a mastiff?'

'Like a mish-mash of all sorts. Mastiff, rottweiler, pit bull.'

'A Molosser.'

'What's that?'

'The type. Big, sturdy, with huge jaws. Ideal for fighting.'

'Definitely.'

'I doubt then it's owned by a kennels. Last thing they want is for their dog to be seen in public. Daren't risk it being confiscated. People who take their dogs out we class as status group. The type who strut the dog round their estate, frightening old ladies. Maybe will roll their animal with other dogs on a patch of waste ground. A kennels will have invested hour upon hour training their animals – fed them special diets, all sorts. Did you say you were a Detective Inspector?'

'Yes.' He waited for a response but none came. 'Why?'

'Seems unusual to have someone of your rank working an attack in a local park. No offence, but we sometimes have trouble getting a handful of constables to assist in a raid where we know, for a fact, the organisers are into all sorts of stuff.'

Jon closed his eyes for a moment, tired of the subterfuge. 'It was my dog that was attacked. He's in the vet's now, following a blood transfusion.'

'Sorry to hear that.' Genuine sympathy in his voice.

'Cheers. And the young girl I mentioned? It was my daughter. She was right there.'

'Jesus.'

'Nick, this animal, it was advancing towards my girl. I saw it begin to crouch. Do you think it could have been about to attack her and Punch — my Boxer — intervened?' He listened as the other man drew in breath.

'The prime target of these trained fighting dogs is other dogs. Unprovoked attacks on people are extremely rare, thank God. More likely, your dog was trying to ward it off and bang, the thing went for it.'

'To think it could have been my daughter…'

'As I said, very unlikely.'

Jon considered the answer. Maybe he's right; the guy's an expert, after all. 'You were mentioning something about status groups.'

'Yup. To your organised guys, people from status groups are muppets. Can't control their dogs, no appreciation of the animal's pack mentality or how to show it dominant behaviour. Now that is when you get those incidents of the animal chewing up a three-year-old because she toddled into the back garden.'

The man's words made sense. The dog that attacked Punch, the way it released its grip when whistled: it was highly trained. So what the hell was it doing running around on a golf course?

'Sorry, Jon,' the RSPCA inspector said, 'I've really got to go.'

'OK. How can I get hold of you, Nick? If you're on the road up here.'

'I'll give you my mobile. Maybe I should take yours as well.'

Once the call was over, Jon tipped the phone from one palm to the other, considering Maccer's advice once again.

Take the hit. Risk Parks being pissed-off about the mess you've created. Start using the resources at your disposal. See how serious the situation really is. The National Crime Agency. What had Maccer said? Powers like the Gestapo's. His eyes narrowed. Rick Saville, his partner at work, had come to the Major Incident Team via the graduate fast-track programme. The training involved rotations in many departments throughout the police service – intention being to prepare the officer for the supervisory role a senior rank entailed. During a rotation with the MIT, Rick had felt the buzz of a murder investigation and had dropped out of the programme. But not, Jon thought as he lifted his phone, before he'd completed a stint with the Agency.

'All right, Rick?'

'Yeah!'

His partner's voice was full of cheer. A moment later, Jon heard the sound of a young boy's laughter and realised why. Zak, an angelic-looking four-year-old with the sweetest of natures, had come about through Rick donating sperm to a lesbian couple. Rick got on well with them and they frequently dropped the lad off at Rick's flat.

'Got Zak here! Haven't I, little fella? Got you here!'

Jon smiled at the sound of Rick's gooey voice. Shame, he thought, I'm about to put a frown on your face. 'Rick, you did a stint with the NCA, didn't you?'

'Yeah, when it was known as SOCA. Four months'-worth.'

'Have you got an in with them? Anyone I could contact?'

His partner's voice was now more serious. 'I should think so. Why?'

Jon bowed his head. 'I need some help.'

Rick spoke away from the phone. 'Zak, go and jump on Andy, will you? Good boy.' His voice came back stronger. 'What's up?'

'I'm not sure. Could be something and nothing. Could

be a lot worse.'

'Go on.'

'You know my visit to Ireland – '

'Oh shit. The people in the nightclub made a complaint, after all?'

'No.' He looked at the tightly drawn curtains and lowered his voice. 'Punch has been attacked. We were walking him near the golf course. Some beast of a dog got hold of him. He's at the vet's now.'

'Christ, Jon. Is he OK?'

'Hopefully. He needed a blood transfusion. All kinds of stuff. This thing that attacked him – a bloke in a van whistled it back. I chased the vehicle on foot – managed to get a look at the number plate. It was from Ireland.'

'You think it was them? From that nightclub?'

'Maybe.'

His partner was silent for a few seconds. 'They know where you live.'

'If it was them.'

'What was he called again? The bloke you chucked over the bar?'

'That's the thing. I only know the nightclub's name. Darragh's. But a quick search on the system…' He checked the door was closed. 'I need to know exactly who he is – what he might be part of.'

'Oh.' Rick replied. 'I see what you're getting at. And you don't want this in the open until you know.'

'Precisely. If he's part of anything bigger and the nightclub's a front for other stuff, which I think it is, the NCA may have something on him.'

'I'm coming over.'

'What? No need, mate, honestly.'

'How's Alice and Holly? Where were they when this happened?'

'Close enough.'

'Holly saw it?'

Jon wondered what to say. My daughter was inches

away from being mauled. I was too far away to stop it. If Punch hadn't...' 'She didn't see all of it – but, yeah. She's pretty upset.'

'I'm coming over. Don't mind me bringing Zak, do you? Andy's got to work this evening.'

There was a knock on the door half an hour later. Dusk had fallen, but Jon had instructed Alice to keep the hallway light off. That way, no one out on the street could get a good idea of who was in the house.

He approached the door in the semi-darkness. 'Rick?'

'Yup.'

Jon slid the bolt across and opened up.

'You OK?'

'Yeah,' Jon replied, giving a tight smile. 'Come in.' He waved them across the threshold, unable to resist a swift scan of the street before closing the door behind them. 'Hiya, Zak. Holly's in the kitchen.'

Rick set off down the corridor, Zak balanced in the crook of his arm. As usual, Jon found himself studying the tousled locks of fair hair hanging down over the little boy's collar with concern. He wasn't sure which school the two mums were planning on sending Zak to, but he was fairly sure they couldn't afford to go private. He thought of the standard haircut for so many lads round Manchester. Cropped short at a barber's, then what was left of the fringe plastered down their foreheads with cheap gel. They would look at Zak and think just one thing: he's different. And when their parents whispered to them that the blond-haired kid lived with two women, Jon knew the baiting would begin.

Rick pushed the kitchen door half-open and thrust Zak through the gap. 'Red alert, it's a Zak-attack!'

Holly immediately dropped her felt–tip pen. 'Zak!'

The two of them met halfway across the lino floor, Holly hugging the younger child before adopting her motherly tone. 'Would you like to do colouring with me?'

Zak grinned back, happy to do anything.

'Come on, then,' Holly instructed, taking him by the hand and leading him to the chair next to hers.

Jon watched from the doorway as Rick stepped over to Alice. She had a strange smile on her face. Pleasure and anxiety fighting for control. Jon was just able to see her eyes glistening before they both embraced. Funny, he reflected, how Rick was able – without a word – to trigger emotions in her that she's able to hold back with me. They embraced for longer than usual before Rick leaned back to look into her eyes. 'You OK, gorgeous?'

She nodded, smiling again. 'Coffee?'

'Yes please.'

'Jon? Why don't you two go through to the telly room? Does Zak want some tea? It's just beans on toast. I was doing some for Holly.'

'You sure?' Rick replied.

''Course.'

They headed into the telly room and Rick gestured at the closed curtains. 'Is this all because…?'

Closing the door, Jon nodded. 'It's a nightmare. I'm ninety-nine per cent sure whoever was in that van isn't in a hurry to come back.' He held up a finger and thumb, a sliver of air between them. 'But there's just this tiny doubt…'

Rick sat on the sofa. 'Did you get a look at them?'

'I did the driver.' Jon sank on to his saggy armchair with the threadbare arms. He thought about the man at the wheel. Straggly auburn hair, nose that looked like it had been broken a few times, muscular shoulders. 'We were inches apart. I had hold of the van door's handle. Nearly yanked my shoulder out when he accelerated away.' The fingers of his left hand caressed his right wrist, which still throbbed. The swelling wasn't going down. 'His face is filed. In here.' He tapped his temple with a forefinger. 'The other one was still in the rear of the van with the dog. The thing was going crazy.'

'And it was a big animal, you said.'

'Fucking huge. Not tall like a wolfhound. But big, you know? Muscles jumping off it. No flab. It had this spade for a head... Anyway, the NCA. Can we tap into it?'

Rick thinned his lips. 'It'll be bastard tricky. The whole system is audited for lawful business use.'

'The PNC has security measures, too – but you can glean intelligence without necessarily leaving big footprints behind you.'

'No, I mean it's really pegged down. Every section is password-protected, all searches on them logged. Every email and phone call is stored and goes to hard disc.'

'Really?'

'Really. But if you need information – for legitimate reasons – it's awesome. The whole Proceeds of Crime Act – the powers it bestowed...' He shook his head. 'It's incredible. You know about SARs, right?'

Suspicious Activity Reports, Jon thought. 'That's when a business has to get consent, isn't it? Like a guy walks into an Aston Martin dealership wanting to pay cash. The onus is on the dealership to approach the NCA for consent to sell it.'

'Not just a business like a luxury car garage. Banks, building societies, solicitor's firms. Any institution handling cash transactions.'

'Over what sort of amount?'

Rick smiled and sat back. 'Any cash transaction, whatever the size.'

'You're joking?'

Rick opened his palms. 'What part of the term 'police state' don't you understand? There was a joke going round when I did my stint there. People thought Parliament only opposed the Act for as long as they did because so many of the Honourable Members were shitting bricks about how their own private dealings could be exposed.'

Jon snorted. 'Many a true word said in jest. So go on. SARs...'

'Right. ELMA is the database for all SARs. Password-protected, as I mentioned. But once you're in ELMA you can start refining your searches. Takes a bit of training, but you can go a hell of a lot deeper. Addresses related to an individual, bank accounts, companies the person does business with, names of the people in those companies, their bank accounts. It goes on...number of any passport or driving licence used as identity in any transaction.' He opened his palms again and tickled the air with his fingers. 'The web just spreads and spreads.'

'To other countries as well?' Jon asked.

Rick draped an arm across the back of the sofa. 'You're thinking about your recent trip, aren't you? I know the Agency maintains contacts across the world. Our man in Columbia, our man in Belize, and so forth. There's probably an entire team with Ireland as their remit. I imagine they'll know the names of all the major players from memory – accessing the system may not even be necessary.'

Jon tipped his head and groaned at the ceiling. 'I don't have a name.'

The door opened and Alice came in with a couple of drinks. She placed them on the coffee table and slumped down on the sofa next to Rick. He regarded her for a moment then dropped his hand to start massaging the back of her neck. Her eyes half-closed in appreciation.

'Try not to stress about this,' Rick said quietly. 'We'll get it sorted out.'

Jon watched fondly as she leaned slightly toward his colleague. Physical contact between them was so relaxed they were more like brother and sister, he thought, slightly relieved at the fact Rick was gay. If it was any other man, my hackles would be up. He glimpsed the face of his watch. Shit! The nurse said the vet's shut at six. He jumped to his feet.

'What?' Alice asked, the queasy look back on her face.

He held up his hands. 'Nothing. The vet's – I wanted

to look in on Punch. They shut at six.'

Rick glanced at his own watch. 'That's now.'

'I know – maybe I'll catch it before it closes. Ali, is that OK?'

She looked at Rick. 'You can stay a bit, can't you?'

'I'm not going anywhere.'

She looked back at Jon. 'Yes.'

He hurried out into the hallway. 'Daddy's popping out for five minutes!' he called through to Holly, yanking his jacket off the end of the banister.

CHAPTER 11

The sky was clear and a frost was already forming on the tiny patch of grass that was their front garden. He stepped onto the pavement, eyes sweeping the road.

A man was walking towards him, head down, shoulders hunched against the cold. Jon stood before his gate waiting to see if he recognised him. Six feet away, he looked up. The face was familiar – the bloke lived about six doors down. 'Evening.'

'Evening,' the man replied, pace not slowing. 'Going to be a cold one.'

'Yup.' Jon turned right and was on St Andrew's Road in minutes. As he approached the semi-detached house in which the practice was based, he could see the ground floor was dark. He glanced up at the first-floor windows. A light was on. The shadowy form of someone moved behind a thin curtain.

She soon appeared in the next window, this one with nothing to obstruct his view. The young woman opened a cupboard, removed a mug and began to prepare a drink.

He considered knocking on the door, the urge to see Punch was so strong. He thought about how fast his dog's ribs had been rising and falling. Little shallow gasps that seemed likely to stop at any moment. He squeezed his eyes shut but an image of the thing that had attacked his dog was waiting in his head. He blinked it away, but it was replaced by the look of fear on Alice's face, the grief on Holly's. My family. No one attacks my family. If I ever get my hands on the fuckers in that van. He let his train of thought run, picturing his fists slamming into their faces. He nodded to himself. It would be methodical. The driver first, one punch straight to his nose then an upper cut to snap the head back. If he was still standing, another to the side of his head. Once he dropped, it would be the turn of the guy in the back of the van. Jon allocated him the face of the nightclub owner. Again, one directed at the nose. Instant result – blood and tears so the bloke couldn't see the next blows coming. He realised his breathing had picked up and his weight had gone on to the balls of his feet. Stop it, he told himself. Don't let revenge fantasies take over.

The nurse was no longer at the kitchen window. Probably just putting her feet up, he thought. Seeing what's on the telly. I can't disturb her now. It wouldn't be fair. Besides, they'd have rung me if there was anything to report. He squinted to make out the opening times on the notice below the brass plaque to the side of the front door. 8.00 a.m.

Turning to go, he thrust his hands into his pockets. His fingertips immediately brushed against something soft and he pulled it out before thinking. The flap of Punch's ear. Earlier, he thought. I shoved it in my pocket earlier. At the golf course. Was that really this morning? It felt like a distant memory.

He contemplated the triangular piece of flesh. There'll be payback for that, he said to himself, dropping it in the little bin at the top of the vet's path. I need the name of the nightclub owner. I have to know who the bastard is. He racked his brain for anything. A memory of the noticeboard beside Clifden's metallic monument.

Something about fundraising for a new roof for the town's Gaelic Football Club. He remembered the police officer saying how Darragh always put his hand in his pocket for local projects – including the sponsoring of that year's Christmas lights. It was exactly the type of thing a local paper would report. What was the name of that one I flicked through in Mannion's Bar? *Galway Advertiser*, that was it.

'It's me!'

Rick peered down the corridor from the kitchen doorway. 'Make it in time?'

'No.' Jon slung his jacket back over the banister. 'But I've thought of something.' In the kitchen, Holly and Zak were sitting at the table, bowls of ice cream with sprinkles before them.

Alice looked across from the corner chair. 'Have you been running?'

He nodded. 'Freezing out there.' He turned to Rick, but his partner spoke first.

'I was thinking. You know all the building work in Manchester before the recession? City-centre flats by the thousand – remember how ridiculous it got? During my stint with the Agency, they were looking into loads of the deals – '

'Tell me in the telly room,' Jon cut in.

Rick's eyes moved briefly to the youngsters and he nodded.

Once inside, Jon shut the door. 'Go on.'

'Finance for a lot of it was from investment companies that were traced back to Ireland. Suspicion was the money had come from the IRA's coffers. There were layers upon layers – including offshore accounts – the investigation was still ongoing when my rotation came to an end.'

Jon sat down in front of his computer. The letters IRA hung heavy in his mind. *Is that who I've messed with?* He felt nauseous.

'Thing is,' Rick continued. 'The guys I know who are still in the Agency, I could ask them if it's possible to have a dig round tangentially.'

Jon glanced up at his partner. Tangentially. 'You and your big words. In plain English, mate?'

Rick held a finger in the air. 'You're already looking into this area.' He wormed the finger a little to the side. 'A few related searches just over here would go unnoticed. They'd just be among dozens of avenues in an ongoing investigation. You could do it so it didn't show up on any audit. Not unless they were going over it in forensic detail.'

Jon grinned, feeling a little better. 'You know? Maybe there is something to this business of recruiting smart-arsed graduates.'

Rick cocked his head to the side. 'Maybe.'

'Mind you, this old plodder thought of something else,' Jon announced, pointing at his computer.

Rick stared at Google's homepage. 'You've lost me.'

Jon tapped in the words, *Galway Advertiser* and hit search.

Rick placed a hand on the edge of the desk and leaned forward.

The paper's homepage was dominated by a report about the murdered British soldier. Conjecture was now flying around over who'd carried out the killing. Unionist politicians were poking the finger at Sinn Féin, claiming the party was inextricably linked to the IRA. A video clip of Martin McGuinness started up and they listened to the deputy First Minister of Northern Ireland rebutting the accusation. Since the Good Friday Agreement, he asserted, the IRA had surrendered its weapons and was no longer active. A journalist recounted the known breakaway groups from the resistance movement – including the Real IRA, Continuity IRA, Irish National Liberation Army, Og Laigh na hEireann and Irish Republican Liberation Army.

Jon moved the cursor to the newspaper's own search box and keyed in 'Clifden Christmas lights sponsor'. A single result came up.

Darragh de Avila sparks Clifden's Christmas Season

There he was, standing proudly next to the town's plane-wing memorial.

Jon pressed his fingertip so hard against the plasma screen, the man's face dissolved into a splodge of black. 'Darragh de Avila? I fucking got you.'

CHAPTER 12

'De Avila. What sort of an Irish name is that?' Jon asked.

Rick frowned. 'There was an Eamon de Valera, that famous guy from Irish history.'

Jon kept staring at the screen. 'Eamon de who?'

'You're the one with Irish ancestry,' Rick replied incredulously. 'Your grandpa never tell you all about old Eamon?'

Jon reached for the mouse. 'Never met my grandpa, mate. Not so as I remember, anyway. Or my grandma before she died. More weird shit in the Spicer family, I'm afraid. My mum refuses to go into it.'

Rick's voice was more serious. 'Well, de Valera was, I'm pretty sure, the Irish republic's first ever Prime Minister and President in the forties and fifties. Helped kick us Brits out.'

'Bet there's a few statues to him, over there.'

'No doubt.'

Jon reflected on his knowledge of the political set-up in Ireland. Could fit on a bloody postage stamp, he thought, recalling the audio clip of McGuinness. He glanced at his colleague. 'Do you know how it all works over there? DUP, Sinn Féin, Good Friday Agreement? All that stuff?'

'The Good Friday Agreement is basically a power-sharing deal between the biggest political parties in Northern Ireland.'

'Right. So how come Sinn Féin is a political party in Northern Ireland and also in Ireland itself? It confuses the hell out of me.'

His colleague smiled. 'That's the crux of it, mate. Sinn Féin wants an Ireland as it was – one nation, free of British rule. The unionists in Northern Ireland, like the DUP, want to remain part of the United Kingdom. The Good Friday Agreement was an accord – brought about by years of wrangling – where the unionist parties and Sinn Féin agreed to share power in Northern Ireland's assembly.'

'Stormont.'

'Correct. The unionists only agreed to it when they were assured by Sinn Féin that the IRA had handed in its weapons and disbanded.'

'Sinn Féin being part of the IRA?'

'Sinn Féin being the political wing of the IRA.'

'And have they really disbanded?'

Rick let his hands rise and then fall. 'Who knows? Not many believe the IRA would have handed in its entire arsenal. And now you've also got all these IRA offshoots who never wanted to go along with the Good Friday Agreement. A lot of people also believe the main players in the IRA are just maintaining the ceasefire while they gauge if Sinn Féin's policy of engaging with the political process will really bring them power. If not, the guns come back out: the big nasty ones they never handed in.'

Jon turned back to the screen. 'De Valera, de Avila – they don't sound Irish.'

'Isn't there a legend that those types of name in Ireland date back to when the Armada was wrecked off Ireland's coast? Spanish sailors getting frisky with the lovely local maidens?'

Jon glanced to his side. 'Did you ever read normal books when you were young – or was it just encyclopedias?'

Rick grinned. 'The newspaper article describes de Avila as proprietor. Doesn't mean he's the actual owner.'

'That's what everyone seemed to describe him as,' Jon answered, thinking about Siobhain's call and his conversation with the uniform in Clifden's police station. Could it have been an officer in the Irish police who'd passed his identity on?

'OK,' Rick replied. 'Let's assume he is the owner and let's assume he's behind what happened in the park.'

'Then I'm in the shit,' Jon stated, joggling the mouse so the cursor arrow stabbed at de Avila's head. 'He's got good enough connections to get the attack arranged in hours. That van either crossed from Belfast in the last few days or it was here already.'

Rick retreated a couple of steps to sit on the arm of the sofa. 'Why do you think that?'

'I blagged it with the ferry companies operating the Dublin–Holyhead route. Neither had any vehicle with the van's registration on their manifests. I also had an ANPR search carried out.'

Rick looked even more uneasy. 'And?'

'After the attack, the van didn't head for the motorway. Which means the driver is savvy enough to keep off them – or he's based locally and didn't need to go on it.'

'Or,' Rick held up a finger. 'There's option two. The whole incident has no connection whatsoever to you smacking those guys over in Clifden. That would explain why the van wasn't on the ferry and why it doesn't appear to have fled Manchester. Just local shitheads.'

Jon weighed up the likelihood. The voice he'd heard in the back of the van had sounded like Darragh's. But that was mainly because of the Irish accent. He thought back to the look of panic on the driver's face when he'd caught them up at the roundabout. The man at the wheel didn't even contemplate jumping out to fight – it was as if the plan was accomplished and all he wanted to do was get away. 'I don't know.'

Rick leaned forward. 'You've got to go to Parks with this. Just to find out what's going on.'

Jon grimaced. 'I really don't want to be her syndicate's resident pain-in-the-arse. You know how it ended up with Buchanon. And before that, McCloughlin. If she hadn't stepped forward to take me in…'

'You've got no other choice.' Rick stood. 'And she'll definitely prefer you being straight with her. Especially with the ANPR check and any other unauthorised stuff you've been up to.'

Jon crossed his arms and said nothing.

CHAPTER 13

They woke early. It had tried to snow in the night; a sprinkling of tiny white balls that covered his rear yard. Pausing on the back step, empty plastic milk carton in one hand, Jon searched for the trace of any footprints in the delicate layer. Nothing.

He dropped the crushed carton into the recycling bin, reflecting on the night that had just passed. Neither he or Alice had slept well. Time and again he'd woken as she'd restlessly moved around in the bed. The scene from the park seemed to be stuck on a loop in his head. The moment the beast had brought its huge muzzle level with Holly's face...

At some point, the slam of a car door ripped him from his troubled slumber. The engine had continued to chug. Jon was almost certain it was a taxi, but he had to see. After all, the van's engine had been a diesel. He slipped out from under the duvet.

'What is it?' Alice immediately whispered.

'It's OK,' He lifted back a corner of the curtain. The black cab was clearly visible under the streetlight, engine idling as the driver spoke into his handset. 'Just a taxi.'

Alice lay rigid, staring at the ceiling. 'We can't go on

like this.'

'I know.'

'When you said to Holly the van would never return, I so wanted to believe you.'

He sat on the edge of the bed and placed a hand on the huge swell of her belly. 'First thing tomorrow, I'll tell my boss what's been going on.'

He walked slowly across the yard and opened the kitchen door, painfully aware there was no Punch following him in. Normally his dog would be barging past, heading straight for the food bowl in the corner. Jon looked wistfully at the empty dish. The vet's would be open at any minute.

Alice and Holly were sitting at the table. His wife was contemplating the cup of coffee before her. A large bag packed with toys, books and activities for Holly was on the floor. The skin below Alice's eyes was a purplish colour and her shoulders were hunched. He moved behind her and placed a hand across the back of her neck. 'You'll be able to relax once you're at your mum's. When you've set off, I'll swing by the vet's to check on Punch.'

She leaned her head back as he stroked his thumb up and down. 'Give him a big kiss from me.'

'Will he come home today?' Holly asked tentatively.

'We hope so,' Alice replied.

'Would you like that?' Jon asked. They'd told their daughter that Amanda, Alice's mum, was still feeling poorly and needed to be looked after for the day. 'Then you can be looking after your granny and your dog.'

Holly nodded vigorously, attention back on her bowl of Honey Hoops.

Jon glanced into the waiting room at the veterinary practice. He was first of the day. 'Morning. Is it OK to look in on Punch?'

The nurse he'd seen through the window the previous

evening stood up. 'Come through. I was expecting you last night.'

'I got here just after you'd closed.'

A pained expression crossed her face. 'You should have knocked; I'd have let you in.'

'Well, I figured nothing serious could have happened.'

'No. I've just looked in on him myself.'

Jon hesitated. 'How does he seem?'

She see-sawed a hand. 'No change, really. Pulse and breathing have steadied. He's sleeping.'

'That's good?'

'To be expected. Given the level of trauma.'

He followed her down to the surgery and she stepped sideways to allow him access to the bank of cages. His dog didn't appear to have moved from the afternoon before. Leaning closer, Jon could see his breathing was more normal. The flesh around his gums was a shade darker, too.

'He's still very poorly, as you can see,' the nurse said. 'When Valerie comes in, she'll assess him properly. Perhaps X-ray his neck to see if there's any damage to the vertebrae there.'

Jon gazed at his dog. Please don't let there be anything wrong, he thought. 'And the foreleg? Where it was crushed?'

'She'll look at that.'

'OK – when would be a good time to phone?'

'Half-twelve?'

'No problem. Half-twelve it is.' He turned back to the cage. 'Can I stroke him?'

'Of course.' She reached out, popped the clips and swung the door open, taking care not to snag the drip-line running through the bars.

Jon placed his hand on Punch's head. 'Hang in there, boy,' he whispered. 'We'll take you for a nice holiday, soon. Steak for every meal, OK?'

CHAPTER 14

Jon walked between desks, eyes shifting to the glass partitions of his DCI's office. She was in there.

Exchanging greetings with various colleagues, Jon got to his desk on the far side. No sign of Rick yet. A spoon clattered in a bowl and, at the next table, DI Elmhurst placed a box of Shreddies in her lower drawer while looking across at Jon.

'Aren't you on holiday, soon?'

'Tomorrow,' Jon replied, turning his computer on. 'I need to clear a few things first.' He picked up the message slip which had been placed at the top of his in-tray. Call Clive Knott at Intelligence. The guy's after a FWIN, Jon thought, as he put it back. 'Where's Ryan?'

She glanced at the empty desk facing hers. 'Running late. Traffic on the M62. Coffee?'

'Oh bollocks, I meant to get some more. We're out.'

She lifted out a large jar from a shopping bag at her feet. 'Ta da!'

'You're a star,' he replied, wondering how much their syndicate's coffee kitty must now owe her. He took his jacket off, eyes straying to Parks's office once again. Let's get this over with, he thought. Her door was ajar and he knocked on the glass before poking his head through the gap. 'Morning, boss.'

'Jon,' she nodded, sitting back. 'Need a word?'

'Please.' He coughed awkwardly. 'Do you have a minute?'

She gestured to the chair on the other side of her desk. 'What's up?'

He closed the door behind him and turned round, registering the row of photos lined up on a lower shelf. 'I've got a bit of a situation.'

'Something to do with you charging out of here yesterday?' She raised an eyebrow. 'I nearly called you to make sure everything was OK.'

He rubbed his palms together. 'Yes. I'm hoping it will all be a false alarm. Really, there's every chance that's the case. But, I need to be – '

'Jon. Start at the beginning. And sit down.'

He perched on the edge of the seat and breathed in. 'Sorry. I really didn't want to bother you with this…'

'It's not a problem, I'm sure.'

'Right.' He turned his hands over and examined the myriad scars etched into his skin. Here we go. 'I went over to Ireland recently. It was as a result of a call I received from a female who identified herself as Siobhain. She informed me that Zoë, the partner of my younger brother, Dave…' he glanced up, to check she was aware of his brother's murder. She gave a small nod.

'Following Dave's death,' he continued, 'Zoë was unable to cope. She left their son, Jake, and disappeared. The boy now lives with my mum and dad. In some four years, the only time we heard from her was via two postcards. In the first, she stated that she was proceeding to Connemara in Ireland in order to try and ascertain the whereabouts of an old friend living in that part of the country. The name of that friend was Siobhain.'

'The same Siobhain who called you?'

'I can only assume so. Her second postcard was from

the city of Galway itself. She was staying there for a bit before proceeding to Clifden – the town on Connemara's coast where she had reason to believe Siobhain resided.'

'OK. And Jon? You can drop the formal language. You're not in court.'

'Right. Sorry.' He flexed the fingers of his right hand, realised he'd formed them into a fist and quickly straightened them. 'Siobhain informed me – said – that Zoë was mixed up with some dodgy characters and needed someone to get her out of there. She was working in a nightclub called Darragh's.'

'Who, Siobhain?'

'No, Zoë. I don't know anything about Siobhain, not even her phone number. She called me from a payphone.'

'OK. Who are these people Zoë's mixed up with?'

'That's the problem. I'm not sure. Siobhain made out the nightclub owner is strictly small-time, smuggling pirate DVDs, perhaps other stuff.'

Parks's voice was now more wary. 'Pirate DVDs have been identified as a major source of revenue for paramilitary groups over there.'

Jon nodded. 'Well, anyway – I drove across, but there was no sign of Zoë in the nightclub. None of the staff would admit to knowing her. I then got into an altercation with some of those staff – '

'Meaning?'

He looked up at her. 'The doorman of the club swung at me. More than once. I retaliated and he ended up on the floor. A baseball bat was then produced by the owner. I disarmed him and…you know…had words.'

'Did you strike him?'

'No. And there was a nightclub full of witnesses who can verify that. But I realised then that I was…the situation I'd got myself in was bad. I went into the back office, removed the security tapes – I don't know why – and left.'

'Where are these tapes now?'

'I chucked them in a bin.'

Parks stared at Jon, one manicured nail tapping. 'Jesus Christ, Jon. There's more, isn't there?'

He nodded. 'This was on Saturday night, four days ago. Yesterday, my dog was attacked – '

'What breed?'

Jon blinked. 'Sorry?'

'Breed?'

'Boxer. He's a Boxer.'

'Carry on.'

'He was attacked by some type of fighting dog. Kind of mastiff Rottweiler cross. Huge thing – it was approaching my daughter. Had got to within a few feet of her before Punch – my dog – ran at it.'

'You think it was going to attack your daughter?'

'Yes. But the thing heard Punch coming and rounded on him instead. It took my pet apart.'

Now she looked outraged. 'Where was its bloody owner?'

'I was just getting to that – '

'Is your dog OK?'

'No, he was very badly mauled. They're doing more tests this morning. He went into shock, lost a lot of blood.' Jon frowned. Parks was now upright in her seat, finger tapping faster. Shit, he thought. She's absolutely furious. I'm fucked. 'The...er...the animal that carried out the attack was then called back to a van. I gave chase and was able to note the registration down. It was from County Galway in Ireland.'

Her finger stopped moving. 'Ireland?'

'Yes.'

'When exactly were you over there?'

'I arrived Saturday evening.'

'I don't suppose you were handing out cards with your address on.'

'No – I mentioned my surname to a uniform in the town's police station, along with the fact I was a copper from Manchester.'

'Anyone else?'

He shook his head. 'I know the drinkers in a bar saw that my car was British. The only other people in that town who know my identity would be Siobhain and Zoë. I didn't see either of them.'

'What about this Siobhain? You're sure she actually knows Zoë?'

He thought about her asking if he'd really done those things to Salvio. Apart from Rick, only Zoë knew about that. 'Yes. She was able to mention some specifics that prove it.'

'I only wish you'd come straight to me with this.'

He wasn't sure what to say: the woman now seemed more sympathetic. Parks turned to her computer for a moment. 'After the incident in Clifden, you drove straight to…where, Dublin?'

'I slept in my car that night, somewhere just along the coast, then drove to Dublin the next day. I was on the ferry by the afternoon.'

'And your dog was attacked Tuesday morning, three days after the Clifden incident,' Parks stated, reaching for her mouse. 'Do you have the van's registration?'

'Yes. But I searched yesterday. Nothing on the PNC, nothing on the ANPR cameras on the M60, nothing with the ferry companies crossing from Dublin.'

Parks's eyes met his. 'Really?'

'Yes – sorry. I know that I wasn't authorised to – '

She waved a hand. 'I'm treating this as an official incident, Jon. Those searches won't be a problem.'

'That's…appreciated,' Jon replied. 'The guy at Intelligence who requested the ANPR check is wanting a reference number.'

'He'll get one. Now, what else have you got on these people in Ireland?'

Jon sat forward. 'The nightclub owner is called Darragh de Avila. All I've been able to glean is that he's a businessman who regularly supports local fundraising events.'

'But may also have sidelines in smuggling counterfeit DVDs and God-knows-what else.' She pushed a pad of paper towards him. 'Jot down his name there, will you? And that van's registration.'

Jon did as asked. 'So what's next, boss?'

Her attention was on her screen. 'We get this character thoroughly checked out.'

Jon's eyes settled on the wires trailing from the back of her computer. The intelligence systems she was going to access. All that power – and it's on my side. He wanted to raise his arms in triumph.

'There's been no complaint made against you via the Irish police,' Parks announced, 'nor would I expect one, given the nature of the people you had this fracas with. You're on holiday this week, correct?'

'Yes, from tomorrow. Center Parcs.'

She pursed her lips, still looking at the screen. 'Why didn't you take today off and have the entire week to yourself?'

Jon felt his head drop a notch. 'I've used up my holiday allocation. We've got a fortnight in France this summer.' Or we did, he thought. Until all this happened.

'Center Parcs,' his DCI murmured. 'I didn't know they allowed dogs there.'

'You have to book a special lodge.'

'How is your daughter with all this?'

'She seems relatively OK – so far.'

'And your wife?'

'Worried sick, to be honest. Neither of us slept last night.'

'And you rushed out of here yesterday because…?'

'Turned out to be nothing. My daughter was asleep and dreamed the dog that attacked Punch was looking in through the front-room window. She's seems OK now, but I guess we'll have to wait and see if the dreams turn into a regular thing.'

'Are they at home now?'

'It's our daughter's half-term. We thought it best the two of them stay at my wife's mum's today. She lives over near Worsley.'

'How much work have you got on at the moment?'

'You mean screamers?'

She nodded.

'There's the armed robbery on that social club in Miles Platting. Same MO as the two others last month. And the carjacking in Timperley. The one that left the vehicle owner in intensive care.'

'Nothing DI Saville can't tread water with for a few days.'

'I suppose – '

'Go on, Jon. Bring me details of any other things that have to be actioned before the weekend and get yourself home. I'll let you know as soon as we know more.'

Unable to believe how well everything was going, Jon stood. Parks was now busily typing away. Less than a minute ago, he thought, she seemed ready to bite my head off. Now she's my biggest ally. He looked bemusedly at the photos lined up on her shelf. Among the shots of her children was one he hadn't noticed before. It was of a dog, one of those comical-looking things with a moustache and bushy eyebrows. Realisation dawned. 'That's a nice-looking dog.'

She paused in her typing to look lovingly at the image. 'He's a salt and pepper miniature schnauzer.'

'What's he called?'

'Dennis,' she said proudly. 'He's my best boy.'

CHAPTER 15

Out in the incident room, Rick was just taking off his jacket, shirt neatly pressed and hair artfully arranged so that several short strands went against the direction most of the spikes were pointing. How long does he take each morning in front of the mirror? Jon wondered, thinking about the cropped hair on his own head. Three seconds to rub dry with a towel and that was it. He held up a hand in greeting.

Rick nodded back before shooting a questioning glance at Parks's door.

Jon held up a thumb. 'I needn't have worried.'

'How do you mean?'

Jon noticed the cup of coffee next to his phone. Nice one, Rachel. He took a sip. Still hot, too. 'Dog lover,' he whispered with a smile.

'You what?' Rick sat.

'She's a dog lover, mate. As soon as I mentioned my Boxer had been attacked, that was it – she started pulling out all the stops.'

Rick looked mystified. 'That swayed it for her?'

Jon gulped back the rest of his drink. 'You prefer cats to dogs, don't you?'

Rick nodded. 'But what's that got to do – '

'You wouldn't understand,' Jon grinned, stepping away from their desks. 'Coffee?'

'Yeah,' Rick replied, still looking confused. 'Cheers.'

Jon crossed to the brew table and flicked the kettle on. Reaching for a clean mug for Rick, he assessed the situation as it now stood. I should call Alice, he thought. Let her know that everything's going to be sorted. As he spooned coffee from their syndicate's jar, Paul Evans – the detective who'd dug out the details for the RSPCA's chief inspector the day before – wandered over.

'Morning, Jon.'

'Hi Paul – thanks for the contact, I had a decent chat with him yesterday.'

'Still looking into the dog-fighting stuff?'

Jon tipped his head. 'You got something?'

'There's an incident in with the overnights. Caught my eye.'

'Go on,' Jon replied, splashing a load of milk into Rick's cup.

'It's actually under abandoned or stolen vehicles. A van that someone tried to torch on playing fields in Offerton, Stockport way.'

That's about ten minutes from my house, Jon thought, turning to face his fellow detective.

'The calibre of criminal we have to deal with today,' Evans sighed with mock regret. 'Just gets worse and worse. These particular playing fields are directly behind a fire station. Firefighters put the vehicle out and a couple of uniforms have just checked it over. In the back of the van is a very large, dead, dog.'

Jon licked his lips. 'Where's this again?'

'Offerton – opposite a community place that got closed with all the cutbacks: the Dialstone Centre.'

Jon vaguely knew it. Stockport Rugby Club's ground was a short distance away. 'Did the van have Irish number plates?'

'I think the report said they'd been removed. I've got it up, now.'

He led Jon over to his computer, slid into his chair and traced a finger down the screen. 'Yup – plates are missing.'

'Nothing else on the van?'

'Just that it's a white Ford.'

Same model as the one I chased, Jon thought. It's got to be the one. 'Ping that over to me, would you Paul? Cheers.' He hurried back to his desk, grabbing the coffees on the way. 'I think we've got something,' he announced, plonking the drinks down and logging on to his computer. He went to his emails and brought up the one at the top.

'What is it?' Rick asked, coming round the desks while looking suspiciously at the coffee Jon had just made.

'Could be the van from yesterday. Someone tried to torch one over near Stockport. Firefighters put it out.'

Rick whistled. 'How soon did they get to it?'

Jon scanned the report. 'Not sure. But the carcass of a large dog was in the back.' He scrolled down until the radio room's number for Stockport police station came up. 'Hello, DI Spicer, Major Incident Team, here.'

'Sergeant Maughan speaking.'

'Morning Sergeant. You've got an abandoned vehicle on your patch. Can I give you the FWIN?'

'Go ahead.'

Jon read it out. 'Can the officers attending make sure the scene is secured and then await my arrival? We'll be there in fifteen.'

'Will do.'

Jon hung up and looked at Rick. 'Drink up, mate, we're heading out.'

They were on the road less than five minutes later, morning traffic heavy in the opposite direction. Soon they joined the A6 and from there Jon knew it was a straight run through Levenshulme and Heaton Chapel to Stockport itself.

The road curved round and suddenly low winter sun

was blinding him. He flipped the visor down and glanced at the dashboard. One degree. It had been a cold bastard of a winter. 'Can you give Alice a buzz, mate? Tell her everything's being sorted.'

In the passenger seat, Rick reached into his jacket. 'Do you want me to mention the dog in this van?'

'No – not yet. I want to be sure first.'

Rick keyed in the number as Jon cruised along in the outside lane, occasionally resorting to the blue lights behind his radiator grille to clear dawdling cars from his path.

'Alice, hi, it's Rick. Are you OK? Good. Listen, Jon's driving. We're on our way to an incident. But he's seen Parks. Apparently, she's a fellow dog-lover.' He paused. 'Dog-lover, yes. She has a dog.'

'Miniature schnauzer,' Jon called across.

'Did you get that?' Rick said. 'Anyway, she's totally on our side. The thing's got priority status.'

Jon leaned across. 'Whoever this guy is, we'll know everything about him very soon. So don't worry, babe.'

Rick listened for a second and smiled. 'She says to concentrate on your bloody driving. And she loves you, God knows why.'

Jon smirked. 'Love you too, babe. See you later!'

Rick hung up and stared out the window. 'You know, one thing's bugging me in all this: the Zoë factor. What do you think has happened to her now?'

'How do you mean?'

'Since you turned up in Clifden.'

His mind went to the curiously quiet town. The sense that, somehow, the place itself had been watching him. The way everyone insisted they'd never heard of Zoë or Siobhain. It was all a touch surreal. 'You reckon, by going over there, I've just made her situation worse?'

'It's possible.'

Jesus, he thought, Rick's right: she could be in some back room right now, having the shit being beaten out of her. 'Maybe,' he said quietly, 'she's got away.'

'And if she hasn't?'

He didn't want to contemplate it.

'What if Siobhain rings again? Or Zoë does, asking for your help.'

Jon wanted to push the thought away. There's enough on my plate already. You know what you'll do, a part of him said. You'll go back for her. Because if you don't, you'll never be able to look at Jake again without feeling guilty.

Stepping Hill hospital was on his right. He indicated left, passing through some traffic lights onto Dialstone Lane. 'Somewhere along here.'

Rick pointed. 'There you go. Lisburne Lane.'

He turned into a narrower road, houses on either side. Moments later, he was parking outside the playing field's entrance. Fifty metres across the grass was a grubby white van, paintwork blackened by smoke. Scene of crime tape cordoned it off.

The sun was barely visible above the tops of the houses which bordered the expanse of grass. Shadows caught in the tyre tracks that led to the vehicle. He tested the ground with his feet. Solid. 'Must have been driven here early evening, before the ground froze. Obviously dumped in a hurry, oblivious to the fact they'd parked directly behind a fire station.'

'Which means they couldn't know the area,' Rick concluded.

A patrol car was parked on the edge of the grass, a couple of uniforms sitting inside. Jon placed a hand on the roof and leaned down to the partly open window. He wanted to shake his head. So bloody young. 'Morning, lads. That my van?' he asked, holding his warrant card up.

The one in the passenger seat clocked his rank and scrabbled for the door handle. 'Morning Detective. Yes it is – secured as requested.'

As he got out, flakes of sausage roll fell from his tunic.

'Bit of breakfast while we waited.'

'And why not?' Jon smiled. 'This is DS Saville.'

'Sir,' the constable nodded at Rick. 'Shall we show you across?'

Jon contemplated the question. No point more people than necessary poking around. He shook his head. 'May as well stay warm in your car. What do we need to know?'

The one who'd been in the driver's seat produced his notebook. 'It was set alight at 6.30 p.m. last night, or thereabouts.'

'Anyone see the vehicle's occupants?'

'No. Firefighters spotted the flames through their canteen windows on the first floor. They ran a hose across the training area behind the station and gave it a good soaking. It was our first job of the day when we came on duty this morning.'

'So it was standing there through the night?' Rick mused.

The driver nodded. 'They kept an eye on it in the fire station. No one's tried to tamper with it.'

'They were long gone, I imagine,' Jon murmured to Rick. 'Soon as they saw the flames had taken hold.'

'What's it being linked with?' asked the officer. 'Seems odd there was a dog in the back.'

Jon turned to him. 'What does the animal look like?'

'Big, ugly and part-cooked. Could feed an entire village with the amount of meat on it.'

Jon gave a nod. *I think we've struck lucky here.* 'OK, we'll take a peek.'

They trudged across grass still encased by a thick layer of frost. Jon thought he could feel blades snapping underfoot. The van was no more than ten feet from the fence. 'No wonder they put it out,' he observed. 'Would have been a fire risk for the station itself.'

The water sprayed on to it had collected into pools and then frozen in the night. Micro-lakes of milky ice. Judging from the smoke damage to the van, the fire had taken hold properly before being extinguished. Jon took a moment to examine the grass near the driver's door. Any footprints had been obliterated by the hosing-down the vehicle had received. The rear door was ajar. Below it, Jon could see a small triangle of plastic. All that remained from where the registration plate had been wrenched off. He circled round to the front of the vehicle. No plate there, either.

'Is it the van?' Rick asked.

'Looks like it,' Jon replied, ducking eagerly under the tape and snapping on a pair of latex gloves.

'Wish they made winter versions of these,' Rick complained, doing the same.

Jon peered through the window into the driver's cab. The fire had obviously been set in the footwell – a mound of charred and soggy cloth filled it. Flames had spread to the seats' upholstery which, he guessed, would have spewed thick smoke. He looked for any sign of a tax disc on the inside of the windscreen. Nothing. Using one finger, he pulled tentatively at the handle of the door. It swung open and the smell of petrol and burnt plastic enveloped him.

Rick had opened the door on the other side of the cab, and using the tip of a biro, sprang the glove compartment.

'Anything?' Jon asked.

'A road map of Ireland.'

'Has to be it,' Jon breathed, lifting the floor mat so he could examine the metal of the door frame. Punched into its surface were various digits and letters. Jon noted down the main one at the top and stood. 'Let's see this dog then.'

They met at the rear doors and Jon swung the right hand one open. Gloom filled the blackened interior. Halfway along the bare floor was a large object. Jon squinted to make sense of what he was seeing. They'd wrapped the body in a carpet – possibly what had been used to line the floor. Thick shoulders and a square-shaped head with a squashed muzzle poked from the partly open folds. The animal looked as if it had died in the act of snarling.

'Check the size of those teeth,' Rick murmured. 'Is that it?'

'Hang on.' Jon reached in, unlatched the other door and swung it open. The amount of light now allowed a much clearer view. The carpet appeared to have been doused in petrol or some kind of accelerant before being set alight. What he could see of the dog's huge carcass was badly burnt. 'Still can't tell.' He stepped onto the footplate and climbed into the claustrophobic space. Head ducked low, he glanced uneasily at the blackened walls, fume-filled air making his nose itch. As he reached down to unfold the carpet a thought popped into his head: in a horror film, this is when the thing's eyes snap open.

Rick suddenly tensed. 'It moved!'

Jon's arm shot back, elbow connecting painfully with the side of the van. His partner creased up laughing.

'Twat,' Jon cursed, examining the smear of soot now on his coat-sleeve.

Rick fought back his laughter. 'You'd have done exactly the same to me.'

Chuckling in agreement, he peeled back the flaps to reveal the entire corpse. The flames hadn't taken hold properly at the far end of the carpet and the animal's coat was still intact. Tiger-like stripes covered its rear legs, long tapered tail lying across them. 'Definitely the one.'

'Christ.' Rick's voice was now serious. 'What type of breed is it?'

'No idea,' Jon answered, jumping down onto the grass and reaching for his notebook and phone. 'But I know a man who might.' He keyed the number in. 'Inspector Hutcher? DI Spicer, here.'

'Hello, Jon. Nice crisp morning here in Manchester.'

'Whereabouts are you?'

'Somewhere called Blackford Bridge, not far from Bury. Know it?'

'Roughly.' He turned to Rick. 'Your mobile has a decent camera, hasn't it?'

Rick nodded.

Jon spoke into his phone once again. 'Could me and my partner pop over? We're taking some photos and I'd like you to see them.'

CHAPTER 16

Jon peeled the blackened gloves off, hands immediately feeling colder as damp skin made contact with chilly air. 'I reckon about nine stone,' he said, thinking how much effort it had taken to slide the carpet with the remains of the massive dog nearer to the van's doors.

'Christ. Plenty of adults don't weigh that much,' Rick replied, examining the photos on his phone as they walked back to the edge of the playing fields.

The two uniforms climbed out as they got closer. 'Find what were you looking for?' asked the driver.

'I think so.' Jon answered. 'Scene-of-crimes are on their way – can you two remain here until they arrive?'

The constable exchanged a quick glance with his colleague. 'Sure.'

Of course you can, thought Jon. Sitting in a toasty-warm car, listening to the local radio station – a morning's work doesn't get much easier. 'Only one of you actually needs to be here – the other can start knocking on doors.' He circled a finger at the houses which surrounded the playing field. 'I'll let you two toss a coin to see who does the footwork. We shouldn't be long.'

Half an hour later, they were making their way along a

main road bordered by a tree-lined slope. Jon looked into the woodland, glimpsing a dirty brown river in the valley below. The road kinked to the left, signs for Bury Golf Course on the bend.

'A few hundred metres more,' Rick announced, eyes on the street atlas. 'Meadow Road.'

Jon slowed the car as a turning came into view. 'This?'

Rick craned his neck. 'Yup.'

They turned into a road with a moderate incline that was in severe need of a new layer of tarmac. The car's heater was on and, as they negotiated the many potholes, an unpleasant odour began to fill the vehicle.

'That'll be the sewage works,' Rick commented.

They descended further into the valley, a row of low circular-shaped concrete structures coming into view on their right. After another fifty metres, they reached a fork.

'Left here,' Rick announced, folding the *A to Z* shut. 'It's at the end.'

Jon continued along the overgrown lane until a derelict mill came into view. It was a familiar sight: eight or so floors, row upon row of smashed windows, vegetation spilling over from collapsing gutters, a tall chimney with the name of the mill owner spelt out in white bricks down the side. Knowles and Son. A common name for the region, Jon thought, reflecting on how dynasties rose and fell. I wonder what the descendants of the millworkers do now? Probably employed by the local Tesco's. He pictured a line of women toiling at the tills, hands repeating the same movement over and over again. Not that different to what the previous generations did.

A police vehicle and several unmarked cars were parked at the open gates. From somewhere nearby came the sound of rushing water. With the river so close, Jon thought, the mill had probably been powered by a waterwheel. A massive thing mounted on the rear of the building.

To the side were several large sheds. A police officer

was warily approaching. 'Yes, gents?'

Jon removed his warrant card. 'DI Spicer, DS Saville, MIT. Is Nick Hutcher about?'

'Right – he said you were on your way. The fight was in here.'

'Was?' Rick asked.

'We missed it,' the officer responded. 'Place was deserted when we arrived.'

They rounded the corner and Jon saw the low buildings were arranged to form a three-sided courtyard, the open end of which was closed off by a very new chain-link fence.

Jon stared through the strands of metal. In the far corner two tyres were suspended beneath a crude wooden frame. The rubber was ripped and frayed. Overhead, thick cables had been attached from one side of the courtyard to the other. Dangling from each one was a thinner wire ending in a karabiner-type clip. The doors to two of the outbuildings were open.

The officer pointed. 'The one on the far side.'

Jon and Rick slipped through the open gate and made their way over. A group of three men were inside. Jon knocked a couple of times on the rotting door frame. 'Nick Hutcher?'

A tall, craggy-faced man with short greying hair and a kink in his nose turned. He was wearing jeans and a dark-green fleece. 'DI Spicer?'

Jon nodded. 'And DS Saville. Good to meet you, Nick.' He looked about. 'I take it this was a kennels?'

'That and a fight venue,' the RSPCA officer answered. There was a hint of weariness about him, as if he'd seen enough scenes like this to last a lifetime. But when they shook hands, his grip was strong. Plenty of fight in the bloke yet, Jon thought.

'How's your dog?'

Jon dropped his hand. 'Hanging in there. Stable, they said this morning.'

'A terrible thing to have happened. I'm sorry.'

Taking in breath, Jon nodded. 'He'll pull through. I'm more worried about the effect it'll have on my little girl.'

Nick shook his head. 'Bloody animals. The owners, that is,' he added hastily. Jon held a hand towards his partner. 'This is Rick.'

Hutcher gave Rick's hand the same treatment. Jon held back a smirk as his colleague tried to suppress a look of discomfort.

'What's this for, then?' Jon asked, turning to a treadmill.

'To get their stamina up,' Nick replied. 'They'll run the dogs on it, raising the incline, increasing speed. Can't exactly exercise them in the local park, after all. Once they're in the pit, there's no place to hide – the animal has to be in good shape.'

'And the set-up outside?' Jon asked.

'All part of it. The tyres you saw hanging above the ground are for biting on.' He led them outside and pointed to the tyres' frayed edges. 'They can do a lot of damage, Molosser breeds.'

Jon tried not to think about what had happened at the golf course.

Rick pointed to the overhead cables. 'And those?'

'Dog runs. See the wire hanging down? Each animal has its collar attached to the clip at the bottom. The looped end allows the dog to run back and forth below the cable – but not off to the side to attack its neighbour.'

'Very organised,' Jon stated. 'Have you got whoever owns the premises?'

'Nah. Probably rented to someone whose details will turn out false. Even if we get who it is, we can only charge them with keeping a premises and possessing training equipment. The actual fight's already taken place.'

He took them over to the other open doorway. The poorly lit room smelled of blood. In the middle of the floor, waist-high panels of chipboard had been arranged in a square.

Jon approached the construction, noting the closely spaced screws running down each corner. It had been built to withstand a battering. He peered over the barrier at the carpet lining the floor of the pit. Patches of blood covered it and he saw spatters on the inner walls. He probed at a particularly thick smear with a knuckle. Dry but with a little give at the centre. 'When was it, do you reckon?'

'Within the last forty-eight hours, I'd say.'

In one corner, a white line ran across the carpet to form a triangle with the base of the two converging walls. He looked at the opposite corner and saw the same marking there.

'The pit must be twelve feet in diameter with walls two and a half feet high. Only people allowed in the ring are the referee and each dog's trainer,' Nick announced grimly. 'The ref will call time out and one dog is released. It has to cross its scratch line into the main part of the arena, showing its desire to fight. Generally, they meet around the middle like a pair of steam trains. The ref allows fighting to continue unless some issue like fanging occurs.'

Rick looked to his side, eyebrows raised.

'When a dog puts a tooth through its own lip, impeding its ability to bite,' Hutcher elaborated. 'They'll use breaking sticks to prise their jaws apart. Each dog is returned to its corner and the problem sorted. Then the other dog is released first and it must come out of its corner to show willing. The fight goes on until a dog won't cross its line, is killed or the trainer withdraws it. The referee has no power to stop a fight.'

Jon pictured the encounters. 'Don't the dogs ever go mad and start on the people also in there?'

Nick gave a sad shake of his head. 'Unfortunately not. At least not with pit bulls. They're man-friendly. They can be easily trained to never go for a human. We bust one kennels in Stoke where the owner had a Japanese toza patrolling the pit bulls' cages. You see, the pit bulls would probably wag their tails and allow themselves to be stolen. The toza, on the other hand, had been trained to go for anyone who wasn't the owner. Took a sleeping dart before we could go in.'

Jon placed his elbows on the edge of the pit and stared into it. 'They just keep going?'

'To the death. And all to please their owner. Anything to please the twisted piece of shit who's sick enough to play on the animal's loyalty.'

Hearing the venom in the man's voice, Jon glanced to his side. Nick was surveying the blood-soaked scene with disgust. 'Got dogs yourself?'

Nick looked at him. 'Sorry?'

'Have you got any dogs?'

He thought for a second. 'Seven, at the last count. The downside of spending too much time in rescue centres.'

Jon smiled. Thought you had.

'With non-pit bull breeds,' Nick continued. 'You can never predict what the animal will do. They might flip and latch on to the ref, they might refuse to fight. Makes betting awkward.'

The thing that got to within a couple of feet of my daughter was no pit bull, Jon thought. 'The creature I'm interested in, it was a fighter, no doubt. But when the whistle came from the back of the van, it released my dog immediately.'

'That's strange,' Nick murmured. 'Just a whistle was enough?'

Jon nodded.

'And it wasn't a pit bull?'

'No – not pure, anyway.'

The RSPCA officer gestured to the door. 'Let's get in the light so I can see these photos. Setting other breeds against each other is definitely a trend we're seeing more and more of. Tozas or mastiffs crossed with pit bulls. Canary dogs are another one that's increasingly popular. But as I said, you never know what type of animal will result. For a dog to be in the middle of an attack then release on a whistle: not even pit bulls will do that.'

'Well,' Jon replied. 'This one did.'

As they stepped back into the courtyard they saw another couple of men entering through the gate. They were gripping the corners of some heavy-duty plastic sheeting. 'Found one, chief,' the stockier man puffed, struggling with the weight. Jon saw the skin on his bald head was bright red.

Nick immediately started across. 'Where was it, Mark?'

'In the ravine at the edge of the river. The vegetation was all crushed where it had rolled down.'

They placed their load on the floor and opened the sheeting. Lying on the expanse of plastic was the carcass of a large, fawn-coloured dog. Its head was the shape of a mallet – almost as wide as it was long. A muscular neck then merged with a broad chest. Jon tried to assess its height – probably about half a metre. Its pig-like eyes were partly open and Jon saw they had the dull, milky gaze of something that had been dead a while. 'I'd say it's been there over twenty-four hours. If this was the summer, there'd be fly infestation by now.'

Nick nodded in agreement. 'It wasn't in much shape,' he stated, kneeling down and pressing a finger into the blubber on its torso. 'Poor thing took a hammering. Obviously didn't want to give up, though.'

Jon's eyes lingered on the deep rips to its shoulders, head and neck. Dried blood and dirt matted its fur. 'What do you reckon was cause of death?'

Nick continued to stare downwards. 'My guess is it lost too much blood – it's strength would have failed and the other dog would have got it by the throat. Probably suffocated.'

Jon raised his face to the sky, focusing on a cloud in an attempt to keep the image of Punch pinned to the grass from his mind.

'Or the owner finished it off,' the bald-headed one said.

'These people won't waste time and money on a losing dog.'

Jon took another quick look at the corpse. 'Recognise the breed?'

Nick rubbed a hand against his chin. 'Canary dog crossed with a mastiff, I'd say. Historically, Canary dogs have been bred for their aggressiveness. Pair that with the bulk of a mastiff and you've got one formidable animal.'

'But not formidable enough for what it was up against,' Jon whispered. 'Must weigh ten stone.'

'And the rest,' the bald inspector who'd carried it up replied, wiping sweat from his shiny pate. 'Nearer twelve, my guess.'

Nick turned his head to look up at Jon. 'The word we got was there's a visiting kennels doing the rounds with some kind of exotic breed. Its owners were prepared to give away a twenty percent advantage in body weight, which is unheard-of on the circuit.' He got back to his feet with a wince. 'Bloody knees. Let's see these photos of your animal.'

Rick brought up the first image and presented his handset to Nick. 'Just brush the screen to bring across the next picture.'

Nick examined the image for a few seconds. He held the phone closer then further away. He looked to his colleagues. 'Ever seen something like this before?'

They crowded round, eyes on the little screen. Each one shook his head.

'Well proportioned,' the bald one commented. 'Arched ribcage, retracted stomach. Almost like it's built for distance running.'

'With neck muscles like that?' a colleague replied. 'Look at the bulk around its shoulders and the folds on its throat. Only loose bit of flesh on it.'

'Double chins,' Nick stated, glancing at Jon. 'Ideal protection. Bit like a lion's mane: stops an attacker getting to the throat.' Slowly, he brushed through the other images.

'Curious markings on the legs.' The bald one held a finger to the screen. 'Almost brindled.'

'It was covered in stripes like that,' Jon said. 'Apart from a mask of black covering its face. And it was agile. When it ran back to the van it was incredibly light on its feet. It took off a good distance from the doors, sailed straight inside. More like a pounce, it was.'

Nick worked his way back. 'Bitches are normally less bulky.'

Jon looked at him. 'You mean it's a female?'

'It is. Another feature that's odd is the extremely long tail – tapers to a very fine point. Unusual.'

'Why?' asked Rick.

Nick handed the phone back. 'You'd expect it to be docked, that's all. One less thing for another dog to get hold of. The ears have been cropped to little points, but the tail was left alone.' He shrugged.

Jon crossed his arms. 'So, any idea what it is?'

Nick looked directly at him. 'You know what? Not a fucking clue. Can I see this thing in the flesh?'

The deep rumble was more of a vibration, juddering through the walls and up from the floor. Beyond the double-glazed window of the hotel room, the plane's climb was so laboured it seemed on the brink of giving up and falling back to earth.

Slipping one foot into a high-heeled shoe which was beginning to split down one side, the girl popped a mint in her mouth and turned to the pair of single beds. 'That's eighty quid, then.'

Devlan and Sean stared at her with uninterested expressions. Both wore only boxer shorts. Nervously, she placed a hand on one hip, eyes moving between them.

Eventually Sean swept his straggly auburn hair back and looked across to the other bed. 'Come on, you tight bastard, pay her so she can piss off.'

Devlan raised a hand and scratched at the cropped hair on his head. 'Me? Why me? All I got was her bony arse cheeks digging into me.'

'All expenses paid,' Sean smiled. 'If I came on this tour, you said it was all expenses paid.'

Devlan lowered his arm and examined the thick Celtic pattern tattooed round his bicep. 'Don't remember that including whores.' He reached for the wallet lying on the small table between the two beds while continuing to speak to his friend. 'Can't believe we just shared a spit-roast.'

'You never wore rubbers,' the girl stated. 'It was twenty more each for bareback – I told you that.'

He didn't bother looking at her, two twenties dangling from his fingers. 'Wait until the boys back home hear about this.'

She crossed her arms. 'Eighty.'

He was off the bed in an instant, one hand grasping her throat as he marched her backwards across the room. 'Eighty you reckon? Eighty?' She didn't resist, a look of defeat on her face as she was shoved against the wall. 'Eighty, is that right?'

She shook her head, lips moving soundlessly as her cheeks reddened.

He relaxed his grip, and as she opened her mouth to drag in air, he stuffed the two notes between her lips. 'You'll take whatever I give you, right?'

She nodded, eyes downcast.

'Good girl. Now fuck off.' He pulled the door open.

Removing the crumpled notes from her mouth, she stepped into the corridor. Smirking, he slammed the door shut and jumped back on his bed.

'That wasn't needed,' Sean said under his breath.

Devlan shrugged. 'Rank bitch.'

'We don't need any more trouble.'

'From her? What could she do?'

'Still…'

The sound of another plane taking off started to fill the room. Devlan reached for the bottle of Bushmills on the bedside table.

As he took a swig, Sean sat up. 'We need to ring your dad.'

Wincing, Devlan lowered the bottle. 'I know, just…not yet.'

'Don't make it any worse than it's going to be. You have to tell him what's happened.'

His companion closed his eyes. 'I…fuck!' He swigged sharply. 'I can't believe she's dead, Sean.' He glanced sorrowfully at his mate before staring at the bottle. 'Can't believe Queenie's dead.' He reached for a crumpled shopping bag on the bedside table. Visible through the clear plastic was a tennis ball, its wool-like surface frayed and torn from where Punch had chewed it. He swung it before his face like a pendulum.

Sean watched him for a while. 'Were you going to stop Queenie from going for that little girl?'

The other man was deep in thought.

'Devlan?'

His head turned. 'What?'

'Were you going to stop Queenie from going for that little girl?'

'What do you mean?'

Sean glanced at the bag. I was watching in the van's rear-view mirror, he thought. You let Queenie get to within striking distance of her. 'When you took that Boxer's tennis ball, it was to give Queenie his scent. The Boxer was meant to die, not some wee lass.'

Devlan raised one corner of his mouth in the semblance of a smile. 'Ach – that young girl was in no bother.'

Sean didn't reply. The Boxer was the family's pet, he thought. That little girl would have had the dog's scent all over her. 'Give us a nip.' He held his hand out, face now sombre.

The bottle of whiskey was passed across. Sean took a good gulp, placed it on the bedside table and looked out of the window. Another plane had begun to take off. 'This place is doing my head in.'

Devlan swung his legs off the bed and stood. 'Come on, we're going out.'

'Where?'

'Out.'

'Where out?'

'For a wee drive.'

'In what? We've got no car.'

'Since when's that a fucking problem?'

CHAPTER 17

As they walked towards their cars, Jon turned to Nick. 'So where are your tip-offs coming from?'

'Little weasel in Newcastle who's well into the scene. We got him last year for causing cruelty to an animal. Normally they'd take the fine and carry on as normal. But this guy was carrying a two-year suspended sentence for something else.'

Jon nodded. 'Start snitching or go to prison.'

Nick smiled. 'He's my bitch, now.'

'What's he told you about this visiting kennels?'

'Not a lot. They've fought their dog in Newcastle, Birmingham and now, it appears, Manchester. Looks like it's ripped apart everything thrown at it, so far.'

'Was your man at any of the fights?'

'No. Was meant to be at the Newcastle one, but had to miss it because he was in hospital. Got problems with his kidneys, poor thing.'

'He's no idea where this visiting kennels are from?'

Now at their vehicles, Nick reached for his keys. 'I can try and call him en route.'

'That would be great.' Jon unlocked his Mondeo. 'Just keep behind us. Basically, we're going round to the bottom of the M60.'

They'd barely made it back on to the main road when the sound of Jon's mobile filled the car. He nodded at the cup-holder where the handset was positioned. 'Rick?'

His partner huffed as he reached down. 'What am I – your bloody secretary? Sort your hands-free kit, would you?'

Jon thought about the instruction booklet for the equipment. He hadn't got further than the opening paragraph congratulating him on his purchasing decision before he'd given up. 'I don't know,' he mused, 'you might look quite fetching in a wig and skirt. Nothing too high, though – I don't like tarty.'

Rick was looking at the screen, his middle finger raised at Jon. 'It's Parks.'

'Take it,' Jon said quickly.

'Hi boss, it's DS Saville here. Jon's driving. Yes, of course I can.'

Jon glanced to his side and saw a faint smile spreading across his partner's face.

'OK, OK,' Rick nodded. 'Just that link? What a relief. We hope to be back in an hour or so. See you then.' He cut the call and turned to Jon. 'Darragh de Avila has no link to any recognised paramilitary organisation over there. He doesn't feature on any intelligence system – not with the NCA and not with JTAC.'

The Joint Terrorism Analysis Centre, Jon thought. The body charged with keeping tabs on international terrorist risks. 'He didn't show up on anything?'

'Only two incidents which the police in Ireland had logged.'

'Being?'

'Suspected dog-fighting.'

Jon glanced across. 'Seriously?'

'A couple of raids on premises he owns near Clifden. But not enough evidence to press charges.' He placed Jon's phone back in the cup-holder. 'A relief, yes?'

Jon let his breath out through both nostrils. 'Big relief. Massive, in fact.' His thoughts turned to Punch. So it was simple revenge. Just because I made the guy look like a fool in his own nightclub. Well, the bastard will look a lot worse than that if I ever get my hands on him. He made an effort to relax his grip on the steering wheel, pushing the thoughts of payback from his head. 'Could you give Alice a call? Let her know the good news.'

Back at the playing fields, Jon swung his vehicle on to the verge, leaving room for Nick to park behind him. The two uniforms were back in their patrol car, which now had a white scene-of-crime van parked alongside it. As Jon climbed out, he heard Nick's car door shut behind him.

'Some more info for you.'

Jon turned round. 'You got through to him?'

'Yeah, he's whining and moaning, saying he can't show too much interest in the touring kennels. He's lying, though. They'll all be chattering about this animal.'

'How so?'

'It came over as a Grand Champion. Now it's taken out three other dogs. That's the making of a legend. After what it did to the dog we just saw, no one dares risk their animal against it. Now people will want to breed off it or they'll want it dead. Another thing – I asked him for a description of the animal. A Molosser with a stripy coat were his words.'

Jon leaned against his vehicle. 'You said it came over as a Grand Champion.'

'Probably a kennels from Ireland. My man said a friend who was at the Newcastle fight reckoned that's what their accents were.'

'Whose?'

'The dog's owners.'

'Did he say how many of them were there?'

'Just two.'

Jon felt a flicker of excitement. 'Don't suppose he got

any names?'

'They all hide behind nicknames. Rustler, The Sergeant, Oddbod, bullshit like that. The kennels are called Clock-on. Don't ask me how you spell it – sounds Irish, though. One of the blokes had a Gaelic-sounding name, beginning with D.'

Jon dipped his head, eyes fixed on Nick. 'Darragh?'

The RSPCA officer frowned. 'Might have been. You want me to check?'

'Please.'

Nick removed his mobile from his fleece and pressed a few buttons. 'It's me.' He rolled his eyes. 'I know, I know. You're ill. These Irish kennels. Was the name Darragh? Maybe? That's no fucking use to me. Keep your ears open. Anything else on this, my phone rings with your name on the screen, OK?' He cut the call and hunched a shoulder. 'Says it might have been. One of those weird Irish names, were his exact words. He'll ask his mate next chance he gets.'

Darragh, Jon thought. It had to be him. He felt the tingle in his spine he always experienced when closing in on a suspect. 'Want to see the animal?'

'Too bloody right.'

Jon paused at the patrol car's window. 'Anyone in the surrounding houses see anything?'

The driver looked up. 'Afraid not. Curtains drawn, tellies on.'

The sun was now about as high as it was going to get – perhaps a third of the way up the pale-blue sky. Their shadows stretched far away behind them as they made their way across. Twenty metres off from the burned-out van, Jon realised who the scene-of-crime officer was. Nikki Kingston. Shit. How long, he wondered, since that thing happened between us?

His mind went back to the night in the Bull's Head. Five years? More? They'd been trying to catch a serial killer dubbed the Butcher of Belle Vue. The name came about because the killer removed large swathes of his victims' flesh before dumping their bodies on waste ground around that part of the city. Nikki was working the forensics. He couldn't help a small smile of pleasure catching the corners of his mouth. Apart from the flirting around, she was brilliant at her job. When she had come up with a key piece of evidence, what was meant to be a congratulatory kiss had escalated into something more. Jon remembered her look of irritation when he'd pulled his head back.

She was wearing a white oversuit and was on her knees, examining where the van's registration plates had been removed. She leaned back on her haunches, then, by pushing a hand down on the van's bumper, laboriously rose to her feet. Bloody hell, Jon thought, she's pregnant. A tiny part of his chest twinged.

She saw him approaching and something flitted across her eyes. Moving to the perimeter tape, she pushed the hood off her head. Dark corkscrew curls sprang out.

Your hair, Jon thought, it gets me every time. 'Nikki – it's been a while.'

'Hello, Jon,' she answered with the faint hint of awkwardness. 'It has.'

He couldn't stop his eyes from dropping. Even beneath the voluminous folds of the forensics suit, her swollen stomach was obvious. He considered her raucous sense of humour as he wondered what to say. 'You been on the pies?'

She placed a hand on her bump, blowing a strand of hair away as she did so. No wedding ring, he noticed, waiting for her riposte.

'Only when you leave any.' She directed a meaningful glance at his belly.

Jon looked down at his waistband with dismay. No way I'm getting a paunch, he thought. He heard her laugh.

'That had you worried.'

Now feeling sheepish, he raised his chin. She was looking at Rick. 'Good to see you.'

Rick stepped forward, smiling. 'You're looking great, Nikki. How long before…'

'Ten weeks,' she smiled back, eyelids lowering at the thought. 'Ten weeks before I can put my feet up.' Her eyes flashed. 'Not in stirrups, mind. On the bloody sofa. If I pop on my first day of maternity leave, I'll be so pissed off.'

Jon grinned. The woman was five foot two of infectious spirit. 'Nikki, this is Nick Hutcher, he's chief inspector of the RSPCA's dog-fighting unit. Can he take a look at the beast?'

'Be my guest.' She started walking away, speaking over her shoulder as she went. 'If a girly's that big, I dread to think what a boy's like. Its knackers will be the size of two tennis balls.'

The RSPCA officer had a bemused expression on his face. 'She's got a way with words. I was thinking as we drove over; why did they abandon it?'

Jon weighed things up. Time to lay my cards on the table, he thought. 'I'm fairly certain this animal is the same one that attacked my dog yesterday. And the Irish connection could fit with some people I suspect might be looking to level scores with me.'

Nick scratched at his head. 'You need to explain.'

'I caught up with the van the animal jumped into. The driver must have realised I'd seen the vehicle's registration – which, incidentally, was Irish. They also knew I'm police.'

Nick's gaze went back to the vehicle. 'Was it was dumped in a hurry, then?'

'So much so, they didn't think to check what that strange-looking building with the tower was on the other side of the fence.' He nodded at the fire station.

Nick whistled. 'You're saying you got a good look at their vehicle – forcing them to get rid. Except that left them with the dilemma of what to do with their dog.'

'And,' Jon added, 'I'd got a very good look at that, too.'

Nick was silent for a second. 'If they made the decision to sacrifice the animal, that wouldn't have been easy. If this is the Grand Champion everyone's talking about, any litter from it would have been worth thousands.'

Rick shifted his weight from foot to foot.

'What are you thinking, mate?' Jon asked.

'I don't know. I can appreciate the two blokes in the van needed to make themselves scarce, but surely there was an alternative to killing their prize dog?'

Nick shrugged. 'They certainly wouldn't have wanted any other kennels getting their hands on it. Maybe it was the only option they had.'

'How would it have been done?' Rick asked.

'All these people have a vet's kit. A first-aid pack to stitch up any damage sustained during the fights. Probably gave it an overdose of painkillers. Kindest way to do it.' He gave Jon a cautious look. 'If I were you, I'd sort out some precautions.'

'How do you mean?'

'I know these types and, believe me, they will be fucking furious.'

'Good,' Jon grunted. 'I intend to cost them a lot more, yet.'

Nick's eyes narrowed. 'I can believe that.' He approached the rear doors, leaned forward and was silent for a few seconds. 'What an incredible physique. You said it was light on its feet?'

Jon stepped closer. 'That's right.'

'Yet it's got such amazing muscle bulk in the shoulders and neck.' He hooked his fingers into its mouth and prised the stiff jaws apart. 'My God – the size of those incisors.'

Jon looked away. *Those things were clamped on my dog's throat.*

'See the gaps between each one?' Nick asked, struggling slightly to close and reopen the jaws. 'Inverted scissor bite. Its jaw muscles extend up and round the top of the head: this thing is really quite alarming.' He straightened up.

'What will happen to it?'

'Don't know,' Jon answered. 'The incinerator?'

'Could I take it? We can store it at one of our centres while I try and work out what – if any – breed it is.'

'You're welcome to it.' Jon turned away. 'I'd be happy to never set eyes on it again.' Nikki was near the driver's cab bagging up some evidence. 'Anything?' he called, wandering across.

She shook her head. 'Not a lot. Some bits of newspaper from under the floor mat. But that's about it.'

'Any details visible on them?'

She examined the fragments through the thin layer of clear plastic. 'A date; sixth of June.'

'Recent, then,' Jon replied, stopping at her side so he could look over her shoulder. His eyes slid to the thick curls just inches from his face.

Nikki squatted down and clipped the lid of her equipment box closed. 'Sorry to not be of any more use. What's it all about, anyway?'

Jon waved a hand. 'It was, er…' He glanced to the rear of the vehicle where Rick was chatting quietly to the RSPCA officer. 'It was my dog. The animal in the back of the van attacked my dog.' His eyes touched hers.

'Your Boxer? Punch?'

He nodded, looking again at the vehicle to avoid her face. She held up a hand and he reached down to help her to her feet. 'Is he all right?' she asked, letting her fingers slip slowly from his.

'Hopefully.' He heard the faint tremor in his voice and cleared his throat. 'He's being cared for at a vet's.'

'So now you're trying to figure out who owns the van?'

'That's the idea.'

'I bet it is,' she breathed. 'So.' Her voice picked up. 'Family OK?'

Hardly, he thought. My wife's so wired she's about to snap and my daughter's having nightmares about that thing in the van. 'Good, thanks.' He nodded at her tummy.

'We're expecting our second in a couple of months.'

'Really?' Nikki's smile didn't quite convince. 'And how's Alice?'

Jon thought about her having to spend the day at her mum's, unable to remain in her own house. I should ring her, check everything's fine. 'She's doing well. And you?' He struggled to phrase the question. 'Is...how's the daddy-to-be handling it all?'

Nikki shrugged nonchalantly. 'I wouldn't know. When I said I was keeping it, he ran a mile.'

'That was good of him.'

She let out a little snort. 'Better off without him. You know me – I always pick them.'

The observation hung between them and Jon looked away. 'Well...we'd better press on.' He pointed at the equipment box containing her evidence. 'Let me know, yeah?'

'Will do.'

Jon walked back to the rear of the van. 'Rick, we should get back to the station. Nick? How do you want to play it?'

'I'll get a work vehicle sent over from our nearest rescue centre to collect the carcass. Then I'd better return to those kennels.'

'Can you find your way back?'

'Satnav.'

Jon nodded. 'Are you sticking round Manchester?'

'For tonight. Then back down to Sussex.'

Jon thought of the RSPCA officer sitting in a sterile hotel room. 'I'd offer to take you out for a beer, but with all this business with my dog...'

'Don't worry. Two of the guys based up here are showing me a particular pub. The Marble Arch? Apparently it brews its own beers.'

Jon pictured the venerable old boozer with its ornately tiled ceilings. 'Your colleagues have good taste.'

Nick smiled. 'That one called Mark? He loves the cider

they do there.'

'Well, another time, it would be a pleasure to take you out myself.'

'Cheers. I'm sure I'll be back in this neck of the woods before long.'

Jon extended a hand, readying himself for the steel-like grip. 'Thanks for your help.'

As they shook, Nick's eyes shifted to the dead dog. 'I'll get back to you with anything I find.'

Once they were safely out of earshot, Rick gave Jon a smirking glance. 'Your hand hurting?'

'Yeah, I noticed you kept far enough back to just give him a wave.' He flexed his fingers and examined them for any damage. 'Bloke could squeeze blood from a stone.'

Rick chuckled as he bowed his head, voice turning serious. 'You reckon the nightclub owner is behind this, then?'

Jon nodded. 'We've got the same type of van. Same type of dog. The only thing that's confusing me is the time line. When I was in Clifden in Darragh's club, that dog and its handlers were over here – up in Newcastle and down in Birmingham. So, are the handlers just mates that he was able to call on to do his dirty work? Or did he pop over here for the fights themselves?'

'If he did,' Rick answered, 'and he's travelling under his own passport, we'll be able to track his movements.'

'True.' Jon thrust his hands into his pockets. 'Including how he got back to the Irish republic.'

He considered the nightmare process for when a suspect fled to another country within Europe. First step would be to make a Request for Mutual Legal Assistance. That meant going to the CPS who, if they agreed to pursue it, would then approach the Home Office. The official at the Home Office would then contact a counterpart in the country concerned who, in turn, would contact someone in that nation's police force.

But, as Jon well knew, any enquiry was only as good as

the officer conducting it. And he would be relying on a copper in another country to build a strong enough case for Jon to eventually apply for a European Arrest Warrant. He groaned at the prospect.

'You had a bit of a chat with Nikki.'

Jon registered the expressionless tone. His colleague knew how close Jon had come to being tempted all those years ago. 'We were going over the forensics – or lack of.'

'Yeah, she was also flashing you those big brown eyes of hers.'

'Was she?'

'Who's the father?'

'She's not – ' He stopped himself.

'Go on.'

Sighing, Jon continued. 'She's not involving him. Apparently, he buggered off.'

'So just discussing forensics, then.'

'For fuck's sake, Rick. I've worked on and off with Nikki for years. How could I not ask after the fact she's pregnant?'

His partner gave him a wary look. 'That woman would love to get a hook into you.' He grasped an imaginary rod and started reeling.

'I see. Like I'm just some brainless fish.'

Rick smiled in reply.

The silence between them was broken by a muffled warble. Jon removed his phone and glanced at the screen. Anonymous. 'DI Spicer speaking.'

When she spoke, it sounded like she was in the next street. 'Was that you in the dark blue Mondeo? I was on my way to Darragh's – you drove straight past me.'

He came to a halt, staring straight ahead. 'Siobhain?'

'Yes.'

'How did you get this number?'

'I rang your house. Your wife answered.'

Alice? Jon frowned. What the hell is she doing at home? 'You spoke to my wife?'

'Yeah – she gave me your mobile. So I rang it.'

Treat this woman, Jon thought, like she's a suspect. You have no idea what her agenda is. 'What's happened to Zoë? Is she all right?'

'She's…she's doing OK.'

'Doing OK? What does that mean?'

'He slapped her about some. Wanting to know who the hell you were.'

Was that how he found out where I lived so quickly? Jon thought, rubbing at the back of his head. 'How bad is she?'

'She'll be OK.'

The cowardly fucker, Jon thought, picturing Darragh de Avila.

'That night, I was on my way to find you,' Siobhain went on. 'But you zoomed off at a hundred miles an hour.'

Jon's step faltered. Somehow, he thought, your words don't ring true. The gush of a pre-prepared lie. He'd heard it in interview rooms a thousand times before. 'No one knew of any Zoë.'

'She's here! You must come back. As soon as she's on her feet, they're sending her to Belfast with that delivery.'

Jon started walking again. 'Who are you?'

'What?'

Jon sniffed. 'It's a simple question. Who are you?'

'I'm a friend, that's all. Just looking out for her and keeping my own head down.'

'You say you live in Clifden. You say your name's Siobhain. No one knew of you, either. I don't know a damn thing about you.'

'I am Siobhain. I knew Zoë when we were in Manchester. How else would I know about you? About what you did to Salvio? Zoë told me.'

'So you say. Tell me more about Zoë. What's the name of her kid?'

'Jake.'

'How old is he?'

'I don't know. She said he was two when she left Manchester. Six?'

Six and a bit, Jon thought. You really have spoken to her. 'Why doesn't Zoë call me herself?'

'He keeps a close eye on her. Checks her phone, has someone watch her. You know the type of man.'

Jon thought about Darragh. Anyone prepared to hit a woman was, ultimately, weak. Weak and insecure. What's more, Jon smiled to himself, Darragh himself would know it. Deep down. When he was alone, looking in the mirror, he would see that weakness in his own eyes. Jon carefully filed the knowledge. 'Are they a couple?'

Her laugh was full of scorn. 'He doesn't let anyone get close to him.'

'Where is he now?'

'About, I think. He's got a place nearby.'

'In Clifden?'

'Yeah.'

Jon realised Siobhain's local knowledge could be useful. 'Is he there at the moment?'

'He comes and goes. I've not seen him today.'

He thought about Alice, back in their home for some reason. 'I need to know if he's there.'

'I'll find out for you.'

'Ring me back as soon as you know.'

'So will you come?'

'Do you know what's happened over here?'

'No,' she replied, uneasily. 'What?'

'Doesn't matter.'

'Will you not come and get her? She's no one else.'

'You want me to stroll back into that nightclub and just pluck her out of it?'

'Can't you?'

'They won't let me back in there – you must know how things ended up.'

'There is some talk.' It sounded like she was smiling. 'Conor Barry, the guy on the door, has bandaging to his nose.'

'Are the police involved?'

'The Guards? That lot will never involve them.'

That's a relief, Jon thought. 'I'll never be able to – ' He stopped himself. Why am I even discussing this?

'We can sort something, tell him we need women's stuff from the chemist. He'll let her nip out for that.'

'He'd believe that? After me turning up the other day?'

'There'll be a chance to get her out. At some point.'

'He'll know you helped her.'

'I don't care. I hate this town. Soon as Zoë's safe, I'm off too.'

Jon sighed. 'Listen – find out if he's at home then call me back.' He cut the connection and started scrolling for his wife's number. 'It was that dodgy girl from Clifden.'

Rick lifted his eyebrows.

'Alice is at our place, she just gave that Siobhain my mobile.' Jon looked up at the sky waiting for his wife to answer. 'Alice, hi babe. Why aren't you at your mum's?'

'We'd forgotten Holly's Nintendo,' she said breezily. 'I just popped back.'

'But we agreed – stay away until this thing is sorted.' The line beeped. Another caller, trying to get through.

'Isn't it?' she replied. 'Wasn't that what Parks's phone call earlier was about?'

Her words were catching and he heard the jangle of keys. She's on the move, he thought. The line beeped again. 'Yes – but I didn't say it was safe to go home.'

'Well I'm setting off back to Mum's, anyway. When will you be there?'

'Not sure.' He could hear her opening their front door. 'Sixish, hopefully.'

'Right. I'll – ' She stopped talking.

A pang of disquiet coincided with another beep from his phone. Piss off calling me, would you? 'Alice are you still there?'

'Someone's at our garden gate.'

'What do you mean?'

'A man. He's...he's looking at me.'

'Alice,' Jon kept his voice low and urgent. 'Get back in the house.'

'Can I help you?' His wife's voice had a hard edge. 'What do you want? What the bloody hell do you want?'

Jon started running for his car. 'Get inside and lock the door!'

'You bloody well leave my family alone, do you hear?'

'Get in the fucking house!' As he opened his car, Rick was also on the phone. 'Are you inside?' Jon demanded.

'Yes.'

'Bolt it.'

'I have.'

'I'll be there in ten.' He started the engine.

Rick dropped into the passenger seat, talking fast. 'Yes – all units. Everything. Thirty-seven Arkville Road, Heaton Moor. It's an officer's home residence, I repeat, officer's home residence.'

CHAPTER 18

Rick called Alice's mobile as Jon sped along Dialstone Lane, siren wailing. 'We're on our way, Alice. Can you see what he's doing?' He glanced at Jon. 'She doesn't want to go near the windows. In case he throws something.'

Jon leaned across and asked loudly, 'Did you hear our front gate open?'

Rick shook his head in reply.

'Tell her to look through the letterbox.' He got to the traffic lights leading out on to the A6. Red. Fuck. In front, a stream of cars was crossing in both directions.

'Did you hear that, Alice?' Rick asked. 'Yeah – just a quick peep.' Holding his hand on the horn, Jon went the wrong way round a pedestrian island and forced his way out into the junction. Cars started pulling up and Jon manoeuvred between them.

Rick had bowed his head, phone pressed against his ear. 'Is he still there? He is? What's he doing?'

Now clear of the mess, Jon accelerated sharply.

'Standing there?' Rick said. 'That's all? He's looking up at the first-floor windows. OK, that's cool Alice. What does he look like?' He listened for a moment. 'Gingerish hair, quite stocky. Dark jacket. Right, we'll be there soon.'

Jon glanced at the dashboard. Sixty-five miles an hour. A speed camera went off behind him.

Rick spoke again. 'Where's he walking? Along the pavement? A car's pulled up?'

'Description,' Jon hissed.

'Can you see the type of car, Alice? Only the back? It's white. OK, that's good. Is it a hatchback? A hatchback. Great. Toyota maybe. It's driving off now? Don't worry — hold tight. We'll be there in...' He looked at Jon.

They were now approaching the point where the A6 passed the centre of Stockport. The white town hall was on their right, colonnades and ornate edging shrouded behind anti-pigeon netting. Jon lifted a hand, three fingers outstretched.

'Three minutes. I need to make another call, OK?' Rick hung up and selected another number. 'Les, DS Saville again. A white hatchback, possibly a Toyota. Two male occupants in the front. Passenger has gingerish hair, stocky build and is wearing a dark jacket. Proceeding from the area of Arkville Road, Heaton Moor. Cheers.' He clutched the phone between his knees.

'Streets are like a rabbit warren round ours,' Jon growled in reply. 'I can't believe she was shouting at him. Asking what the bloody hell he wanted.'

Rick glanced up. 'Jeez, that's India 99.'

Jon could hear the muted thrum of the Air Support Unit in the sky above. He swung the car into Arkville Road. The street was already clogged with patrol cars, doors wide open, lights silently flashing. Another police vehicle roared round the corner behind them. Jon turned his siren off and pulled up. Alice was in the front garden, pointing off to the side as she spoke to a uniform who, in turn, was busy relaying the information into his handset.

Producing his badge, Jon negotiated his way past the officers clustered on the pavement. 'Cheers, boys, I appreciate you getting here so fast.' He walked up to Alice. 'Are you OK?'

She managed a weak smile. 'Fine.'

He quickly rubbed a hand up and down her lower back. 'You did well, babe.' He found himself glancing about, as if some tangible trace of the men might remain.

'You seem more freaked out than me,' Alice said.

The officer who'd been speaking into his handset gave a cough. 'Sir, India 99 had been called out to an incident in Beswick. That was resolved and the pilot offered to divert here. They're sweeping the immediate area.'

Jon glanced up at the police helicopter working its way back and forth like a bird of prey quartering its hunting ground. Once more he felt a wash of excitement at knowing so many resources were there for him.

Rick appeared at his side. He wrapped an arm round Alice's shoulders and gave her a squeeze. 'Hey, nice going. Cool as a cucumber.'

A flush appeared on her cheeks. 'I only went inside and locked the door. Hardly gave you much to go off.' She glanced at Jon. 'I'm sorry.'

'About what?'

'Having a go at the person. It's just...all that's happened. I don't know, my temper snapped. I couldn't hold back.'

Don't worry, thought Jon. If it was me, I'd have hurdled the garden gate to get at him. 'Let's head in. I could do with a brew.'

Alice looked over to the group of uniformed officers. 'Can I get any of you a tea or coffee?'

They held up their hands, politely declining.

'What's my husband been saying about my brews?' She protested light-heartedly.

Several smiled, replying that they had other calls stacking up, moving back to their cars as they did so. The officer who'd been talking into his handset caught Jon's eye. Discreetly, he pointed a forefinger at the sky.

Jon gave a little shake of his head.

The officer immediately turned away. 'Give it one more

minute, lads. Then you can call it a day.'

Once in the house, the three of them walked down the corridor to the kitchen. Outside, car doors slammed and engines revved. Jon crossed the room, flicked the kettle on and reached down three mugs from the cupboard. The hair of the man I saw driving the van was tinged with red, he thought. 'So this guy, Alice. You got a good look at him?'

'Yes. About six foot tall. In his early thirties, heavyish build.'

Could be the same bloke, Jon thought, plonking a teabag in each cup and turning round. She was sitting at the table, Rick slumped in the corner chair. 'What about his hair?'

Her eyelids lowered. 'Kind of a ginger colour, wavy.' Her eyes reopened. 'It was tied back.' She brushed at her neck with a forefinger. 'Stubby little ponytail. And his jacket was a black leather one. The ponytail almost touching the collar.'

'Good,' Rick encouraged.

Jon leaned against the sideboard. The driver of the van was also mid-thirties and he had longish, straggly hair. Tied back, it would have formed a short ponytail. The only other feature Jon recalled was his flat nose – as if the bridge of it had been flattened on more than one occasion. 'What about the shape of his face, Ali? Anything stand out?'

'I don't think so,' she murmured. 'Fairly ordinary-looking. Squarish jaw. I just remember his eyebrows were quite bushy.'

'Nothing else?'

'Not that springs to mind.'

'How about his nose? Thin, fat, hooked, pointed?'

She shook her head. 'No, I don't remember. It couldn't have been especially unusual.'

Jon fished out the tea bags and added a splash of milk to each mug. What, he wondered, are the chances of it being the same man? Visual recollections were so subjective; different people registered different features. I'd focused on the broken nose because it was a clear indicator the man was no stranger to fighting. If it was the same man, who the hell was driving the car that had pulled up? Darragh?

'Do you think it was one of them?' Alice asked.

Jon placed mugs in front of her and Rick. 'My instinct is, they're already back home in Ireland. But I can't say that for certain.'

She reached for her tea, a vertical furrow forming between her eyes. 'This isn't over, then. They're coming to our house now. Christ, Jon.' Her eyes sought out his. 'They're coming to our house! Why?'

He sat at the chair next to hers and took her hand in his. 'We don't know that, Alice. I mean...' He struggled to find an alternative explanation for the man's presence. 'The Bramleys' next door is up for sale – maybe this guy was making sure the neighbours aren't a bunch of nutters. In which case, you just cost the Bramleys a potential buyer.'

She didn't smile. 'Why didn't he answer me, then?'

Jon leaned back, casting a glance at Rick. Help me out, here, for fuck's sake.

Rick registered the look and blinked. 'You did start laying into him, Alice. Demanding to know what the bloody hell he wanted.'

She looked over her shoulder at Rick then turned back to Jon. 'Why does this feel like I'm in an interview room at the station? You two, a double team.'

Jon saw the guilt flare on Rick's face. 'Until we have more facts, there's no point panicking.'

Alice searched out his eyes. 'You really think this had no connection to what happened to Punch?'

Jon felt his heart lurch yet again. Punch. I was meant to call back late morning. 'I just don't know. All we can do is take precautions and try to carry on.' He reached for his phone. Whoever had been trying to call earlier had left a message on his answerphone. The first three digits were the same as his home number: the call had been local. The vet's, he thought. It could be the number for the vet's. He was about to ring his answerphone when another call came in. Anonymous. Siobhain again? 'DI Spicer.'

'It's me. He's here.' Even slightly out of breath, her Irish accent was coming through strongly.

Jon's eyes bounced between Alice and Rick. 'Where — at his house?'

'It's one of those apartments where he lives. He arrived late last night.'

'You're sure?'

'Yes.'

'He's in his apartment right now?'

'Yes.'

Jon shook his head. Who'd just been standing on the pavement outside, then? Was it the mate from the van? 'Who's he with? Is he on his own?'

'No. There were a few there. A bit of a party, it was.'

A party. Jon felt his teeth grind together. The fucker was having a celebration, was he? Raising a glass to his little achievement. Jon wanted to smash his fist into something. 'Is the other one there?'

'Which other one?'

'I don't know his name. The one with gingerish hair. His mate.'

'Denis? Not sure.'

Denis, Jon thought. 'OK, leave it with me.'

'Does that mean you're coming?'

Jon allowed himself a glimpse of Darragh's face, blood pouring from a mouth of broken teeth as he brought his heel down on it one more time. Glancing guiltily at his wife, he cancelled the image from his mind. 'I said leave it with me.' Before she could say anything else, he pressed red and began to turn the phone over in his hands. 'Seems Darragh is back,' he announced. 'Arrived in Clifden late last night.'

Alice sat forward. 'That was the Irish woman again?'

He nodded, accessing his answerphone and lifting the handset to his ear. The message began to play.

'Mr Spicer? It's Valerie Ackford. Could you please come to the veterinary practice? It's Punch, he's…please come. As soon as you possibly can.'

CHAPTER 19

Jon hesitated at the front step of the vet's. What did she mean? It's Punch, he's...please come. Why didn't she say what it was about? He can't be dying. They said he was stable...that he was – '

The door opened and he looked up to see Valerie standing before him. 'Please, come in.'

Jon suddenly felt like his leg muscles had been struck by a wasting disease. 'Is he...' His jaw was numb, his tongue clumsy. He tried again. 'Is everything all right?' Valerie placed a hand on his arm and he wanted to shrug it off. Don't say it isn't, he thought. Don't.

'Mr Spicer, Punch's condition has deteriorated. It can happen as an animal starts to come out of shock. I'm very sorry, but his system is simply shutting down.'

Jon couldn't move forward. He hovered in the doorway. 'Well, what...how can you reverse that?'

Slowly, she shook her head. 'We're past that now, Jon. The best thing is for you to just be with him.'

'What do you mean, just be with him?' His head dropped. I know what you mean, he thought. His vision started to swim and he had to wipe at his eyes.

She squeezed his arm in reply. 'Come on, come with

me.' She took his hand and led him down the corridor. The nurse glanced up and immediately turned away, a tearful look on her face. He felt sick as they reached the treatment room. I don't want to go in there. I don't want this to happen. 'Can't you do anything?'

'I'm sorry,' she whispered. 'Come.'

He felt a tug on his hand and stepped forward once again. The room was bright and he could hear music from the radio. Piano, melodic and beautiful. Whatever that is, Jon thought, I never want to hear it again. He became aware of a rapid rasping sound and turned to the cage as Valerie unclipped the door.

Jon looked at her. 'What do I do?'

'He's not in pain – I've made sure of that. Just…stroke him. Talk to him. He may well recognise your voice.' She stepped past and left the room.

Jon sucked in breath and forced his gaze to the cage. He looks like he's fast asleep, he thought. Not dying. Not about to die. Punch was lying on his side, position unchanged except for the fact his neck was arched back. His muzzle was pointing to the back of the cage, as if an interesting smell was located there. Jon saw his breathing was laboured, ribs rising and falling, stuttering, almost stopping before finally moving again.

He stepped closer, grasped the corners of the blue carpet at the base of the cage and swivelled it round. The movement had an echo of another; the van, he realised. Dragging the beast towards the light. He regarded his dog's face. The eyes were shut, tongue lolling from slack jaws. Jon draped a forearm across his dog's shoulder and let his fingers rest lightly on the fluttering ribs. Cold, he thought, you're so cold. He lowered his forehead and brought his nose into contact with Punch's ruined ear. 'I'm here, boy,' he murmured. 'Daddy's here for you now. It's OK. You're a good boy. Daddy loves you.'

He didn't know how long he stayed like that. The piano faded away and was followed by something with violins.

At some point Punch's breathing slowed and finally came to a halt. He kept whispering all the same, hand running back and forth, back and forth. When he did lift his face, Punch's coat was matted with his tears.

He wiped at his eyes and looked around. The cupboard units are all still here. The tap and the sink. That little cardboard box is on the work surface. Music is coming from the radio. Nothing, he realised, has changed: except Punch is now dead. He closed his eyes and held the thought. Punch is dead. Punch is dead. He visualised a dark space – somewhere safe and quiet – and pushed the thought as far in as it would go. Then he cupped a palm over the side of Punch's face, ran the tip of his thumb slowly down the smooth groove of fur between the animal's eyes and walked out of the room.

Valerie was in reception, sitting at the computer alongside the nurse. They looked round at his approach.

'He's gone,' Jon announced. 'Slipped away.'

Valerie nodded, getting to her feet. 'I'm so sorry.'

He gave a quick shake of his head. 'No – I want to thank you. Both of you. I know you did everything possible.' He looked at the workstation and back at Valerie. 'Can you make arrangements…I don't know what the procedure – '

'Yes,' she replied. 'There's no need to rush, though. Why don't you – '

'I'd like him to be cremated,' Jon cut in, the cliff edge overlooking Edale clear in his mind's eye. Strange, he thought, realising part of him always knew that's where Punch would end up. He pictured the numbers of walks they'd enjoyed together up there, Punch trotting happily alongside, occasionally turning his eyes upward. Just checking, the look said. Just checking you're still here. Us two, in this perfect place together. Jon closed the thought down. 'Doesn't matter what the ashes are in. Cheapest pot will do. Can you add the costs to our bill?'

'Of course,' she replied. 'It sounds like you've – '

'I have. It's what I want. It's what Punch would want. Shall I call you tomorrow?' He could tell she was taken aback at his businesslike tone.

'I'll be in touch, don't worry. I only wish...'

Now it was his turn to squeeze her arm. 'Thanks again.'

He walked quickly down the corridor and let himself out. Turning left on the pavement, he slid his mobile from his pocket and called home. 'Alice?' He swallowed hard. 'He's dead.'

'Jon.'

'His body couldn't cope. It just shut down.'

'Oh, Jon. I don't know what to say...are you all right?'

He thought how her words confirmed what never needed to be said. They might have referred to Punch as the family dog but, if the truth be known, it was really his. 'I'm OK. A bit shaky. I'm going for a walk.' He looked up at the pale sky. 'Just to try and get my head straight. I won't be long.'

'That's fine. Rick's here. Mum's happy hanging on to Holly. I'm really sorry, Jon. I'm really so sorry.'

'Thanks. I'll see you in a bit.' He snapped his phone shut and continued towards the golf course. The car park was a quarter full. He crossed the asphalt at a quick pace, strode down the grassy bank and came to a halt where the attack had taken place the day before.

The grass looked as if it had been gone over by the groundsman; no clue as to what had happened there remained. Jon walked over to the screen of bushes, sat down on a tree stump and rested his forearms across his knees. So, he asked himself, clasping his hands together, what's your next move? You've a pregnant wife and young daughter. If your lives can ever return to normal, you're going to have to start using your brain.

CHAPTER 20

Silence as Alice and Rick looked up. He stepped into the kitchen, concentrating on keeping it together.

Alice rose and walked towards him, both arms out. He closed his eyes and bowed his head, leaning in slightly so her hair was pressed against his face.

After a few seconds, she leaned her upper body back and he felt the hard ball of her pregnancy push against him. She regarded him anxiously, tears spilling from her eyes.

'I'm OK,' he replied, wiping them from her cheeks.

She sighed, hands sliding down to his waist. 'Are you hungry?'

He considered her question. 'No. But a coffee would be great.'

She gave a small smile. 'Rick?'

'Yeah – another coffee would be great, thanks.'

She began to make them all drinks. 'It doesn't seem real. Our whole life – it's like we've woken up in a parallel universe.'

Jon watched her. It's real, he thought, taking a seat.

She placed the drinks on the table, pulled a chair between the two men and took hold of Jon's hand. 'Where did you go? I was getting worried.'

'The golf course. Somewhere quiet to sit and weigh everything up. Work out what to do,' he circled his free hand in the air, 'with this situation.'

Alice looked uncomfortable. 'With Zoë?'

He sighed. 'Her, yes. But Darragh as well.'

Alarm showed in her eyes. 'What do you mean?'

He looked down at the table as he spoke. 'I've been thinking it through. He's just lost his prizefighting dog because of me.'

'My heart bleeds,' Alice retorted angrily. 'How will he ever cope?'

Jon lifted his eyes. 'That's exactly what worries me.' He saw her pupils contract as the focus of her thoughts turned inward. She was picking up the thread.

'But they killed Punch! Their dog is dead, and now so is ours. We're even.'

'No.' He kept his voice low. 'It's not. Punch was payback for what happened in his nightclub.' He saw her eyes flick away for an instant. A spark of resentment. 'I'm sorry, Ali. If I knew what was going to –'

She rubbed briskly at his hand. 'It's all right. We can't turn the clock back. But you're saying it isn't over? He's back in Ireland and still planning to attack us again?'

Jon flipped his other hand palm up. 'I just don't know.'

She turned her head. 'Rick? Is this...do you think what Jon's saying – is he right?'

Rick was studying Jon. 'What else is on your mind?'

He shrugged. 'I haven't got a lot further than that. What's your take?'

Rick took a long breath in. 'I agree that with characters like him – small-time criminals – it's how their minds work. It's all about reputation. Threats to it, real or imagined.'

Alice slid her hand off Jon's. 'So you're saying he's right. He's going to come back?'

'He could well do.'

She pressed a finger against the table. 'Then we get the Irish police involved. Have them haul the bastard in – charge him with… I don't know, attempted murder of Holly. Christ, that dog was about to attack her!'

'I've been considering it,' Jon muttered. 'But it's a non-starter.'

'Why?' Her eyes glittered angrily. 'Tell me why.'

'Shit, Ali. This whole bloody mess – '

'Just tell me.'

'Because I lack any kind of hard proof.'

'You got the registration of their van! You saw the driver. The van's then abandoned and set on fire with that thing in the back of it!'

Jon pursed his lips. 'It's not enough to bring charges against Darragh. Not as it stands.'

'But you're a policeman.' She looked from him to Rick. 'You know full well he's behind it. I don't understand how you can't – '

'What do I do?' Jon interrupted. 'Explain to DCI Parks that we've no hard evidence, but could she ring the police station in Clifden and ask them to arrest him? Tell Darragh that, if he's planning anything else that might endanger our daughter, he really should strongly reconsider – '

'All right, Jon,' Rick cut in. 'You've made your point.'

He blinked a couple of times then placed a hand back on hers. 'Sorry.'

'Then forget the Irish police,' Alice said. 'If they won't take action, we do something.'

Jon stared mournfully at her. 'Ali, we face the same problem: proof. And even if we managed to collect any, the process involved in arresting someone beyond Britain's borders is a nightmare. We'd still be relying on the police in Ireland to help build our case.'

Alice ran her hands through her hair. 'I can't carry on living like this.'

They sat in silence for a few seconds before Rick said, 'There could be a way to sort it out.'

Jon's eyes went to Rick. 'How?'

'Threaten to hit him where it hurts most – his wallet. You go over and tell him Zoë's coming back with you and things end there. If he says no, you explain that – as a policeman – you'll make sure his business suffers. You'll bring in the National Crime Agency, if needs be.'

Jon was looking at Alice. Tension was pulling at her mouth and pinching the skin at the corners of her eyes. She's coming apart at the seams, he thought, putting an arm round her and wrenching his eyes back to Rick. 'Carry on.'

'OK, you ask for a meeting with him. But it must be in private. You tell him that, if Zoë leaves with you, he's free to tell his people anything he wants. It's all about not losing face, remember? You begged him. You pleaded and apologised. You offered money. Anything Darragh wants you to say, you say it. What's crucial is Darragh comes out of that meeting the victor, not you.'

'What you're suggesting,' Alice whispered. 'The man was prepared to let a fighting machine loose on our daughter – and Punch. How do you know he wouldn't do the same to Jon?'

Rick reached out and squeezed her hand. 'You have to remember, Jon's police. Behind all this, he's a British police officer.'

'And they just executed a British soldier – the one kidnapped outside those barracks in Belfast!'

'No.' Jon cut in. 'That's completely different, Ali. You're talking about Northern Ireland and you're talking about dissident republicans looking to derail the peace process. Darragh is a small-time criminal in a tiny town in a far corner of Ireland. He has no link to any paramilitary activity whatsoever.' She still looked frightened. 'Alice – the guy is a crook. He's a crooked businessman. His priority is to guard his business. I think Rick's right – he won't jeopardise everything over Zoë.' 'Could you do that?' Alice asked. 'Let him humiliate you?'

Jon sat back and spread his palms. 'If it makes this thing go away, yes.'

Both men looked at Alice.

She glanced from one to the other. 'What?'

'What do you think?' Jon asked gently.

'I trust you two. If you reckon it'll work, then so do I.' She flinched. 'How long will you be leaving me and Holly on our own?'

Jon's eyes closed for a moment. Good point. Darragh might be back in Clifden, but he obviously knows people over here… He drummed his fingers on the table. 'Center Parcs,' he announced, raising his eyebrows. 'You go to Center Parcs tomorrow as planned – but you move lodges. We don't need the one that allows dogs. Book into another, but in your maiden name.'

Rick was nodding. 'And you go in my car. Darragh's seen that you own a Mondeo. So you leave it here on the drive.'

Jon regarded his colleague. 'Rick – there's no need – '

'There is.'

'OK, thanks. It would be safe, wouldn't it? Different lodge, different name, different car. Who's going to find her?'

'Nobody,' Rick responded.

Alice lifted a finger and rubbed at the edge of her eye. Jon watched her anxiously. 'Ali, none of this happens unless you're happy, OK?'

She nodded. 'There are other things to consider. As I said, how long do you go for? We have to agree on a limit.'

'She's right,' Rick stated.

'Well,' Jon replied. 'I'm due back in work on Monday. Today's Wednesday. Say I left tomorrow – I'd stay until Sunday evening at the latest.'

'Three nights,' said Rick. 'Should be enough.'

'And Zoë?' Alice asked. 'Does she come back to Manchester?'

'I don't know,' Jon replied. 'What do you reckon?'

She let out a growl of exasperation. 'I'm so angry with her. She never thinks of anyone but herself.'

Jon nodded wearily. 'If she's using drugs again, she can have a flight anywhere she wants but Manchester. We've got Jake to consider in this – not to mention my mum and dad.'

'And if she's not on them?'

He shrugged. 'Let's cross that bridge when we come to it.' His eyes fell away. He found himself looking at Punch's basket in the corner, bowls for food and water beside it. It hit him like a donkey's kick. He's gone.

'And when you get there?' Alice asked. 'What if Darragh refuses to meet you?'

Jon sat back. 'Well, I had an idea the first time I was over there. You know how we've got Dave's stuff up in the attic; the bits and pieces left in their flat when Zoë disappeared?'

Alice gave a nod.

'There's a decent photo of her up there, I'm certain. What if I make up a load of missing-person posters? Pin them up all round Clifden. Get a cheap pay-as-you-go mobile and put its number on the posters. If she is working for Darragh, it'll embarrass him into agreeing to meet up. He has his reputation as a pillar of the community to protect, after all.'

Her smile was cautious. 'I can see that working.'

'So...' Jon paused. 'Do we have a plan?'

Alice brushed at the table. 'You're not wanting revenge?' She looked into his eyes. 'Are you?'

He kept looking back. 'No, babe. I don't want revenge.'

'Jon, they just killed your dog. I can't bear to even think what their animal would have done to Holly. You must be...surely, there's...'

'I know they did. But I can't let it get to me. There's us to think about. You and Holly.'

She stared at him as the seconds ticked past. 'If you go over there to settle this, it has to be peacefully. There can be no grudge, no feud. I can't carry on like this – curtains drawn, jumping at every knock on the door. Do you understand?'

'I do. Look.' He raised his fingers. 'Steady. I'm in control. That side of me – it's in the past.'

'You won't resort to violence?'

'No.'

'Promise me.'

'I promise I will not resort to violence.'

'I don't know,' Alice's voice was faint. 'You make it all sound so simple.'

'There's no reason it shouldn't be.' Jon raised himself in his seat and injected some optimism into his voice. 'Know what? I might even try to see my grandad. Last time, I didn't have a chance to speak to him.'

'You're there for three nights, no more,' Alice stated.

'With me watching your back in the office,' Rick chipped in.

Jon thought for a moment. 'Rick, if word of this does get back to Parks, you knew nothing. This was me acting on my own, right?'

Rick gave a reluctant nod.

Jon placed both palms on the table. 'I'll get on the computer. See what time flights leave tomorrow.'

Alice slid her chair back. 'I'll call Center Parcs and change our booking.'

They all got to their feet and regarded one another for a moment, coffees untouched on the table. Rick extended both arms. 'Group hug?'

As the three of them embraced, Alice said, 'Are you sure this – doing this – is the right thing?'

Jon looked down at the crown of her head. 'It's the only way to get our lives back.'

'Rick?' she asked.

'It'll be fine.'

'Sure?'

'I'm sure.'

Above her, the two men's gazes met. Each spotted a glimmer of uncertainty in the other man's eye.

PART II

CHAPTER 21

Jon could just see the underside of the wing above the small window next to him. The aircraft began to taxi towards the runway as the pilot continued his pre-flight commentary.

'So, we'll be taking off in a north-easterly direction towards Stockport, then turning back to pass over Manchester, Liverpool and along the Welsh coast. After flying over Anglesey, we'll cross the Irish Sea, then over Dublin and Athlone before touching down in Galway where, I gather, the sun is trying to come out. Flight time is one hour.'

Jon's eyes went to the sky above Manchester airport. Unbroken grey in all directions. The small plane was only a fifth full, businessmen mostly, by the look of them. His passage through the airport had been smooth: the woman at the check-in desk had weighed his holdall with the usual questions about whether he'd packed it himself.

'I have,' Jon replied, thinking about the items of riot of gear he'd spirited from the station the previous evening. When he'd mentioned to Rick that he intended to take some things, his partner had looked horrified.

'What sort of stuff are you talking about?'

Jon had glanced down the corridor in the police station, picturing the storeroom where the equipment was kept. 'I don't know. A stab-proof vest for starters. Armour for my forearms, elbows, shins and knees. Pepper spray. Maybe an Asp.'

Rick had come to a halt. 'You promised Alice there'd be no violence, Jon. So why are you planning to enter that town like the bloody Terminator?'

'Oh come on, I'm talking about stuff I can slip on under my clothes. Just for self-defence. Then, if something does go wrong, I can get myself out.'

'You think it'll go wrong?'

He looked into his partner's eyes. 'Mate, let's not pretend this plan is without risk. It makes sense to take every precaution we can.'

'But without mentioning any of this to Alice?'

Jon glanced up at the ceiling. 'It only occurred as we were driving in. And no, I don't think mentioning it to Alice would be a good idea. With the pregnancy and everything, she's stressed out enough as it is.'

After he'd put the protective gear in the boot of his car, he'd gone back into the station to find DCI Parks and inform her all ongoing cases were safely with Rick. She'd immediately asked after Punch.

'I'm afraid he didn't pull through,' Jon replied.

She stared at him with growing horror. 'You mean...'

'Just after lunch.' He brushed the air with one hand. 'It was very peaceful – he didn't ever come out of shock. Not fully, anyway. The vet says he wouldn't have felt a thing.'

She came round from behind her desk.

What, Jon thought, is she doing? Oh Christ. She's going to give me a hug. He watched in horror as his boss clasped an arm around him, hand pressing against the middle of his back. 'That's terrible Jon, I'm so sorry.' She leaned her head against his upper arm. 'I can't imagine what you're feeling. They become a member of the family, don't they?'

'He was...at the end of the day, he was a mate. One of my best mates.'

'The companionship, I know,' she said soothingly. 'At least it was painless.'

Jon remained rooted to the spot, head bowed. He pictured the scene from the main incident room. This must look so bloody odd. 'Yes.'

She lifted her head, gesturing with the index finger of her free hand. 'Try to enjoy your break at Center Parcs. Things must seem awful now – but they won't be for ever. Remember that, OK?'

Now guilt began to well up. The woman is doing her best to comfort me, he thought. And here I am bullshitting her. 'Thank you.'

She returned to her chair. 'We can pursue it, you know. At least pass everything we have to the police over in Ireland. I know they were very interested to hear about that van.'

Jon pondered recent developments. The Vehicle Identification Number he'd noted down from the van's doorframe had tallied with that of one which had been stolen from outside a garage in Galway a month before. Whoever had stolen it must have then switched plates; the registration Jon had noted down at the roundabout belonged to a separate vehicle.

Thinking that official enquiries could jeopardise the plan, Jon replied, 'I'm not sure what involving the Irish police will achieve at this stage – we haven't really got the evidence.'

Parks lifted a palm. 'Elmhurst and May will be picking up the case once they've finished testifying in court. They should be on it by Friday.'

Shit, thought Jon. That's the last thing I want. 'OK – I'll think about it while I'm at Center Parcs, if that's all right?'

'Perfectly,' she replied. 'See you next week. And Jon? Just...I don't know. I'm so sorry about Punch.'

'Thanks.' He left her office and returned to his desk. Rick was sifting through the files for the cases they were currently working on.

'What was that all about?' Rick murmured without looking up.

Jon sank onto his seat and also started moving paperwork around. 'Bloody nightmare. She was trying to make me feel better about Punch. Told me to try and enjoy my break at Center Parcs. Now I feel like complete shit.'

'No other way,' Rick whispered. 'We just have to make damn sure she never finds out what we're up to.'

Jon's mobile started to ring and he scrutinised the screen. Nick Hutcher. 'Hi there, Nick. I thought you'd be in the Marble Arch by now.'

'They're picking me up at eight.'

Jon glanced at his watch. Twenty minutes' time.

'You rushed away from those playing fields. Everything all right?'

Jon nodded. 'Yeah, it was a false alarm.'

'How's your dog doing?'

'He didn't make it,' Jon replied, clearing his throat.

'He died?'

'Yes.' He heard the other man breathe out.

'Really sorry to hear that, I honestly am.'

'Thanks.'

'What…was it from the injuries?'

'Basically.'

'You'll want to find those people from the van, then. I have something for you. About the breed of dog.'

Jon sat forward. 'Go on.'

'Are you near a computer with internet access?'

His monitor came to life as he jiggled his mouse. 'I am.'

'OK. Google these two words. First is 'La', second is 'Tauromaquia. I'll spell it for you.'

Jon typed it in and pressed return. Top hit was an Amazon entry. He read the text. *La Tauromaquia, Francisco*

Goya y Lucientes. The Disasters of War. Spanish entertainment and other prints.

'Got the results?' The RSPCA officer asked.

'Yeah, some kind of book, is it?'

'Go to the second result. The profile on Goya.'

Jon clicked on it and a screen came up titled, *The Genius of Goya*. Below was a menu of his many artistic works.

'Go to the bottom one, etchings.'

Selecting that option brought up a new list. 'Have done.'

'Now click on the third, La Tauromaquia.'

A string of thumbnail images formed a row across the screen. Most seemed to be scenes of bullfights from another era – elaborately dressed men on horseback leaning from the saddle to stab at bulls with lances. Another image showed an unarmed man crouched before a charging bull as if readying himself to vault clean over the animal.

'Know much about Goya?' Nick asked.

'No.'

'Me neither. These sketches were done in the early eighteen-hundreds. They're all about bullfighting at that time. So you've got matadors going about their business. But scroll across to the twenty-fourth print.'

By moving the bar at the base of the screen along, more images were revealed. Number twenty-four appeared to be of a man on horseback observing a bull. The animal's head was low to the ground as it tried to ward off several smaller animals.

'Enlarge that and tell me what you think,' Nick instructed.

Jon clicked on the image and it took over the screen. The quality was poor but now Jon could see that the creatures swarming round the bull were dogs.

'Look familiar?' The RSPCA officer asked.

The coats of two seemed pale, but the one partly behind the bull's rear leg was covered in faint stripes. A fourth, darker, animal had latched on to the bull's face and appeared to be hanging on for dear life. All the dogs had spadelike heads and long, thin tails. Lowering his phone, Jon tilted his head so he could see Rick. 'Check this out,' he said, lifting his handset back up. 'They're the same as the animal that attacked Punch. What are they?'

Rick was now looking over his shoulder as Hutcher replied. 'The breed is called Alano, or Alaunt in older records. This is some story, mate. Are you ready?'

Jon leaned back in his seat. 'Yup.'

'Right, history. It's an ancient breed, origins unknown. Some sources indicate they were first brought into Europe when the Alanos – a nomadic tribe – invaded Iberia in the four-hundreds. The Roman Empire was starting to lose power and the Barbarian hordes were moving in, including the Alano people.'

'Bloody hell,' Jon stated.

'I know. It's thought the breed is the ancestor of most Molosser breeds today, including the Great Dane, Cordoba Fighting Dog, Fila Brasiliero and Canary Dog – the type we found at the mill earlier on.'

Jon continued to stare at the image. 'You're saying these things date back some fifteen hundred years?'

'Correct. They were used as war-dogs because of their fearless natures. They'll attack anything – regardless of size – and fight to the death. The Spaniards used them alongside their soldiers for centuries. Later, they were used in bullfighting.'

Jon swallowed, the image of the creature stalking closer to his terrified daughter crystal-clear in his mind. His eyes went to the framed photo beside his monitor. Punch, you never stood a chance.

'Now,' Nick continued. 'Their use in bullfighting was outlawed in the 1880s and their numbers plummeted. Some were kept for hunting wild boar and cattle – the dogs can keep up a steady gallop for miles, apparently. Another quality is that they'll hold on to their prey, but release it when ordered to do so.'

'The whistle,' Jon said. 'When the guy whistled, it let go.'

'What I thought. And the long tails? They act as a rudder when pursuing their quarry. You also said it jumped into the van from some distance?'

'Yes.'

'These things can climb trees, Jon, they're so agile. They don't bother with barking in an attack situation and the destructiveness of their bite is legendary. With the modernisation of Spain, the wild boar population pretty much died out and, for most of the twentieth century, the breed was believed to have become extinct. Then, in the late 1980s, an enthusiast called Carlos Contera started scouring rural Spain to see if any still existed. It took him months, but in an isolated valley in northern Spain called Encartaciones, he found a small population. They were being used to herd a type of half-wild cattle that still live in the area. Contera had their DNA analysed by the Faculty of Veterinary Medicine at the University of Córdoba. When their authenticity was verified, he started to restore the breed.'

Jon shook his head. 'Nick – I don't know what to say. You must have been at this for hours.'

'Not really. A colleague had an inkling about the breed. Most of the information is on Contera's own website. Anyway, it's been a pleasure; I'd never heard of these things until this afternoon. Nowadays there are a few hundred – used for cattle herding only. They're not kept as pets and they're never entered into shows.'

'Understandable.'

'True. The colouring of the one that attacked your dog is known as negro y atigrado, which translates as black and tigered. A fit, yes?'

'Definitely,' Jon agreed. 'But if there's only a few hundred of these things being kept as working dogs in rural Spain, how did one end up in the back of a van in

Manchester?'

'I've already emailed Contera. Hopefully, he'll get back to me very soon.'

The hum of the aircraft's engine picked up. Jon dipped his head and watched as the propellers first blurred then became all but invisible. His seat seemed to press into his back and the plane surged down the runway, a haze of heat emanating from the roaring engines. Then the floor tilted and suddenly they were rising into the air.

He looked down at the ranked formations of houses below. The M60 came into view, a grey ribbon with curling offshoots. By a big roundabout he could see the pyramid-shaped building housing the Co-operative Bank's call centre. Then everything went white. Seconds later, the plane emerged from cloud into a world of bright blue. For the first time in weeks, he felt hot sunshine against his face.

Alice glanced at her watch then up at the dull grey sky. 'His flight should have taken off by now.'

Rick was bent over, squeezing Alice's bags into the boot of his BMW 1 Series. 'Right, that's everything.' He closed the hatch, stepped round and held the key fob out. 'So you're OK with the controls? You know how the buttons on this thing works. You press – '

'Rick,' Alice stopped him. 'You've explained already. I've got it.'

He smiled. 'Sorry. Nerves.'

'About Jon?'

'No, that old meathead can look after himself. About you two.' His eyes slid to Holly, who was in the rear seat, studying the pages of a comic. Speaking softly, he added, 'How's she been with all this?'

Alice hunched a shoulder. 'Better than I thought. She's obviously upset Daddy's not with us, but then again, that's nothing new with the ridiculous job he insists on doing.'

She grinned briefly.

Rick shook his head. 'I know. What a way to make a living – the idiot. Seriously though, are you OK with everything?'

'I don't know,' she sighed. 'One minute I am, the next I find my hands are trembling. I can't wait for this weekend to be over.' Her eyes lifted anxiously to the sky again.

'I know what you mean. But he knows what he's doing.'

'Yes. I have to keep telling myself there's a difference between the Jon of old and the Jon of now.'

'Being?'

She tapped her temple. 'Now he uses this. Before, it was fists first, questions later. Must be something about getting older.'

'Well, it certainly took a long time happening to him,' Rick smiled.

'He gave me this.' She held out a black leather pouch, the silver neck of an aerosol can visible inside.

'Pepper spray?' Christ, he thought, how much stuff did Jon sneak out of that storeroom?

'He said if that guy shows up again, blast him in the face with it.'

She dropped it back into her handbag. 'I'll keep it in its little holster thing. Don't want to confuse it with my breath freshener.'

'For God's sake, don't do that,' Rick coughed. He looked at the car parked on the drive and then at the house. 'Timer switches for the lights all on?'

'Check.'

'Directions printed off?'

'Check. And all emails from Center Parcs and recent internet searches deleted off the computer, as ordered.'

'OK. Call me later, right?'

'Yes.'

After they'd hugged, Rick tapped on the BMW's rear window. 'Have a great time, Holly. See you soon!'

He watched the car right up until it reached the end of the road and started indicating. Then he turned to the house, failing to see a black Golf as it pulled out and followed his BMW round the corner.

CHAPTER 22

By the time the pilot announced that the plane was about to start its descent, the layer of cloud below the aircraft had begun to fracture. Through the gaps, Jon glimpsed dull landscape and the glint of a distant lake. Visibility hazed out. They emerged in the cold shadow of cloud, faded fields rising to meet them. Jon compared the density of housing around Manchester to the sparse clusters of dwellings below. Far off, the horizon was pimpled by distant peaks.

Walking across the tarmac, he eyed the pale green corrugated metal of the terminal. This place, he thought, isn't much more than a large shed in a field. Inside, he was surprised to see two Garda officers with a sniffer dog. Tail swishing from side to side, the Labrador nosed at everyone's hand luggage as they filed into the baggage reclaim room. Jon couldn't resist bending down to quickly ruffle the animal's ears.

He stood apart from the other passengers, most of whom were now talking into mobile phones as the conveyor belt clanked into life. The dog's handler got it to jump up on to the belt and it worked its way eagerly along the procession of luggage.

Once beyond the solitary person at passport control, he searched for the Car Hire desk in the main part of the terminal. An Avis sign was by the exit doors. Once two Germans in suits had collected their vehicle's keys, Jon stepped up to the counter. 'Hi. Is there a Car Hire 3000 around here?'

'That's us,' the woman smiled. 'We all share the one office. What's your name?'

'Spicer.'

She looked at several sheets pinned to the wall. 'Ah, yes. A Ford Focus, three days' hire, with the option of extending that, if needed.'

Out in the small car park, he searched for anything that was pale blue. There you are, he thought. And a car with Irish, not British number plates. That's good news: it won't stand out this time round. The key didn't seem to work in the door and Jon was about to set off back to the terminal when he tried the handle. The vehicle had been unlocked all along. Remember, he told himself, you're not in Manchester now. Things are different here.

On the passenger seat, a photocopied sheet of Galway's road system showed him how to get on to the N59. Twenty minutes after crossing over the River Corrib, he again passed the roadside sign welcoming him to Connemara. The landscape immediately grew more rugged.

When he reached Clifden, he drove straight past the police station, eyes cutting momentarily to the entrance. The place could have been closed. In the town square he continued round until the metallic airplane-wing monument came into view. Its smooth, shiny surface contrasted with the somewhat dated brick buildings all around. A foreign object, thrust into the centre of somewhere it didn't belong. Know the feeling, Jon thought, as he slotted the car into one of the many spaces available. In front of him were two buildings: Darragh's to the right, Joyce's Hotel to the left.

Once again he had the feeling he was the focus of unseen eyes. He glanced up at the rows of blank windows staring down. What time is it? he wondered, glancing at his watch. Half-eleven in the morning. Except for a family speaking French or Spanish, the pavements were deserted. He watched the woman pause outside a souvenir shop. The young girl holding her hand began to swing her leg to and fro and Jon found himself thinking about Alice and Holly. They'd be on their way to Center Parcs by now.

He slid his holdall off the rear seat and slipped through the doors of Joyce's. Thick reddish carpets and dark, wooden walls interspersed with head-high lamps. Their cloth shades were too thick, shrouding little bulbs which struggled to properly light the foyer.

'Good morning, sir.' The young man behind the reception desk wore a dark green waistcoat over a white shirt.

'Hello,' Jon nodded. 'I haven't got a reservation. Is there any chance...'

'That's fine.'

Thought it would be, Jon thought, glancing at the rows of hooks behind the desk. From almost every one there hung a key. 'Do you have any rooms overlooking the street?'

'Not at the back? It tends to be quieter there.'

'The front is great, cheers.'

'How many nights, sir?'

Jon pondered the question. They'd agreed a maximum of three. But, that suddenly seemed a bit generous. A desire to be back in time to join Alice and Holly at Center Parcs bit. 'Two, please,' he replied, thinking he could extend it by another night if necessary.

Room 17 was towards the end of the second-floor corridor. He examined the enormous brass key-fob. Not much smaller than the plaque outside Valerie Ackford's veterinary practice.

The door opened to reveal a room with the same

chintzy feel as the foyer – floral pattern on the eiderdown and frills on the pillows of the double bed. The armchairs either side of a coffee table by the window had lacy coverings over the headrests.

Dumping his holdall on the bed, he checked his phone had reception before tossing it beside the bag and crossing to the window. The view of the high street was a good one. Directly opposite was a small black-fronted pub called Lowry's. He noticed the empty bottles arranged on the other side of its narrow, dim windows. Looks like a nice quiet place for a beer, he concluded.

By opening the window a crack, he was able to see down to the entrance of Darragh's some thirty metres along the pavement. Perfect.

Pulling the window closed, Jon examined the holdall. OK, he said to himself. Time to get started.

The zip opened with a low burring noise and he removed the layer of clothes at the top. Below it was the body armour from Longsight station. A stab-proof vest embossed with the Gear-Tech logo. The item was thin enough to sit beneath a shirt without being obvious. He removed kneepads and forearm and lower-leg protectors, knocking a knuckle against the hard plastic panels. Strong enough to absorb the impact of a baseball bat. A pair of lycra shorts, the groin area reinforced with hard casing. Beside them was a little leather holster with the can of pepper spray inside.

Wrapped up in a T-shirt was the Asp – a telescopic truncheon that, when extended, measured twenty-one inches. He held the black rubberised handle in the palm of his right hand and brought the handle down in a short chopping movement. The rod of high carbon steel inside extended itself with a cold snicker. The business, he thought, twisting the handle and collapsing it back.

Next, he removed an A4 plastic file. In a Perspex sleeve inside were a hundred sheets of paper. He slid them out and examined the uppermost one. A colour photo of Zoë was at its centre. Jon guessed the hills in the background were those of the Lake District; he knew his brother had spent a summer up there, squatting in an empty holiday home. Above the image of her smiling face was a single word: MISSING.

He looked into her eyes. True, they were a bit sunken and the lines running from their corners were too deeply etched for a woman in her twenties. But Jesus, he thought, considering what she'd gone through, it was amazing she was able to smile at all. And it was a genuine smile, too. A tiny wedge of sunlight catching in each eye, the lock of dark purple hair hanging between them shimmering.

You found happiness once, he thought. You and my brother. Perhaps it was just for that single summer. A dozen or so weeks spent walking the hills, maybe earning cash on local farms. Lazy evenings watching the sun set. Another image abruptly appeared. Zoë, in a house somewhere close by, lying in bed with two black eyes, clutching her ribs every time she coughed.

He thought about the last time he'd actually seen her. The half-derelict tower block in Manchester, specks of Salvio's blood dotting his clothes. Tears had been coursing down her face as her arm had scrabbled beneath her bed. Still on her knees, she'd held up the file.

'It's got all Jake's records from the hospital and that. Dr Griffiths's number, everything. Here.' He remembered her thrusting it towards him, a look of desolation on her face. 'You'll look after him, right? I can't. Not now, not on my own.'

Jon read the text below her photo once more. *Zoë recently came to Ireland. Last known place: Clifden. If you have seen her or know where she is, please call the number below.*

He removed the pay-as-you-go mobile from his coat pocket. Cheapest model he could find, now with thirty pounds' credit. He placed the handset next to his usual phone and then ferreted about in the holdall's side pocket for the little box of drawing pins. That's it, he thought. Everything I need to get the wheels turning. He stepped over to the window and looked down on the empty street. A trilling noise rang out from the direction of the bed.

CHAPTER 23

'Everything OK?' Rick asked.

'So far, so good. I'm sitting in my hotel room which overlooks the high street. The entrance to the nightclub is just a bit along.'

'Perfect, then.'

'Any trouble at t'mill?'

'Not a thing. Parks isn't even in today. Off on some conference. It's uncannily quiet, actually. Elmhurst and May are due to start tracking Darragh's movements in and out of the UK. But they won't even be close to liaising with the Irish police until after the weekend.'

'Good.'

'What are you going to do first?'

He sat down in the chair by the window. An elderly man was making his way along the pavement on the other side of the road, legs bowed as if he'd suffered from rickets as a child. He opened the door of Lowry's and the dark interior swallowed him.

'Plaster this town with posters. If that doesn't lead to anything, I'll start handing out flyers in his club. Basically, I'll make it so Darragh's life is far easier if he deals with me.'

'Deals with you.' Rick snorted. 'Let's hope that's not what he tries.'

'I'll be OK. It's not like the security he employs is a problem. One guy with a useful feint. And now I know that's all he's got.'

Rick was silent for a couple of seconds. 'Keep in touch, yeah? And I'll see you on Monday.'

'That's the plan. Speak to you soon.' He cut the connection, brought up Alice's number and pressed green. She picked up on the third ring. 'Hi. Have you got there?'

'Yup. Safe and sound.'

Jon felt a little knot of tension suddenly go slack. 'And you've switched to a different lodge?'

'Yes – like you said. And checked the booking's in my maiden name. How's it looking there?'

'Quiet – like last time. Except the shops are open. Where's your lodge?'

'By the village bit, next to the lake. Holly's feeding the ducks.'

Jon smiled. 'Good. Enjoy yourselves and I'll see you soon.'

'Are you driving back to Roundstone?'

'Maybe this afternoon. I'll see how things go here.'

'Be careful, OK?'

'I will.'

'Love you.'

'Love you, too.'

He flipped his phone shut. Right, he thought, getting to his feet. Let's start pinning posters up.

The glass front of the noticeboard to the side of the plane-wing monument was secured by two little clasps. Inside was the same collection of notices. He studied the newspaper clipping about the roof appeal for Clifden's Gaelic Football Club. When he'd read the piece online, he'd missed a small mention towards the end of the article. Actual building work was being generously carried out at a reduced rate by Darragh de Avila's construction company,

Convila.

Interesting, Jon thought. The guy has fingers in more than one pie. After pinning a poster over the article, he made his way to the post office, where the lady inside allowed him to put one up. The duty manager of the Supervalu supermarket directed him over to the Community News section of the noticeboard in the foyer, where he pinned up another.

Jon found himself glancing at the faces of the few customers queuing at the tills, half-expecting to catch them nodding and whispering in his direction.

When he got to Mannion's Bar, his eyes went to the A-board on the pavement outside. Soup and a roll was on offer again. He pushed open the door and stepped inside. The same girl was behind the bar and he saw a slight flutter of her eyes before she resumed her chat with a solitary man at its far end.

'Hi there,' Jon announced. 'I was wondering which soup is on today.' She looked at him blankly and he touched a finger against his chest. 'I was in here last Saturday.'

She removed a pen from the pouch of her apron. 'Last Saturday?'

Yeah, Jon thought, like you didn't recognise me just now. 'Yes, you had cream of mushroom on that time.'

'Ah, well, Thursdays it's chicken.'

'Lovely, I'll have a bowl and one of your rolls, too.' He held up the sheaf of posters. 'And would it be OK to pin one of these up?'

Her eyes flitted to the pub's large noticeboard just inside the door. 'A poster?' 'Yes.' Jon slid out the top one and laid it on the bar. Off to the side, he saw the old man crane his neck. 'It's my brother's partner. We don't know where she is.'

She made an O with her mouth and held up a forefinger. 'You said you were looking for holiday properties.'

That's right, thought Jon. And you're shit at pretending to only just remember that piece of information. 'I was — but the other reason I was over was to try and track down Zoë here.' He glanced at her image. 'Do you recognise her?'

He saw her swallow before her eyes dropped to the poster. Her brow wrinkled slightly. 'I've never seen her in here.'

In here, Jon thought. Did I ask you to be that specific? 'What about the town in general? In the supermarket, perhaps.' He made sure they had eye contact. 'Or in Darragh's?'

'No.' She shook her head. 'I don't recognise her.'

'OK,' Jon drew out the two syllables, keeping his eyes on her all the time. 'But can I put a poster up?'

She seemed relieved at the prospect of him moving away from the bar. 'Sure you can. Anything to drink?'

'A pint of fresh orange juice and lemonade, cheers.'

He ate his soup in silence, aware of the pay-as-you-go phone in the pocket of his jacket. Relax, he told himself. No one's going to ring straight away. The barmaid remained behind the pumps, talking with the old man in hushed tones. Jon gave up trying to listen when he realised they were speaking in Irish.

Pushing his empty bowl aside, he downed the last of his drink and examined the black-and-white photos on the walls once again. The captions described a 1919 flight by Alcock and Brown which had made it across the Atlantic before crash-landing in Derrygimlagh Bog, on the edge of Clifden. Hence the plane-wing monument, Jon concluded, getting to his feet. 'Where are the toilets, please?'

The barmaid gestured to the swing door at the other end of the bar.

'Cheers.'

The toilets were old-style, a bare concrete floor and individual urinals stretching from the floor up to chest height. Each must consist of about half-a-ton of porcelain, he thought, positioning himself before the middle one.

He was halfway through relieving himself when he heard a tapping sound to his left. There was a window at the urinal's far end, the upper pane held partly open by a metal strut. A blurred arm was beyond the frosted glass. A couple more taps before the hand reached up. Fingers with lilac-coloured nails dropped a scrap of paper through the small gap. Footsteps quickly receded.

Jon stared. That was more than strange. Zipping up his fly, he approached the tightly folded piece of paper on the windowsill. He checked over his shoulder to make sure no one had entered the toilets behind him then plucked it from the tiles. The scrap opened out to reveal a single line hastily scrawled in red biro.

Pony sale tomorow morning de Avila at the back

Did the note mean Darragh would be sitting at the rear of the event? Is that where he wanted to meet; somewhere public? But why the subterfuge about delivering the message?

No, whoever dropped that note through the window was tipping me off about something while not wanting to give their identity away. Siobhain, maybe? Or even Zoë? Someone's following me, that's for sure.

Back out in the pub, he glanced across at the barmaid who was midway through pouring the old boy another beer. Her nails weren't painted. 'See you again.'

'Thanks,' she smiled. 'See you.'

Once outside, he stepped over to the kerb and turned round. The table he'd been sitting at was in full view from the street. He walked to the narrow alley running down the side of the pub. Twenty metres along was the frosted window of the toilet, upper pane slightly ajar. Whoever wrote that note is very familiar with this place, he thought.

Continuing on up the high street, he spotted a few notices in the window of a small bookshop.

The elderly lady inside said he was welcome to pin up a poster in the window before she wandered into the back office mumbling about Blu-Tack.

Jon surveyed the little shop. On the circular table in the centre of the room, several hardback books had been stood on their ends. A small notice before them had the handwritten words, 'Local Interest'.

The title of the smallest book caught his eye. Ireland's Western Shore – Graveyard of the Armada. He picked the book up and scanned the preface. It described how, in the winter of 1588, the Spanish fleet had fled Drake's forces and attempted a return to Spain by sailing round the tip of Scotland and down Ireland's west coast. But a huge storm had blown in from the Atlantic and smashed two dozen ships on the unforgiving coastline. Thousands of Spaniards had perished.

Jon recalled the dramatic painting in the back office of Darragh's nightclub. The title was something to do with the wrecking of a ship. He tried to remember what the vessel had been called, but it wouldn't come. A quick check of the index revealed all manner of names: *Annunciada, Bautista, San Esteban, La Girona, Encoronada, Duquesa, Trinidad.* None seemed right.

The shop owner walked back in with a bulb of Blu-Tack in her hand. 'Here you are. Whichever space you fancy.'

'Don't suppose you've seen her?' he asked.

'No, sorry,' she replied. 'I wish I could be more help.'

Jon studied her kindly face. No way she's being anything less than honest, he thought. 'By the way,' he asked, 'is there some sort of a pony sale round here tomorrow?'

She pointed to the junction. 'There most certainly is. Connemara ponies. Back along the Galway road, just past the Garda station. You can't miss it – look for where all the horseboxes and four-wheel drives are parked.'

'Thanks.' He continued his circuit of the town square.

Two shops along, his eyes widened. It was an art gallery; paintings on display were moody seascapes. The exact same style as the one in Darragh's office. Jon squinted at the untidy signature in the corner of the painting. F. Whelan.

The tall man inside the shop reminded Jon of Roald Dahl's Big Friendly Giant.

'Fergus?' the man said in answer to Jon's question, accent distinctly English. 'He's a member of the travelling community. Comes by every so often in the summer to collect the proceeds of any sales.'

'Any way to get hold of him in the meantime?'

'Sorry. I've no idea where he spends his winters.'

Damn, thought Jon. The painting in Darragh's office was enormous in comparison to the ones this man had for sale. It was probably requested specifically by the nightclub owner. 'I saw another painting the other day. My guess is Fergus was asked to paint it.'

'You're looking to commission him yourself?' The art gallery owner was reaching for a pen.

'Well...perhaps. But I'm also very interested to know more about what it depicted. It was of a ship being wrecked on a rocky shore. I can't remember – '

'Where was this painting?'

'In that nightclub round the corner.'

'Darragh's?'

Jon nodded.

The gallery owner put the pen down, folded one hand over the other and scrutinised Jon. 'May I enquire if you're here on holiday?'

Jon hesitated. 'Yes.'

'Take my advice. Stick to admiring the landscape and enjoying the odd pint in a quiet pub. Steer clear of that club and the people involved in it.'

Jon acted confused. 'Really? Why?'

The other man turned back to the catalogue on his desk. Jon waited a few seconds before deciding their conversation was going no further. 'Nice paintings, by the way. That Whelan person's.'

'Aren't they?' he replied, without looking up.

Once out on the street, he called Rick. His colleague's answerphone clicked in. 'Hi mate, it's me again,' Jon announced. 'If you get a chance, can you have a little dig around on that interweb thingy? I'm beginning to think there really is some kind of link between the de Avilas and the Armada. And no, I'm not losing my marbles. I saw a painting in Darragh's office about a ship with a Spanish name being wrecked. That and the RSPCA inspector discovering that the Spanish army used to use Alanos as war dogs. I don't know – maybe a Google search will throw up something. Speak to you soon.'

At the entrance of Darragh's nightclub, he pinned a poster on each door, driving the drawing pins as far into the wood as they'd go. Try prising those back out with just your nails, he thought, walking back to his hotel.

Up in his room, he resumed his seat by the window, laid both phones on the table and removed the small note from his pocket. The words were neatly spaced and rounded to the point of being slightly childish. He noted how the word 'tomorrow' was missing an 'r'. No full stop, either. Whoever wrote it, he guessed, hadn't gone far at school. Zoë, he remembered, had spent her childhood in care. Never the basis for a decent education.

Dropping the note on the table, he sat back and waited. After forty-five minutes, his legs were twitching with nervous energy. He stood and rocked on the balls of his feet, looking restlessly round the room. Pony sale. The words were ricocheting round in his head. What did the message mean?

If I was at home, he thought, I'd get changed and go for a run. He kicked his shoes off then removed his socks, fleece top and T-shirt. Next he took the large towel out of the bathroom and laid it out on the expanse of carpet at the foot of the bed.

After circling his arms back and forth, he dropped into the press-up position and pumped out a set of fifty. Chest muscles throbbing, he positioned the desk chair at the end of the towel and adopted the press-up position once again, this time with his feet up on the seat of the chair. He completed another thirty-one, breath becoming laboured and shoulders burning as he forced himself to complete a few more.

As soon as he reached thirty-five, he shoved the chair away and began a series of squat thrusts. After that, he laid on his back and completed seventy abdominal crunches. On his feet, he shook his arms loosely at his sides, feeling the blood surging through the muscles of his upper body.

His head turned to the little pay-as-you-go phone. Is the bloody thing working? Picking up his normal phone, he dialled the other handset's number. Moments later it started to ring and he cut the call. Course it's working, he thought. Give the posters a bit more time. It's not like the streets are heaving with people.

After wiping himself down with a wet flannel, he put his clothes back on and started pacing the room. I can't bloody stay here, he thought. What can I do? But he knew the answer already. He looked at the jacket slung across the bed. Car keys are in the side pocket. He pictured the narrow, twisting road to Roundstone. You're off to meet your grandad, he said to himself, scooping up both phones.

'Dad, he's here.'
  'Who?'
  'That fucking great peeler. The one from England.'
  'What do you mean, he's here?'
  'Here, in Clifden. Walking round the place pinning up posters.'
  'Oh my God. What kind of posters?'
  'Not about the tapes. Missing-person posters.'
  'Zoë?'

'Yes.'

The old man moved the phone to his other ear, got slowly to his feet and walked stiffly to the plate-glass windows of the restaurant. Beyond the faint reflection of his fleshy face, the streets of Dublin were busy. Lunch hour was almost over and office workers were heading back to their desks. His beady eyes settled for a moment on his Maserati parked directly opposite. A bastard warden was peering through the windscreen. Check all you want, he said to himself, knowing the disabled badge was on the dashboard. The beauty of having a doctor keen to show his gratitude, he thought.

'I'm on my own here, Dad. You're in Dublin. Fuck-knows where Devlan is. The guy walked straight through Conor. What if he comes back to the club tonight? I need Sean. Where the hell are they?'

'I'm having trouble getting hold of them.'

'Well, I'm not opening the club. If it's not open, he can't get in.'

He moved towards a quiet corner of the restaurant, away from the smattering of other diners. 'You'll be open as usual. Clear?'

'Jesus!'

'Clear?'

'Yes. Where are they? I pay Sean's wages, not Devlan.'

'Manchester, apparently. I'll get hold of them, don't worry.'

'You need to. Quickly.'

'They'll surface soon. The fight's on Saturday. No way they'll miss that.'

'Those damned dogs. If he spent more time on proper business – '

'It is business. You know your brother's not good with books, like you. But these fights aren't just a sideshow, Darragh: that's why I let him keep organising them.'

'So what's this tour of England achieved?'

'Spreading the word, Darragh. Creating interest. Soon

as we have a litter, we've got potential buyers in Newcastle and Birmingham, is what he said. Meanwhile for you son, it's business as usual. A tan – and one here on his own – is not a problem for us. No one can be allowed to think that.'

'He's also police.'

'I know. But it's still business as usual. I'll get you Sean back.'

'OK. And I need to talk to you about Anderson Court. The bank called me back – there'll be no more loans – '

'Later.'

'You said that last time.'

'Listen, I'm about to meet some people about these properties haemorrhaging us money.'

'Who are they?'

'Turkmen.'

'Who?'

'They're from Turkmenistan. They've got cash.'

'What kind of cash?'

'They control a supply route coming out of Afghanistan – '

'Heroin, you mean?'

'They're drowning in cash and they're looking for places to invest. They're also very interested in the Alano – so I've invited them to the fight on Saturday. VIP treatment, the lot.'

'Dad, I wish you'd mentioned this. I need time to think. The whole point of my business plan was to move us into legitimate streams of revenue. Whoever these people are – '

'Time is something we don't have, son. If we can seal the deal with these guys, we're out of the woods with those bloody buildings it was your stupid idea to buy.'

CHAPTER 24

The circular tablet inscribed with the word 'Roundstone' came into view. Jon felt his palms moisten. Why, he asked himself, are you nervous? You're meeting your grandad; he'll be pleased to see you. He nodded. Course he will be. You're family. But it's not only that, another part of him responded. This is the first step in discovering what happened with Mum.

He got out of the vehicle and studied the sky. On the horizon, a few shafts of sunlight had broken through, mottling the distant ocean with a silver sheen. Slowly, Jon walked along the high street, crossing over when he reached O'Dowd's. The lights were on and he could see a couple of figures at the bar. I could pop in, he thought. A quick pint to gee me up. He regarded the steep side road. No. Best to do this with a clear head and no alcohol on your breath. First impressions and all that. He walked up the incline, the little bungalow gradually coming into view.

There was a car parked on the driveway. A battered old red Nissan, brown patches of rust discolouring the wheel arches. Jon stopped at the foot of the drive and looked at the windows. The curtains in one room were closed, the rest of the house dark. He took a quick breath and approached the porch. The door was ajar and the old armchair Malachy had been sitting in was empty. Jon looked at the moth-eaten old blanket stretched over it, and as he reached through the gap and knocked on the inner door, he realised his mouth had gone completely dry.

After a few seconds he could see a figure approaching. The door opened to reveal a kind-faced woman somewhere in her fifties. Her brown hair was cut short and swept to the side. Jon saw a few strands of white running through it. She was wearing dark blue trousers and a white tunic with some kind of badge.

Jon glimpsed the name Eileen Mahon. One of Mum's sisters is called Eileen, he thought. Possibly the youngest. She was looking at him with a quizzical expression. 'Yes?'

The muscles round his mouth felt stiff and unresponsive as Jon tried to smile. 'Hello.' He gestured behind him at the road. 'I was…I'm here, because I was – '

'Is it Jon?'

He met her eyes and saw a range of emotions in them. Pleasure, surprise, alarm. 'Yes.'

She looked at the empty armchair. Then her eyes went to the road, as if searching for someone else.

'I'm here on my own.'

Her gaze went back to him and a muscle beside her eye twitched. 'Look at me, just standing here. Come in, come in.' She stepped back and waved him into the little hallway. 'The kitchen is in front. Will you have a cup of tea?'

'Yes, thank you.' Jon stepped inside, recognising the same dusky smell that had permeated Mannion's Bar. He continued towards the doorway at the end of the corridor. There was a room on his left with an old sofa, a television and a wooden sideboard. A multitude of framed photos covered it. He heard the chink of cutlery in the kitchen and looked uncertainly over his shoulder.

She waved him on. 'Kieron, my son. Kieron? We have a visitor.'

Jon stepped into a small kitchen that appeared

unchanged from the fifties. A cast-iron stove took up the middle part of the far wall. At the stone sink in the corner, a man somewhere in his early twenties was washing up. Heavy features and thick black hair.

'Hello there,' he nodded.

'Hello.' Jon checked the room again. Where, he wondered, is Malachy?

Eileen stepped round him. 'Kieron, this is your cousin, Jon. Mary who lives near Manchester — it's her oldest son.'

Jon saw the other man's eyes widen a fraction before he turned to remove a tea towel from the thin metal bar running along the front of the stove. He dried his hands slowly then turned back, now in control of his face. 'A pleasure to meet you, Jon.' A hand was held out and they shook.

'Good to meet you.' He turned to Eileen once again.

Seeming to read his thoughts, she nodded at the doorway. 'Your grandfather is having his nap. I call in each day to make his tea. Kieron works nearby, so I feed him, too.'

Jon glanced at the clock on the wall above the window. Ten to five. They eat early.

She took the tea towel from her son's hands, wrapped it round the handle of a huge kettle sitting on the stove's hotplate then poured boiling water into the teapot on the middle of a small table. 'Sit down,' she said, gesturing at one of two chairs as she replaced the kettle.

Wedged in the gap between the ancient-looking stove and the row of cupboards lining the adjacent wall was an old wicker chair. Beneath it was a basket filled with hard lumps of peat. On the floor on the other side of the stove was a blanket on which a black-and-white Border collie lay. It looked up at Jon with a semi-interested expression.

Jon unzipped his ski jacket. The kitchen was warm as toast. Hanging it on the back of a chair, he turned round. 'Sorry to just turn up like this. I'm actually staying in Clifden and drove over on the off chance. The lady in your village shop told me this is where Malachy lives.'

Eileen smiled. 'So you're alone?'

'Yes.' Jon sat down, brought his knees together and slid his palms between them. 'Mary doesn't know I'm here.'

Eileen's face tightened. 'Well, it's lovely to see you, so it is. It must be over thirty years. How old are you now, Jon?'

'Forty-three.'

'Oh Lord!' She rolled her eyes, removing another cup from the shelf near the sink. 'You were knee-high to a grasshopper when I last set eyes on you. For Martyn's christening in Scotland. Jeanne's oldest? He lives in Boston, now.'

Jon gave a little shake of the head. 'Sorry, I don't remember. Jeanne is the oldest sister, is that right?'

Eileen's smile slipped a fraction before she spoke. 'It is. Jeanne, then Una, then Mary, then Nial, then me.'

'So Jeanne lives in Scotland?'

'Yes – near Glasgow. Her husband works on the oil rigs.'

'What about your other sister and brother?'

'Well, Nial's still in Roundstone. He runs the hotel.'

'And Una?'

Eileen removed a packet of biscuits from the cupboard, tore it open and tipped the contents on to a plate. 'Una died back in 1982. A traffic accident out in Guatemala where she was working for a mission.'

'I'm sorry.' Jon dropped his head, thinking about his own Mum's devout Catholic beliefs. Suddenly, a thought occurred: are they even aware my brother's dead? 'I didn't know. I didn't know about Grandma either – not until I found her grave in the little cemetery by the beach.'

There was silence for a few seconds. 'Mary didn't tell you?'

He looked up to see troubled expressions on both their faces. 'She doesn't talk about this side of the family. Never has.'

Kieron looked to his mum for a response. She became

aware of the plate of biscuits in her hand. 'Here.' She put them in front of Jon. 'Do you take milk and sugar?' She picked up the little jug next to the teapot.

'Just milk, thanks.' As she poured, he took the opportunity to look around the kitchen more carefully. Kieron had gone back to washing up and Jon took in his muddy overalls and stout work boots. The young man's shoulder muscles bulged through his clothes and heavy forearms protruded from his rolled-up sleeves. Nailed to the wall above him was a crucifix.

'So are you in the medical profession?' Jon asked Eileen as she slid a cup towards him.

'That I am. District nurse for the area south of Clifden.'

'Same as Mum,' Jon said. 'Though she worked in a hospital. Did you train in Manchester, too?'

Eileen's eyes clouded as she turned away. 'No. Galway for me.'

How come? Jon thought. If the family was happy to send Mary away to train in Manchester, why not you as well? After all, you could have shared a flat. Unless Mary being in Manchester is somehow part of the rift that opened up. Along with her getting married to a non-Catholic from Salford. 'I actually came past last Sunday morning. Malachy was sitting out in the front porch. We didn't speak, but he seemed well.'

'Oh, he is that.' Her tone was that of a teacher referring to an unruly kid. 'He's slowed down a lot since Mum died. Mind isn't what it was. But he still gets about – drinks beer in O'Dowd's often enough.'

'Really?' Jon grinned. 'He manages that steep road?'

'Nick, the barman drives him back. Whenever that might be.' She rolled her eyes again.

'And you live in Roundstone, too?'

'Yes – down near the church. It's only a two-minute walk.'

Kieron pulled the plug in the sink and turned round. 'You know the mountain? Out there to the left?'

Jon frowned. Did he mean the craggy great hill overlooking the village? Or the range of distant peaks across the bay?

'Errisbeg Hill,' Eileen cut in. 'We in the village call it the mountain.'

The one overlooking the village then, Jon thought. A good hour or so's climb, I should think.

Kieron continued with a note of pride in his voice. 'Malachy would be up and down that twice a day checking his animals. Once in the morning and again after lunch. Sometimes carrying an animal down on his back if it needed attention.'

'He was a sheep farmer, then?' Jon asked.

'He was. Knew the name of every lamb, the ewe that had given birth to it. Every ewe's mother. Would be up there all the hours God sent making sure they were OK. Didn't matter how heavy the rain, how skinning the wind. After that he ran the village butcher's shop. Until the rules about only using government-approved abattoirs.'

The younger man stepped over and picked up a cup of tea. One minute he's not saying a word, Jon thought. Now there's no stopping him.

'He used to just slaughter a sheep round the back of the shop, butcher it and sell the meat. Now? Animals have to be shipped over to Galway for the chop before being driven all the way back here. Makes no sense. Then they said you could only have stainless-steel work surfaces. Refitting the shop would have cost thousands. It was cheaper just to close.'

'I thought it was only Britain that had ridiculous regulations like that,' Jon replied, spotting the collie's ears going up. The animal's tail started to wag as a door opened. Jon heard a shuffling in the corridor, punctuated by an occasional click.

'That'll be him,' Eileen said. 'Get ready.'

Kieron adjusted the thin cushion on the wicker chair by the stove. A couple of seconds later, the man Jon had seen in the porch entered the room, a walking stick in one hand. His eyes darted to Jon, but showed no recognition.

'Dad,' Eileen said in a voice that was slightly raised. 'This is your grandson, Jon. Mary and Alan's oldest boy. The one who's a policeman in Manchester.'

His eyes, bright and beady, went back to Jon.

Placing his hands on his knees, Jon stood.

A burst of Irish came from Malachy.

Eileen shook her head. 'No.'

With one hand held out, Jon had to watch as the old man asked something else. Eileen shook her head again then answered briefly in the same language. Another question from Malachy. 'No,' she replied. 'And don't be speaking the Irish in front of him. It's not polite.'

Malachy seemed to think a moment before he turned to Jon. 'You are most heartily welcome in my house.'

Bloody hell, Jon thought, as he felt his hand being pumped up and down. I forgot his accent's so strong.

'Will you stay for your tea?' he asked. 'Eileen, get another plate out. What is it that we're eating?'

Eileen rolled her eyes yet again. 'Would you listen to him? Offering food to everyone who steps through the door when he doesn't know if there's a bite to eat in the house.'

'Ach, I do. I can smell it, sure enough.'

He made his way over to the corner chair, the collie dog muzzling at his free hand. 'Hello there, dog, hello.' Turning round, he lowered himself into the chair. Hands dotted with liver spots cupped the end of his stick. He looked at Jon with a glint of mischief in his eye.

Kieron had removed a bottle from a cupboard. He filled a tiny glass and put it on the corner of the stove. Malachy nodded. 'Thank you lad. Will you be having some of the whiskey, Jon? Are you a drinking man?'

Jon sat back down. 'Well, I'm driving. But a little one sounds good.'

Malachy winked. 'To go with your cup of tea there.

Kieron? Pour him a drink. So are you staying in Roundstone?'

'No – Clifden. I'm only over for a few days.'

'Ah, Clifden, yes. The big town. You should be staying here. There's a bed waiting for you in Roundstone. God knows there are enough O'Coinnes living in the place.' He gave another wink.

'Thanks,' Jon smiled, taking the glass Kieron was holding out. 'Cheers.'

He took a sip as Malachy did the same. The old man's eyes closed and he smacked his lips. Jon felt fiery tendrils curling down his throat and seeping into his stomach.

'Will you have something to eat?' Eileen asked, wrapping her hand in the tea towel and opening the main compartment of the oven. The window misted at Jon's side.

'No – thanks, I couldn't. You weren't expecting me.'

She took out a baking tray which held an impressive lump of gammon. Ceramic pots containing mashed potato and roughly chopped carrot followed. 'Nonsense, there's plenty here.'

Jon eyed the meat. It looked delicious. 'Are you sure?'

Nick Hutcher glanced at his watch. Twelve minutes past six. He decided to check his emails a final time before turning the machine off.

In the hour since he'd last looked, another eleven messages had arrived. Most were just reports more junior inspectors had copied him in on. Something from Lucy in the legal department outlining her concerns over certain legislative changes. Below that message was one from someone whose name he didn't immediately recognise. Carlos Contera. The guy in Spain who'd been restoring the Alano breed.

Hutcher clicked on the email and started to read.

Dear Mr Hutcher,

Thank you for your message, I found it very interesting. And thank you for your kind comments. I believe it is the most impressive breed of dog there is on earth.

Yes, there have been a few enquiries from individuals with a desire to purchase an Alano.

Because of my worries about what the dog would be used for, I decline these requests. The only exception is if a local farmer wishes for a dog to do work they are suited to – and that is cattle herding.

The photo you sent me of the carcass in your possession is without doubt an Alano. I believe it is one of a pair stolen from my farm almost one year ago. This can be proved by sweeping the dog for a microchip. All my dogs are microchipped. The two missing dogs are –

Female – AH23
Male – AV8

Please can you confirm if it is AH23 in your possession. I will be prepared to pay all necessary costs to have the remains returned to me. You said the dog was found in Manchester, in the north of England, but I have had no enquiries from your country about purchasing an Alano.

I keenly await your response,

Sincerely yours,

Carlos Contera

Nick looked at his watch again. Simon, the vet at the Manchester rescue centre holding the dead Alano, would have already left for the day.

He clicked on reply and began to type.

Dear Carlos,

Thanks for your reply – your English is far better than my Spanish! I will find out as quickly as I can if it is AH23 and ensure the remains are kept safe. I hope to have an answer for you tomorrow morning.

In my original email to you, I think I caused some confusion. I was not asking if you had received any enquiries specifically from Britain about purchasing an Alano. I was more interested if you'd received an enquiry from anyone non-Spanish. If you have any records on this it could greatly assist in the police investigation being conducted.

Best wishes,

Nick Hutcher

He pressed send then brushed a forefinger across his lips. The one found in Manchester had to be AH23, no doubt about it. But that meant the male – AV8 – was still out there somewhere. And it would be bigger, stronger and more ferocious than its dead mate.

CHAPTER 25

Kieron took the chair next to Jon as Elaine went to work on the joint of gammon. She passed over a plate piled high with food. Malachy immediately piped up from his corner chair. 'Now is that enough for you? Has she given you enough?'

Jon regarded the four thick slices of meat with relish. 'Loads, thanks.'

As a plate was put in front of Kieron, Jon realised there wasn't a chair at the table for Eileen or Malachy. He started to get up. 'Here, I'm in someone's seat.'

Eileen batted a hand. 'Nonsense. Dad likes to eat in the corner and I never sit.'

Certain they were just being polite, Jon sank back. Kieron was now tucking into his food as Eileen cut up some meat into smaller squares and put a half-full plate next to Malachy's shoulder. She retreated to the corner opposite Malachy, put her plate on the worktop and, still standing, began to scoop up mashed potato.

Jon sensed this really was the usual routine. For a few minutes the only sound was the scraping of cutlery.

Malachy finished first. Sitting back with a sigh, he said, 'Ach, that was a lovely bit of meat, thank you, Eileen.'

She nodded in reply, still busily eating.

'Does the fire need more turf?' Malachy asked, leaning forward and using the end of his stick to turn the handle of the stove door. 'It does.'

Jon peered into what appeared to be a mini-furnace. Malachy reached down to the basket beneath his chair and tossed in a couple of lumps of dried peat.

'You'll be baking us in our clothes,' Eileen complained.

'What?' Malachy asked as the door clanged shut.

She glanced at Jon with a pained expression. 'He doesn't feel it.'

Beside him, Kieron murmured, 'Shall I open a window, Jon?'

'I'm fine,' Jon answered, hoping his forehead wasn't shining with sweat.

'What was said?' Malachy asked, chin jutting forward.

Jon looked over. 'Eileen was asking if I'm warm enough.'

The old man nodded sceptically, the impish look back in his eye. 'Did she now? Don't believe a word my daughter says. She's mad, you know.'

'Dad!' Eileen protested with a smile.

Malachy poked the tip of his tongue out from the corner of his mouth. 'I'm the only one around here who still has his wits.' His face grew a little more serious. 'Doesn't he look like Orla's brother's grandson, Joseph?' he asked Eileen, nodding at Jon.

Eileen tutted. 'He does not, Dad.'

'He does – the one who went to live in Yankee land.'

'You're thinking of Jeanne's youngest, Martyn. The one who lives in Boston.'

Malachy looked confused. 'Did not Joseph move there?'

'No,' Eileen replied, taking his plate. 'Joseph drowned, remember? In that storm off Croaghnakeela Island?' She glanced at Jon. 'Joseph was a fisherman.'

'Oh, so he did,' Malachy said, voice now subdued.

'Well, he looks like him.'

Jon gave a cough to break the silence. 'Kieron says you used to go up and down Errisbeg Hill four times a day when you farmed sheep.'

Malachy's head came back up. 'You mind your step on the mountain. The mists can close in. There's many a path that leads only to a drop. Have you been up?'

'No. It looks a good climb.'

'It is, so. The views from the top are finely. The sea on one side and all the bog spread out below you on the other.'

That word again, Jon thought. 'What is this bog?'

Kieron sat back. 'The bog. It's the only thing between us and Clifden. Did you not take the bog road here?'

'I don't think so. I came along the one that hugs the coast.'

'Well, there's a short cut. Takes a third of the time. Follow the high street as if going back towards Galway. The road takes you inland. A mile out of Roundstone is the turning for the bog road. Little thing, it is. On your left. It gets you to Clifden in about twenty minutes.' He smirked. 'If Mum gets called out to a patient, she won't drive it at night. Too scared. She prefers the coast road which takes three times as long.'

Eileen waved a hand. 'I'm not the only one who won't use that road after dark.'

Jon looked from Kieron to Eileen. 'Is it haunted or something?'

'It's a lonely place, the bog,' Eileen replied, gathering their plates and avoiding eye contact. 'Mile after mile of marsh, dotted with hundreds of little lakes. You wouldn't want to break down on it. Not alone anyway.'

'They say phantoms haunt it,' Kieron added melodramatically, a smile playing at the corners of his mouth. 'White shapes in the mist that rises there. Of course, they might be grazing sheep.'

'Do you like a story, Joseph?' Malachy asked, signalling

with his glass to Kieron.

'It's Jon,' Eileen cut in.

'Do you like a story, Jon?'

'Yes,' he grinned. 'I hear enough working as a copper.'

Eileen gave a hoot and a clap. 'I bet you do.'

'Well,' Malachy announced, as Kieron refilled his little glass then gestured with the whiskey bottle to Jon.

'No, thanks,' Jon whispered.

As Kieron retook his seat, Malachy continued. 'There used to be a house on the bog road. A kind of inn, run by two sisters, Anna and Kathsha Connelly. It was known as the halfway house. Folk travelling to and from the market in Ballinaboy – pedlars, packmen and the like – would sometimes call there if a storm blew in.' He took a sip of whiskey. 'This was in the days when Ballinaboy was bigger than Clifden. Before they built that road across.'

'The N59?' Jon asked.

Next to him, Kieron gave a nod.

'These two sisters were wicked,' Malachy continued. 'If a fellow arrived and he was the only one staying, they'd murder him in the night, rob him of his takings and throw the body in the lakes. One hot summer, the level of the lakes dropped right down and some little girls and boys, out herding ponies, saw something in the water. Taking it for a dead swan, they went closer. But it was a naked body. And then, in the water below, they saw the skeletons of many more. The yeomen were sent out and the two sisters were taken to Galway gaol and hung.'

Jon smiled. 'Is that true?'

Eileen sighed. 'There might be a scrap of truth in it, somewhere. The remains of the house can still be seen, though. Kieron and some of the others who graze sheep out there use it for a pen, nowadays.'

Jon looked at the younger man. 'So you farm sheep too?'

He nodded. 'Look for where the road rises up slightly and the big lake with an island of dead trees in its middle.

Cormorants nest there. What's left of the halfway house is on your right.'

'You mentioned ponies,' Jon replied, thinking about the sale the next day. 'Would that be the Connemara ponies I've heard mention of?'

'Yes,' Kieron replied. 'You've bred them in your time, haven't you Malachy?'

He flicked a finger as if warding off a fly. 'Only for a bit of fun. Nothing serious.'

'Connemara ponies,' Kieron said, turning to Jon. 'Tough little animals but very gentle. Ideal for learning to ride on. People come from far and wide to buy them. It's something to see, the auction.'

Eileen was filling the kettle again. She nodded at the plate of biscuits. 'Have another, Jon.'

He glanced at the mound of custard creams. 'I couldn't eat another thing,' he said, patting his stomach and glancing at his watch. 'In fact, I should get back. Thanks so much for the food.'

'That's a pleasure,' Eileen replied. 'Will you not stay for a cup of tea?'

He contemplated for a moment whether to mention why he needed to be back in Clifden. No, he decided. It's too soon to start going on about a possible junkie relative who was partner to my dead brother. 'No, thanks, I'd better be going.'

'Will you come back to us? What is it that you're doing in Clifden?'

Jon reached round for his coat. 'Trying to find someone, actually. The last place we think she lived was Clifden.'

'Police work?' asked Kieron.

'Kind of,' Jon replied, standing up. He stepped over to Malachy. 'It's great to meet you. Is it OK if I call again?'

He reached out and gripped Jon's hand with both of his. 'You're always welcome here. Come for your tea, tomorrow, why don't you? It's not a nice thought, you in that town eating alone.'

Jon smiled uncertainly, eyes moving to Eileen. She nodded back. 'Well,' he said. 'I'd like that.'

'Don't be shy,' Malachy added. 'If I've hit the hay – '

'He means if he's in bed,' Eileen interjected.

'Just let yourself in,' Malachy continued. 'The door's never locked and you know where the kettle is.'

Jon closed his other hand over Malachy's, feeling the bones beneath his papery skin. 'Thank you.' After shaking hands with Kieron, he turned to Eileen.

She gripped him by the shoulders and went up on tiptoes to plant a kiss on his cheek. 'Lovely to see you, Jon. Let me show you out.' Once they were in the corridor, she lowered her voice. 'Will you mention me to Mary? Tell her I sent my love.'

Jon paused at the front door. 'Of course. I'm not quite sure how to go about telling her I've been.'

She placed a hand on his arm. 'You'll find a way.'

'She's never told us, you know. Why she cut off all contact with Malachy and Orla. With all of you, in fact.'

Eileen's gaze shifted uncomfortably to the road outside. 'That's something you'll have to discuss with her.'

Except she refuses to talk about it, Jon thought. 'See you tomorrow.'

She smiled in reply and he set off down the drive. The day had started to fade and he looked towards the sea. On the horizon, a glowing band of yellow seemed to be fighting for survival between the dark sea and slate sky. As he passed the construction site for the huge house opposite, the black lettering on the digger caught his eye. Convila. He came to a stop. Darragh's construction company; the same one doing the repairs to Clifden's Gaelic Football Club. He pictured the nightclub owner. Get yourself everywhere, don't you?

The turn off for the bog road was almost apologetic: all the road markings encouraged drivers to continue to the

N59 a few miles north. Set back was a modest sign, quietly announcing in small letters that Clifden was thirteen kilometres in the direction it pointed.

Checking there was still sufficient daylight left, Jon took the turn and found himself on a single lane of unmarked tarmac. He surveyed the landscape. Encroaching on each side of the road was a layer of snakelike grass, curled over and collapsed in on itself. Beyond, the brown tundra was punctuated by rushes, outcrops of rock and stumps of wind-blasted trees, sparse branches furred with moss. There was, he thought, something prehistoric about the terrain.

At the side of the track, sheep silently regarded his passing with slit-shaped pupils, jaws grinding slowly as if grimacing with disapproval. Then Jon began to spot the glint of water. Puddles at first, followed by dark fingers or ragged little ponds. There didn't seem to be any bank or drop dividing land from liquid – the wiry turf simply vanished beneath the inky expanses.

The pools grew in size, opening out into lakes, surfaces rippling in the breeze. The road twisted its way through the watery maze and Jon marvelled at how a route had ever been plotted through. The craggy top of Errisbeg was now on his left. Aside from the thin strip of tarmac, he could see absolutely nothing to suggest the presence of man.

After a few more miles the road started to rise, passing between two outcrops of rock before levelling out on a rough plateau with a wider swathe of grass on each side. The nearest lake had an island in its middle. Trees were clustered on it, branches heavy with bunched, black forms. A pair of wings flapped. The cormorants, Jon thought, slowing to a crawl. He scanned the ground to his right for the halfway house, unable to see anything but lichen-covered rocks. Then he realised some of the stones weren't randomly placed.

He pulled over and climbed out. Silence engulfed him.

He stepped off the road and crossed the springy turf to the building's remains. Now closer, he could see the last remnants of what had once been several rooms. The stones had lain there so long they appeared fused with the ground. Moss had crept over the upper ones, further blurring their outline.

He stepped through a vague gap that may have once been a doorway. A few crushed cans of cider to his left, along with some charred pieces of wood and an old tyre. He realised the rear walls of the ruined dwelling stood higher and he moved towards the most obvious room.

A section of metal fence, buckled and rusted, barred his way. Twine and barbed wire attached it to a couple of wooden stakes driven into each side of the doorway. Jon looked inside and saw clumps of sheep's wool and piles of droppings. His eyes picked out a kink in the wall. A hearth, maybe?

He pictured the house as it once was; a lone traveller warming his hands at the flames, oblivious to the fact that, once asleep, he would be robbed, murdered and dumped in a nearby lake.

His eyes swept the water encircling Cormorant Island. The surface was brooding and still. This entire place, he thought, is silent as a grave. From far away, came the faint hee-hoo of an unseen bird.

CHAPTER 26

There was a muddy pick-up truck in the space he'd last used. After parking next to it, Jon entered the hotel lobby and approached the front desk. A young woman was now on duty. 'Evening,' Jon said. 'Room 17, please.' As she turned to retrieve his key, he added, 'Don't suppose I have any messages?'

She ran a finger across the cards in a small wooden box. 'Nothing for 17.'

The door to his room clicked behind him. He removed the phones from his ski jacket and threw it on the bed. Slumping into the window chair, he checked both handsets. No message on either. He brought up Alice's number and pressed green. After three rings, she picked up. 'Hi there, how's it going?'

'Great. I took her for a swim. She loved the slides – not that I tried going down them.'

'I should think not. The size of your tummy, you probably wouldn't fit.'

'Such a charmer.'

He laughed. 'You know I love you. What's Holly up to now?'

'Watching a bit of telly.'

'Tell her I say hello.'

'It's Daddy. He says hello, sweetie.'

'Hi Dad!' Her voice sounded so far away. Jon felt a wave of sadness go through him. 'She sounds happy.'

'She's loving it. How's it going with you?'

'Yeah, interesting. I've already had a mysterious message.'

'Someone saw the posters?'

'No, someone saw me. I was in the toilets of this pub and a note was shoved through the window from the alley outside.'

'What did it say?'

Jon slid the bit of paper from his jeans pocket. 'Pony sale tomorrow morning, de Avila at the back.'

'He wants to meet you?'

'He could just ring me if he wanted to meet. I think it's someone tipping me off. About something the bloke will be doing at the sale. The handwriting looks female. My money's on it being Siobhain.'

'But surely she could have just rung you.'

'Not if she wants to keep her phone number hidden from me. To do that, she'd have to use the payphone near the post office. This place isn't big: I could get there in about ten seconds, wherever I am in this place.'

'I don't like her sneakiness.'

'We'll meet eventually, I'm sure.' He crossed his legs and looked at the street below. 'I met Grandad earlier.'

'You did?' Alice gasped. 'Go on.'

'He's certainly a character.' Jon grinned as he recalled the old man playfully insisting he was the only sane one in the house. 'I had to really pay attention, his accent's so strong. They speak differently, too. All, will I be doing this, will you be doing that. It was great.'

'Suppose it was too soon to raise the subject of your mum?'

'Definitely. He seems pretty together. Although he got my name wrong a couple of times and I don't think he has any memory of calling me a wee fuck.'

'Was anything at all said about your mum?'

'No. Well, not to me. His youngest daughter, Eileen, and her son, Kieron, were there. She appears to cook him his tea most days. They spoke a bit of Irish when Malachy first shuffled in and found me sitting in his kitchen. That was about Mum, I'm sure. Eileen said no to everything he asked.'

'She lives nearby?'

'Just round the corner. So does Mum's brother, Nial. He runs the hotel, she said.'

'Weren't there two other sisters?'

'Yes, Jeanne, who lives in Scotland, and Una. She died in the eighties. A road accident in Guatemala. She was out there working as a missionary.'

'Oh.'

'I don't think they know our kid's dead, either.'

'That's no surprise. But it sounds like you all got on.'

'Alice? You'd have loved it. They were so keen to just chat. No telly on in the background, or music playing. Told me this old tale about two sisters who murdered passing travellers – '

'Oh, that's Holly calling me.' She spoke away from the phone. 'Coming, sweetie. Are you going back?'

'Yes – they asked me for tea tomorrow.'

'Take some flowers for Eileen.'

'Will do. Listen, I'd better go, as well. I've got some more posters to hand out.'

'Be careful, OK?'

He glanced to the body armour laid out on the bed. 'Don't you worry.'

After stripping down to his underpants, Jon slid on the lycra shorts with the built-in groin protection. Like wearing a cricket box, he thought, reaching for the stab-proof vest. Next, he strapped on the arm and leg protectors. From his holdall he took out a large shirt and baggy pair of beige cargo trousers.

Once they were on, he looked at himself in the full-length wall mirror. If you weren't searching for it, the protective gear was all but invisible. Holding up his injured hand, he examined the puffy flesh around his knuckles. When he curled his fingers to make a fist, the pain in his wrist increased. He knew it would be useless in any fight. He examined the pepper spray and Asp. Do I take them? No, he decided. I can't see me needing them tonight. He laced up his shoes, put the ski jacket back on and headed for the door, a sheaf of posters in his hand.

Voices were coming from Mannion's Bar so he pushed the door open and stepped inside. All eyes went to him and he heard several conversations grind to a halt. As he crossed the room the noise levels began to recover.

'Evening,' he nodded at the barmaid.

'Evening,' she replied, attempting a smile. Her eyes slid towards the men lining the stools before her. Jon examined the row of profiles. Weatherbeaten faces and heavy features. The fingers grasping the glasses looked leathery and tough. Jon placed his own scarred hands on the wooden surface. 'Pint of Guinness, please.'

She nodded and began to pour.

Jon regarded the nearest man. 'Looks like there'll be a heavy frost again.'

He continued staring straight ahead. 'Aye.'

'Still, this cold snap can't last too much longer, surely.'

'There's a while of it yet.' He glanced at Jon. 'Is it you who's been putting up the posters?'

Jon noticed several heads turn in his direction. 'That's right. Have you seen her?'

Slowly, he shook his head. 'No.' A finger moved in the direction of his drinking companions. 'None of us have. Are you sure she was here?'

'That's what I've been told. Working in the nightclub, Darragh's.'

The barmaid placed his pint down. 'Have you spoken

to him?'

Jon nodded. 'He says she doesn't work there.'

'Well,' a man three stools along said, looking at his drink. 'There's a misunderstanding taken place somewhere.'

Jon studied the row of men, trying to fathom if they were being straight with him. The whole bloody town can't be in on this, can it? He lifted his pint and took a long pull. 'Mind if I hand a few more out?' he asked, removing the roll of posters from his pocket.

She shrugged. 'Go ahead.'

He made his way round the bar, leaving a poster on any occupied table. People's conversations paused and Jon caught the odd quiet comment being made behind him.

'I wonder who she is.'

'Have you ever seen her?'

'Pretty-looking thing, isn't she?'

Back at the bar, he drained the rest of his pint, thanked the barmaid and made for the door. He continued past the plane-wing monument and looked across at Darragh's. The place was well and truly closed. He glanced at his watch. At least two hours to opening time, he thought.

The little pub called Lowry's only had three people in it, and one was standing behind a bar that couldn't have been much over ten feet long. Jon ordered another pint of Guinness then made his way over to the corner seat by the window. The assortment of empty bottles lining the sill was from another era. Cure-all concoctions sold by wandering pedlars, Jon thought. Maybe some met their fate on the lonely bog road.

Just after ten o'clock, a light came on behind the windows set into Darragh's front doors. Someone must have entered from round the back. The right-hand door opened and the girl he'd seen in the rear office stepped out on to the pavement. What, Jon thought, was she called? Hazel, that was it. She emptied the contents of a dustpan into the gutter, turned round and spotted the poster pinned to the door that was still closed. She looked at it for a few seconds before going back inside.

Next, Darragh appeared. His head tilted to the side before a hand went out and the poster was ripped off.

Interesting, thought Jon.

The nightclub owner then bent forward and started trying to prise the drawing pins out with his fingernails.

Jon smiled to himself. Think you'll need a knife, mate.

He gave up and said something to Hazel who was standing next to him jiggling about in the cold. They vanished back inside. You missed the one on the other door, Jon thought.

Hazel reappeared with a small implement and began levering one of the upper drawing pins out.

He set off across the road, and by the time he'd reached the other side, Hazel was prising the final drawing pin out. 'Excuse me.'

Her neck stiffened and she became very still.

Jon kept his distance. 'I'm not here to cause any trouble.'

Hurriedly, she started working the tip of the blunt knife under the last pin.

'Listen, I'm only trying to find Zoë. You work in that place. Please, tell me what's happened to her.'

She straightened up, now happy to leave the pin in the door. Jon stepped to the side so he could see her profile. Her lips were working back and forth as if she was trying to suck some kind of an answer from her teeth.

'It's Hazel, isn't it? Come on, Hazel. No one can hear us. Tell me what the hell is going on.'

She turned to him and he saw that fear had made her face ugly. She rolled her eyes upwards and Jon realised there was a small CCTV camera mounted on the wall directly above her. She widened her eyes; a silent demand that he acknowledge its presence.

He gave the tiniest of nods.

The stubby knife was then jabbed in his direction. 'Get

out of my face, all right?'

He moved back and raised both hands. 'OK, OK. No bother.'

Still pointing the blade at him, she retreated into the open doorway. Jon began to turn on his heel and quickly said, 'Call the number on the poster. Please.'

The right-hand door banged shut, revealing the other poster still pinned to it. Wow, Jon thought as he crossed back over the road. She knows something, I'm certain. And she would have told me if she wasn't so scared of her boss finding out. He slipped back into Lowry's where his pint was still waiting.

After another twenty minutes went past, two people approached the front door from the left. Jon recognised the older, chubby barman and another man, hair cut in a Mohican style, tramline running through the stubble on the side of his head. You're new, Jon thought. Maybe the DJ? They looked at the poster on the right-hand door before opening it and going in. Hazel emerged a minute later and was halfway through removing it when the woman who did the tickets arrived. They spoke briefly, then both went in.

Soon after that, the first customers showed up. Jon wondered how word had got round that the club was open. Another four filed inside. Still no bouncer, Jon thought. Shall I wait for him to show? A group of eight arrived, six girls and two blokes. That's enough, Jon decided, slipping out of Lowry's.

The ticket woman's mouth opened as he stepped through the door. He dropped a five-euro note on her little table. 'I'll keep my coat on.' Pushing through the inner doors, he glanced about. Everyone was sitting down except for a couple of girls at the bar. Jon marched straight across the dance floor, watching the barman's eyes widen. One of the girls looked round. Jon recognised her as the flirtatious one from his first visit. Her eyes dropped slowly down him before an eyebrow went up.

'Don't mind if I hand a few of these out, do you?' He slapped a poster on the bar.

The bloke behind it stared back, saying nothing.

Jon turned to the girls. 'Ever seen her in here, ladies?'

They studied the photo before shaking their heads.

'Do you come here much?' Jon asked the one he recognised.

She looked back at him and blinked. 'Would you be chatting me up, now?'

'He's in the fucking club.' Darragh's eyes were on the TV screens, mobile phone pressed to his ear. His head jerked to the side. 'Hazel, lock that door. Now.'

She hurried across the office and bolted the door giving access to the bar.

'Make sure the back one is secure, too,' Darragh ordered before speaking into the phone once more. 'He's just put one of his posters on the bar. They were pinned to the front doors, too.' He listened for a second. 'Conor? No, he's not here yet. Usually gets here around eleven. Dad, you've got to get them back.'

Hazel reappeared.

'Has he rung you?' Darragh asked her, irritably.

'Who?'

'My fucking brother, of course.'

She shook her head.

Darragh turned back to the screens and spoke into his phone. 'What's he doing now? I'll tell you: he's walking round the club putting posters on every table. He's asking questions, pointing to her photo. Now he's coming back to the bar. He's looking straight at the camera. For fuck's sake, Dad, the bloke's waving at me, pointing at the phone number at the base of the poster.'

'Where is the bastard staying?'

'How do you mean?'

'Is he booked into a hotel?'

'Yes – Joyce's, next door.'

'Have his room searched. And his car. Our priority is those tapes.'

'OK. Should I ring him?'

'No. I'll be back from Dublin tomorrow. Make no contact with him before I get back.'

Jon dropped his hand and set off across the dance floor, back through the foyer and towards the doors to the street. As he neared them, a figure appeared. The bouncer. He looked up and saw Jon striding straight at him. Taken by surprise, he didn't have time to quell his initial reaction: to step back.

The guy's got no stomach for any more trouble, Jon realised. He brushed past him, taking in the strips of bandage plastered across the bridge of his nose. 'Relax,' Jon said, setting off back to the hotel. 'I only want to speak with Darragh. Tell him to give me a ring, would you?'

CHAPTER 27

'Ignore my calls again, you'll find the shit getting kicked out of you. And it'll be my boot that's doing the swinging.'

'Sorry, Dad.'

'You think I couldn't, do you?'

'I'm sorry, Dad.'

'We've got this big fight here on Saturday. I'm bringing some extremely important associates over from Dublin and you're still pissing about in Manchester – '

'We got into a spot of bother. Queen Meabh…she's dead.'

'What was that?'

'Queenie – she's dead. Sean put her to sleep, Da. He had to.'

'You sound like you're almost crying, son.'

'Da, she's dead. We had no other choice – '

'Stop your fucking snivelling. Now!' There was a pause. 'Tell me what happened.'

'That peeler? The one who threw Darragh around? We let Queenie on to his dog as payback. He caught up with our van, somehow.'

'You used Queenie on his dog? What, in a fight?'

'No, in a park.'

'You let Queenie out in a park?'

'To show him, Da. When Darragh told me what had happened – '

'You ever do something like that again, I will break your fucking knees, as God is my witness. Something that crude. Is that what I taught you?'

'No.'

'How did I teach you?'

'To be subtle.'

'Subtle, sure. Can you even spell the fucking word?'

'Eh, Da?'

'Doesn't matter. When we need to deal with…an issue, we move carefully and we move quietly. Understand?'

'You mean like that time with – '

'No names, Devlan. Not over the phone. But you know what I'm talking about.'

'Sure Da.'

'We've survived here, in our little corner of Ireland, because we're clever. Is releasing a dog like Queenie into a park anything other than pig-shit fucking thick?'

'Da, he threw my brother over the bar. In front of everyone.'

'And you know why he was in the club?'

'Why?'

'He was looking for a girl. Now Devlan, you wouldn't know anything about that? A girl who's gone missing?'

There was a pause. 'No…no, I don't.'

'Sure?'

'Yes!'

'OK, we'll speak no more of the matter. You said Queenie is dead?'

'I whistled her back and we drove off. I don't know how, but the peeler caught us up. He saw Queenie, the van's number plates, Sean's face – '

'Where is he?'

'Sean? Here, with me. I didn't know what to do. Darragh said the peeler is in some murder team – '

'Major Incident Team.'

'So we knew they'd be after us. We had nowhere safe to put Queenie, the van's plates had been switched – '

'Just put Sean on, will you?'

A moment of muffled noise.

'Gerrard, it's Sean.'

'What have you let that gobshite get up to?'

'Well…' A slight cough of embarrassment. 'After the peeler had seen us…I don't know Manchester, neither does Devlan. We couldn't keep the van, didn't know what to do with Queenie – the kennels we'd fought wanted the dog for themselves – '

'So you fucking killed her?'

'There was no other option. We couldn't let anyone else get hold of her.'

'How much did getting that pair of animals over from Spain cost me?'

'I don't know. A lot.'

'A lot? More than the monthly wage bill at Golden Fields. Jesus, I can't believe this. Where are you now?'

'Lying low. Some cheap hotel near Manchester airport.'

'What's left to do?'

'Nothing. We're just waiting on new passports – with what's happened, we can't use our own.'

'Where are you getting them?'

'Grennan – he's sorting two.'

'He's a good man. Will you have them for Saturday? I want the pair of you back here.'

'Yes.'

'This fight? Bone Yard kennels are coming down from Belfast with four dogs, a couple of tozas are being brought up from Limerick, there's money flying in from Dublin, Liverpool, all over. Plus I've got these three from overseas – property investors, they are.'

'You're not cancelling?'

'No. Why?'

'Well – with losing Queenie.'

'Cuchullain's stomach is fine again.'

'Is he shitting OK?'

'Sure he is – Denis has been running him hard these last two weeks.'

'And he's back to his old self?'

'He is. Sean, you're the one with a brain between your ears. Keep Devlan from doing anything else stupid. Have you got that?'

'I have.'

'Good. Now, put him back on.'

Another pause. 'Hi Dad.'

'He's back in Clifden.'

'Who?'

'The British policeman, Spicer.'

'Fuck!'

'He was in the club again last night.'

'In the club? Did he touch my brother?'

'No. Darragh kept in his office. Conor showed as the policeman was leaving. He's got a pair of bollocks on him, I'll give him that.'

'Da – I know where his wife and daughter are.'

'What?'

'He tried hiding them away. But I got Grennan to put a watch on their house.'

'You know where they are?'

'Yeah. At a holiday-camp place called Center Parcs, not far north from here. We could – '

'You'll do nothing, son, do you hear me? I'll get this thing sorted. You and Sean just make sure you're back here first thing tomorrow morning.'

Both sides of the road leading out of Clifden towards Galway were solid with parked vehicles – mostly four-by-fours with empty horseboxes attached to their towbars. Fragments of straw scattered the road. A tannoy system sent the sound of a man's voice drifting towards Jon on the light breeze.

Shortly after the police station, a wide entrance led into a large courtyard bordered by small industrial units. At its centre was a hangar-type building with a sign on its front. Connemara Pony Sales. Now Jon could hear the whinny of animals between the stream of words blaring from the speakers. The sharp smell of sawdust caught in his nostrils.

He looked at the units lining the outer edge of the park, most of which had their shutters down. Clifden Plant and Tool Hire. Paul Acton and Sons Motors. Frank Ryan Kitchens. DA Services. A clatter of hooves, and Jon was forced to step quickly aside as a man led a pony round the corner. The animal's head was held high, whites of its eyes showing.

The side of the building consisted of a row of narrow pens, each of which held a pony, some grey with white mottles, others varying shades of brown. They stamped nervously on the sawdust-covered floor, emitting shrill sounds or leaning across the uppermost railing to brush muzzles with their neighbours.

Quietly assessing them was a motley collection of people. Ruddy-faced men wearing green body-warmers or grubby fleeces, dirt and fragments of hay clinging to their elbows. Jon took in the assortment of hats – including flat caps, similar to those worn by older folk around Manchester but enlivened with colourful strands of thread. He saw a black trilby, woollen caps pulled low over heavy brows and, towering above its neighbours, a fur Cossack hat. At the far end of the building, he could see bodies pressed into a section from where the auctioneer's amplified voice rang out.

The space itself was too crowded for him to get in; steep wooden tiers rising up, people perched on every available inch, many with mobile phones pressed to their ears. Spotlights shone down into the ring.

Jon thought about the handwritten note. De Avila will be at the back. By standing on tiptoe, he was able to scan the uppermost rows. No sign of him there. Jon turned back to the ring itself.

A pony with a number painted on its flank was being led round. In a little balcony above it there sat a stern-faced man. Behind him a sign in red block letters read, All buyers please to call to sales office.

'Two thousand six hundred we have, two thousand six hundred, I have no advance on two thousand six hundred? It's two thousand six hundred, any advance on two thousand six hundred? I have an advance? Thank you sir. Two thousand six hundred and fifty, I have two thousand six hundred and fifty on my left, last time, all finished? Two thousand seven hundred, I have. Any more than two thousand seven hundred? She's in the market at two thousand seven hundred. All done now? Last time, two thousand seven hundred. Sold there at two thousand seven hundred.'

The man on the balcony brought the hammer down with a loud crack, cupped his hand over the mouthpiece of his headset and spoke into the small microphone on the counter in front of him.

Jon felt someone brushing past. Turning round, he saw a few empty spaces on the uppermost row. He climbed the steep steps, nodding thanks to a woman in riding trousers who'd shifted sideways on the rough wooden bench. Leaning the back of his head against the bare plaster wall, Jon surveyed the audience more carefully.

The people standing closest to the ring were exclusively men; expressions serious, none speaking. They studied the dappled grey pony now being led into the ring by a man wearing a long green coat. He soon retreated to the gate and, left alone, the pony lowered its nose and blew twin craters in the fresh sawdust. Its coat was thick and shaggy, similar, Jon thought, to that of Highland cattle. Mud had turned the long strands on the underside of its belly into a mass of spikes and its tail hung almost to the ground. Earlier this morning, Jon thought, you were probably standing ankle-deep in a boggy field. It raised its head, ears swivelling independently of each other as the auctioneer began to speak.

'OK, you'll have seen the notes for this magnificent filly. Starting at three thousand five hundred euro, three thousand two hundred and fifty, three thousand, two thousand seven hundred and fifty, two thousand five hundred, two thousand two hundred and fifty...'

Jon's eyes drifted across the crowd again. The note said de Avila would be at the back. He leaned forward, stealing a glance along to the corner of his row. Apart from the lads, there only appeared to be couples or women with younger females, probably their daughters.

He felt someone sitting down next to him and turned. An oldish man, late fifties or thereabouts. The end of his nose was bulbous, the skin blotched an unhealthy red. His grey, wiry hair looked dry and Jon saw the collar of his threadbare coat was flecked with dandruff. Keeping his eyes on the ring, the man inclined his head slightly and spoke from the corner of his mouth. 'Jon Spicer?'

Jon immediately got a whiff of his breath. Bit early in the day to have been drinking. He frowned. 'Yes?'

The man laid a manila folder on the bench between them, tapped it twice with a forefinger and spoke again. 'Some commercial details and other information for you. It'll be worth you taking a look at the back, behind this building.'

With that, he got to his feet, made his way to the end of the row and walked down the steep steps. His place was immediately taken by a couple of teenage girls.

Jon placed the folder on his lap and half-lifted the cover. Some kind of printout. Columns of figures, each one preceded by a euro sign. The top of the sheet was marked with the word, Convila. The name of Darragh's construction company. He glanced to his side but the other man had already disappeared from view.

Jon squeezed past the girls. An exit sign led out to a side area clogged with more four-wheel drives and horseboxes. At the rear of the building was another row of pens, these holding a collection of older-looking ponies, many with ribs and hip bones visible beneath their flanks.

In the far corner, a large lorry for transporting horses was parked up. Two men were discussing something at the ramp leading into the vehicle's rear. Extracting his phone, Jon pretended to take a call, absentmindedly looking over as he talked quietly into the mouthpiece.

Lettering on the side of the lorry read, Golden Fields Farm, Clifden. Directly above him, a tannoy speaker relayed the auctioneer's voice. Feigning difficulty at hearing his imaginary caller's words, Jon moved to the side.

The younger of the two men gave a shrug and walked down the ramp. He stopped at a grimy Volvo estate, opened the door and began to climb in.

'OK, OK,' the older man said, voice heavy with defeat. 'I accept.'

The man straightened up. From a pocket, he produced a thick wedge of notes, peeled a few off and handed them to the other man who, with a look of disgust, shoved them in his trouser pocket. They walked over to a horsebox and lowered its rear door. The older man got in. Seconds later, he emerged with a thin pony that had a pronounced hobble.

'No, not the lorry. Put it in number four.' The younger man nodded in the direction of the pens.

Jon circled round the back of the building until he reached the other corner. Another man was leading a decrepit-looking pony to the rear stalls. This side of the courtyard was also packed with vehicles and horseboxes. Wherever that lorry was heading with its cargo of knackered animals, Jon thought, it's not setting off until after this auction is over. He quickly checked his other handset. Still no messages. Damn it. A notice was on the door of the sales office; the auction finished at midday.

Jon walked back to the centre of Clifden and drove his hire car to the Aldi on the opposite side of the road to the auction. Perfect, he thought, parking in the corner and reaching for the folder.

First were the financial records for Convila. Subsequent sheets listed a variety of projects. He scanned each one's title. Phoenix Gardens. Emmet Street. Anderson Court. Abbey Row. Hanover Quay.

Judging from the columns of figures, all the projects were running at a major loss. He looked for a business address for Convila, but it didn't feature.

The next sheet was a printout of a website's home page. Golden Fields Farm. Jon glanced across the road. The name on the side of the horse transporter behind the auction. He read the introductory paragraph.

Offering a total solution to your pet food manufacturing needs, Golden Fields Farm is one of Europe's leading producers of premium dry foods.

Creating your own label product is easy with us – from product development right through to manufacturing, packaging and despatch.

In partnership with us, you will also have access to our state-of-the-art facilities, the expertise of our in-house nutritionists and the finest ingredients available.

No matter what size, shape or colour of product you have in mind, we can create it for you. And with three extruders now fully operational, we are able to meet the tightest of deadlines too.

The sheet stapled to it was a printout of the company's 'contact us' screen, including a phone number, email and postal address. Below that were directions for arriving by road.

Follow the N59 out of Clifden, heading north towards Letterfrack. Three miles outside of Clifden, take the first right after Lough Breenbannia. Golden Fields Farm is the first property on your left.

Next sheet was another financial report, this time for Darragh's Nightclub. Who was the old boy that stank of booze? Jon wondered. And how did he get hold of all this stuff? Overheads included council tax, heating, lighting, staff pay and wholesale drinks costs. Profits were negligible over the winter months, picking up in spring and peaking during the summer. Nowhere near enough, Jon thought, to justify the piles of cash Darragh had been counting in the back office.

He selected Rick's number on his mobile. 'Hi mate, everything OK back at the ranch?'

'Fine,' Rick replied. 'You?'

'Yup. Some interesting developments.'

'Parks hasn't cottoned on you're there. Yet,' Rick whispered. 'At least, she's said nothing to me.'

'Good news.'

'So, what are these developments?'

'I've been slipped a load of information on de Avila. Company accounts, business addresses, that kind of thing.'

'The nightclub?'

'That, but other stuff, too.'

'Who gave it to you?'

'I don't know. An old guy. Looked like a bit of a tramp, to be honest. He just asked if I was Jon Spicer, dumped it on the seat next to me and buggered off. First is a building company called Convila. It's got an involvement with the following projects: Phoenix Gardens, Emmet Street, Anderson Court, Abbey Row and Hanover Quay. But there's no business address, VAT number or anything listed.'

'Financial figures?'

'Yeah – and they aren't small. Anderson Court alone has cost Convila nearly three hundred thousand euro in the last half of the previous financial year. Can you run the names past your contact in the NCA?'

'With pleasure,' Rick replied.

'Cheers. There are a few other things too. Golden Fields Farm, a pet food manufacturer.' He read out the address and turned to the final sheet. 'And I've got four names listed – no idea what they're to do with. First is Tommy Hammel. Then there's a Geordan and Fionna Reilly – I'll spell them. Last is a Francis Collins. Then it just says Castlebar, 1993.'

'OK, I've noted them down. What about the nightclub?'

'It's making peanuts, mate. Hardly covering its costs. My guess is that it's a front for other things.'

'Should you still be doing this?'

'What?'

'Digging around out there. Hundreds of thousand euro property developments are not the kind of operation small-time criminals are involved in.'

'We don't know what connection de Avila has to them – could just be the on-site security. Anyway, I'm being careful. But if your contact can get on the system and run any of his tangential things, it would be useful.'

'I'll give him a buzz. Have you spoken to Alice?'

'Yeah – they're fine, cheers. How're Sophie and Ryan's enquiries going into how de Avila got in and out of the country?'

'They've only got a bit of time on it today. Then they're not back in work until Monday.'

Jon realised almost half of Friday had gone already. Time was flying. 'I want to be back Sunday morning at the latest. Preferably Saturday so I can make it up to Center Parcs for our last night there.'

'Flying back with or without Zoë?'

'Give me a chance, mate. I haven't even set eyes on her yet.'

CHAPTER 28

By half-past twelve, the procession of ponies being led out to horseboxes had dwindled. Twenty minutes later, Jon heard the sound of a large engine revving. The horse transporter appeared at the retail park's entrance and Jon immediately started his car.

The transporter turned right, heading away from Clifden and along the N59 towards Galway. It reached the outskirts of the city almost an hour and a half later, signalled left and turned into a large industrial park. Jon noted the name: Menlo Estate. The transporter passed by numerous premises before halting at an anonymous-looking building at the far end. The metal gates were swung open by an overweight man with a bald head.

Jon came to a stop and began to fiddle with his phone, eyes on the lorry as it swung round and started to reverse towards a head-high sheet-metal gate topped with barbed wire. Jon noted the small sign just below the roof: DA Services. The same, he thought, as that little unit on the industrial park in Clifden.

The bald-headed man was now opening the side gate and, as he pulled it back, Jon glimpsed the metal screens forming corridors into a covered area. Numerous dents –

none much more than knee-high – had disfigured their surfaces. Hooves and horns, Jon thought, realising he was looking at a lairage: the area where animals were held before being prodded forward into the slaughterhouse itself.

The driver of the transporter had climbed out of his vehicle and was undoing the catches at its rear. I don't need to see this, Jon thought, putting his car in gear and swinging it round. The main road had just come into view when his phone started to ring. Jon glanced at the little screen. Nick Hutcher, the RSPCA man.

'Nick, hi there,' Jon said, pulling onto the gravel verge.

'Hello. Are you able to talk?'

'Yup.'

'Good. I've got a meeting in a few minutes, so can't stay long.'

'I'm all ears.'

'I've been in contact with the guy out in Spain who breeds Alanos.'

Jon slid his hand down the outside of the steering wheel, feeling the stitches in the material catching against his palm. 'Anything?'

'Yes. He had two dogs stolen from his farm last year. All the animals are microchipped and so I had the carcass up in Manchester scanned – it's the female he lost, AH23.'

'Nice name.'

Hutcher grunted. 'I asked him about that. Stands for Alano Hembra – female Alano, number 23. Now, he's had various purchase enquiries from overseas, but he only sells to local farmers for obvious reasons. I asked him if he kept a record of these enquiries and he does. Two from Finland, a few from Russia and America, one from Saudi Arabia. But these were all for single males. Only two enquiries have been for a breeding pair. One from Italy and one from – wait for it – '

'Ireland.'

'Correct.'

Jon clenched a fist. The evidence against de Avila was mounting up. 'What was the enquiry – letter, email, phone call?'

'Phone call. Young-sounding bloke, said he was called Mickey.'

'Right,' Jon scoffed. 'And he wanted the dogs for?'

'His collection. Contera told him Alanos can't be kept with other dogs. The bloke said he'd keep them in a secure run, at which point Contera informed him Alanos aren't suited to being confined, either – and politely refused his request. The bloke said money was no object. Contera has had silly amounts offered by Russians and he let the Irishman know he's not restoring the breed for financial gain. Less than a month later, two animals vanish. It was a professional job – alarm systems were disabled. Bolt cutters were used to gain access to the kennels.'

'Seems this Mickey doesn't like being told he can't have something.'

'Looks that way. And that still leaves AV08 unaccounted for.'

'What?'

'Alano Varón. Male dog, number eight.'

'Well, I'm also unearthing some interesting stuff about de Avila.' He glanced in his rear-view mirror. The roof of the abattoir was just visible. 'Don't suppose you know much about horses and ponies?'

'In what sense?'

'Unwanted ones,' he replied. 'What do horse- and pony-trekking places do when their animals get past it? Is there any kind of system?'

'It's illegal to dispose of any large animal yourself. Different councils have different rules for dead pets. Of course, in the old days, it would be the knacker's yard for horses, donkeys and ponies. In fact…bloody hell…'

'What?'

'Well, it was largely an Irish thing; the collection and disposal of unwanted horses.'

'You're right.'

'I've got to dash. Oh, and I called my contact in Newcastle back. Not much more on the Irish kennels. His mate didn't think the name was Darragh, though. Thought there was a 'v' in it somewhere, almost like devil. Not sure if he's just pulling my chain with that, to be honest.'

Jon was back in Clifden by three o'clock. He swung into Aldi, grabbed a sandwich and drink from the chiller then wolfed them down in his car. Still nothing on the pay-as-you-go mobile. This was getting annoying.

He continued north out of town on the Letterfrack road. After a few minutes he saw a large lake on his left, spiky reeds clustered at the edge of the dark water. The right turn appeared soon after. A people carrier was parked up a hundred metres ahead next to an old beige Honda. A couple of dark-haired young men were standing on the grass verge smoking.

Jon pulled over and lowered his passenger window. 'Is Golden Fields Farm near here?'

'The farm?' The man's accent was heavy. Eastern European, Jon guessed. 'Is here. This is farm.' He glanced over his shoulder.

Jon realised there was a gap in the row of conifers that formed an impenetrable screen at the side of the road. It was an entrance, leading to some large buildings set back in the surrounding fields.

At that moment the driver's door of the people carrier opened. A ginger-haired man wearing combat trousers and a faded red sweatshirt got out. Peeling white letters across the sweatshirt's front spelled Golden Fields. He approached Jon's car and spoke with exaggerated slowness. 'Are you here for work?' He pointed at the side of the road. 'Park it there and I'll take you along.'

Jon assessed the situation. May as well go along with this, he thought. As he reversed in behind the people carrier, more men began climbing out of it, some in tracksuits, some in jeans and T-shirts. He wandered over and joined the group.

'OK.' The man in combat trousers announced. 'I'll take you to the front office. Watch for lorries, they never pay attention to this.' He slapped a hand on a circular sign to the side of the entrance. The words read, Dead Slow.

'Patrick, how are you?'

The young Garda officer stopped in his tracks, mobile phone at his ear. 'Mr de Avila, hello.'

'Can you talk, Patrick?'

He glanced across the car park at the station, turned round and returned to his vehicle. Once back inside, he hunched forward, the fingers of his free hand picking nervously at the edge of his seat. 'Go ahead, Mr de Avila.'

'We have a problem, Patrick. The British policeman whose details you so kindly gave to Darragh.'

The officer closed his eyes for a moment. 'Yes?'

'He's back in Clifden.'

'He is?'

'Judging from the posters all round town, yes.'

'I didn't know.'

'You do now.'

'Yes.'

'I don't want him here.'

'What's he done now?'

'He's causing my family inconvenience, that's what.'

'Has he assaulted anyone else? Something we can actually use?'

'No.'

'I'm not sure what can be done, Mr de Avila. Not if Conor Barry is unwilling to press charges. I mean, if he's only –'

'The night he paid a visit to our nightclub, he stole something.'

'Really? He stole something? Well that changes everything. I'll come round right now. You just need to file a report – '

'I will file no report. He stole a pair of security tapes. The footage on one of those tapes could be very damaging to us.'

'With respect, Mr de Avila, it's probably for the best I don't know what that footage – '

'I want you to get the tapes back from him and instruct this man to go home, back to Britain.'

Patrick felt a dribble of sweat begin to make its way down the inside of his arm. He rubbed agitatedly at his shirt. 'But Mr de Avila, if I approach him, he'll know I have a connection to you – '

'The footage on those tapes includes you.'

'Me?'

'Calling in at the office to collect your cash from Darragh.'

'You filmed...' Patrick looked nervously towards the police station. 'Oh Jesus.'

'We're in the same boat here, Patrick. Now, the longer he stays, the greater the risk he's exposed to.'

'Risk? What will you do?'

'Nothing, if he returns those tapes and goes home. I can keep my head, Patrick. There's no need to worry about me.'

A short silence. 'Where's Devlan? I've not seen him or Sean for a while.'

'They'll be back very soon. And then things will change.'

'He's police, Mr de Avila. If anything happens to him – '

'Then retrieve those tapes and ensure he returns to Britain where he'll be safe and sound. Make sure he's gone by Saturday. I've guests arriving at the farm and if he's still making a nuisance of himself by then, I won't be responsible for reining in Devlan.'

'Mr de Avila, I can't guarantee he'll be gone. As I said, how can I raise it with him – '

'Are you enjoying that extension on your house? Does little Roisin like playing in her nursery there?'

The officer bowed his head. 'Mr de Avila, I can pass you information. Be your eyes and ears in this place. But I've no influence further than that – '

'Don't annoy me now, Patrick.'

'Mr de Avila, please. You know I always do what I can...' He paused. 'Mr de Avila? Are you there? Hello?'

He slowly lowered the phone to his lap. His hands started to shake violently as the spectre of his dead uncle rose up in his head. Seamus Coffey. A sergeant when Patrick had joined the Guards. It was Seamus who'd taken Patrick aside the night he was filing a drink-driving charge against Devlan. Quietly, he'd advised Patrick to forget about it. The envelope of cash that had turned up shortly after from Gerrard de Avila was a surprise – and one that came in useful. Then Gerrard requested something else; just a criminal records check for a businessman in Galway. Patrick had passed the information on. More cash arrived: more requests followed.

It was the death of Seamus that first gave Patrick an inkling of how perilous his own situation was. Seamus liked to sink a few drinks when he was off duty. More and more, before he died, he liked to finish off the night sinking them in Darragh's. Patrick had heard the rumours about how his uncle never seemed to hand any cash over the bar. He'd also heard that, sometimes, Seamus even drank in the back office with Gerrard de Avila himself.

Then the accident had occurred. True, Seamus lived alone. True, patrol cars sometimes had to drive him home when he was too drunk to walk. Leaving the gas rings on one night was hardly a surprise. Then waking up, full of a hangover, and turning on his bedside light...

Oh God, Patrick thought. What have I got myself into?

CHAPTER 29

As they walked along the driveway's verge, a lorry trundled past them, exhaust fumes mingling with the pungent, meaty aroma emanating from the factory itself. Like a packet of beef and onion-flavour crisps, Jon thought. One that's been left out for too long in the sun.

The lorry came to a halt alongside a cabin. The barrier lifted and it continued into a courtyard ringed by a combination of old and new buildings.

'Weighbridge,' the ginger-haired man announced, nodding to the smooth slab of concrete set into the driveway alongside the cabin. 'Every vehicle gets recorded going in and out. By the way, my name's Denis.'

Jon looked at him. Siobhain had said Denis was back in Clifden: this wasn't the man who'd been driving the van in Manchester. Was there some kind of mix-up?

'What was the farmhouse,' Denis stated, pointing to the old stone cottage to their right. 'Now the reception and farm manager's office. You go there to pick up your wages.'

They rounded the corner and Jon could see the lorry was now backing towards a bay at the front of the modern building. A couple of fork-lift trucks were waiting, roof lights flashing.

'This here's your raw materials store.' The man led them to what appeared to be an old barn flanking one side of the courtyard. Its open design gave them a clear view of the bags and sacks piled inside.

'Flexible intermediate bulk containers – or big bags as we call them. Full of stuff like rolled peas and corn, alfalfa pellets, sunflower seeds.' He gestured to the nearest one. 'Fork-lifts can hook them up by the loops on the sides.'

Identical, Jon thought, to the bags builders deliver sand and the like in.

The ginger-haired man walked over to another section and rested a hand on a paper sack. 'These – fifteen-kilogrammers – have things like your shrimp meal, fish meal, meat and bone meal, vitamin and mineral powder. Right, any questions?'

Most of the potential employees stared back at their guide with blank faces. Jon wondered how much of the speech they understood.

'Good,' Denis said. 'Any of you drive a fork-lift?'

A few hands went up.

'Better money,' he stated, 'if you can. Right, I'll take you over the main facility itself. It's where everything gets mixed together and cooked. Like baking a huge fucking cake, so it is.'

He led them to where the lorry had backed into position. The driver was unlatching the rear doors. 'Just in time,' Denis said. 'Follow me up these steps, mind you keep back from the edge.'

They climbed up to a walkway that curved round the rim of a conical stainless-steel vat. The top was about three metres in diameter. Placing his hands on the railings, Jon was able to peer down into it. In the gore-spattered opening at the bottom were four layers of fierce-looking blades. The smell rising up reminded Jon of when, during a walk near Hathersage, he'd almost stepped on a sheep's corpse crawling with maggots.

'This is the macerator,' Denis announced. 'Think of it as a giant food blender, but with carbon-steel blades that cost a fucking fortune. All the soft crap from an abattoir? The stuff you can't sell to people – intestines, offal, eyes, brains, bollocks – it ends up in Dolavs: those things.' He pointed to the large plastic container balanced on the stumpy tines of a fork-lift. The vehicle was backing slowly away from the lorry. 'Into the macerator it goes and then we switch it on. But what do we always do before turning a food blender on?'

The man driving the fork-lift yelled out. 'Put the fucking lid on!'

'Good man, Olav. Put the fucking lid on.' He gestured to the circular piece of metal suspended by chains above their heads. 'Otherwise, this place ends up coated in the worst smelling layer of shit you can possibly imagine. Think scraping up a mud pie made by Satan himself. Right, let's move before he tips out.'

They proceeded down the other set of steps into the building.

'Right lads, two ways in,' Denis pointed. 'Big doorway for the fork-lifts, small doorway for people. Use the big doorway and you'll get mown down sooner or later. Once we're inside, stick to between the yellow lines, clear?'

He waited for a series of nods then swept aside some hanging plastic strips. One by one, they filed in behind him. Jon found himself in a large airless building with an incredibly intricate system of tubes hanging from the ceiling about twenty feet above. Punctuating the erratic pattern were rows of fluorescent strip lights. The temperature was uncomfortably hot and it only seemed to magnify the unpleasant smell he'd noticed drifting across the fields.

Raising his voice over the loud hum of machinery, Denis continued. 'OK, so we've got all the ingredients for whatever's being made.' He led them to a perspex screen. Behind it, three long nozzles stuck out from the side of a machine. 'The dies on the end of the nozzles decides the shape of biscuit produced. Today we're doing dog-bone shapes, as you can see. But it could be little fish shapes if it's cat food – hearts, clovers, circles, swastikas, if you wanted them. Dogs, they like stuff which honks a bit. Like a bone that's been buried for a while. That's what it is today, if you can smell it.'

Smell it? Jon thought. It's been making me want to retch for the entire bloody tour.

'Once they're coated, the conveyor whips the biscuits off to the dryer.'

They all walked towards a vibrating box that, Jon guessed, was the width of his house. Metal ladders and walkways encased it. As they got closer, Jon saw the ladders led down as well as up.

'When this facility was built,' Denis stated, 'we couldn't get planning permission to go higher than ten metres. But this dryer has six decks; first two are above ground, the other four, below. Follow me.'

Their footsteps began to clang as they trooped along the grid forming the walkway to the first set of steps. Now within touching distance of the dryer itself, Jon could feel the heat coming off the sheet-metal casing. He looked between his feet and saw the huge piece of equipment was sunk into a gigantic concrete pit.

'As you can see,' Denis called up, already on the walkway below. 'Dust is the main problem we have.' He ran a hand along the railing and held up orange-coloured fingers. 'The machine breathes the stuff out. It clogs up the ventilation system, collects in the grips of your work boots, gets fucking everywhere, so it does. As we get lower, you'll see there's also the problem of condensation – moisture dripping down.'

They dropped deeper, light now provided by wall-mounted bulbs covered by metal grilles. Oxygen levels seemed to be diminishing with every step. Seven flights of steps later, they reached the bottom.

'And this is it,' Denis shouted above the din of machinery. Leaving the steps, he crossed to the middle of the pit and extended both arms. 'The arsehole of Connemara.'

Jon stepped off the final stair and looked up at the underside of the giant dryer. Drips fell steadily from the huge girders that supported it. He realised the concrete floor was awash with a brownish sludge. The walls were glistening and, peering at where they met the floor, he could see dozens of tiny lumps dotted about.

'When it's on,' Denis said, 'someone needs to scrape this floor clean every hour.' He pointed at the drain by his feet then raised his hand and rubbed a thumb and forefinger together. 'You want good money? Lots of cash? This is your job.'

'These are dead mice?' Someone asked, nodding down at the little lumps in the corners.

'Baby ones,' Denis replied, moving back to the steps. 'They build their nests in the crevices and cracks, but the little ones often fall out.'

Arsehole of Connemara, thought Jon. Spot on.

As they filed towards the office, Jon brushed a palm across his head to dislodge the last few powdery flakes from his hair. Once inside, he thankfully breathed in air that wasn't heavy with the smell of putrid flesh. They were directed to a row of plastic chairs lining the wall to the left of the door.

'Emily? Have you the forms for me?'

The woman behind the desk placed a batch of clipboards on the counter. 'Make sure they give back all the pens.'

'You've seen our advertisements, so you know we pay more than any other place round here,' Denis announced, handing clipboards out. Jon saw a pen was attached to the top of each one. 'Fill in your details,' Denis said slowly. 'If you have a phone…' He held up a thumb and forefinger to the side of his head. 'Phone? Yes?' He pointed to the bottom of the form. 'Write the number down. We have overtime shifts. More money for you if we can call and get you in.' He worked his way down the line to Jon.

'No thanks.' Jon shook his head.

The man's eyes reduced to slits. 'You don't want the work?'

'I already have a job,' Jon replied. He stood. Confusion now filled Denis's face.

Jon stepped to the side so he could address the woman behind the desk directly. 'Tell Darragh de Avila that Jon Spicer was here having a good look round. He knows who I am.' His eyes went back to the man. 'Cheers for the tour, mate. It was very interesting.'

As he walked back up the drive he realised his clothes were coated in a film of the orange powder. No wonder the smell's staying with me, he thought irritably, checking his mobile once more. Ten minutes, I reckon. Ten minutes before Darragh rings me wanting to speak. He swung his car round. A lorry was heading towards him. It indicated right and turned into the farm's driveway. Milky liquid was seeping from its rear doors and Jon wondered how long it would be before the pony carcasses from Darragh's abattoir arrived for processing.

Back in Clifden, he slowed down at the junction with the high street. Twenty minutes, he thought. De Avila's now had twenty minutes to ring me. In fact, he's had all of yesterday and this morning, too. He thought about how time was ticking by. The chances of getting Zoë out and being on a flight home tomorrow were shrinking. Agitation needled him. What the hell was going on here? It seemed the man's business interests extended throughout the town and beyond. Like some kind of octopus, Jon thought. Maybe, he decided, it's time to give him a stronger poke.

He drove back to the business park where the auction had been held. Almost every vehicle was gone. He steered his car through the entrance and continued to the far end. Jon could see a man bent over the bonnet of a car parked inside the unit for Paul Acton and Sons Motors.

On his left, the pens were empty except for two young men. One was scraping up manure with a shovel, the other was hosing down the gutters. Jon came to a stop beside the small Nissan in front of DA Services and climbed out. The shutters were lowered on the business unit, but he could hear music playing inside.

He rapped his knuckles on the metal door set into the corner of the screen. No reaction. Glancing over his shoulder, he could see the two youths clearing up were now watching. He waited for a pause in the music then kicked his foot against the metal. The entire thing rippled with the impact and, a moment later, the music dropped in volume.

A voice called from inside. 'Who's there?'

Jon booted the screen again.

'For fuck's sake.'

Footsteps on the concrete floor and the screen's inner door opened a fraction. Jon placed his foot in the gap so it couldn't be closed again then hooked his fingers round its edge and yanked. The door swung fully open, half pulling out a young guy. He struggled to regain his footing, neck arching to look up at Jon.

'Who the fuck are you?'

Jon pushed the guy backwards. 'Wouldn't you like to know.' Inside, overhead strip lighting shone down on a row of computer monitors. Each one was sitting on a humming piece of computer equipment. On the shelves lining the back wall were boxes of blank DVDs and empty cases. Well, well, well, Jon thought. The pirate video operation Siobhain mentioned.

'What do you want?' the young man asked uneasily, fingers twitching at his sides.

Jon stepped over to the nearest piece of equipment and picked up the DVD case next to it. The image on the cover was high quality. *Snuggledown*. Disney's next big release. I was thinking of taking Holly to see this, Jon thought. 'This isn't even out in the cinemas.'

The man's eyes cut to the open door and he said nothing.

Dropping the case back on the table, Jon glanced at the man. 'Who makes the deliveries for you?'

'What?'

'When a batch of DVDs are ready, who delivers them to wherever they're sold?'

'I only mind the gear.'

'You never help load up a van?'

He shook his head.

'Never deal with anyone, is that right? Never even seen who you work for. What do you do, just pass the discs through the letterbox when someone knocks? Sounds a slow way of loading a van.'

He shrugged.

'Ever see a girl called Zoë driving? English girl?' The young man kept quiet as Jon began to survey the room. 'I don't know how long burning a copy takes, but I'm guessing you manage hundreds each day?'

Licking his lips, the guy shrugged. 'I only mind the gear. I don't know.'

'Yeah?' Jon replied. 'Then why don't you run along to your boss and tell him today's output has been interrupted.' He stepped over to the first plug on the wall and flicked the switch. The whir of the nearest two machines died and the monitors went blank. He continued round, cutting the rest of the power. 'You can tell him it was Jon Spicer. Tell him I'm here for Zoë. He knows how to get hold of me.'

The other man picked his denim jacket off the back of a chair and slipped through the door.

'Room 17, please.'

The girl handed Jon his key with a smile. 'You have a

message.'

'Oh?'

She reached below the counter and produced a white envelope. 'It was dropped off earlier.'

'Thanks.' Jon examined the wording on the front. Mr Spicer. Urgent. 'Who by?'

'A gentleman – I'd say in his fifties,' she replied. 'He didn't want to leave a name.'

'Red nose?' He wriggled the fingers of one hand at the side of his head to indicate an untidy frizz. 'And wiry grey hair?' She tried to suppress a smile. 'Had his coat seen better days?'

'Actually, he was wearing a suit. But that sounds like him.'

Once in his room, he looked around with a puzzled expression. Has someone, he thought, been in here? The bed had been straightened, as usual, but a pair of his jeans were lying crumpled in the corner. He checked the wardrobe, thinking he'd stacked his tops further back on the shelf. Shrugging, he placed both mobiles on the little table then sat in the chair overlooking the street. He studied the handwriting on the envelope. Cramped and on a downward slant. The pen stroke underlining the word 'urgent' had been finished with such haste the ink petered out like the tail of a speeding comet.

He peeled open the flap and extracted a single sheet of paper.

I believe this will be of pertinence in your investigation of the de Avila family.

My investigation? So he knows I'm a policeman, Jon thought. Someone is passing information to him.

A dog fight has been arranged for tomorrow at the de Avila property, Golden Fields Farm.

Jesus, thought Jon. I've just been there. Can this be for real? He read on.

It will be attended by several notable figures from both Belfast and Dublin. The farm is reputed to be a location de Avila has used in the past to settle business issues – vis-à-vis Tommy Hammell, for example.

I believe the fighting is due to commence early afternoon. I know in the past the nightclub has been used by de Avila for the purposes of hospitality the evening before such events.

I wish you every success with your project and remain your loyal assistant in the matter.

Project? Jon thought. Odd choice of word. But then again, who uses 'vis-à-vis', either? He reached for his mobile and selected Nick Hutcher's number. 'Hi mate, I hoped you might be out of that meeting.'

'Yup – just grabbing a cup of tea.'

'I've been given some more information about de Avila. No idea how solid it is, but the rest of the stuff has turned out useful. It's about a dog fight.'

'Yeah? Whereabouts?'

'Here, in Clifden. I've got a location and a date, but no exact time. Early afternoon is all.'

'OK – that's no major problem. Where exactly is it taking place?'

'A facility used for making pet food, believe it or not.'

'I've heard of stranger.'

'But probably not smellier.'

'Sorry?'

'I posed as a job applicant and was shown round this place earlier today. I thought Manchester had a monopoly on dark satanic mills.'

'Grim was it?'

'Disgusting. I'll never be able to look at a dog biscuit

again.'

'Ironic place to have a fight – though I suppose the dead dogs can just be recycled there and then.'

Not just dead dogs, he thought, eyes shifting to the name on the piece of paper. Tommy Hammell. He remembered the slurry of meat from the Dolav flopping against the sides of the giant vat. The sound from inside as the blades had started to spin. Another thought hit him. Zoë. He closed his eyes for a moment. Oh, Jesus, there'd be no trace of her left. No, he said to himself. Don't be ridiculous. Darragh might enjoy knocking women about, but he isn't a killer. No way.

'You still there, Jon?'

'Sorry, mate. Miles away. Is it enough for you to act on? I would love to disrupt this guy's big day.'

'I can certainly put a call in to the ISPCA.'

'Irish Society for the Prevention of Cruelty to Animals?'

'You're picking up on this animal protection business, aren't you? This could be an event featuring that other Alano, you realise?'

'I wondered as much.'

'Leave it with me – I'll call you back.'

Jon cut the call and brought up Rick's number. 'Am I still in the clear with Parks?'

'Yup,' his partner replied. 'Anything on Zoë?'

He shook his head in exasperation. 'Nope.'

He brought Rick up to speed on the theft of AH23 and AV8 from Contera's farm in Spain then lifted the sheet of paper. 'Anything from your mate in the NCA on that information I gave you?'

'He hasn't had a chance to start checking yet. One thing he mentioned though – his main point of contact in Ireland is within the Criminal Assets Bureau – the equivalent of the NCA's Proceeds of Crime Department.'

'OK.'

'A part of the Criminal Assets Bureau is a system called

CARIN. This is the good news; it's an informal enquiry system for tracking suspicious activity – dodgy financial transactions and the like. When he gets a chance, his contact in the Bureau is going to dig around in the weeds and see if anything on de Avila shows up.'

'That's great.'

'Oh – and Sophie got a hit from a ferry company.'

'She did?'

'There was a de Avila on a crossing on the second of February. Dublin–Holyhead.'

'From Dublin? That doesn't fit with what Hutcher told me. He said when dogs are brought across, it's from Northern Ireland to avoid customs checks.'

'He was a foot passenger. No vehicle involved.'

'Oh.'

'You don't reckon it could have been someone else on that ferry?' Rick asked. 'Another family member or something?'

Jon tapped his forefinger on the gearstick. 'I suppose it's possible. But Siobhain said to me he's…' His finger stopped moving. 'Christ, I assumed when she said he was back, she was talking about the de Avila I saw in Manchester. Maybe she wasn't.' The prospect of there being another family member he didn't know about loomed in his head. 'What were the details of this foot passenger?'

'I don't know. She just said it was a D. de Avila.'

'Has to be Darragh,' Jon said. 'I mean, there can't be that many people with the exact-same name. Not travelling on ferries within the time frame we're interested in. I reckon the van came over separately – probably driven by that other guy from the Clock-on kennels or whatever they're called.'

'I'll be sure to not tip off Sophie until you get back.'

'Cheers. After that, the Bureau can raid every premises of his they can find, for all I care.'

'OK – I'll sit on it until Monday. You will be back by

then, won't you?'

'I bloody hope so. Thanks Rick. Last thing – while that contact in the Bureau is poking around, see if he can keep an eye out for anything on a DA Services. It appears to be an abattoir just outside Galway, based on an industrial park called Menlo. There's also a little business unit with the same name here in Clifden. That one is being used to produce pirate DVDs.'

'How do you know?'

'I just walked in and saw all the equipment.'

'What – the door was open?'

'No, some kid let me in. I sent him off to tell Darragh that production was being suspended.'

'Jon, you'll be seriously pissing this guy off.'

'No choice, mate – nothing else has worked so far. Listen, I'd better go. Talk later.'

He checked the time. Just after half-four. I wonder what sort of a day Alice and Holly have had? He brought up her number and pressed green. Her answerphone message kicked in. 'Hi babe, it's just me. You're probably still out and about. The pony sale was interesting, some real characters milling around. Anyway, still no contact with Zoë. If I haven't heard from Darragh by tonight…' He sighed. 'I'll be really pissed off. Anyway, I'm popping back to Grandad's now, might be the last chance I get to see him. Speak to you later.'

As he lowered his phone, the smell from the pet-food factory caught in his nostrils. He sniffed at his fingers, hand and then his sleeve. I bloody reek of death, he realised, walking towards the shower.

He made a short detour via the Aldi and picked out a bunch of purple flowers. No idea what these are, he thought. But I'm sure Eileen will like them. The only single malt in the alcohol section was a Scotch. Can't see Malachy going for that, he thought. He selected a bottle of red and white wine instead then headed for the tills.

The turning for the bog road was a short distance beyond Clifden. Jon slowed his car, remembering how easy it would be to miss it. About a mile out of town a small sign caught his eye. Connemara Gaelic Football Club. The place de Avila's company was due to re-roof. Good old Darragh. Always ready to help the community out, he thought as his mobile phone started to ring.

CHAPTER 30

He stamped on the brakes and reached into his jacket. Hutcher's name was on the screen.

'Hey, Jon, your tip-off is a good one! The ISPCA already had word there was a major event taking place, they just weren't sure of any details.'

'So it is going to be in that pet-food factory?'

'They're confident enough of it to be arranging a raid in conjunction with the Garda. Remember the name of the visiting kennels touring England?'

'Yeah – Clock-on, or whatever.'

'My contact recognised it straight away as Gaelic. Clochán. It's the old name for Clifden.'

'De Avila,' Jon stated, thinking the guy wasn't turning out to be the small-time criminal Siobhain said he was.

'I think you're right. Seems now – with this trip to England – the bloke's indulging in a bit of international dog-fighting activity. That's a worrying development.'

'He certainly seems ambitious.'

'This one at the pet-food factory? He must be planning to fight the male Alano, AV8.'

Jon tapped away on the top of his gear stick once again. If Darragh is arrested, there's nothing stopping Zoë from leaving Clifden whenever she wants. He smiled. This could be just what I need. 'When's the raid taking place?'

'They're going to wait until they reckon everyone who's been invited is there. Rumour has it there are dogs en route from a well-known kennels in Belfast.'

'Excellent. Can you see if they'll do me a favour?'

'Jon? If your intelligence turns out to be correct, no favour you ask will be too big. They've been trying to bring down Clochán kennels for years.'

'I only want to go along on the raid. A background observer. It would be so nice to see de Avila being led out in cuffs.'

'I only wish I could be there, too. This sounds like it could be a big one.'

'I'll give you a full report, don't worry.'

Hutcher laughed. 'I'll pass your number on. Someone will give you a buzz.'

'Gerrard, how can I be of help?'

'How are you, Brendan?' Even though the person on the other end of the phone couldn't see his face, Gerrard forced himself to smile. The obsequiousness of doing so made him feel ill.

'Busy. There's plenty going on here, as you can imagine.'

He fanned his thick fingers and ran them across the smooth wood of the table in his hotel suite. Behind him, notes trickled from a pair of shoulder-high speakers barely an inch thick. The sound was so clear, the pianist could have been in the room. 'I don't doubt that. Margaret well?'

'She's fine, Gerrard. What can I do for you?'

Gerrard thought about Patrick – the young Garda working out of the station back in Clifden. The man had called earlier in tears, sobbing down the phone like a woman, saying he was out of his depth, that he didn't know what to do, pleading for permission to not get involved. The young officer was weak and ineffectual,

Gerrard had thought contemptuously. And – at some point in the future – he would pay for that. 'I've never asked for favours, you know that Brendan.'

'That's true. But you're asking for one now?'

'A quiet word is all I want you to have.'

'About?'

'I've a situation and I'm reluctant to take it up with…the proper channels.'

'Those being?'

'The police.'

'And what is this situation?'

'There's a British policeman showing his face in Clifden. He's got it into his head a girl he knows has been working in one of my businesses there.'

'Which one would that be?'

'The nightclub. The one my son, Darragh, runs. This policeman is acting on his own, I'm certain. A few nights ago he marched into Darragh's office demanding the return of this girl. He refuses to believe she isn't there.'

'Is she there?'

'No! But the prick won't accept that. Things are starting to escalate, Brendan. He's making a nuisance of himself – thumped the doorman, threatened my son. Now, I don't want to ruin the man's career over a moment of madness on his part – '

'Doesn't sound like you, Gerrard. Getting soft in your old age?'

Gerrard forced another smile, toes curling in his shoes. 'It's not like that, Brendan. Far from it – '

'What is it you want me to do?'

'Have him removed back to England. Oh,' he gave a little shrug, 'and ask that he return some property of ours that he took. Then we can forget about the whole thing.'

'What property?'

'Two security tapes from the nightclub. The things are of no value – it's a point of principle. He stole them and I would like them back.'

'And how do you propose that I arrange all this?'

'Come on, Brendan. You have an office in Stormont these days. The parliament in Dublin is riddled with your people. You've got clout. A quiet word, that's all I'm asking.'

'Am I missing something here? Why don't you speak to this person? If the girl he's looking for isn't there, make that clear to him, demand your bloody cassettes back and tell him to be on his way.'

'The man won't listen to reason, Brendan. That's the problem.'

'And on what grounds do you think we could have him removed?'

Gerrard felt the blood rising in the back of his neck. 'On the grounds the bloke is looking for trouble – and, before long, he's going to fucking find it.' His outburst was met with silence. Gerrard took a deep breath in. 'Brendan? Sorry, that sounded worse than intended. What I meant is that – ' He paused. 'Brendan, there's an event taking place at the farm tomorrow – '

'I don't get involved in that kind of activity any more.'

'I know. But there are people travelling in from all over. Campbell's coming down from Belfast. Brendan, if these people get wind that there's a British policeman throwing his weight around here, I can't guarantee his safety.'

When the other man spoke, his voice was quivering with anger. 'Do you realise the shit flying round this place? A British soldier has been tortured, executed and dumped. The unionists are on our backs. Those cunts are threatening to walk out of this place. Their Tory mates in Westminster are beginning to nod their heads in agreement. Now Downing Street is demanding answers and we have no idea – not a clue – who did it.'

'Surely everyone knows it wasn't the IRA?'

'Does that matter to the unionists? Continuity IRA, Real IRA, Provisional IRA – it's still the IRA to them because that gives them the exact excuse they need: no power-sharing with Sinn Féin because we're just a mouthpiece for terrorists.'

Which is absolutely true, Gerrard thought. 'So there's not even a whisper who was behind it?'

'There's no longer any communication between us and those mad bastards who only want to carry on fighting. For them, we sold out when the party signed up to the Good Friday Agreement. To them we're worse than the bloody unionists. We're traitors, Gerrard. We've entered the political process. As you've just said, we've got offices in Stormont.'

And don't forget, Gerrard thought, your big salaries and cars, fat expense accounts and civil servants to do your bidding. Meanwhile, out in the real world, the rest of us are seeing our businesses going tits up. 'That's a bad state of affairs.'

'So you can see how your little problem compares?'

My little problem, Gerrard thought. You weren't so dismissive when you used to come down here, sit in our nightclub, enjoy drinks on the house then go on to a prime spot to watch the fight. Bastard.

'Why can't you use the Guards to sort this, anyway?'

'You know that isn't my way.'

'But trying to get a senior Sinn Féin official to pull a few strings is?'

'Jesus, Brendan – it's just a call to someone in London. A word on to whoever this guy's boss is in Manchester, that's all.'

'Sorry, Gerrard. You need to sort this out yourself, I haven't the time.'

The line went dead and Gerrard carefully placed his phone on the table. He interlinked his fingers before his face. 'Haven't the time?' he murmured, sitting perfectly still. The waves of fury refused to fade.

CHAPTER 31

By the time he found the turning for the bog road, the sun was low in the sky. The land became spiked with reeds and soon Jon could see fingers of water reaching out for the narrow strip of asphalt. He tried to imagine driving along it in the dead of night. One thing was for sure, he thought, you'd take it bloody slow. The twisting road had no markings and he realised how easy it would be to come off it and plough into the marsh itself.

Far ahead, he caught the wink of approaching headlights. As the road carved its way between the expanses of water, the lights would disappear from view, only to appear again slightly closer. Eventually, he was able to see the vehicle itself. A battered old Land Rover. Finally they met and, as the last metres closed between them, both vehicles slowed to a crawl. Jon moved the outer tyres of his car on to the grass verge, the Land Rover doing the same. As they inched past each other, the driver solemnly held up a hand. The gesture, thought Jon, was part-greeting but part-something more: a signal to go carefully. He nodded back and the other vehicle was soon just twin dots of red in the gloaming.

***

'Hey brother, it's me.'

'Devlan! Why've you not been returning my calls?'

'Been busy.'

'Sorry to hear about Queenie.'

'That fucking British peeler – it's his fault. I'll be there tomorrow, Darragh. And I'll break his fucking face, so I will.'

'Dad's getting it sorted, Devlan.'

'Is he now? How come Conor left me a message saying this peeler's been visiting other places of ours?'

'What do you mean?'

'Don't try to bullshit me. He's been to Golden Fields, pretending that he was after work. Conor told me about the message he gave to Emily. "Tell Darragh, Jon Spicer has had a look around."'

'Well…he did, yes.'

'The fucker. And Conor mentioned something about the unit in Clifden.'

'Um…yeah.'

'What did he do? Tell me!'

'Shoved Roy out of the way and marched in.'

'Who's Roy?'

'Denis's youngest. We pay him to keep an eye on the machines. Spicer pulled all the plugs out, told Roy production has been suspended.'

'Jesus, I do not believe this. And you never told me about the fucking security tapes he took, did you?'

'I didn't know he had them – not when I left you that message. I only found out after.'

'Conor said you've had his car and room at the hotel searched.'

'Yeah, no sign of them.'

'Where's he getting his information?'

'Wish I knew.'

'The Guards?'

'No. Dad checked with our man at the station.'

'Who, Patrick?'

'Yeah.'

'He didn't even know Spicer was back in town until Dad told him. A big clue would have been all the posters that have been plastered round the place.'

'There a phone number on these posters?'

'Yeah, I've got it right here. He'd stuck a poster to the front doors of the club.'

'Give it me.'

'What will you do?'

'Call the fucker, of course.'

'What will you say?'

'Not sure. I just want to hear the guy's voice.'

'Dad said you're to sit tight. Do nothing until your flight in the morning.'

'Just give me the fucking number, Darragh.'

As Jon pulled up outside Malachy's bungalow, the last of the sun was catching on the distant peaks. In the purpling sky above, stars were beginning to emerge.

Eileen's car was already there and he could see lights on behind the closed curtains. He walked up the driveway, glancing over his shoulder at the building site opposite. The letters on the side of the dumper truck were just visible.

His hand was on the handle of the porch door when a succession of high notes pierced the air. Someone's mobile, he thought, before his eyes widened. The pay-as-you-go! Putting the bouquet of flowers on the ground, he scrabbled to get the phone out of his pocket. 'Hello?'

Silence.

Jon frowned. 'Hello?'

No reply.

He held his breath. Was someone there? It sounded like the call was connected. He strained to make out any noise. Was that someone breathing? 'Hello? Can you hear me? If you have information about Zoë, there's no need to worry, your identity will be safe.'

A chuckle, menacing and low.

Jon held the handset away from his face for a moment. Was it a kid, mucking about? He pressed it back against his ear and continued to listen, the presence of the person at the other end of the line becoming more sinister with every second. 'Hello?'

A sudden howl caused him to flinch. The line went dead. Jon lowered his shoulders and stared at the handset, the noise still resonating in his brain. That wasn't a kid. It sounded like an adult. He wanted to wipe his ear, as if the deranged shriek had dirtied it. He brought up the last call received function. There it was: anonymous. 'Wanker,' he muttered, retrieving the flowers and opening the door.

'The tax man, was it?'

Jon's heart missed a beat. Christ, it was Malachy, sitting there in the shadows. The old man was slumped in his chair, staring out across the still bay. 'I didn't see you there.'

The old man raised a small glass and took a sip. 'Kieron found a dead ewe. Out at the tamhnóg by where Mattie cuts his turf.'

Jon frowned. 'Is that somewhere along the bog road?'

Malachy sat forward. 'Eh?'

Sensing their wires were crossed, Jon held up the flowers and bottles of wine. 'It's Mary's son, Jon. I ate with you yesterday. I've brought some wine with me.'

Malachy sat back. 'Jon! A thousand welcomes to you. There I was thinking you were Joseph, the pair of you are so similar.'

Joseph, Jon thought. The grandson of Orla's brother. The one who drowned out at sea. A bit freaky he keeps mixing us up. He turned slightly and regarded the ocean. 'What's that mountain range on the horizon called?'

Malachy gazed fondly at its faint silhouette. 'The Twelve Bens. And further north, across the bog, you have the Maumturks.'

Great names, Jon thought, looking back at his

grandfather. 'I went to the pony sale earlier. It was really interesting.'

'Oh, the sale, yes. You get some funny fellows along there. Did you speak to anyone?'

'No. I just watched.'

'Well, tell them your mother is an O'Coinne if anyone asks. People like to know your family in these parts.'

The front door opened and light spilled into the porch as Eileen looked out. 'I thought it was you I heard talking.' She tutted at Malachy. 'Don't be making him stand out in the cold while you drink your whiskey. Jon – come in, come in.'

'Malachy?' He looked down at the old man. The sheep dog was lying across his frayed slippers 'Are you staying outside?'

The old man gave a nod. 'For a few minutes yet. You go in. Eileen, pour the man a drink now.'

She rolled her eyes and they walked down the corridor.

'I wasn't sure if you prefer red or white, so I got both,' Jon announced. 'And these are for you.'

She looked over her shoulder at the flowers he was holding up. 'Irises! That's so kind, Jon. You didn't need to.'

'Yes I did.'

Kieron stood as they entered the kitchen. 'Jon, hello.'

'Hello,' he replied, placing the bottles on the worktop and shaking hands. 'How was your day?'

'Not bad, thanks. Lambing season is not far off – then things get busy.'

'I bet.' Jon's mind went to a previous investigation. One that took him to a hill farm on the lower slopes of Saddleworth Moor. 'Do you gather all the animals in for it?'

'Now we do,' Kieron replied, examining the bottles with a look of curiosity. 'Wine.' He glanced back at Jon. 'A bit of a treat.'

Have I, Jon thought, made some kind of faux-pas? 'I

thought…you know…a glass would be nice.'

'It will be,' Eileen cut in. 'Usually we only have it on special occasions. But this is special enough. You were telling Jon about the lambing season.'

The younger man nodded. 'It used to be that the women would live out in booleys – the nearest to here is Scailp.'

'Scailp is at the foot of the mountain,' Eileen explained, stirring a large saucepan on the old stove. 'It's a pasture for sheep and cattle.'

Jon took a seat. 'And what's a booley?'

'A hut,' Kieron replied, rummaging around in the drawer for a corkscrew. 'Walls of rocks, roof of branches and reed straws. The women would stay there and wean the lambs, the men would go out in the evening, collect the milk and bring it back to the village for churning. When it had become butter, it would go in wooden kegs to Galway.'

'How recently were things done like that?' Jon asked.

Eileen thought a moment. 'Orla, used to help when she was young. That would have been up until the Second World War.'

Jon shook his head in wonder.

Kieron pointed. 'Which colour will you have Jon?'

'Red, thanks.'

'And how was your day?' Kieron asked, passing him a glass.

Jon lowered his eyes and examined the ruby liquid, unsure of how much to say. 'The person I'm looking for in Clifden is a relative, of sorts.'

Eileen turned her head. 'Who?'

Jon raised his eyes. 'You know I had a brother?' He watched Eileen's expression as she registered the fact he'd used the past tense. She doesn't know, he concluded sadly.

'David?'

'Dave – or our kid, as we called him.' He took in a breath. 'Well, he died a few years back.'

Eileen held a hand over her open mouth.

'I'm sorry,' Jon said. 'With this issue Mum has, I wasn't sure if you'd know or not…'

'We didn't know.' She reached out and rested a palm on his shoulder. 'What happened?'

Jon kept his eyes on his glass. 'I'd prefer to tell you another time. But he left behind a young boy, Jake. He's now six and lives with Mary and Alan.'

'With Mary and Alan?' Eileen whispered.

'Jake's mother had her fair share of problems. With Dave gone, she couldn't cope and – well – pretty much fled, leaving Jake behind. All I've heard of her since then is a couple of postcards. She was coming over to Galway to look for a friend she used to know back in Manchester.'

'What's her name?' Eileen asked.

'Jake's mum? Zoë Butler. Then, literally a week ago, this friend Zoë came looking for rang. She said Zoë had found her, but had got herself into some trouble and needed someone to get her out of Clifden. She said Zoë was working in the town's nightclub.'

'Darragh's?' Kieron said, rolling his wine round in the glass.

Jon looked across at him. 'You know it?'

'Yes. Some of the younger ones drive over there at the weekends for the dancing.'

'How long's it been open?'

'Ten or so years? I take it you didn't find Zoë there?'

Jon leaned back. 'No. The owner, Darragh de Avila, claimed to know nothing about her.'

Kieron nodded slowly. 'A man with his fingers in many pies. That family are a bad lot.'

Sighing heavily, Eileen addressed Jon. 'If you'll learn anything from this visit, Jon, it'll be that we Irish can bear a grudge. For generations they can fester. So as a family eventually has no idea why they dislike another so.'

'But we know they're bad,' Kieron retorted, looking from his mother to Jon.

They, thought Jon uneasily. 'Go on,' he prompted.

There was a bang as the front door shut. Malachy's walking stick thudded along the corridor and, a moment later, he appeared in the doorway. 'Have they given you something to drink?' he asked, eyes going to Jon's glass. 'Ach, so they have.' He started across to his corner chair, sheepdog trailing behind. Jon reached down to try and stroke it, but the animal shrank from his fingers. There's only one person who's allowed to stroke you, he thought.

Malachy lowered himself into the chair, 'Now, Jon. Don't be shy. Help yourself to more when you want.'

'We were talking about the de Avilas, Grandad,' Kieron said.

'Oh, them.' Malachy's face soured as he produced the glass from the pocket of his cardigan. 'A little nip would sit well in there. Well, there's not much I can do about Gerald now.'

Kieron stepped over and took the glass. 'Gerrard, Grandad. It's Gerrard who's building that house. Gerald died over ten years back.'

'And the world's a better place for it,' Malachy replied, hands now resting on his walking stick.

'Malachy!' Eileen admonished.

He brought the stick down with a little bang. 'And I outlasted the bugger! How's that, Jon?' He poked the tip of his tongue from the corner of his mouth. 'I outlasted him!'

'Grandad's talking about Gerald de Avila,' Kieron said, filling the glass. Jon took a look at the label. Redbreast. A pure pot-still Irish whiskey, twelve years old. Thank God I didn't get him a bottle of Scotch. 'Gerald cheated Grandad out of some ponies when they were younger.'

'He did, so,' Malachy muttered. 'Terrible man.'

'In those days the family were just slaughtermen – when Gerrard took over the business, he moved it to the big place they have near Galway.'

'An industrial park called the Menlo Estate?' Jon asked.

'Yes. It's where I have to send my sheep for slaughter. So the family is still making money out of ours. Since Gerrard's been head of the family, they've moved into other areas, I hear.'

'I noticed the name on that digger outside. Convila.'

'That's their construction business,' Kieron nodded. 'But it's Darragh who's really behind it all.'

'The one I spoke to in the nightclub,' Jon stated.

Kieron nodded. 'We were at college together in Clifden. Then he went on to University in Cork where he got all his exams in business studies. He's the brains in that family – got his brother's share, too.'

Jon looked up sharply. 'His brother's?'

'Darragh has a twin, called Devlan.'

Jon repeated the word in his head. Devlan. Nick Hutcher's words came back. His snout in Newcastle thought the Irishman's name sounded something like 'devil.' 'He's got a twin? I didn't realise. What's he like?'

'They're not identical, for a start. Devlan is loopers. I used to play Gaelic football with him for Clifden – until he was banned for life. Waited for a fellow in the club car park once, clubbed him half to death, so he did.'

Jon stared at the other man. 'Someone from the opposition?'

'No – our bloody captain! Argument over which position Devlan had been told to play in. But that's Devlan for you – he's happy to go for you, but only if your back is turned. Should have been locked up when he did that.'

'Why wasn't he?'

'The other fellow wasn't for pressing charges.'

Jon's mind was leaping ahead. Shit, he thought. Why didn't I see it? Maybe Darragh would lash out at a woman, but it was obvious he wasn't a truly violent type. The demented shriek from the phone call he'd just received echoed in his head. Jesus Christ, the brother might still be in England. Alice. Holly. He got up.

'Are you OK?'

He looked at Eileen, saw her concerned expression. I need to speak to Rick. See if he can find out if that ferry booking Sophie unearthed was for a Devlan, not Darragh. 'Sorry, urgent call I need to make.' He retrieved his phone from his jacket. 'Can I use the front room?'

Kieron pulled the kitchen door open. 'Of course.'

He stepped into the corridor then through to the next room, closing the door behind him as he brought up Alice's number. 'Come on,' he murmured as it began to ring. 'Alice! It's me.'

'Hi. What's wrong?'

He made an effort to relax. 'Nothing. Just checking how you guys are. Did you have a good time today?'

'Yeah, it was nice. Just wandered around, really. Fed the ducks, played hide and seek in the woods. Holly's been asking after you.'

'Tell her I'll be back soon.'

'Still no word from Zoë, then?'

'Not directly. Sometimes I think the wheels are beginning to turn – but then I realise I've made no progress at all.' He sat down in the armchair by the sideboard covered in photographs. 'I don't know. I'm beginning to wonder if she's really here. I've been round the entire town handing out posters – no one admits to recognising her. And there's been nothing from Siobhain. God knows what her agenda really is.'

'Something's definitely not right with her.'

Jon reached out and examined a photo in its silver frame. He made sure his voice was casual. 'How busy is it there?'

'Fairly quiet, actually. About half the lodges seem empty.'

'Probably the recession. And the lodge you moved to. It's booked under Lorimer, not Spicer, isn't it?'

There was a pause. 'Yes. Why?'

Jon bent forward to look more closely at the black-and-white image. A christening by the looks of it. From the stiff clothes and rigid expressions, he guessed it was taken some time ago. 'You know, making sure the precautions we agreed are all in place.'

'Jon, you're sounding cagey. What's going on?'

She reads me like a bloody book, he thought, straightening up. 'It seems Darragh has a twin brother. It could be that this brother was the one over in England.'

'A twin?'

'Yes.'

'But he's back in Ireland now?'

'I'm not one hundred percent on that.'

'What? He might still be here, in England?'

In Manchester, Jon thought. Having had to kill his prizefighting dog. 'It's a possibility.'

'Bloody hell, Jon.'

He raised a hand at the empty room. 'It's not anything to panic about. You and Holly will be fine where you are, I'm certain. But if you want me to come home, I'll get the next flight.'

'I'd feel a lot happier if you weren't ringing me from another country.'

'Right, I'm on my way.'

She sighed. 'No. I mean…I don't know. You're sure we're safe?'

'If I wasn't, I'd already be on a plane back. How could anyone possibly trace you?'

'You're the policeman – you tell me.'

He weighed it up. 'They can't. It's fine.'

'As long as you're certain about that,' she said uneasily. 'What's next?'

'I don't know. Give it a bit longer, I suppose. Something has to happen soon.'

'You didn't plan for two brothers.'

'No, but it doesn't really change anything. I'll just be putting the proposition to another person as well.' Three, actually, he thought. Since it seems like the dad is also part of things. God, what am I getting into here?

'It's your decision. You're the one with the experience in this sort of thing. But I don't feel comfortable.'

'It'll be OK, honestly. I'll be home by Sunday night, if not before.'

'Call me first thing tomorrow, OK?'

'Will do.'

He hung up, eyes quickly scanning the other photos. Assorted portraits. A family pose on a flowery sofa in what was obviously the photographer's studio. White teeth and immaculate hair. That'll be the branch of the family who live in Boston, Jon thought, bringing up Rick's number. 'Hi mate, how's things?'

'All OK, here. You?'

'Yeah – still poking around without much to show. One thing, though. It looks like Darragh de Avila has a twin brother called Devlan.'

'Really?'

'And he might still be in the Manchester area.'

'Manchester area?'

'I have a nasty feeling Darragh was never in England. I think it's Devlan behind the incident on the golf course.'

'Shit.'

'Exactly – that ferry booking. The one for the foot passenger Sophie found – '

'Dublin–Holyhead, second of February?'

'Yup. See if it was for a Devlan de Avila. Also, it would be great if she can search for him on anything returning to Ireland. Plane or ferry.'

'She's not back in until Monday now.'

'Bollocks, I forgot it's Saturday tomorrow.'

'I could check.'

'No – that might look dodgy if Parks found out. I'd prefer you keep well clear.'

'My contact in the NCA called just now. No good news, I'm afraid. It's turning out to be a nightmare working out who's really behind those property developments.'

'It's not Darragh de Avila?'

'He can't say. They're all holding companies or registered with subsidiaries which are linked to offshore companies. It's all been set up very carefully. He said he needs something more if he's to dig any deeper.'

'More? Like what?'

'The name of the family's accountants would be ideal. Something to give him a way into their arrangements.'

Jon crossed his legs. I don't like the sound of this.

'And I just did a quick internet search on that name – Tommy Hammell. I don't suppose he's a professional children's entertainer living in Florida?'

'For all I know, he is.'

'Well, that was the website which topped the search results. But a few hits further down was a newspaper story from the Dublin's Evening Herald. It's six years old.'

'What's it about?'

'Tommy Hammell, aged thirty-seven, convictions from the courts in Dublin for fraud. Con-artist by the looks of it.'

'And?'

'He disappeared. Given his background, the police don't expect him to show up.'

Jon frowned. Why the hell was the guy's name given to me in connection to the de Avila's business dealings? What did the letter delivered to the hotel say? Something about the pet-food factory. 'Is he listed as a missing person?'

'The Garda were treating his disappearance as suspicious. Money left in his bank accounts, summer holiday booked and paid for, that type of stuff. Last activity on his credit card was to fill his car up with petrol at a station on the N59.'

Jon felt his armpits prickle. The road that connected Clifden to Galway. 'Let me know what else you find.'

'You're persisting with this? What if there's some connection between Hammell and the de Avilas?'

Jon wiped a hand over his mouth as he thought about

his phone call with Siobhain. Strictly small-time, she'd said. Nothing to worry about. She must have known that wasn't true. 'Listen – I'll give it one more day. I can't just leave Zoë here. Not at the mercy of this bloody family.'

CHAPTER 32

The lock on the hotel door clicked and Devlan de Avila looked up. 'Where the fuck have you been?'

Sean Doyle paused in the doorway. 'Walking.'

'Walking?'

'You know, exercise? Fresh air? Talking of which…' He crossed the room and opened the window. 'This place stinks.' He turned round and eyed the other man's socks.

'Yeah, well, we'll be home soon. Hazel will put on a wash for me.'

'You could use some of the stuff I bought. Wash some things in the bath.'

'I've never washed a pair of socks in my life.' The shopping bag rustled as Devlan's fingers squeezed the tennis ball inside it. His fingers relaxed. Then he repeated the action again, an intense expression on his face.

Sean looked on uneasily.

Abruptly, Devlan put the bag to one side, sat up and scratched at the stubble on his face. 'We're going out.'

'Yeah?'

Devlan nodded. 'To do a little job. I spoke to Darragh just now. That English peeler wants a fight, so he does.'

'How do you mean?'

'He's been out to the farm and he turned up at the unit

in Clifden – sent word to Darragh that business is suspended.'

Sean slowly lowered himself into a chair.

'What are you fucking smiling for?' Devlan growled. 'You think this is funny?'

'No. But the guy has some brass neck on him, you have to admit.'

'You reckon? We'll see.' He reached a foot down and shoved it into a trainer.

'What are you thinking?'

Devlan got his other trainer on and stood. Nodding at Sean, he said, 'You need to get your throwing arm in.' He stepped over to the table in the corner. Beer bottles and crumpled cans covered it. He picked up two empty litre bottles of San Miguel.

The questioning expression on Sean's face was replaced by a troubled look.

Devlan bared his crooked teeth with a smile. 'We're going to visit the wife and daughter up at that Center Parcs place. Show them how you do things Belfast-style.'

Sean Doyle sat back and draped his forearms over the chair's arm rests. 'Don't be fucking stupid, Devlan.'

The other man's eyes lit up. 'No man crosses my family like he has.'

'Your dad himself said to sit tight. When's our flight? Ten hours' time? We'll be back in Clifden soon. Just calm your jets.'

'Fuck that. We're going to find which bungalow they're in, Sean, and we're going to burn the bastard down.'

'We're not.'

'We fucking are.' He yanked the liner from the litter bin under the table, spilling rubbish onto the floor. 'Are you up for it?' he asked, putting the two empty beer bottles inside.

'You after killing his family, now?'

'Not kill them. They'll get out fine. This is a warning.'

'This is fucking madness, more like. Listen to yourself.'

'What?' Devlan's eyebrows lifted. 'You'd take it, would you? What he's doing, you'd take someone doing that to your family? The bastard made us kill Queenie.' He raised his hand and wiped spit from his lower lip. 'You're happy with that?'

'You know I'm not. That was a very special dog. The hours I spent training her. But there'll be a time and place to settle with him.'

'I'll do it myself then.' He grabbed his jacket from the chair in the corner then jabbed the hand holding the bin liner at Sean. The bottles inside clinked as he spoke. 'Dad's not around forever, you know that. More and more he's looking to hand over to Darragh and me. And when he does, I want people who I know will defend the interests of our family like it's their fucking own. Because that's how it works. Look out for us and we'll look out for you.'

The two men stared at each other in silence.

Sean's upper lip bulged as he ran his tongue across his teeth. 'You're going against your dad on this?'

Devlan hesitated a moment. 'People need to know we don't fuck around. This guy is making us into idiots.'

'Your dad will go ape-shit – with the both of us.'

'Will he?' Devlan sat on the end of the bed. He shook his head. 'He's old, Sean. He's not got that same…' He struggled to find the right words. 'You know the story when that guy from Dublin tried to cheat Dad out of all that money?' He grinned. 'Dad fed that fucker into the macerator, sent him back to Dublin in bags of dog biscuits. No messing!'

Sean inclined his head. 'True.'

'It should have all been sorted with this peeler days ago. Dad's good at the talking, fair play to him. But people will be starting to wonder if that's all he can do.'

Sean's heel began to jiggle up and down. 'I don't know.'

'Listen, mate. When Dad starts handing over more stuff to me, I'll need someone to run the kennels, know what I mean? Take charge, like. Those plans to establish our own, Irish, line of Alano? We can get another bitch from that person in Spain. We can get as many as you need. Start touring the rest of Europe, not just Britain. The Germans, the Dutch, the Finns? Fight all them lot. That's the direction you can take it. Become a world force, like.' He nodded at the other man. 'You. It can be you that does it.'

Sean kept quiet.

'Come on,' Devlan urged. 'What do you say?'

Slowly, the other man's eyes went to the bag sitting between Devlan's feet. 'Petrol bombs? Hardly the style your old man favours, is it?'

Devlan looked down at the bottles. 'You got a better idea?'

Sean looked off to the side. After a second, he said, 'Maybe.'

'What Seany-boy?' There was a playful note in Devlan's voice. 'Spit it out. Come on, fella!'

The other man sighed. 'We're just putting the frighteners on them, right?'

'Yeah, course. That's all.'

Sean sat forward. 'That Sergeant in the Guards. The one who started demanding bigger and bigger pay-offs.'

Devlan shrugged. 'Who?'

'The one who died? The gas leak in his house?'

'Seamus Coffey?'

Sean spread his hands in reply. 'We do that up in Center Parcs. But we leave a window open – let them know what could have happened.'

Devlan de Avila's lips parted in a smile.

The drive up to junction 40 of the M6 took them less than ninety minutes.

'There's your turn-off.' Devlan nodded at the sign the car's headlights had picked out. He looked back at the CDs on his lap. Luther Vandross. Barry fucking White. What sort of a prick listens to shite like this? It was a bloke, wasn't it? Whose car this is?'

'Yeah, a bloke,' Sean replied, steering down the slip lane.

'Was he a nigger?'

'No, white.'

Devlan flipped the cases over his shoulder and reached into the glove compartment once again. 'George Michael? He's a fucking bum-bambit.' The CD clattered against the back windscreen. 'Elton John? No, No! Barbara Streisand. No!' Both CDs flew into the rear of the vehicle. 'We're in a faggot's car. That's what this is. I do not fucking believe this.' He reached up and tore the little air-freshener off the rear-view mirror. 'Going to have to disinfect ourselves, Sean. Could be all sorts of germs in here. Thank fuck we're wearing gloves.' He started eying the interior of the car with disgust.

Sean glanced across. 'What if he's been using it for a bit of car-park shenanigans? Sucking off other fellows right where you sit?'

Devlan practically levitated from his seat and Sean burst out laughing.

'Shut your fucking mouth, will you?' Devlan screamed. 'Say any of that stuff again and I will bury a screwdriver in your fucking ear.'

Sean regarded the other man uneasily, the laughter dying in his throat. 'OK, mate, OK. Just having a laugh with you.'

Devlan was now trying to minimise how much of him was in contact with the seat. 'Not funny. Seriously, it's not. How much fucking further?'

A few minutes later they reached a floodlit entrance with barriers across the traffic lanes. Continuing past, they followed the road through the forest. A small side lane appeared on their left and Sean turned down it. A hundred metres later, they spotted a lay-by.

'That'll do,' Devlan said.

He climbed out and removed a canvas B&Q bag from

beneath his seat. They set off into the mass of pine trees, picking their way across the needle-covered forest floor until the faint outline of the perimeter fence loomed before them.

They edged closer, keeping a careful watch for any guests among the dense trees on the other side. Distant laughter and the sound of bicycle bells. A procession of lights flashed past; teenagers racing along a dark woodland trail. Once they had disappeared, Devlan and Sean jogged up to the twelve-foot-high fence, strands of razor wire looped along its top.

Devlan removed a pair of wire-cutters from the bag. Each snip caused the surrounding fence to reverberate with a sound like giant bangles shaking. Sean prised the flap back and, in seconds, they were through. 'You think we'll find their bungalow?'

'We'll fucking find it,' Devlan growled in reply. 'When we get to the main bit, we split up.'

Forty minutes later, Devlan's phone started to ring. 'Yes?'

'She's here. I can see her.'

'Where are you?'

'By the main lake, next to a kiddies' play area. The shops and stuff are right behind me. She's here, with the little girl. They just came out of a restaurant. Where are you?'

Devlan checked his surroundings. 'Not sure. There's a wooden sign with an arrow for the main village up ahead.'

'Now they're walking away. Could be heading back to their accommodation.'

Devlan started striding along. 'Don't lose them.'

'We're just putting the frighteners on them, yeah Devlan?'

'Dead on. Just sending a message, like.' He cut the call, trying to keep his face straight. Can't be marching along with a big grin, he thought. People might take you for a loony.

CHAPTER 33

'Well,' Malachy slapped his hands against his thighs. 'It's time I hit the hay. Are you sure you've had enough to eat there?'

'Absolutely stuffed,' Jon replied, placing both hands on his stomach. He sat back, smiling from the tales he'd heard. The time when Malachy's father, Phelim, noticed a hare behaving oddly when he was out cutting turf on the family's bank at the edge of the bog. The animal had repeatedly lowered its head and pointed its ears toward a distant rock. Eventually, Phelim had laid his spade down and followed the animal. In a hollow beneath the giant stone there was a badly decayed corpse. It turned out to be the body of an old man called Mícheál who, the villagers worked out, must have lost his way crossing the bog on his way home from the workhouse in Clifden during a particularly violent storm. To this day, Malachy had stated, the spot was known by the locals as Dead Man's Grave. As for hares, he added, many refused to eat them, believing the animals had supernatural powers.

Jon glanced at his watch. Just after ten. His thoughts turned to Clifden and he felt his cheerfulness fade. Time to go back to that club and hand more posters out. Maybe sit at the bar this time and refuse to move until Darragh showed his face. 'I should be going, too. Eileen, thanks for the food. It was delicious.'

She batted a hand in his direction. 'Will you come back for your tea tomorrow?'

'If I haven't found Zoë, I'd love to.'

'She'll show up sooner or later, I'm sure,' Malachy said, struggling to his feet.

As Jon pulled into Clifden's town square, he glanced at the dashboard clock. Eleven fifteen. That's what comes of being too chicken to drive the bog road at night, he thought. An extra forty minutes to come by the coast.

There was an unusual amount of cars parked about. Must be because of the pony sale, he thought, lifting the batch of Zoë's missing posters off the passenger seat and examining the vehicle registrations as he walked along the pavement. Many featured letters that marked them out from different counties.

Looking further up the street, he could see a few figures outside Darragh's. He paused before the entrance to his hotel, wondering whether to head up to his room and put on the protective gear. Not worth the hassle, he concluded. The bouncer isn't interested in another clash.

The girl on duty in the hotel foyer was waving a brown envelope at him. My God, Jon thought, don't tell me someone's actually come forward with some information on Zoë's whereabouts. 'That something for me?'

'Yes. It was here when I arrived for work.' Her eyes went momentarily to the posters in his hand. 'Any luck?'

'Nope,' Jon replied. 'Have you ever seen her?'

She shook her head then leaned forward. 'Listen,' she whispered. 'Don't think people in this town aren't grateful about what you're doing. They are.'

Jon blinked. 'Sorry?'

'Standing up to that family the way you are. They've been a blight on this place too long.' A male member of staff appeared from the dining room area. Seeing him, she placed the envelope on the counter then reached for his room key. 'Just be careful. Please.' With that, she retreated into the rear office.

Jon watched her go then looked down at the envelope. 'Jon Spicer' had been written across the front and he realised the handwriting was familiar. The same methodical style as on the note pushed through the toilet window of Mannion's Bar. Siobhain again, surely.

He took the stairs two at a time, opened the door to his room and sat himself down in the corner. Once the little table lamp was on, he held the envelope up and traced the contents with a fingertip. A flexible piece of card. He tore open the envelope's flap. A photo, but one with a good third of it snipped off.

Jon examined what was left.

The shot was of Zoë, standing next to Clifden's plane-wing monument. She was wearing a black polo top. Though the lettering on the left-hand side of the chest wasn't fully legible, Jon knew what the word said: Darragh's. So she has bloody worked there, he thought. Which means all the arseholes in that place have been lying to me. Sunlight made her hair – dyed dark red in the picture - glow. Probably summer tourist season, Jon thought, judging by the ice creams people in the background were enjoying.

Turning the photo over, he saw the same childish handwriting on the back.

Please don't give up on her now. Siobhain.

He studied the image once again. She looked happy – and healthy. Wide smile, those prominent incisors standing slightly in front of her other teeth, like two volunteers stepping forward for a task. And there was an arm around her, the person's hand dangling forward. The fingernails were varnished a plum colour. Same shade as the person's who'd dropped the note through the toilet window of

Mannion's Bar. Siobhain.

So Zoë was here, he thought. I don't know when exactly, but at some point she was here. This proves it. The knowledge gave fresh impetus to his wavering resolve.

He removed the sheets of paper from the manila file given to him at the pony auction. What sort of a family am I dealing with here? He flicked over the uppermost sheet listing the nightclub's profit and loss. Below it were photocopies of the printouts about the various property developments. Phoenix Gardens. Emmet Street. Anderson Court. Just figures: no company details, nothing to give an insight into the de Avila's exact involvement.

As he went to place them on the table, the sheet on Anderson Court tilted towards the lamp's soft light. Jon's hand hung in the air as he looked down. There were fine indentations on the surface. He held the sheet closer to his face. Letters. A piece of paper had been placed on the Anderson Court printout at some point and something had been written on it.

He reached to the desk behind him and grabbed the pencil off the hotel notepad. By scribbling lightly across the sheet, faint white letters started to appear.

query €60,000 planning fees with Blackman & May

Just the one tiny slip up, Jon thought. Rick's mobile was on answerphone. 'Sorry mate – I know it's late. When you get the chance tomorrow, can you ask your contact in the NCA to run a check on a company called Blackman and May? No idea who they are, but I think they're linked to one of these big property developments. OK? Cheers, speak soon.'

He jogged back down the stairs, crossed the foyer and stepped onto the street. As he neared the nightclub, he saw Hazel. She was standing next to the ginger-haired man from Golden Fields Farm. The girl spotted him approaching and, biting on the nail of her thumb, whispered something.

The man from the pet-food factory looked over his shoulder and turned round. Conor Barry stepped out from the doorway onto the pavement, closely followed by a third man. Jon looked him up and down. The bastard is an inch or two taller than me, he thought, and probably a stone or so heavier.

Jon stepped up to him. 'So you're the one who's been building all the dry-stone walls round these parts.'

The giant's face remained blank.

Right, Jon thought. That joke fell flat. 'Evening gentlemen. Darragh around?'

Conor Barry stepped forward, eyes gleaming. 'Fuck off, you cheeky English prick.'

A sudden show of bottle, Jon thought. Now you have two others with you. 'Conor. How's the nose? It looks sore.'

The girl suppressed a smile, moving back towards a notice that said, Private Party. For the crowd going to the fight tomorrow, Jon realised. The bouncer murmured something and the ginger-haired man nodded, not taking his eyes off Jon.

'So I take it you won't be letting me in then?' Jon asked, cocking his head.

'Come on and try,' Conor smiled.

Jon felt a part of his brain suddenly switch on. Go on, the voice in his head urged. Lay the little fucker out. Just smash him in the face, you know it'll feel so good.

At the edge of his vision, the girl started edging across the pavement. He flexed the fingers of his injured hand and remembered his promise to Alice: no violence. 'It's OK,' he said to her. 'I don't want any more trouble.' He turned to the three men. 'I just want to know where Zoë is.'

They stared back at him in silence.

'Look, I know she was here.' He held the photo towards them. 'Tell Darragh to cut the crap.'

Not one of them moved.

Jon sighed. 'You've got my mobile number – it's on all the posters. Tell Darragh I want a word. Tonight.'

The girl glanced at the line of men and gave a cough. 'I'll…I'll tell him – '

'Shut up!' Conor hissed.

Jon shrugged. 'There's no need for this.'

Conor pointed a finger. 'Fuck off back to Britain before we send you back there in a box.'

'Really?' Jon grinned. 'And how will you do that?' He stepped closer as a Lexus pulled up alongside them. The door opened and a couple started to get out from its rear.

The ginger-haired man placed a hand across Conor's chest and pushed him back a step. 'Mr Campbell, go straight in.'

The man's eyes bounced between Jon and the group before he ushered his female companion forward.

Jon took in his appearance. Late fifties, but very trim. Hair cropped short and a nasty scar running down the back of his head. The woman he was with looked to be in her early forties and had obviously had a boob job. As the Lexus pulled away, Jon clocked the dealership's sticker in the rear window. Belfast. Another punter for tomorrow's fight. He caught the ginger-haired man's eye. 'I'll see you tomorrow.'

His eyebrows dipped in confusion.

Jon gave a little salute and set off back to the hotel.

Devlan leaned to the side, the pine tree's bark rasping against his coat. Down a shallow tree-lined slope was the rear of the lodge where Alice and Holly were staying.

'What's the time now?' he whispered.

Sean was stretched out on his back, gazing up at the pine canopy. Stars twinkled through little gaps in the feathery foliage. 'When you last asked ten minutes ago, it was almost one.'

'Right. And the last light went off before midnight.'

'And we need to be at the airport check-in by four,' Sean added wearily.

'Let's do it. Kitchen area is immediately on the left. I open a window then keep watch while you do the gas, yeah?'

Sean nodded as Devlan blew into his hands. 'Fingers are frozen. You?'

Sean flexed his fingers in and out, his latex gloves making the faintest of squeaks. 'Not so bad.'

'Good. You can do the door lock, then.' He handed Sean a key ring that held an array of thin, spiky implements.

They made their way down to the lodge. Identical ones on each side formed a rough semicircle. When they reached the back patio, Devlan listened at the sliding doors. After a minute, he held up a thumb and Sean skirted round the plastic picnic table and chairs to join him. He sank down on to his haunches, worked a length of metal into the keyhole and teased it to the side. Something clicked.

'Bingo,' he edged the door open a little. They both listened for another minute then Sean reached through, peeled the curtain back and ducked his head fully inside. He looked back out. 'No carpet,' he mouthed.

Devlan gave a nod.

Sean eased the glass door open another ten inches and slipped through the gap. Devlan followed him in. A living area with an L-shaped sofa filling one corner. A floor-to-ceiling print of a forest on the wall directly opposite, tree trunks rising up out of the skirting board. To their left was the kitchenette; soft light glowing from the cowling above the gas rings. Very kind of you, Devlan thought, gesturing to Sean to stay put.

Stepping onto a striped rug, Devlan padded silently across the room, pausing to examine the items on a coffee table. A Nintendo DS and a copy of *Red*. Perched on a cushion at one end of the sofa was a small beanbag dog.

He stepped lightly across the floorboards to the door leading into the side bedroom. It was ajar but there was no sound of breathing coming from inside. He peeped round and saw the bed was empty. He made sure every window was firmly shut.

Back in the corridor, he noted the low ceiling dotted with recessed light fittings. This place will fill up in no time. He was about to wave Sean over to the kitchenette when the bedroom door at the end of the passageway swung open. The little girl stepped out, the hem of her purple nightie swaying slowly as she came to a halt and stared straight at him. He stared back. She blinked, yawned, and, moving like an automaton, shuffled into the bathroom. A trickling sound started.

How the fuck, Devlan thought, did she not see me? He looked to his sides and realised: his back was pressed to the wall bearing the giant forest print. Dark clothes, he realised. I blended right in.

A few seconds later, she reappeared, turned right and disappeared back into the dark bedroom. The door closed. He flicked a hand at Sean, who slid round the kitchen counter. The spring in the dial for the oven creaked slightly as he turned the gas on full.

Smiling to himself, Devlan picked up the little toy dog perched on the sofa cushion, yanked the head off and put both pieces back.

Out on the patio, Sean inched the door shut.

Devlan pointed to the corner of the lodge. 'They're both in that bedroom.'

Sean turned, seeing its window and the curtains behind it were closed. 'So you opened a window in the other bedroom?' he whispered.

Devlan was already making for the trees.

'Devlan,' Sean hissed, following him up the slope. 'You left a window in the other bedroom open?'

'Yeah,' Devlan said over his shoulder. 'A window in the other one open.'

CHAPTER 34

Squinting at the mobile's glowing screen, Jon saw Alice's name. Christ, he thought, sitting bolt upright in the bed. It's three fifteen in the morning. 'Alice?'

'Jon? Oh, thank God you answered.'

'Alice?' People were talking excitedly in the background. A car engine revved. Is she outside? 'Are you OK? Where's Holly?'

She was speaking quickly to someone, words too muffled to make out. Suddenly her voice was back in his ear. 'Jon? Something's happened…'

'Where is Holly?'

'She's here, with me. It's OK.' Her voice was breathless, agitated.

His chin dropped and he saw how the slight ripples in his stomach were lit a faint blue by his phone's screen. 'Alice, what's going on?'

'There's…we had a gas leak.' She started talking away from the phone once more. 'Thank you, that's very kind. Holly? It's hot chocolate. You'll like it. Stay there a minute while I talk to Daddy.' Her voice grew louder once more. 'We're outside with blankets wrapped round us.'

A voice called out in the background. 'It's safe! It's

safe! Relax everyone.'

Jon fought to keep his voice under control. 'You said a gas leak?'

'Yes. We were fast asleep. There's a family in the neighbouring lodge, they have a teenage lad, he came back late: got the wrong lodge. Tried to open our front door. It woke me up. The whole place was thick with it.'

'Slow down.' Jon turned his bedside light on. 'Your lodge was full of gas?'

'I grabbed Holly and we got out. The place was…we were choking.'

Jon climbed out of bed. 'Who's there now? Who's with you?'

'Everyone in the cul-de-sac is up. Night staff from the office are here – one just came out and said it's safe.'

Jon was walking around, scratching at the back of his neck. 'I don't get it – '

'Excuse me?' Alice was speaking to someone else again. 'Yes, it's our lodge. Me and my daughter. What was it?'

More talking. Too many people close by, all of them speaking, everything just a jumble of syllables. Jon wanted to scream down the phone for them to shut the fuck up. He could make out Alice's voice. She sounded indignant. 'He's taking me back in, Jon. They've opened all the doors and windows. Everything's been opened.'

The background noise grew fainter and he guessed she had stepped through the door. A male voice started to speak.

'It was the dial for the oven. This one here, right in the middle? It was turned to full.'

'But that's impossible.' Her words were incredulous.

'Well…' The man sounded embarrassed. 'I've checked the utility room with a reader. This was the leak, madam. Right here.'

A siren note of panic started up in Jon's head. 'Alice!' He took his boxer shorts and jeans off the back of the chair and threw them on his bed. 'Alice!'

'Perhaps,' the man continued, 'you were planning to put a casserole on? Could you have forgotten?'

'No. No, I couldn't.' Alice now sounded uneasy. 'Has someone...was a door or window open?'

'No, everything was firmly locked.'

Her voice came back down the line. 'Jon, did you hear that? I don't get it, the man is saying the oven – '

'I heard.' Jon pulled a clean T-shirt off the wardrobe shelf. 'I'm coming home.'

'You're what?'

'I'm coming home.'

'When?'

'Now. First flight I can get. This isn't right.' He heard a beep. 'What was that?'

'The man's walkie-talkie. Someone's telling him the fire brigade are here.'

Jon used his free hand to try and get his boxer shorts on. 'Alice, look around you. Can you see anything? Any sign someone was in there.'

'I have done, there isn't – oh my God.'

'What?'

'It's Holly's dog. That beanbag one she got from McDonald's?'

'What about it?'

'The head's been pulled off. Jon – it was on the sofa. I saw Holly put it there. Its head's been pulled off.'

Jon gave up trying to get a foot through his underwear. 'Alice. You and Holly: get out of there.'

'What?'

Shit, he thought, sitting down in the armchair. They're so bloody far away. He spoke slowly and clearly. 'Get your handbag and walk out while there are still lots of people around. Is the fire engine there?'

'Yes, it's pulling up outside.'

'While it's busy, just take Holly and move. Get on the motorway and don't stop driving, OK?'

Her voice went very calm. 'It was them, wasn't it?

That's what you're saying.'

'We can't use our mobiles any more, Alice. Not for speaking to each other. Call me from any services. Pull up on the petrol-station forecourt, where it's brightly lit. Let me know you're fine, then get going again. I'm phoning Rick.'

'OK.'

He listened to more sounds of movement, voices rising and falling, the rumble of a diesel engine. He heard Alice's voice. 'Holly? Come with Mummy a minute. No, don't worry about your drink. That's it. Good girl. Jon? I've got her. I'm hanging up.' The line went dead.

Jon put his phone down and searched for something to punch. His reflection glared back at him from the full-length mirror in the wardrobe door. I'm naked, he thought. Naked and totally fucking powerless. A roar of frustration broke from his lips. He breathed in and out several times then called Rick's number. With the handset on loudspeaker, he started to get dressed. Answerphone. He hung up and rang again.

His partner answered groggily. 'Jon?'

'Yeah mate, it's me. Can you hear OK?'

'What's going on?'

Jon wondered where to start. A week ago, I had a normal life. Not now. 'There's been some kind of incident where Alice and Holly are staying in Center Parcs.'

'Say that again. An incident?'

'Just listen, mate.'

'OK.'

'Can you get hold of a car?'

'Yeah, Andy's. He's here.'

Jon crossed the room and started removing the rest of his clothes from the wardrobe's shelves. 'Right. Alice and Holly are fine, but there was a gas leak in their lodge. One of Holly's toys – a little dog – was on the sofa with its head ripped off.'

'Where are they now?'

'I told them to get the hell out. They're heading for the motorway and staying on it. They're going to call me from a service station. I'm on the first flight I can get.'

'Is there one in the morning from Galway?'

'I don't know. There'd better be. Usually, there're two each day.' He started ramming garments into his holdall. 'I need you to make sure they're safe – until I get back. Can you drive up there?'

"Course I can.'

'And I need your opinion about the lodge. Alice mentioned staff from Center Parcs had turned up, and a fire engine was attending. Treat it like a crime scene, mate. If it was them who did this, it changes everything. I am going to nail this family. Really fucking nail them.'

'It doesn't make sense. How could they have found her?'

He was on his knees, searching for his trainers under the bed. 'For all I know, my phone calls are being intercepted.'

'You really think so?'

'I don't know what to think anymore. Just call me when you've had a look around the lodge she was in, yeah?'

'OK, will do. Jon? I'm texting you an address for a website.'

'What is it?'

'The de Avila family history; their ancestor was a Spanish soldier.'

Jon stopped in the act of unplugging his mobile phone charger from the socket near the TV. 'And?'

'You rang asking me to check on a possible link to the Armada. When the fleet was wrecked during that huge storm?'

'Go on.'

'I didn't find much – not until I tried pairing the name de Avila with the breed of dog the RSPCA officer found out about. Alano. Then this particular document came up. If nothing else, it'll give you a good insight to their mentality.'

Jon was scanning the room for any other important items. Car keys, on the coffee table by the window. 'Why?'

'This ancestor, the soldier, he was on board a ship called the *Concepción*.'

'*Concepción*: that was the name of the bloody ship! The one in the painting above Darragh's desk.'

'The guy's account ended up in the University of Galway and it's now been put online. There'll be computers with internet access at the airport.'

'OK, if there's time before my flight, I'll check it out.'

'Jon – it's worth it. You'll see why.'

'Got you. And Rick? Cheers for taking care of things.'

'Call me when you know what time you'll get in.'

'Will do.' He cut the connection and put the phone in his jacket. The other handset bumped against his fingers. Apart from that blood-chilling shriek, not a single call. Nothing from anyone – especially Siobhain. Nothing from her except a dodgy photo taken fuck-knows when.

He peeled back the curtain and looked down on the street. A couple were wandering out from Darragh's and he could hear the faint thud of music before the club's doors swung shut. This place, he thought. He lifted his gaze to the dark sky, conjuring his dead brother's face. Sorry our kid, but I tried. Honestly, I did my best. He surveyed the town's rooftops. Zoë, if you're here somewhere, I'm sorry. But right now? I've got my own family to protect.

The glow from the many lights dotted round the airport merged to form one big shimmering pool. An oasis in the night, Jon thought as he sped along the deserted road. The barriers were up and he drove into the near-empty car park and left the vehicle in a slot near the main entrance.

The terminal building was quiet: one lady behind the information desk and another raising the shutters of a little shop at the far end, the word Bewley's emblazoned across them. He turned to the Avis desk. No one there. A notice on the wall instructed him to drop any keys into the secure box directly below it. Jon slotted them in and wandered over to the departures board.

A 6.25 to Edinburgh. A 6.40 to London. A 7.10 to Birmingham. A 7.35 to Manchester. After that, nothing until the evening round of flights, including one at 7.50 to Manchester.

The clock at the bottom of the board read 4.45. Nearly three hours, he thought, checking his mobile yet again for any missed messages from Alice. Nothing. Surely she'd have passed a service station by now? Can I risk calling her? What if my calls really are being hacked? He put his mobile back down. She'll be driving anyway.

He flicked a glance over the arrivals board. A Manchester flight was due in at 6.45: probably the same plane making the return journey at 7.35. He approached the information desk and placed his hold all and little rucksack on the floor. 'Morning. What time does check-in open?'

'They should be here by 5.30 or so.'

'Any seats on the first flight to Manchester?'

'Let me see.' She tapped away at her keyboard. 'There are.'

'Great, I'll take one.'

Once everything was sorted, he turned round. What the hell do I do now? He needed something to keep his mind from dwelling on where Alice and Holly were. The café shop had a newspaper stand. A single copy of the previous day's Irish Independent was at the top. His gaze went to the nearby shelves. Souvenirs – tins of Irish fudge, knitwear and cuddly toys. He picked off a teddy bear and an oatmeal-coloured scarf. After buying the items along with the paper and a coffee, he sat down at a table. In the right-hand column of the front page was a report on the furore surrounding the murdered British soldier. He scanned the headline.

Investigation stalls, Stormont teeters

According to Sinn Féin, the lack of progress in finding the soldier's killers was due to the fragmented and inchoate nature of what remained of the dissident movement.

Unionist politicians were becoming increasingly vocal in their criticism of Sinn Féin's refusal to condemn the act outright. So far, a Sinn Féin spokesman had only expressed regret at the soldier's death before asserting that the act of an outlaw group shouldn't be allowed to derail the peace process.

A representative for the Democratic unionist Party said there was a fierce internal debate going on over whether they could still share power with an organisation that appeared unable to apologise for the atrocity.

Shaking his head, Jon flipped the paper over and tried to read the sport. He finished a page-worth's of articles with no idea of what he'd just read. His eyes went to his phone as a text came in. From Rick.

www.ucg.ie/celt/de-avila. Check it out.

May as well, Jon thought, if I can get on the internet. He walked into the shop where the woman was kneeling before a fridge, stacking it with cans. 'Can I use one of your computers, please? To go online.'

'Sure,' she replied without getting up. 'They're all ready to go.'

He moved his things to a corner table with a monitor. The homepage was crowded with all manner of advertisements. Tilting the screen of his phone, he typed in the address Rick had sent. A page with just a single result appeared. Jon clicked on it.

My time in Connacht by Francisco de Avila

Funded by the University of Galway and Higher

Education Authority via the CELT project

Translation by Richard Hallam

On the left-hand side of the screen were a couple of tabs. He selected 'Preamble'.

In the autumn of 1588, the remains of the Spanish Armada – having been chased from the Channel by the English fleet under Drake – attempted to return to Spain via the North Atlantic. A powerful series of storms drove the 130-strong fleet onto the west coast of Ireland.

Up to 24 Spanish ships, including several galleons, were wrecked on the unforgiving coastline. An estimated 5,000 Spaniards perished.

Twelve ships were wrecked on the coast of Connacht, the region that encompasses modern-day Connemara. Francisco de Avila was a soldier on board the Concepción of Biscay, an 18 gun vessel with 225 men. It was grounded at Carna, 30 km west of Galway Bay, having been lured to the shores by the bonfires of wreckers from the notorious O'Flaherty clan.

This account describes de Avila's extraordinary tale. The fact de Avila survived to write it was, as the author himself asserts, due only to his war-dog.

Jon's eyes froze. War-dog. Hutcher used that term for the Alanos that Spanish soldiers released during attacks on enemy forces. He went to the next tab, titled 'Text – Part 1.'

Since we sailed from Lisbon to England, I have passed through a great many hardships and misfortunes, from which our Lord, in his infinite kindness, delivered me.

What follows is the truth, by the holy baptism which I have received.

The galleon in which I sailed, the Concepción, had received great injury from many cannon balls. There were still holes through which water entered and no amount of pumping would dry her out. When we passed along the coast of Ireland, a ferocious storm sprang up on our beam with sea buckling to the heavens. Neither cables nor sails could save us. On the shore there was spotted fires and many of the gentlemen and scions of nobility on board demanded we sail for them.

Our Captain, Don Alonso, did yield to their wishes and so our fate was sealed for, to the sides of this shore, were rocks. Within a space of minutes, our ship was broken into pieces. Many I saw drowned, among them infantry, captains, ensigns, commanders and other war officials and noblemen. Those who reached the shore were first stripped then cut to pieces by the savages who waited there. One gallowglass warrior did walk into the shallows where he killed over twenty of my countrymen alone with his axe.

I regarded this solemn scene with my Alaunt, Pio, and I did not know what to do. Death was imminent by remaining on the battered ship, yet the shore was full of enemies who pranced and shrieked with delight at our misfortune.

It was then I saw the cover of a hatchway, the size of a table, that God saw fit to deliver to me. Supplicating Our Lady of Ontanar, I cast myself on to it and beckoned Pio to follow. There came wave after wave and soon we were carried to the shore. Chattering with cold and covered with blood, I emerged, hardly able to stand. A band of the savages approached. But, thanks to the

Most Holy Virgin, His Mother, I had Pio. When I ordered him forth, my dog did create such fear among them, the savages fled back to where their fellows were breaking open chests and whatever they might find. Using this opportunity the Lord had granted, I made off along the shore to some rushes where I was able to hide for the night with Pio for my warmth.

In the morning I ventured back and saw a sight of such grief and pity. Over one hundred dead bodies were being devoured on the sands by sea birds, crows and foxes. Of the Concepción, nothing remained. The sea continued to cast up dead bodies and I began to walk, shoeless and suffering great pain and hunger.

Jon's eyes went back to the mention of the dog. An Alaunt – the older name for what was now known as an Alano. He blinked. It seemed surreal to think the fearsome creatures were beginning to reappear. And the fact one had got so close to Holly…he shuddered. Devlan de Avila. The name burned in his mind's eye. *I owe you so much pain.*

He became aware of a presence by his side. The girl from the café shop.

'Did you want a refill? They're free.'

'Yes,' he replied, realising she was holding a glass pot in her hand. 'Thanks.'

As she walked away, he checked his mobile again then turned back to the screen.

I met a woman of many years, a rough savage. 'Spain?' she asked and I nodded my assent. She directed me to a monastery of monks some four leagues off who might offer me repair. With great toil I finally reached it but all that was inside were twelve of my countrymen hanging by their necks – an act by the Lutheran English who were, I soon learned, abroad on horses searching to make an end of any who had escaped.

I sallied forth into the trees. Later that day I encountered two young men going for plunder at the shore. Though I sought to circumvent them, they changed course towards me, one crying out, 'Yield, Spanish poltroon.' He drew his knife. For ever be His Most Holy Pity for I had Pio by my side. I bade him once more to attack and this time hold on to one of the savages so that I might take his clothes, shoes and knife for myself. I also extracted from him that, beyond the mountains ahead, were good lands of a savage chieftain called O'Rourke, an ally of the King of Spain.

I gave many thanks to God at this news and so I began my arduous walk to safety. Many times I left the road to hide from English horsemen as they rode by. The ground was most rough and often unable to hold any more moisture. If it were not for the fowl and other prey Pio was able to bring back, all there would have been to eat was berries and water cresses which could not have sustained me for the long journey.

Little by little, I continued travelling until, after many days, by the grace of our Lord, I met with a clergyman. He was dressed in savage's clothing, for this is how priests travel so the English should not recognise them. He spoke to me in Latin and, because God gave me grace, I was able to reply in the same tongue. He said he would deliver me to O'Rourke, a great enemy of the Queen of England and all her affairs.

Jon dragged his eyes from the screen and looked around. Tables, chairs, lights humming, fridges purring, ceiling vents sighing with warm air. Modern-day comforts: he shivered at the thought of how brutal life had been. His phone warbled and he snatched it up. Anonymous was showing on the screen. 'Hello,' Jon said cautiously, praying for Alice's voice.

'Have you left? Is it true?'

Siobhain, he thought. I should have fucking guessed.

CHAPTER 35

Jon placed his elbows on the table. 'What do you want?'

'Where are you?'

'The airport. My plane leaves at half-seven.'

'But…you can't go.'

'Siobhain, or whatever your name is, I've had enough. You've been no help whatsoever. I don't believe Zoë's even there.'

'You got the photo, right? She's here – it's where she lives.'

Jon thought about the image in his back pocket. 'That photo is probably years old. You know what I think? You gave it to me to keep your sad little game going for a bit longer.'

'I didn't! It's not a game. She's coming back – they sent her to Dublin on that delivery. But she'll be back. Later on, she will.'

Last time we spoke, Jon thought, you said she was too hurt to get out of bed. 'You're making this up as you go along. I can tell from your voice. I'm not fucking interested, all right?'

'You're just going to leave her here?'

'She's not fucking there, OK? Maybe she was once, but

she isn't now.'

'She is here.'

'And where, exactly, is here? It's half-five in the morning and I can hear music. You're in Darragh's, aren't you? Who saw me leaving? The guys on the door? Did they tell you I'd left?'

'What?'

Jon thought about the times he'd been in the club. The young customer – the flirty one who'd shot me the glances. The one who asked if I was chatting her up when handing out those posters. 'Are you the girl always hanging round in that place?'

'Which girl? I've got to go – '

'It is, isn't it?' He heard a click and the line went dead. 'Typical,' he muttered. 'Pissing me about, as usual.'

***

'Hazel!'

She stuffed the phone back into the pocket of her skirt.

'Hazel! What are you up to?'

She turned her head. 'Sorting out a nail.' The chair swivelled round as Darragh de Avila looked through the doorway into the nightclub's office.

'In my fucking seat, too! You can do that later, people are wanting drinks through here.'

Christ, that was close, she said to herself. She thought of Jon in Galway airport. He can't go now. She examined the edge of her lilac-coloured thumbnail. 'There. Done.' Brushing a strand of dyed-blonde hair from her face, she stood. 'Are we not closing soon?'

Darragh shook his head. 'These boys? They'll drink right through – probably go straight from here to the fight at the farm.'

She placed her hands on her hips. 'That's great. Devlan's going to get home and I'll be asleep on my feet.'

'If you want a little sniff to pep you up, there's some in

the top drawer.'

'Really?' Her eyes lowered to the desk. 'I can?'

'Just make it quick – it's elbow-to-elbow at the bar and I don't need you wandering back in spangled.'

Jon made sure no message had been left while he'd been speaking to Siobhain, then put his phone on the table. He shook his head. That woman is playing me. Fuck knows what she's trying to prove, but that's what she's doing. Next time she rings, I'll just hang up. He glanced about and realised the lights above the check-in desks were now on. Two women wearing white blouses and mauve neck-scarves were sitting there. He glanced down at his holdall. May as well get rid of it now, before the place starts getting busy.

As he crossed the shiny floor, he went over what he'd read. If the de Avilas were really descended from the author of that account, the family's foothold in Ireland had been hard won. Rick was right, it gave an insight into how they viewed the world. He wondered if Francisco made it to the land under O'Rourke's control. The chieftain would probably have welcomed a trained soldier like the Spaniard into his ranks. After all, he also had the dog – and what a weapon that was.

'Morning,' the woman behind the desk smiled. 'Just the one item?'

A few minutes later, Jon resumed his seat. A fresh mug of coffee stood by the mouse mat. Jesus, he thought, nodding his thanks. I'll be ricocheting off the ceiling at this rate. Taking a sip, he turned his eyes to the screen.

Finally, we met with a great lake at the far end of which was a castle. I could see it would be very difficult to take – artillery could not be brought to bear on its walls on account of the marshy terrain.

We arrived at the door to be told the chief was gone to defend a territory from the Lutherans. Though he is a

savage, he is a Christian and sworn enemy of the English heretics, carrying war to them whenever he can.

The Lord, in His infinite pleasure, had already delivered to the castle over twenty of my countrymen, each one a good fellow. They told me all survivors from our fleet were being delivered to the Governor of Connacht who was hanging them at once and people who had sheltered them were being placed in prison where he did them all the injury he could.

The chief inclination of the castle's inhabitants seems to be plunder and war. Whenever the heretics sally forth from their garrisons, the fight with them is immediate. The English have demolished the great majority of their churches, monasteries and hermitages, assisted by natives of the land who are as bad as they.

In turn, the inhabitants of the castle plunder the villages of these savages, if they become aware they do have cattle or other effects worth taking. No day seems to go by without a call to arms passing among them.

The men clothe themselves in blankets and wear their hair down to their eyes. Of Pio, their fascination knows no bounds. He will not let any close, so they sit for great lengths and study the animal, whispering all the while.

After more days passed, the chieftain O'Rourke returned. He is a gentleman and most sturdy soldier. After Mass was said among them, in accordance to the orders of the Church of Rome, he did tell us that a great force from the Governor was coming against him and he intended to fly for the mountains.

I bade him to allow me to talk with my fellow countrymen. We considered our past misfortunes and, in order to not see ourselves suffer more injuries and insults, thought it better to make an honourable end of it here by defending the castle to the death.

The chief, failing in his efforts to dissuade us, lay down provisions and arms for our use, including muskets, arquebuses, cross-bows and other weaponry, before departing with his people. The enemy came in sight the next day, their number greater than one thousand. From across the marshes they observed us but could not get their guns closer. The Governor demanded by trumpet many times that we should surrender the castle so he might pass us back to Spain. This we knew to be the lies of a Lutheran heretic.

Jon was vaguely aware of a series of notes ringing out above his head. A female voice announced that anyone on the 6.25 to Edinburgh and 6.40 to London could proceed to the departure gate. His attention went back to the monitor.

When night came upon us, we knew the heretics would attack. I ventured out with Pio and he soon detected the sound of the English approaching. Their cries of terror when he attacked from the dark! I heard the splash of men as they fled the narrow tracks to become ensnared in the breast-high marsh. His Divine Majesty then pleased us with moonlight and we were able with cross-bows to finish the men where they floundered.

We were besieged for seven more nights and each one Pio returned to me with the blood of heretics on his jaws. Soon they sallied forth no more, and when our Lord saw fit to deliver us severe storms and falls of snow, the Governor was compelled to march his force back to Galway.

Jon sat back, thoughts whirling in his head. The de Avilas had surely read this. No wonder Devlan wanted an Alano so badly. That dog saved his ancestor's life again and again. Jon imagined the delight Devlan must have felt when he realised the breed hadn't died out. He'd have sold his grandma to get hold of one.

The terminal now rang with the sound of footsteps and people's voices. Several men in suits were making their way to the doorway on the other side of the seating area. Leaning forward again, Jon read the last section of the story.

When the chieftain O'Rourke received news the English had retired, he returned and did fête us greatly. To me he gave a sister of his, asking that I marry her. My fellow countrymen chose to make the journey north in order to place themselves in the care of the Bishop of Derry who had offered us passage to the Hebrides and the safety of Scotland. From there it would be possible to journey back home. I reflected that, despite their rough ways, these people were Christian and of such remarkable spirit. Moreover, Spain did not hold much for me, since God had not yet granted me the blessing of a wife. So, I took up the chief's offer with the request that, when circumstances should permit, I would lead a force of men back to the site of where the Concepción was wrecked. There, if God was pleased to allow it, I would revenge the lives of my countrymen cruelly taken by the savages of that place. This account I have wished to write to you.

Signed Francisco de Avila, 19 October, 1589, the region that is Connacht

Jon recalled the sight of the fearsome creature in his local park. I bet Devlan bloody loved that – setting his Alano on the family of a hated Englishmen. And a policeman at that.

He glanced at his watch yet again; the need to ring Alice was so strong it made him squirm. She should have found a service station to call me from by now, surely? He dragged air deep into his lungs in an attempt to stay calm. It was now nearly six in the morning. Plenty of time for Rick to have got to Center Parcs. He selected his colleague's number. 'Where are you, mate?'

'I'm here. I was about to call.' There were people speaking quietly in the background.

'You're at their lodge?'

'Yes.'

'Alice hasn't rung me yet. She was meant to ring me.'

'You told her to get on the motorway and keep driving.'

'I know but…fuck, this is…' He bowed his head. 'What's the score there?'

'I don't like the look of it. You know what bothers me most? That toy dog.'

'Had its head been ripped off?'

'Yes.'

'They tried to kill my wife and daughter!'

'Listen, to me –

'Rick, they tried to kill them!

'Jon, get a grip. Listen to me, I'm calling Alice and Holly. Then I'm taking them somewhere safe.'

'Where will you take them?'

'I'm not saying where. I can't risk telling you – not on your phone. Do you understand?'

Jon sank down in his seat. 'Just make sure they're safe, Rick. Until I get back? Please.'

'Don't worry. I'm heading to my car right now.'

'Rick, I need to speak to them. I need to know they're OK.'

'When we meet, I'll ring you, OK? From a payphone. You have that one call.'

CHAPTER 36

Time dragged so slowly, Jon couldn't say how long it took for his phone to finally beep. A text from Rick.

Alice and Holly with me. Will ring once sure not being followed.

He sat back and let his arms slip off the table. They're safe, he thought, head tilting back. Oh thank God, they're safe.

The tannoy announced the imminent arrival of the Manchester flight. My plane, he thought. Once the thing's been turned around, I'm going back home.

The airport was now in full swing. A man was unlocking the door to the Avis office. Jon was just thinking he should check there was nothing owing on his hire car when his phone rang. Anxiously, he looked at the screen. Anonymous. This better bloody not be Siobhain again. 'Hello?'

'Is that Detective Inspector Spicer?'

The voice was southern Irish and he could hear other people talking in the background. 'It is.'

'Detective, this is Martin O'Donagh from the ISPCA. A colleague asked that I call you about an operation we're conducting today.'

The raid on the de Avila farm, Jon thought. I'd forgotten all about it. He sat up. A row of payphones were to his left. 'Martin, give me your number and I'll call you back.'

The ISPCA officer answered on the first ring. 'DI Spicer?'

'Yeah. It's going ahead then?'

'It is – we've been looking to catch these guys for many years.'

'When's it happening?'

'The first fights are due to take place later this morning. We'll wait until everyone is there and then go in. Rendezvous point is the Garda station at Maam Cross, on the N59. It's about halfway between Galway and Clifden.'

'That leaves you a long drive in.'

'We daren't be any closer – in case word gets to them before we arrive. It's happened several times before.'

'Really? You know this lot, then?'

'Clochán kennels? They don't get much bigger. The Manchester United of the dog-fighting world. We believe it's where many of the pit bulls being fought in your country have come from. If we get a result, Detective, you'll have to come back to Galway for the celebration. You'll not buy a drink all night.'

'Thanks for the offer, but I only passed the message on. Do you know who the main players are?'

'The de Avila son. Fellow called Devlan – he's the one with a passion for dog-fighting. A guy from Belfast seems to be his right-hand man, though we're not sure of his name. Maybe, just maybe, we'll be able to charge Devlan with something after today.'

'I doubt it, the bloke's over in England.'

'He's still there?'

'I'm fairly certain. That's why I'm heading back – '

'You're not coming along?'

Jon sighed. 'Believe me, I wish I could. How many

have you got for the raid?'

'There's twelve of us from the ISPCA and seven Guards. We're hoping for at least another eight Guards from the station in Clifden. Someone's putting a call in now to confirm numbers.'

'Can I ring you back later to see how it went?'

'Of course.'

'Good luck, then.' After hanging up, he glanced through the plate glass separating him from the departure lounge. Passengers were filing out to a small plane waiting on the tarmac. Night had now almost faded and on the runway beyond, the same type of plane that he'd flown in on from Manchester was taxiing towards a man waving a pair of glowing batons.

This is it, Jon thought. Just a bit longer and I'll be on a flight. Back to my family. Home. Manchester. A city I know inside out. And Devlan de Avila? The guy will wish he never ventured out of his little town.

His phone rang and his eyes shot to the screen. Anonymous again. 'Hello?'

'It's me, mate. I'm calling from a payphone.'

Rick, Jon thought. 'Are they...'

'Right here, next to me.'

He felt his chest heave. Rick, he thought, I could pick you up and bloody kiss you. 'You don't know how incredible it feels to hear that.'

'Once the pips go, that's it. We're going somewhere secure.'

'I understand. Can you put Alice on?'

A brief pause. 'Jon?'

'Alice.'

'We're safe, Jon. Do you hear?'

He was grinning stupidly. 'I do.'

'Daddy?' Holly's voice, in the background.

He wiped the tears from his eyes. 'Sweetie, can you hear me?'

'Yes! Uncle Rick is taking us on a secret adventure.'

'You be good, OK? I'll be there soon.'

'I will. Bye, Daddy!' A bumping noise as the receiver was handed over.

'Jon?' Her voice was low. 'Rick's not saying much. What's happening? Was it…had someone been in our lodge?'

'We don't know – '

'Then why all this business with the payphone? I mean, fucking hell, Jon.'

'I'll be there soon. My flight leaves in – '

'If that lad didn't try the wrong door, we might never have woken up,' she whispered. 'And what if I'd turned a light on? If I'd known where the switch was…'

Jon rested his head on his free hand. 'We know exactly who did this. He will not get away with it. Trust me, I won't let that happen.'

'Find him, Jon. Find him and do whatever you have to do. Make sure he never – ever – comes near us again.'

He felt an uncoiling in his breast. Like a whole new part of his heart had suddenly kicked into life, pumping him full of blood. His voice felt hoarse. 'I will.'

A rapid series of pips. Money's run out, Jon thought. We're about to be cut off.

'Don't worry about us,' Alice stated. 'We're fine. We're with Rick, we're safe. Find him, Jon. Do you hear me? Find that piece of – '

The line went silent. As Jon sat down, the doors of the arrivals hall slid apart. At the front of the queue was a man who could only have been Darragh de Avila's brother. The basic face-shape was the same, but sunken cheeks and a harsh jaw eradicated any hint of the childish appearance Darragh possessed. In its place was the whisper of cruelty. Hair was shorn, eyes narrow as they fixed on the official checking passports. Jon guessed he was a good three inches taller than the nightclub owner and more heavily built, too. But it was the unbalanced bulk from lifting weights: too much time spent on his upper body.

Jon hardly dared breathe. It was like observing a wild animal he didn't want to spook. *This is the fucker who tried to kill my family.*

The official handed back his passport and Devlan stepped into the main terminal and turned his back.

Jon watched as another man emerged. The driver of the van. *Jesus Christ, it's the driver of the van!* He started patting the pockets of his jacket, searching for his warrant card. Rucksack. He leaned down, grabbed it and started struggling with the front zip. *What am I doing? I have no power here. Warrant card's useless.* Sliding it into his jacket, he raised his head. Relaxed and confident, the two men were now strolling for the exit doors.

Jon got to his feet and set off at an angle. Their paths would cross at the main entrance. A family with a couple of luggage trolleys cut across him. Jon banged into one, toppling their stacked bags to the floor. Not taking his eyes off the two men, he tried to step over a holdall, his foot getting caught up in one of the looped handles.

'Would you mind where you're stepping?' the woman demanded angrily, looking to her husband for support.

By the time he'd extricated his foot, the pair were almost out of the terminal. Jon skirted round the mess, oblivious to the family's incredulous stares. He was now ten metres from the doors. The two men were climbing into a waiting vehicle.

Starting to jog, he reached the Land Rover just as the rear passenger door slammed shut. Denis was driving: the man from the pet-food factory. They were exchanging greetings as Jon bent forward and rapped his knuckles against the window.

All three heads turned. He watched as the smile fell from Devlan's face. Then the man's upper lip peeled back to expose crooked teeth, bases stained brown with nicotine. A hand shot to the side as he made a grab for the door. Jon smiled. *Come on then.* He shook his arms at his sides. *Out you get.*

The other man on the rear passenger seat reached over and clamped a hand across Devlan's forearm. Something was said and Devlan tried to shake his arm free. Refusing to let go, the other man spoke at Denis. The Land Rover's engine revved. Jon leaped forward, fingers narrowly missing the handle of the door as the vehicle set off, tyres yelping. Through the Perspex flaps making up its rear windows, Jon saw Devlan turn. The man raised a hand, two fingers outstretched as his thumb mimed pulling a trigger.

Jon sprinted after the vehicle but it was accelerating away too fast. Nostrils flaring in and out, he watched it race away. Gradually, his pulse slowed. Alice's words came back to him. Do what you have to do. This, he realised, is my chance. Both brothers are now here.

He turned on his heel, strode back into the terminal and examined the departures board. There it was - the later flight to Manchester. Departing at 7.50 tonight. That gives me twelve hours.

The woman behind the information desk was speaking into her microphone. 'Would all passengers on the seven-thirty flight to Manchester please proceed through to the departure lounge with your boarding cards ready.'

Another half hour, he thought, and I could have been on my way home. He hitched his rucksack over his shoulder. 'I need to catch the evening flight.'

She looked mildly irritated. 'You're booked on the Manchester flight?'

'Yes. Can I transfer to the later one?'

Her lips thinned as she began tapping on her keyboard. 'I'm afraid your carrier makes a surcharge for that. Twenty euro.'

'No problem.'

'Then if I could have your boarding pass and ticket.'

He handed them over along with a twenty-euro note. 'Oh, and I'll need the holdall that I checked in earlier.'

She studied her screen. 'It's already been loaded, Mr

Spicer.'

'Surely it won't take two minutes for someone to rummage around for it? How many bags are there?'

'The flight is almost full. Plus there's the commercial freight.'

Jon glanced at the last people heading through the gate into the departures lounge. An elderly couple. A young woman carrying a baby, husband with a change bag hanging from his shoulder. 'You're saying it will cause a delay?'

'You checked in first thing didn't you?'

He nodded.

'Then your bag will have been among the first items on board. They'll have to empty the entire hold to get to it…'

Jon weighed things up. The Asp, he thought, is inside. Along with the body armour and pepper spray. Everything I need for that head-case Devlan.

'It will be no problem to have it put aside at the arrivals desk in Manchester.'

People were congregating near the gate out onto the runway. He imagined all their travel plans. Relatives waiting, connecting flights and onward train journeys already booked.

'Sir, I need to announce the flight is ready for boarding. Will you collect your bag at Manchester?'

'Fine, I'll pick it up tonight.'

She leaned to her side. 'Flight AE731 to Manchester is now ready to board. Will all passengers proceed immediately to gate number one, thank you.' She took her finger off the microphone button. 'Thank you,' she smiled.

PART III

CHAPTER 37

As Jon steered his new hire car through the series of roundabouts leading towards the River Corrib, he thought about what the ISPCA officer had said when he'd rung him back.

'We're setting off any minute,' the man had replied. 'Going via Clifden station where another eight Guards are waiting to join us.'

'OK, I'm about to set off from the airport.'

'You'll have to catch us up at the de Avila's farm, we can't wait.'

Jon raced along the N59. As the stretches of water bordering the road closed in, he wondered about Devlan's accomplice – the one who'd been driving the van in Manchester. There's something about him.

The junction with the R336 appeared and Jon realised he'd reached Maam Cross. His mobile rang: DCI Parks's name on the screen. That's it, he thought. She's on to me. I can kiss goodbye to my job in the MIT. Probably my whole bloody career. He let the call go through to his answerphone, thinking about his old colleague, Maccer. The one who'd ended up working as a debt collector.

***

The thudding bass had died down at dawn. Now a more relaxed beat permeated through the nightclub into the back office.

Wearing a black cashmere jumper, black pleated trousers and black brogues, Gerrard de Avila stood in the centre of the room, staring at Devlan with a stony face. In the corner of the room Sean Doyle sat next to Conor Barry and the driver of the Land Rover. All three men were keeping their eyes firmly on the floor.

Darragh de Avila was sitting behind his desk, arms crossed, eyes moving uneasily between his brother and father. In the far corner, the barmaid with the dyed blonde hair was preparing drinks.

Devlan dragged on his cigarette, pushed a foot out and brushed ash from the leg of his combat trousers. 'He's gone, hasn't he? Back to fucking England, like.'

Gerrard raised a meaty finger and when he spoke, the rumble coming from deep in his chest. 'I did not give those orders.'

Raising both palms, Devlan said, 'I know, Da. I should have asked – '

'You don't ask, you do,' the old man roared. 'That's the way it works. Turning the fucking gas on. How do you know they're not dead?'

'We opened a window, didn't we, Dev?' Sean interjected.

Devlan started searching for more ash on his trousers as Gerrard turned on Sean. 'And you? What did I tell you to do?'

'Not let him do anything stupid,' Sean mumbled.

Devlan's eyes flashed at the comment. Behind his desk, Darragh shifted uncomfortably in his seat.

'Not let him do anything stupid,' Gerrard repeated. 'Jesus, if you can't do what you're asked, is there any point paying you a wage? Is there any point to you at all?'

Sean Doyle studied his palms. 'Sorry. We were both, you know – he was trying to provoke – '

'At least he's gone,' Darragh said quietly.

Gerrard's head swung in the direction of his other son.

'We've got a club full of punters,' Darragh continued. 'Your men from whatever Stan it is are in the corner enjoying free champagne. Everything's set at the farm. And the English peeler is out of our hair.' He briefly lifted his shoulders. 'Dad, it could be worse.'

'Could it now?' Gerrard asked sarcastically. 'Could it be worse?'

Darragh looked unsure. 'Well…'

'The fucking security tape,' Gerrard bellowed. 'What about that? Didn't think of that, did you?' He shot a furious glance at Devlan. 'Either of you.'

'He hasn't used it yet, Dad,' Darragh eventually replied. 'Maybe he slung it and we needn't worry.'

'Maybe,' Gerrard muttered. 'But I don't like the idea of it being out there.'

'Let's get this fight over,' Darragh replied. 'We can catch up on this peeler later.'

The old man remained motionless. No one spoke. Finally, he grunted. 'Anything else like that.' He jabbed a finger at Devlan. 'Understand?'

Devlan nodded eagerly. 'Sure, Dad. I'm sorry.'

The old man turned to the corner where the driver of the Land Rover sat. 'Denis, everything's ready?'

Behind him, Darragh raised his eyebrows at Devlan. His twin winked back and then looked away.

'It is,' the ginger-haired man replied.

'How's Cuchullain?' Sean asked, sitting up.

The ginger-haired man grinned. 'Peak condition. A Tasmanian Devil on a lead is what he is. The bite on the thing – the crushing power.'

'Has he seen any action this last week?'

'Aye, one of the old pit bulls.'

'Which one?'

'Nipper.'

Sean flicked a hand, indicating the animal was surplus

to needs 'Was he game, like?'

'Aye, he was game all right. But Cuchullain wrecked him, so he did. Got in underneath and fucking wrecked him.'

Devlan slapped a fist into his palm.

'Hold your horses!' Gerrard said, a smile playing at his lips as he patted the air with both palms. 'Save it for the farm.' He noticed the tray of drinks being held out to him. 'That's grand, Hazel.'

Gerrard was about to propose a toast when the phone on the desk rang. He gave Darragh a nod.

'Hello,' the nightclub owner said.

Sean began to ask Denis another question, but Darragh chopped at the air with his free hand. 'When? Right now? How many? OK.' He replaced the phone and looked at his father. 'They're raiding the farm.'

The old man lowered his glass. 'When?'

'As soon as the ISPCA arrive. That was Patrick at the station. Eight of them are waiting to join a group who are due from Maam Cross any minute.'

The old man placed his glass on the desk. 'Clear everything.' He clicked a finger at Denis. 'Call to the farm. Have Liam take the pit down. How many dogs have we there?'

'Six.'

'And the Bone Yard's animals?'

'Them too.'

'Tell those boys to get their dogs away.'

Darragh placed his elbows on the desk and cupped a hand to each side of his head. 'We've got people from all over. Four flew in from Liverpool yesterday. Campbell is down from Belfast – '

'I know,' Gerrard snarled. 'We'll have to tell them another time.'

Darragh lifted his face. 'The Turkmen or whatever they're called.'

Gerrard's neck was puce.

'Where's Cuchullain?' Sean asked.

'At the farm, too,' Denis replied. 'In a pen at the back.'

'They're not finding Cuchullain,' Devlan announced. 'I'm taking him.'

'Where to?' Gerrard asked.

Devlan thought for a second. 'Mum's place at Lough Nakilla? The stables, Da. Or the sheds by the boathouse.'

'Think, son. Information is getting out somehow.' He surveyed the room, eyes blazing. 'Tuck him further away than that. Somewhere well out of the road.' He gave his son a meaningful look.

Devlan raised the corner of his mouth. 'Got you, Da. I know a good spot.' Then he, too, examined everyone else's faces, suspicion making his eyes beady.

'Ach, come on,' Denis protested. 'There's no need to be acting like that.'

'Why?' Devlan sneered. 'Someone who knows our business is whispering.'

Darragh coughed. 'Patrick said word about the fight came from the British police officer.'

'Spicer?' Devlan demanded.

'Patrick says it was.'

Devlan spat on the floor. 'I am going to kill that fucking man.'

CHAPTER 38

Jon dropped his speed as the Garda station came into view. The car park was virtually empty. The raid's started, he thought, lifting his foot off the brake. He followed the road towards Letterfrack. The turn off for Golden Fields soon appeared on his right.

He turned into the narrow lane and saw it was congested with parked vehicles – including two Garda vans. Both were empty, no sign of anything – dogs or people – locked up inside. Parking behind a squad car, he climbed out of the Peugeot, warrant card held out to the group of watching police officers. He recognised the one who'd been on the desk at Clifden's station. 'Patrick, isn't it?'

The young police officer seemed momentarily lost for words. 'It is. Detective Inspector…'

'Spicer,' Jon nodded, returning his warrant card to the inner pocket of his jacket. 'Have you got Devlan?'

The officer's mouth opened and closed. 'Devlan? No.'

Jon cursed. 'Is Martin O'Donagh about?'

'That's me.'

The voice came from near one of the vans. Jon turned to see a man of about thirty with curly blonde hair approaching. 'From your accent and height, I thought it might be you.'

Jon held his hand out. 'Any luck? Did you arrest any of the de Avilas?'

As they shook, the ISPCA inspector nodded at the open doors of the vans. 'They knew we were coming – everything's been cleared, though only just.'

Right, Jon thought. That means the shit's really hit the fan. 'How can you tell?'

'Fresh dog faeces in a shed area at the back. Plus recent scratches in the wood partitions.' He shook his head, walking along the grass verge until they were out of the police officers' earshot. 'They've got someone in their pocket, no doubt about it.'

'Seems so,' Jon replied.

'And I'd say from how close we came, he's based here in Clifden. Apart from a couple of senior ranking officers, no one in this town knew the raid was taking place until an hour or so ago.'

A muddy four-wheel drive pulled in off the main road, the rear compartment taken up by a large wire cage.

Martin O'Donagh made sure the ISPCA tag hanging round his neck was visible as he approached the driver's window. 'Looking for the fight? Did no one tell you it's cancelled?'

The man was thickset, a sparse covering of hair on his bullet-like head. 'What fight?' he asked.

O'Donagh stepped round to the rear of the vehicle where a white pit bull with brown patches round its eyes stared back. 'Lost your way?' he called out.

The driver addressed O'Donagh's reflection in his side-view mirror as he backed the vehicle onto the verge. 'Just looking for a nice spot to walk my dog.'

'That so?' O'Donagh smiled, taking out a pad and pen. He noted the van's registration. 'And you've driven all the way up from County Clare just for that?'

The man didn't reply as he put the four-wheel drive

into first.

O'Donagh gestured with his chin to the main road. 'On your way. There's nothing happening here.'

The man glanced to his side. 'Yeah? Fuck you.'

The jeep roared back towards the junction. 'Latecomer to the party,' Jon stated.

'Shows how close we were,' O'Donagh replied wearily.

Jon glanced towards the farm entrance. 'Any sign of the de Avila family? The son you mentioned, Devlan?'

'None. Never bloody is. They'll be racing all round the county, hiding dogs as they go.'

'You reckon?'

'That or they're perched on their arses in Clifden getting pissed.'

That option suits me fine, Jon thought, turning to the hire car. 'Listen, I'm heading back to Clifden. I have to speak to the de Avila brothers.'

The ISPCA officer looked startled. 'They won't be in the mood for chatting.'

Jon nodded. Neither am I.

Back on the N59, he contemplated where to go first. Would Darragh's still be open? He remembered Siobhain's last call to him at the airport. Zoë was, she'd claimed, on her way back from Dublin, having made a delivery of DVDs. The lock-up by the pony auction place, he decided. Let's see if there's any sign of them there.

Gerrard de Avila flicked a finger. Darragh vacated his chair behind the desk and his father sank into it. 'Another drink here, Hazel.'

She immediately went to the cabinet in the corner.

The old man laced his fingers across his stomach as his bottom lip pushed out. Silently, he contemplated the backs of his hands. 'This tan. The English policeman. He knew about the unit making DVDs. He knew about the farm and he knew about the fight.' His eyebrows lifted. 'I wonder what else he knows?'

Now perched on the corner of the desk, Darragh turned his head. 'How many of us knew the when and where of the fight?'

Gerrard's gaze stayed lowered. 'Not many.'

Hazel held up a bottle of whiskey. 'Darragh?'

He shook his head. She looked over to the far corner. 'Sean?'

Sean held up a thumb.

Gerrard's chin came up, ridges of skin bulging at the back of his neck. He looked at the monitors showing the inside of the club. Some people were still at the tables, drinking and chatting. Others were getting to their feet and heading for the doors. 'This is making us look weak. People are going to start taking us for arseholes.' He turned to Darragh. 'What information do we have on this policeman?'

Darragh ran a hand over his mouth. 'Apart from his home address?'

Gerrard inclined his head. 'Apart from that.'

'We know his parents live in Sale, on the edge of Manchester. He has a younger sister lives in a flat in Chorlton. But Dad, we need to consider things here.'

'Consider? We've been considering enough, son. That's the problem. The time for considering has passed. I think your brother had the right idea with the gas – we need to start doing the business to this arrogant English cunt.'

'Dad – everything we've been working for; it's all been carefully planned. The business we've built, the investments we've made – '

'Like buying all those properties?' Gerrard scowled. 'Would you be meaning those things now draining us fucking dry? Aye, I'm glad I took your advice on investing.'

Darragh's face reddened. 'No one could have predicted the way the market went. We're not the only people caught out.'

Gerrard waved a hand. 'I don't want to hear anything more about it. We should have kept to what we knew.

Even Devlan's plans to breed those Alanos have more potential than your fancy ideas.'

The phone on the desk started to ring. Gerrard kept his eyes on Darragh as his son picked up the receiver. 'Hello. Patrick? What's that?'

The room watched as Darragh's face slowly drained of colour.

'You're sure? Here? Coming to Clifden? OK.' He hung up, eyes staying on the phone.

'Something to share with us, son?' Gerrard growled.

'He's here,' Darragh whispered.

The old man tilted his head. 'Who?'

Darragh swallowed and when he spoke there was a tremor in his voice. 'Spicer. Patrick said he turned up at the farm looking for Devlan. He just set off from there, driving towards Clifden.'

A soft clap filled the room as Gerrard brought his palms together. 'Sean, did you not used to snatch folk off the streets up in Belfast?'

Sean nodded.

'Get who you need, find this fucker and take him somewhere nice and quiet. Time we found out where this boy is getting his information from. After that, we can all have some fun with him.'

Darragh straightened up. 'Dad, hold on. We need to think this through – '

'I have!'

'You want to try and take him now, in the centre of town? There are Guards everywhere.'

Gerrard was out of his seat with surprising speed. The flat of his palm cracked against the back of Darragh's head. The younger man's glasses flew off and he stumbled forward. 'The next person to question me will sorely regret it!'

Darragh reached down for his glasses as Gerrard raised his other hand in Sean's direction. 'Why are you still fucking here? Get me that man.'

As soon as Sean was outside, he slammed the rear doors behind him and started to pace back and forth. Christ, he thought. They'll kill him. His mind raced forward. A murdered British policeman. It would fuck everything up. Realising he was in view of the security camera, he moved round the corner and reached for his phone. 'It's Sean. Yeah, I'm fine. Listen mate, this is really urgent. Have you a number for Molloy? Yeah, it's trouble. Serious trouble. OK.' He waited a few seconds. 'Got it. Catch you later.' Mouthing the sequence of numbers, he pressed them into his handset. 'Brendan? It's Sean Doyle. I know, I know, too long. Yeah, in Clifden still. And you – still with the party, aren't you? Office in Stormont now? Sounds plush. Can I talk freely? OK – there's a peeler here, from England. He's going after the family I work for. The de Avilas, yes. He won't give up and it's starting to go fucking haywire. I've no problem seeing an English peeler suffer, believe me – especially this cocky fucker. But Gerrard de Avila has just lost it. I mean really lost it. We're going to end up with a body here. This thing needs bringing under control.'

CHAPTER 39

Jon passed the Garda station for the second time. The forecourt was still practically empty. All out at the farm, he realised, reaching the site where the pony auction had taken place. He turned the Peugeot round and parked.

Opening the door let in a gust of cold air. Specks of snowflakes were being carried on the breeze. The dark grey cloud layer above seemed to be bulging downward. Jon hooked his rucksack over his shoulder, stepped through the half-open gate on the right and started across concrete still spattered with bits of manure. Most of the industrial units were closed. As he made his way to the far end, the wind caused something to clang softly against the railings in the empty pony stalls.

There was no vehicle outside DA Services and a heavy padlock secured the door. Damn, Jon thought, feeling tiny spots of cold as snowflakes made contact with the back of his neck. She's not here. I doubt she ever was. He walked along a couple of units to Frank Ryan Kitchens. Inside, he could see a grey-haired man bent over a table covered with boxes. He knocked on the door and stood back.

The man approached the door, a screwdriver still in his hand. It opened inwards and he beckoned to Jon. 'Come in out of the cold.'

Jon rubbed his hands together and glanced to his left. 'I was wondering, have you seen anyone at DA Services today?'

The man's eyes narrowed. 'You're the English guy that's been pinning up the posters?'

'Have you seen her? Has she ever been there?'

'No. Not her.'

'But you have seen other people coming and going?'

He gave a cautious nod.

'Members of the de Avila family?'

'Listen, they're a bad lot, that crowd. Best left well alone.'

'How often do they load up deliveries from here?'

'I said, they're best left well alone.' He retreated a step.

'Once, twice a week?'

'Sorry, I've work to do.'

The man's too scared to say anything more, Jon thought. Much like the rest of this town. 'OK, thanks.'

He set off for where his car was parked, step slowing as he came round the corner of the pony auction office. A white van was parked sideways across the gateway, rear doors open, engine idling. Cautiously, Jon continued forward, looking for any sign of the driver.

Movement to his left. Jon turned to see two men walking towards him. For a moment he almost laughed, thinking it was a joke. Both had tights pulled down over their faces, features distorted under the tight layer of fabric. One was a shade under six feet, solidly built, nose squashed to the side. The other was much larger and heavily muscled. Beneath the nylon mask, a mop of black hair was pressing down over his forehead. That's the monster from outside the night club, Jon realised. He was about to say something when he spotted the metal bar in the big guy's hand.

Hey up, he thought. These guys aren't fucking around. He turned towards them and planted his feet a little wider apart. 'Where's Devlan?'

'Waiting to see you,' the shorter one replied. 'Into the back of the van and we can take you for a wee chat.'

Glancing quickly at the van's rear doors, he saw the corner of some plastic sheeting hanging over the footplate. There's no way they're getting me in there, he thought. 'Fuck off. I decide where we meet.'

'In the van,' the man repeated, splitting away from his companion.

Jon judged the distances. I could run at the right shoulder of the one with the crowbar. He'd have to check his step to try and bring the weapon up. Time enough to land a punch on him. If he goes down, it's me and the mate, one-on-one. Except my right hand's fucked.

They were now less than ten metres away, closing on him in a pincer movement.

Jon considered the rucksack hanging from his shoulder. No Asp, no pepper spray, no body armour. Nothing of any fucking use at all. And Devlan's not even here. Time to run. He spun on his heel and sprinted for the small gap between the van's rear doors and the metal gate.

'Go!'

The word was barked behind him. Footsteps as they started giving chase. He reached the van's rear doors and was angling his body to dart through the gap when a blur entered the periphery of his vision. His world lit up and he heard a crashing sound. Staggering back, he realised the noise had been caused by him careering into the metal gate. A figure emerged from the whorls of colour filling his vision. Through the tights stretched across his face, Jon could see the person's nose was heavily plastered. Conor Barry. In his hand was a wooden stick with a flattened end.

The nightclub bouncer grinned and his voice seemed to be coming from the other end of a long windy tunnel. 'Bet you've never had a hurley bat wrapped round your head before.'

The footsteps behind him came to an abrupt halt and

an impact flung his right leg from under him. The crowbar, Jon thought, feeling his left leg begin to buckle. He turned, saw a fist from the shorter of the two men flying directly at his face. Boom, his head snapped back. Do not go down. Whatever you do, stay on your feet. He got a hand to the ground and fought to keep his balance. Conor Barry had turned the wooden stick round – he drove the handle end of it at Jon's chest. Before it could connect, Jon got a hand up and clamped his fingers around the wood. Barry tried to yank it back and Jon used the motion to regain his feet. Spikes of pain tore through his knee as it took his weight. Allowing himself to be carried forward, he pulled hard on the stick, reaching out with his free hand to hook his fingers into the other man's face. His right leg was smashed from under him again. This time both knees connected with the concrete. Still keeping hold of the stick, he searched for the bouncer's eyes with his other hand.

'Get the fucker off of me!'

A crack to the side of his temple. His vision dissolved into a kaleidoscope of colours and a second later his brain registered a heavier impact. The ground? Is that the ground I can feel against my face? I have to get up.

Legs braced in a boxer's stance, Sean Doyle watched the peeler topple to his side, face slapping against the shit-covered concrete. Even though the guy's eyes were rolled back in his head, his arms immediately started moving, palms flattening as he tried to raise himself up. Sean brought his fist back in readiness to drive it into the side of the bloke's head once again.

Next to him, Liam swung the crowbar down into the bloke's ribs and the peeler's torso shifted a good six inches across the ground.

'Get away from him, you bloody animals!'

Sean looked over his shoulder. A man was standing about twenty feet behind them, holding up a phone.

'I've rung the Guards. Now stop, for the love of Christ, stop!'

Thank fuck for that, Sean thought, straightening his legs and dropping his fist. He looked at the other two men. 'Let's go.'

Conor Barry's mouth opened. 'What?'

'You heard him,' Sean snapped. 'He's already made the call.'

'A minute – that's all we need to drag him into the back of the van!' Barry protested, tights covering his face ripped open, jacket missing most of its buttons.

'The Guards are coming!' the man with the phone shouted.

Barry's gaze moved beyond Sean. 'You're Frank Ryan, I know you.'

The man swallowed. 'And you're Conor Barry. So please, just leave him be.'

Sean removed a pair of pliers from his back pocket and lowered a knee, pinning Jon's head to the ground. He slid one blade behind Jon's ear.

'Oh, no. No, no – ' Frank Ryan whispered.

The peeler tried to raise an arm. Sean pressed it back down, then, with one practised movement, he clamped the pliers on soft flesh. 'Just like what happened to his dog,' he announced, ripping the top of Jon's ear off. He tossed it to Conor. 'Something for the boss. Now let's go!'

As the other two men started round the vehicle, Sean brought his lips to within millimetres of Jon's wrecked ear. 'Get out of here,' he whispered. 'Get out now if you want to live.'

He lifted his knee from Jon's neck and started striding towards the van, bloody pliers thrust in the shop owner's direction. 'You saw nothing, Frank. Any different and I'll be taking your teeth with these.'

***

Jon sucked in a mouthful of air. The sound of the van

pulling away was muffled, as if he was lying in the bath, head just beneath the surface. He tried to open his eyes but all he could see was red.

Something pressed on his shoulder. 'Hello? Hello? Can you hear me?'

Jon coughed, the fire in his ribs intensifying. 'I can't see.'

'It's blood. Your ear – it's dripping down your face into your eyes. Hang on.'

Soft pressure against his face. 'There. Try blinking.'

Jon did as asked. Still no good. 'There's a bottle of water in my rucksack.'

'They took it. Wait, there's a tap nearby.'

As the footsteps moved off, he touched his face with his fingertips. The skin round his right eye felt like putty. Where the stick connected, Jon realised. I didn't even have time to duck. Please, God, don't let me be blind.

The footsteps came back. 'Here. See if this helps.'

Coolness once again.

'Now try.'

This time his left eye opened a little. He could see snowflakes falling, concrete peppered with bits of manure and hay, the first couple of business units in the background. Fingers appeared close to his face. He refocused to see they were holding a bloodstained handkerchief.

'Here, press it against your ear. The blood's coming from there.'

Jon took it. Holding it against the side of his head, he raised himself into a sitting position, waves of nausea rising at the back of his throat. 'Did you call the police?'

'No – I didn't have time. You need a hospital.'

Jon swivelled his good eye to the kitchen-shop owner. 'Is my ear gone?'

He nodded. 'The top part of it, yes.'

'My right eye?'

'Swollen shut. The hospital is only up the road – I'll call

for an ambulance.'

'No. Help me to my feet.'

'Son, you've taken a terrible beating. They'll have a trolley for you.'

'Help me up.'

'Bloody hell.' He crouched down and Jon got an arm round his shoulders.

Inch by inch, he regained his feet, pain snatching at his breath. Head pounding, he looked slowly around at the bright green orbs dropping silently from the sky. It was a sight he was familiar with from his rugby-playing days. Late tackles, unexpected punches thrown from behind, knees to the head at the bottom of a ruck. A wet sponge, that's what I need. Something to clear my head. 'Where's that tap?'

'There – set into the wall by the gate.'

'Help me over, would you?'

Leaning on the other man, he tried his weight on his right leg. The knee crunched and Jon pressed his chin against his chest, a low moan escaping him.

'This is ridiculous. Let's just get you an ambulance.'

Jon thought about the chain of events if that happened. Into A&E, bedside questions from the Guards, word sent back to Manchester. A phone call from DCI Parks ordering him home. That's not going to happen, he thought. I'm not giving up now. No fucking way. 'The tap.'

By locking his right knee and dragging the leg behind him, he was able to hobble with Frank Ryan's support, over to the tap. Leaning against the wall, he waited for his breath to slow. Then he turned the tap on, bent forward and held his head beneath the flow of water. The cascade was as icy as he'd hoped. After a good thirty seconds, he lifted his head back up and blinked. Better, he thought, feeling the trickles streaming down his chest and back. Much better. Reaching into his pocket, he brought out the keys to the hire car.

SLEEPING DOGS

'You're driving to the hospital?' the shop owner asked. 'Jesus, let me do it.'

'No Frank, I'm fine.' Holding one hand against the wall, he started hobbling for the gate. 'Thank you.'

'Do you even know where the hospital is?'

I'm not going there, Jon thought. 'I do. You get on — will you be OK?'

'Me? You should be worrying about yourself.'

'I'm fine, honestly. Don't report this, Frank, you've done enough. No more risks, OK?'

The man shook his head. 'You're not fit to drive.'

'I'll manage. Thanks for helping me, I owe you.' He unlocked the car and lowered himself slowly into the driver's seat. Flexing his knee caused the pain in it to erupt again, sharp needles this time, shooting straight up into his scrotum. Will I even be able to work the pedals? Air escaped from his clenched teeth as he positioned his foot over the accelerator. Christ!

The engine started and, aware of Frank watching over the wall, he held a hand up. Then he put the car in gear and slowly moved away.

CHAPTER 40

Rick turned from the plate-glass windows of his penthouse apartment, leaving the view across Manchester behind him. He should have called by now, he thought, looking at his watch. What the hell is taking him so long?

He crossed to the desk in the corner and checked the airport's website once again. There it was. Flight AE731, landed. Flipping his mobile over in his palm, he tried Jon's home number. Answer phone. Again. Just like his bloody mobile. Which would be understandable if he was still airborne, but the plane had already touched down.

He glanced across at Alice, who was huddled on the sofa with her legs drawn up under her, handbag at her side. Holly was perched on the edge of an armchair, eyes glued to the telly.

Rick spoke softly. 'This is bizarre. Are you sure nothing's on your answerphone?'

Alice was biting at her lower lip as she reached into her handbag. 'I'd have heard it ringing. Besides, we told him not to call me, didn't we?'

'I know, but just check, will you?'

She rummaged around and brought her mobile out. After pressing a few buttons her eyes widened. 'Oh my

God!' Her eyes went to Holly, but the little girl didn't seem to have heard.

'What?' Rick asked quietly, moving closer.

'He sent a text, a couple of hours ago.'

'What does it say?'

'Devlan arrived in Galway. Am going back to Clifden. Will get the 7.50 flight this evening.' She looked up at Rick with apprehensive eyes.

'Clifden?' Rick said in a faint voice. 'Devlan is there?' Shit, he thought. This really is not good.

'Rick?' Alice asked. 'Why are you staring at me like that?'

He blinked. 'No...no. It was a surprise. Let me think.' He turned and slowly approached the plate-glass windows. Jon will take this guy apart. He recalled the tower block when his partner had lost all control with Salvio, the pimp who'd tried to force Zoë back onto the game. Jon had knocked his teeth out and snapped his arm, would probably have thrown him from a sixty-metre-high balcony if I hadn't dragged him off. His mobile started to play Saturday Night Fever and he pressed green. 'Jon?'

'No – Andy.'

Andy Burnett, his contact in the NCA. The man was sounding excited. 'Sorry, Andy, I was expecting someone else.'

'Can you talk now? Only I'm having to make this call from the car park.'

'Of course – go ahead.'

'Right. You know how the company names from Ireland and other details you gave me were drawing a blank.'

Rick stopped before the windows, keeping his back to the room. 'Yeah – subsidiaries, overseas stuff...'

'Well, we have a way in.'

'What?'

'That name your colleague came up with – Blackman and May? That was the jackpot. Blackman and May is a

Dublin-based law firm with an office in Galway. Their name featured on a suspicious property deal we looked at in Manchester. Hanover Quay, to be precise. Next to where they're building that big media-city thing.'

'Possible IRA investment?'

'That's what we reckoned at first. But the deal had no paramilitary connection that we could find. However, by using the Blackman and May connection, I could start ferreting round under the aegis of the current investigation.'

'And?'

'They do all the de Avila family's legal work. The thread linking all the bits of the empire together.'

'Empire?' Dread tickled at the back of Rick's mind.

'Oh yes. There's a lot of money in this, spread out in all sorts of directions.'

'For a bunch of dog-fighters, you're making these people sound very organised,' Rick said quietly.

'Oh, don't make the mistake of thinking these guys are a bunch of culchies – '

'Culchies?'

'Irish slang. The Bureau officers I've been liaising with used it. Culchie is a bumpkin, a backward country person. The de Avilas might appear to be culchies – probably happy to create that impression. But don't be fooled. In fact, if your mate is still out there poking at the nest, I'd tell him to get the hell out.'

'No, it's on the house, compliments of Gerrard.' Hazel placed the full bottles of beer on their table and started collecting in the empties.

'Sound,' one of the men replied, eyes bleary from the booze. He leaned back in his chair to look her up and down. 'What's your name, doll?'

'Hazel.' She smiled briefly.

'Hazel.' He thought about that for a moment. 'You deserve a break, Hazel.' He patted his knee. 'Why don't you sit down a minute?'

She found his Liverpool accent hard to understand, but the look in his eyes was obvious enough. 'More people to serve.' She glanced to the corner where Darragh was talking to the three Turkmen Gerrard had been so keen to impress. A hand slid round the back of her knee, a forefinger trailing upward.

'Come on. Five minutes.' He started to pull her closer.

'And leave all our other customers thirsty, now?' She tried to step away.

'Stevo.' The voice came from across the table. Same type of accent. The man placed his elbows on his knees, dense tattoos more like a shadow across both forearms. 'That's Devlan's girl.'

The hand immediately dropped and the man looked up at her. 'No offence, yeah? I was just having fun, like.'

''Course.' She returned to the bar, slipped behind it then through to the back office. As she started placing the empties into the stacked crates on the floor, Gerrard continued speaking behind the desk.

'Devlan, where are you? OK. Things are grand – they found nothing at the farm. We got all the dogs away – including the ones from the Bone Yard Kennels. Yeah, they're still here. And the Dublin lot. It's drinks on the house. No, we're putting it down to bad luck, but word will get out it was the Englishman behind the raid. The damage to us is done. The Turkmen? No, I'm not going out there.' He glanced awkwardly at the security monitors. 'I can't face it. Besides, Darragh has a tongue on him for that kind of stuff. Why are things grand? I'll tell you, son – he came back. The peeler. Here to Clifden.'

She risked a glance across. The old man was looking up at the ceiling, an ugly smile on his face.

'I sent Sean to get him. Just waiting for his call, now. Aye – don't worry, we'll keep him hidden away until you're back. Cuchullain? Why bring – ' A quiet chuckle sidled from the corner of his mouth. 'You and that Francisco story. I suppose it would be kind of fitting. Don't come with the dog yet – the Guards are still sniffing around. Right, see you soon.'

He replaced the receiver, raised himself to his feet and blew his cheeks out. 'I'm hitting the hay for a few hours. Tell Darragh I'll be at the house overlooking the bay.'

'OK, Mr de Avila.' She watched him walk wearily to the back corridor. As soon as the rear door banged shut, she made for the toilet, reaching for the tiny mobile phone hidden in her pocket. Door locked, she keyed in Jon's number. The answer phone clicked in. 'Shit,' she cursed under her breath. 'Why aren't you answering?'

She jiggled her knees up and down, fingers pinching at her lower lip before she lifted the phone and keyed in a new number. 'Uncle Bernard, it's me, Siobhain,' she whispered. 'I'm in the club. I've made a terrible mistake. I didn't mean for this to happen. That man, the Brit? The one you met at the pony fair to pass on all the information I'd got for you? He's not really a freelance journalist.' She wiped a tear from her eye. 'I'm sorry, Bernard, I lied to you. I've got him – us – into real trouble. Oh God. They're after him now to find out how he knows all the things he does...' She squeezed her eyes shut and tears rolled down both cheeks. 'I don't know what to do. He's not answering his phone, I can't warn him to get away – '

The music grew louder as the door from the bar banged open. 'Hazel!' Darragh's voice. 'What the fuck are you playing at?'

'I'll try to come and see you,' she hissed. 'Not sure how soon.' Hiding the phone in her pocket, she spoke at the back of the door. 'Changing my tampon, if that's OK with you.'

'Well, are you done?'

'For fuck's sake.' She flushed the toilet, yanked paper towel from the dispenser and opened the door. 'That fast enough for you?'

Darragh looked her up and down, eyes pinched with

suspicion. 'Not with this lot in here. Get some more champagne from the back.'

Rick rolled his eyes at Alice. 'Work call,' he said, trying to sound exasperated. 'Just need to sort something out.' He wandered into his bedroom, closed the door and sat down heavily on the end of the double bed. 'What...how big an empire does it appear to be?'

'Right,' his contact in the NCA continued. 'I'll start with the most recent investments. All legit. The names you gave me – Phoenix Court, Emmet Street, Anderson Court – are all Irish. Offices and residential developments in Galway and Dublin. Only the last one, Hanover Quay, is Manchester. As I said, part of that massive regeneration you've got going on out in Salford. Collectively, these things would have had a value touching the millions, if the whole property market hadn't crashed. Now the banks aren't lending. Building work on most of the Irish ones has ground to a halt and their values are plummeting.'

'Where've they got the money to be getting into this sort of stuff in the first place?' Rick asked.

'I'm getting to that. Then there's the construction company, Convila. That is actually registered to Darragh de Avila. Along with the nightclub, it's about the only things they own with the de Avila name featuring.'

'And both types of business are good ways to launder cash,' Rick cut in.

'Correct. We taught you a bit during your time here, didn't we? Beneath that is what underpins the entire operation. By the way, the boys I know in the Bureau? They're very keen to open a file on the de Avila family. They were able to tell me that, originally, the de Avilas owned a knacker's yard. Over time, it evolved into an abattoir. It appears to have been in the family for donkey's years, pardon the pun. In the wake of foot and mouth, EU laws were passed changing the rules on where animals could be slaughtered. Suddenly the de Avilas were quids in:

there was only one other place in the Connemara region authorised to do it. And the owner of that, out of the blue, apparently decided to commit suicide.'

Rick raised his eyebrows. 'He did what?'

'You heard. Just when business got really lucrative, he tops himself.'

'How?'

'A pile of neatly folded clothes and an empty bottle of whiskey were found on a secluded beach near Galway, his car parked nearby. No body was ever found.'

'That...' Rick struggled for words, 'that...'

'Stinks. I know. So, our mysterious family now have a monopoly on all the processing of meat in the area – which is big on sheep and cattle. Plus they're the place you take those Connemara ponies when they need the chop. The outfit is registered as DA Services, the de Avila name vanishes off the books, but Blackman and May remain as the company lawyers. Then comes another very fortunate development.'

Rick's eyes turned back to the Manchester skyline and he watched as a distant plane began its approach to the airport. Bloody hell, Jon, what have we got you into?

'There was a smallish factory up in Mayo, the county above Galway. It produced dry pet food – biscuits and the like. Turning a small profit, but nothing major. The de Avila family bought it for a song and relocated the entire thing to just outside Clifden. Invested in brand new machinery, named the place Golden Fields Farm.'

'Fuck,' Rick whispered. 'Vertical integration.'

'Very good, mate. So now, rather than sell all the shit that isn't fit for human consumption to pet-food places, they have one of their own. Turnover gradually increases as they win contracts to supply the major pet-food labels and supermarkets' own brands. And that's what is on the books. My guess is a heck of a lot more cash is being generated by that place – and they've used it to buy the properties we were talking about.'

'Which are all legit,' Rick added.

'Exactly. Classic stuff, isn't it? Use your ill-gotten gains to move into above-board stuff. They'll be standing for public office next.'

Rick got up and walked slowly over to the bedroom window. The plane was now descending and he tracked its outline as it got closer and closer to the horizon. Eventually the chequered expanse of the Cheshire Plain swallowed it. 'Cheers, Andy, I owe you for this.'

'There's more.'

Rick dragged a hand over his face.

'That's the dodgy business stuff – oh, and loads of holiday properties they rent out around Clifden. As I mentioned, this isn't information I've dug up all on my own. The lads in the Bureau have discovered no paramilitary links to the de Avilas, which is why they've stayed off the radar so long. All that's on them are some charges of cruelty to animals. None have stuck, but they're known to be well involved in the illegal dog-fighting scene.'

'We've worked that much out.'

'OK. You also gave me some names – Francis Collins, Geordan and Fionna Reilly and a Tommy Hammell.'

'I found a bit on Tommy Hammell – a con-artist who was been missing a while.'

'The Bureau don't expect him to ever turn up. He had a long record for financial scams, most in Dublin.'

Rick felt queasy. 'And somehow his name links in with the de Avilas.'

'Not as worrying as Francis Collins. Did you look him up on the internet?'

'No. Who is he?'

'Was, not is. Collins was on the IRA council. You need me to explain what that is?'

'Please.'

'OK – the IRA is headed by a seven-man army council. It is, shall we say, alleged that Martin McGuinness and

Gerry Adams of Sinn Féin were part of the council for years. Maybe still are. Of course, nowadays Sinn Féin – as the political wing of the IRA – has representatives in all levels of government. London and Ireland, north and south of the border. MPs, TDs, Assembly members at Stormont, dozens of councillors. They've embraced the political process and the tactic's working. A united Ireland, free from British rule, could actually happen.'

'Though not helped by breakaway groups killing British soldiers.'

'True. In fact, events like that are about the only thing that could ruin Sinn Féin's strategy.'

'So, this guy Collins. What happened?'

'Shot to death while driving his car down Castlebar High Street in County Mayo back in 1993. Geordan and Fionna Reilly were innocent bystanders, killed when Collins's car mounted the pavement. Collins's death was blamed on the loyalist movement. So a load of fresh fighting broke out, even though no loyalist group ever took credit for his scalp. Many came to believe it was really the work of British security forces.'

'You're not saying it was the de Avilas? I thought they've always kept well out of this shit?'

'I'd agree, but you need to know something. The pet-food factory they bought in County Mayo? It belonged to the late Francis Collins.'

'Oh my God.'

'That's what I'm saying, Rick. This colleague of yours? He really should not be over there provoking these people.'

By the time he reached Roundstone, the vision in Jon's good eye was going again. Concussion, he realised. Hope it doesn't make me puke. His right leg had gone beyond numb: now it was frozen stiff. Prodding it with his fingers, he felt nothing. The limb of a dead person, he thought. Grafted to my thigh.

Bracing himself for the rip of pain he knew the effort would bring, he turned the wheel to take the sharp left up past O'Dowd's bar. Reaching the top of the little incline, he breathed out with relief. There was Malachy's bungalow. He pulled into the drive, came to a stop, opened the car door and vomited on the drive.

The realisation he'd actually made it caused something in him to buckle and collapse. Fatigue flooded him and new spots of pain began to register all over his body. Summoning the very last of his strength, he looked at himself in the rear-view mirror. Trickles of dried blood had formed a latticework of red across his face. The handkerchief was stuck to the side of his head, welded in place by the thick, red clot that had soaked through the fabric. His right eye was almost completely shut, the skin tight and discoloured.

White dots drifted and floated before his eyes, and as sleep folded itself around him, he couldn't tell if the snowflakes were beyond the windscreen or only in his head.

CHAPTER 41

Rick paced up and down the pristine white interview room. In the main office, he could see Border Agency officials going about their business. A voice announced the arrival of a flight from Cape Town. Airports, Rick thought. A never-ending hive of activity.

As he waited for the official to return, he ran over the last part of the phone conversation he'd had with his contact in the NCA. Burnett had warned Rick that, given the extent of the de Avila family's activities, a major investigation was being opened by the Bureau.

Rick had composed himself before walking back into the living area. He'd talked Alice through the security system for admitting people up the final flight of stairs leading to the penthouse apartment then raced over to Manchester airport.

The door swung fully open and the Border Agency official stepped back in, a canvas holdall hanging from one hand. He placed it on the table and regarded Rick with a glum expression. 'Here it is.'

Rick lifted the luggage tag. Flight AE731.

The man placed his hands on his hips. 'On your head be it –'

'I've said,' Rick cut in impatiently, examining the bag, 'he's my partner, he's not going to lodge a complaint.' He looked at the other man. 'Two minutes?'

The official backed away. 'I'll be outside.'

Rick opened the zip. On top of the badly folded clothes was a knitted woollen scarf and a teddy bear. It was wearing a green jumper with a clover-leaf emblem on the front. Carefully, Rick lifted them out and placed them on the table.

Below the scarf was a folder. Rick opened it up and saw the financial records Jon had described over the phone. He flicked through to the final sheet. On it were four names. Tommy Hammell, Geordan and Fionna Reilly, Francis Collins. Rick placed it to one side.

Next he started removing the T-shirts. He spotted a mobile phone, a basic model by the look of it. After turning it on, he found his way into the recent calls folder. None made and only two received. First was Jon's mobile, second was anonymous, received yesterday, early evening. He put it next to the bear.

Probing deeper, his fingers nudged something hard. He removed the Asp and glanced nervously at the closed door. Next he found the forearm and shin protectors, both carrying the stamp of Greater Manchester Police. A glance in the washbag revealed the slim can of pepper spray.

He got to the bottom, where a few slightly crumpled posters lay. After reading the text, he pulled his mobile out and called the number at the base of the poster, eyes on the handset next to the bear. A few seconds later, it started to ring. Rick hung up, tapping the top of his handset slowly against his chin. Christ, Jon, where are you?

He looked at his watch. Four fifteen. The evening flight to Manchester leaves at seven fifty. If Jon's name hasn't appeared on that plane's passenger list by seven, he thought, I'm going to have to call Parks.

Brendan Molloy's footsteps echoed softly as he strode

down the long, empty corridor. On reaching a door near its end, the Sinn Féin official stopped. Flexing his shoulder once, he knocked.

'Come in.'

He opened the door and entered a large office. On the far wall was a painting of Eamon de Valera. Next to it was a photo of Bobby Sands, the leader of the 1981 IRA hunger strike in Her Majesty's Maze prison, Belfast. The man had starved to death shortly after being elected as a member of the UK's parliament.

Standing in the corner before a filing cabinet was a silver-haired man in a tailored shirt, the sleeves of which were untidily rolled up. He glanced over. 'Anything, Brendan?'

'Not so far, Rory. Not for want of trying.'

The man shoved the drawer shut, making the entire cabinet wobble. He locked it, turned to the ten-foot-high window and stared down at the manicured lawns to either side of the wide road leading up to the front of Stormont. 'Shit.'

'The touts we have in the Continuity IRA and INLA have been pulled in. No one has a clue.'

The other man smoothed his tie. 'Someone fucking knows who killed that soldier.'

Brendan nodded. 'Something else has come up.'

Sinking into the leather armchair, Rory laid a palm on his desk. 'I'm guessing it's not good news, either.' He nodded at the chair opposite.

Brendan sat down and crossed his legs. 'I got a call earlier about a situation in Clifden.'

The man behind the desk raised an eyebrow. 'Clifden?'

'Connemara.'

The older man looked bemused.

'I know, I know,' Brendan replied. 'It's a way away. But this could prove a worry. There's a policeman from Britain out there. From a couple of checks I've made, it would appear he's acting entirely alone. He's ruffling the feathers of the de Avila family.'

'Who?'

The man waved a hand. 'Bunch of culchies, but they run things down there.'

'Connemara? What's to run? Is it not only bogs and mountains?'

'And holiday homes. They own a fair number. Plus an abattoir outside Galway…' He clicked his fingers. 'You know the pet-food factory Francis Collins owned?'

The other man shook his head.

'Well, remember after Francis was killed, we had to sort out his affairs? The operation he had cleaning red diesel and selling it in Northern Ireland – Pat took that on, with a percentage going to Francis's widow. Same thing with his properties in Belfast and Derry – McCague bought them. Gerrard de Avila offered to buy the pet-food factory, saved it from just closing down. I forget what he paid for the machinery, but the cash was appreciated by Francis's widow.'

'No, I wasn't aware. So he owns a few businesses.'

Brendan cleared his throat. 'What they really are is dog men, Rory. Have you heard of Clochán kennels?'

The man shook his head.

'It's very well regarded in dog-fighting circles. They breed a lot of animals and also host events at venues they own. Popular with some of our lot and unionist crews alike. It's regarded as a neutral venue, where they can all go for a bit of sport.'

'You mean betting money on pit bulls?'

'Mainly that breed.'

'Jesus Christ, this is exactly the kind of shit we should be nowhere near.'

The other man's eyes slid briefly to the side. 'My contact says the de Avilas are fast losing patience with this Brit. He's worried we could end up with another body.'

Rory sat up. 'Hang on. Are these fuckwit de Avilas with the party?'

'No, they've always kept well out of politics. No involvement. But that hardly matters, does it? An English policeman murdered while on holiday in Southern Ireland? It'll be another gift for those fuckers down the corridor.'

The silver-haired man looked up, as if searching for cracks appearing in the plaster high above his head. 'Who is this idiot policeman?'

'He's called Jon Spicer. A detective inspector with Manchester police. He's gone to Clifden searching for some sort of a relative, convinced she's been working for the de Avila family. They own a nightclub in the town.'

'Has she?'

Brendan hunched a shoulder. 'I don't know. But this policeman won't give up.'

'Where are you getting this information from?'

'A man called Sean Doyle. Used to box for the Holy Trinity Club in Belfast. Was showing great promise until they realised something's up with his brain. Blackouts in the ring.'

'Is he someone we can trust?'

'Yes.'

'Is he with the party?'

'Yes – but he's not been about. A few years back, he got in with the de Avilas because he loves dogs. Knows a thing or two about getting the animals fighting fit. When he moved down there and started working for the family, I kept him on the payroll – he's a useful guy to have around. Did a lot of good jobs for us in Belfast.'

'And you're sure he can be trusted?'

'Oh, there's no doubt about that.'

CHAPTER 42

The sound of trickling water began to register. Jon lay still, listening to the droplets fall, trying to gauge where he was. Still at the pony auction place? He could vaguely recall getting over to the tap in the wall and leaning forward to hold his head under the ice-cold flow. *Did I pass out? Is that the noise I can hear?*

A voice spoke quietly. 'Just call for an ambulance, Kieron. The man's been unconscious too long. He could have bleeding on the brain, anything.'

Jon felt something warm dabbing at the side of his head. *I'm lying on my back,* he thought. *Somewhere soft, not concrete. A bed.*

A male voice. 'He was able to speak when we brought him in. He said no ambulance, no police.'

'He was practically unconscious in his car, Nial! I'm not going to take the instructions of someone who's half-concussed. Kieron, give me your phone! If you won't call for help, I will.'

With an effort, Jon licked his lips and the talking immediately stopped. He opened his right eye to see three blurred forms looking down at him. Kieron, Eileen and another man. *Of course,* he thought, *I made it to*

Malachy's. He tried to say hello, but all that emerged from his mouth was a rough croak.

Kieron waved a hand, his fingers blurring and multiplying in the air. Jon closed his eyes again. 'Would you give him a drink, Mum? He's trying to speak!'

'I'll wet some cotton wool.' He heard the scrape of a glass, and moments later, felt cold water dripping between his parted lips. He washed it around the inside of his mouth and swallowed. Oh my God, that was good. 'Thanks,' he whispered. 'Think I could drink a jug of that.'

Forcing his good eye open, he saw the older man leaning through the doorway. 'Malachy! He's awake!'

Like bomb-bursts in his head, the words made him wince.

'Sssshhhh!' Eileen whispered. 'Keep your voice down. How are you feeling, Jon?'

He blinked. 'Big, big headache. Probably will get worse when I sit up.'

The shuffle of footsteps as Malachy appeared. 'Oh, he's back in the land of the living. You poor boy.' Jon shifted his head slightly. There were tears in the old man's eyes. 'We thought we'd lost you there.' He got to the side of the bed and placed a hand over Jon's.

Jon smiled as best he could, feeling the syrupy urge to sleep closing back over him. He was vaguely aware of his grandfather holding a bowl towards Eileen.

'Here – give him some of the carrageen for his strength.'

She scowled. 'He wants tea, Dad, not that stuff.'

Jon tried to lift himself up a little and felt the surge of blood behind his swollen eye. 'No – I'm starving, I'll eat it.'

His aunt looked sceptical. 'Are you sure?'

'He just said,' Malachy cut in. 'Feed the boy.'

Lying back, Jon nodded.

Eileen's voice again. 'Open up, then.' A blob of something that had the temperature and texture of blancmange was put in his mouth. 'He makes it from the seaweed. It is packed with goodness, though.'

He heard Malachy pipe up. 'You eat that, Joseph. It will do you a world of good, so.'

'It's Jon, Dad, remember?' Eileen stated. 'Not Joseph.'

A slight delay before Malachy spoke again. 'You take it fine and easy.'

Jon broke the cold lump up with his tongue. It tasted both milky and salty. 'Nice.'

Pleasure suffused Malachy's voice. 'Feed him the rest, Eileen and then let the boy sleep some more.'

Devlan thrust his hips harder, repeating the movement, increasing the speed of it so Hazel's head was driven further into the pillows bunched at the top of the bed.

All the time, he stared at the wall, visualising the peeler from Manchester. The man, cowering in the corner of the big shed out at the pet-food factory. He imagined Cuchullain's chain wrapped round his hand, the links of it digging into his skin as the animal strained at the other end of it, muscles in its huge neck quivering. And he wouldn't bark. Not when his prey was so close. And it would be his silence that would be the thing that terrified the peeler most. The man would be shrieking for mercy as he finally released the clip on Cuchullain's collar.

Devlan shuddered, eyelids lowering. He let his weight go forward onto Hazel's back and rested there for a few seconds. When he straightened up, her face was still buried in the pillows. He reached down and patted her head. 'I needed that.'

She made a noise of agreement and he sat back on his heels, reaching for the corner of the duvet to wipe himself clean. She fell onto her side, hair still covering her face. He slapped her thigh. 'Stir yourself. Dad'll want some food when he wakes up.'

'Fuck's sake, I've not even slept yet.'

'Not my problem.' He climbed off the bed and put his boxer shorts and jeans back on. Then he slipped out the door, crossing an oak-floored landing to descend a few steps into a living area. A giant wood-burning stove was at its centre. Behind the cylindrical glass of its mid-section, flames rose towards a metal flue that stretched a good twenty feet to a wooden ceiling.

Seated on the leather chairs surrounding the fire were Sean Doyle, Conor Barry and the third man from the pony auction car park. Darragh was sitting at a computer in the corner, a couple of open files next to the keyboard.

'Did you want to bang her any harder?' Conor asked with a grin. 'Sounded like you were trying to drill her through the wall in there.'

Pulling a T-shirt over his head, Devlan walked to the breakfast bar that separated the kitchen area from the rest of the room. Incorporated into its centre was a wine rack, bottles of red filling it. 'I thought you'd enjoy listening. Something for your wank-bank, eh, Conor?' His eyes moved to the sliding doors that led out on to a wide balcony. Below it, the grey sea was pinched with little waves. On the other side of Clifden bay, pinpricks of light winked along the shoreline. He sat down on the bar stool in the corner, lit a cigarette and turned to the group. 'So boys, have you got your story straight? I'm guessing he'll be awake soon.'

The large man looked nervously to Sean, who crossed his arms and said nothing.

'It wasn't my decision,' Conor protested. 'It was his.' He stared at Sean, who just shook his head. 'What?' Conor demanded. 'We could have got him into the – '

'Who? Me and Liam?' Sean retorted. 'Way I remember it, you were busy squealing at us to get the fucker off you.'

'Fuck you, it was me that – '

'What's all this bitching about?'

Heads turned.

Gerrard de Avila was standing in boxer shorts and a crumpled T-shirt at the top of the short flight of steps. Looking all of his sixty-seven years, he made his way slowly down.

Devlan lifted a pot of tea from the counter at his side. 'A cup of scaldy, Da? The boys have something to tell you.'

The old man reached the bottom step and crossed to the breakfast bar. Perching on a stool alongside his son's, he rested a meaty forearm on the granite surface and tapped a finger. 'Where's the girl? Is there no food?'

Devlan looked towards the landing. 'Hazel! Come on!'

Gerrard pointed to the teapot and Devlan filled a cup. Rubbing at an eye, the old man added a couple of sugars, splashed in milk from a plastic carton, then turned to the three men by the wood burner. 'So, where have you taken him?'

Conor's and Liam's eyes went to Sean who uncrossed his arms. 'We didn't get him, Gerrard. A man who was there called the Guards.'

Gerrard lowered his mug of tea. 'What?'

Sean kept his hands flat on his thighs. 'We'd got him to the ground, about twenty feet from the – '

'Ten,' Conor interrupted.

Sean head came round. 'You want to have one with me?'

Conor stared back.

'Come on then,' Sean continued, readying himself to stand. 'I'll break your fucking face.'

Wearily, Gerrard lifted a hand. 'Enough! Liam, what happened?'

The large man licked his lips. 'We had him, so we did. At the pony auction place. But this man showed up with a phone in his hand. He said he'd called already – and the cop shop's practically next door.'

'Who was he?' Gerrard rumbled.

'Frank Ryan,' Conor replied. 'Owns that kitchen workshop there.'

Gerrard exchanged glances with Devlan who gave a knowing nod.

The old man turned back to Liam. 'Carry on.'

'The peeler wasn't that close to the van – we'd have needed to drag him over. I don't think there was time; we had to get away.'

'Away and shite,' Conor muttered.

Gerrard took a long breath in and contemplated the view outside. Devlan slid a small plate towards him. 'Sean had time to get us a souvenir, though.'

The old man looked down at the piece of flesh.

Devlan grinned. 'When Queenie ripped into his dog back in Manchester, she tore off its ear with her first bite. That there's the top of the peeler's ear. Sean used pliers on him.'

The old man nodded appreciatively as Siobhain came down the steps and walked round to the kitchen side of the breakfast bar. 'I might have it with my eggs,' Gerrard said, turning back to the room. 'So, is he still in Clifden?'

'He won't have got far,' Liam replied. 'Conor stopped him with a hurley bat to the face. I gave him a couple of cracks with an iron before Sean clattered him. Fucking class punch, it was.'

'Did the Guards pick him up?' Gerrard asked.

'Not according to Patrick,' Devlan replied.

'The hospital, then?'

'No. And he's not back at that hotel he's been staying in,' Sean answered. 'State he was in, he has to be close.'

For a moment, the only sound was Siobhain as she rummaged around in the cutlery drawer.

'Is he still driving the same car?' Gerrard asked. 'The silver Ford?'

'No, Patrick said he's in a black Peugeot now. One of those little hatchbacks,' Devlan replied.

Gerrard nodded. 'Right, Conor, Sean, Liam, I want that Peugeot found. Nip out the front and start making calls there. Hazel, you go and get some air, too. The food can wait.'

The three men began to slowly stand, looking

confused. Gerrard stared back at them impassively. 'I want a wee talk with my sons here.'

Behind the breakfast bar, Siobhain bent forward to replace the frying pan in the bottom drawer. As she did so, she slid her mobile phone from her pocket and placed it in the drawer before pushing it shut. Then she joined the men as they filed towards the front door.

Once it had closed behind them, Devlan leaned back against the wall. 'You don't trust Sean any more?'

Gerrard hunched a shoulder. 'I don't trust anyone outside us three. And Liam and Denis are our cousins, don't forget. But someone's passing information to that English policeman. He knows far too much.'

Darragh looked up momentarily from his paperwork. 'I agree.'

Gerrard swivelled the plate with the piece of Jon's ear round. 'You've got Cuchullain?'

Devlan nodded as he got off the stool and walked over to the wood burner. 'And the peeler's rucksack.'

'His rucksack?' Gerrard said. 'Have you checked – '

'Yes,' Darragh replied. 'No cassettes inside.'

Devlan picked it off the floor and unzipped the front pocket. 'Passport, plane ticket, wallet.' He flicked the wallet open and held up the photo on the inside cover to his dad. 'Wife and wee girl. Worth a punch in the drawers, she is.' He let out a chuckle. 'The wife, like.'

Darragh shook his head.

'Where's the dog?' Gerrard asked.

'I moved him to Drimmeen.'

Darragh looked across. 'The place due to be renovated in the spring?'

Devlan nodded. 'No fucker lives within a mile of it.'

Gerrard's nostrils widened as he filled his chest. 'Once we know it's safe, take him back to Golden Fields. It's the last place the Guards will think of looking now. We find this person – get the tapes back – then set the dog on him. Once Cuch' is finished, we chuck what's left in the macerator.'

Devlan's face lit up with delight. 'Like that shyster who tried to cheat you that time?'

'Hammell,' Gerrard nodded sombrely. 'Just like him.'

Darragh put his pen down and squeezed his temples with the tips of his fingers. Eyes shut, he said, 'Do you really mean to kill him? An English policeman?'

Devlan looked over. 'He's made us look like cunts for too long, isn't that right Da?'

'It is. He has to be dealt with, Darragh.'

Darragh opened his eyes, gaze directed down at his lap. 'If you're going to do this,' he said resignedly, 'let's try and make it to our advantage.'

Gerrard swivelled his stool round. 'What have you in mind, son?'

Rick sat at his desk in the incident room at Longsight and watched the minute hand creep towards twenty-past seven. With a sigh, he called the Border Agency official again. 'Chris, it's Rick Saville again. Has he checked in? No? And the flight's now closed? OK, cheers.' He pressed red and looked at his phone. 'Sorry, Jon,' he sighed. 'But I don't know what else to do.'

He brought up his DCI's number and listened as her phone began to ring. What a bloody disaster. 'Hi, boss. It's DS Saville here, sorry to disturb you so late.'

'That's all right, Rick. Anything wrong?'

'I'm hoping not, boss. But…but I think there might be. If I'm right, it's really not good.'

'Is this about DI Spicer?'

'Yes.'

'You've been in contact about the gas leak up at Center Parcs? He's yet to return my call.'

Bloody hell, Rick thought. She's already heard. 'Yes. There've been other developments.'

'Go on.'

'Jon's been over in Ireland.'

'I realise.'

'No – I mean he's gone back. I think he's there right now.'

'I was under the impression he was in the Lake District.'

'No, he went back to Connemara.'

'Connemara.'

'Yes – he went back to try and locate Zoë, the female who – '

'I know who she is.'

Rick swallowed. 'Of course. I've been looking into things this end and the situation is far more grave – I mean, the danger he's potentially in. Having found out more about this particular family he's been tangling with, it's far more grave than we realised.'

'The ones who posed no serious threat, according to assessments from both the NCA and JTAC.' Her voice had turned hard and cold. 'That family?'

'Well, those checks, boss, were for links to known paramilitary groups. Which don't exist – the family has always kept well clear of the Troubles.'

'So what have you managed to discover?'

'Where they're based, out on Ireland's west coast, is a town called Clifden. They've quietly built an extensive business network. Jon is digging around out there and antagonising the family in the process.'

'I do not believe this.'

'The two men he suspected of being behind the attack on his Boxer dog, Punch – the ones who may be behind the gas leak in the lodge at Center Parcs too – have shown up in Clifden. Jon was about to fly home, but when he saw them, he changed his mind.'

'How do you know this?'

'He sent a text to his wife earlier today. We were expecting Jon to be on the evening flight back to Manchester. Check in just closed and he's not on it.'

'Wait a minute, Jon was returning to Manchester – '

'Yes, when he heard about what had happened at Center Parcs, he was giving up on his search for Zoë and coming home.'

'And he saw these two men where?'

'At Galway Airport, getting off this morning's flight from Manchester. The text said he was following them back to Clifden for one last try to resolve the situation.'

'Very delicately put, DS Saville, for how we know Jon likes to operate. You realise he's out of the MIT? I was his last chance and he's blown it with me – '

'With all due respect, boss, I'm now more concerned for his life than his career. He's not answering his phone and this family, it seems, might have been involved in a several deaths and disappearances over the years.'

'Deaths? According to?'

'A contact who's been in touch with some colleagues in the Irish police.'

'Details.'

'A con-artist called Tommy Hammell. The owner of a rival abattoir. A couple called Geordan and Fionna Reilly, killed during a hit on a man called Francis Collins who was a member of the IRA's army council.'

'Christ almighty. How long since you heard from Jon?'

'About twelve hours.'

'Meet me at the office.'

'I'm here already.'

'Good. I'll be there by eight. Have we any idea of where he's been staying in this town? Which places he's been visiting? I need every scrap of information you have.'

CHAPTER 43

The dull throb that pulsed slowly behind his temple finally woke Jon up. He kept his eyes shut, gauging how dark the room was. Fairly bright, he concluded, judging by the glow beyond his eyelids.

Bracing himself, he opened his good eye. Sunlight was streaming round the edges of the curtains to his left. From beyond the window, he could hear a diesel engine revving, followed by a voice giving instructions. People working on the site across the road, he thought. What time was it?

He turned his head further, relieved the motion didn't trigger an explosion of pain in his head. A wardrobe faced him. No sign of a clock there. Carefully, he turned his head in the other direction. A bedside table came into view. On it was a bowl, the handle of a spoon protruding beyond the rim. Next to it was a jug of water, a glass and a bedside clock. Ten to nine. Shit, he thought. It's the next day. I've been asleep for hours.

He pushed his elbows back to raise himself up. The throbbing behind his eye picked up pace, but was nowhere near as bad as he expected. Looking past the outlines of his feet, he saw his jacket lying across the bottom of the bed. My mobile is in the inner pocket, he remembered. I must get word about what's going on back to Britain.

Shuffling into a sitting position, he wondered about his knee. Just feels numb, he thought, turning the bedcovers back. The leg had been strapped tight with bandages. I'm in my boxers. They must have undressed me.

The sight brought back another memory. Tentatively, he raised a hand to his left ear. More bandaging, these ones encasing the side of his head. God, he thought, they ripped my bloody ear off.

By leaning forward, he was just able to hook the sleeve of his jacket and drag it up the bed. Sitting back, he took his mobile out. The casing was cracked and the display a blank grey. Pressing the on button caused nothing to happen. The crowbar, he realised, recalling the impact of it against his side. He wanted to groan. And the other phone's with my luggage in Manchester.

Peering over the edge of the bed for his rucksack, he realised the men who'd jumped him had taken that, too. My passport, wallet, plane ticket – everything is gone. An echo came to him of one of their voices. The man's accent wasn't local, though. It had none of that lilting softness. Harder, snarly. Belfast, that was it. He was from northern Ireland.

Behind the bowl of the blancmange stuff were several framed photos. More relatives I don't know. One image was of four girls perched in the undulating dips of a large, smooth rock. They were wearing damp-looking bathing costumes. A thin strip of white sand stretched away behind them to a grass-covered headland. Gorteen Bay, Jon thought, looking closer. And that's Mum, second on the right. It must be of all of the sisters.

The bowl of cloudy-white jelly caught his eye. Crystals of partially melted sugar dotted its surface and Jon realised how famished he was. He lifted the bowl and starting spooning lumps of it into his mouth. He raised the glass of water, gulped it down, refilled it and drained it again.

The handle of the bedroom door creaked and the

Border collie's snout appeared in the crack. The door opened wider and Malachy looked in, eyes widening when he saw Jon sitting there.

'All's well, dog, all's well! The boy is awake!'

Jon nodded back. 'Morning Malachy, I am.'

He shuffled in, walking stick clutched in one hand. 'And how are you feeling?' he asked, dragging the chair from the corner over and plonking himself down. 'Any better?'

'Much.' Jon smiled, glancing down at the empty bowl. 'I don't know what's in that pudding you gave me.'

'The carrageen?' Malachy replied. 'Isn't it wondrous stuff? You would never touch it as a child, but if you want more you will have it and welcome.' He started reaching for the bowl.

'I'm OK for now, thanks,' Jon replied, a little confused by the answer. 'I take it Eileen's been busy?' He touched the bandages swathing his ear.

'She has,' he nodded. 'I think we emptied O'Dowd's of all their ice, too. She's been putting it on your leg and eye.'

'Really?' Jon replied.

'You don't remember? You were awake when she was doing it.'

'No,' Jon replied, thinking the concussion had wiped the memories clean.

'She called in at the chirp of the sparrow to check on you and now she's out on her rounds. Rest, she said. That eye, though, it looks as full as a tick, so it does.'

Jon traced a finger over the swollen skin. By tilting his head back, he could see a sliver of the room in front. 'But it's still working.' He angled his head towards his grandad. 'Malachy, I need to make a phone call or two.'

He waved a hand. 'Ach, you'll have to go to your Aunt Aideen's for that, you know I don't have one in the house.'

Aunt Aideen's, Jon thought. I don't have an Aunt Aideen, do I? Oh, unless, he's mixing me up with that bloke again. The one who's boat overturned out at sea.

'Right,' he replied, placing the glass back on the bedside table. His gaze settled on the photo his mum was in and an idea popped into his head. No, he thought. That's not fair. You can't take advantage of him like that. He lifted the photo up anyway. 'Are these all your daughters?'

'It is, so,' he answered proudly. 'Sunning themselves at Gorteen.'

Jon studied the image. 'Which one's Una?'

'There she is,' he said, voice constricted by bending forward. A finger was pointed at the girl on the end.

'You must miss her.' Jon looked up.

'I do.' He sat back, rheumy eyes going unfocused as he stroked his beard. 'And Mary too.'

Jon saw sunlight catching in the sparse bristles on the top of his grandfather's head. He swallowed. Should I do this? No, I shouldn't. But if I don't, will I ever learn the truth? Probably not. Mum will never tell me and who knows how long the old boy has left? He looked again at the photo of his mum, one gangly leg skewed to the side, heel jammed into a cleft in the rock. 'How many years is it since you've seen Mary?'

'Mary?' His eyes grew moist. 'It's been too long.' He reached down and started easing his fingers through the soft fur on his dog's neck. 'Too long.' The dog's eyes slowly closed.

Jon thought about his own age. Forty-three. No contact with my grandparents in decades. He shut his eyes too and whispered, 'I wish she'd come to visit.'

'I know, Joseph. It all happened so long ago, there's no sense in it, surely.'

Two words, he thought. I ask two words now and I might just discover the truth. Time seemed to stutter and stall. Do I say them? He kept his head bowed, guilt making the words catch in his throat. 'What happened?'

Seconds slid by. He glanced up. Malachy had raised a hand to his mouth and was tapping the side of his forefinger against his lower lip. Jon realised he was trembling ever so slightly. 'She was such a young girl when we let her go to Manchester. Away from her family. There was blame to be found with us, too.'

He dropped his hand and gave a little shake of his head. For a moment, Jon thought he wasn't going to say anything else.

'But the time for blame and anger is over,' he continued, banging his stick down. 'As sure as I live, it's over. Maybe not with the man who made her pregnant, but with our family it is.'

The man who made her pregnant. Jon looked up, unsure if he'd heard Malachy correctly.

'And that man who stepped forward to marry her? So he wasn't a Catholic. I didn't mind. And I think in her heart, Orla didn't either. Not many would have stood in like he did and been father to another man's child. He's a good man and he loves her. We all know that.'

Jon felt like the room was rushing backwards. He raised his eyes to the ceiling, trying to fight the feeling. The man who made her pregnant. Mum was carrying someone else's child, that's what Malachy had said, wasn't it? She was carrying someone else's child and another man stepped forward, was prepared to marry her and treat the baby as if it was his own. He breathed in and out, aware of every beat of his heart. 'This man. The one who married Mary, you mean Alan?'

'Yes – the one who worked on the docks there in Manchester. Alan.'

My father, Jon thought. Who I thought was my father, but who isn't at all. He let his head hang forward, the sheer weight of realisation too much. And behind the heaviness, he sensed something else. Something that spun and whirled and twisted with chaotic force. It's all been a lie. The basis of my life – who I am – it isn't true.

Malachy put his hand on Jon's. 'It looks like you're beaten by the sleep again. I shall leave you be.'

'OK,' Jon whispered.

'Shall I fetch you more of the carrageen? For beside your bed?'

He shook his head and then heard the scrape of the bowl as his grandfather slid it from the bedside table. 'There's more in the fridge when you want it. Now come on dog, away now.'

Once the door had shut, Jon tipped his head back and closed his eyes. Alan. Are Dave and Ellie also his? They must be; Mum had been married to him a few years by the time they were born. Maybe that's why there's such an age gap between me and them. The one who isn't Alan's is me. Only me.

He threw the bed covers aside, the white of the bandaging around his knee stark against the covering of black hair on his legs. I need to get out, he thought. I need some space.

Darragh placed his phone beside the computer keyboard and looked across at Gerrard. 'That was Patrick. He's just come out of a meeting. They've been given orders to find Spicer.'

'Who?'

'Every available officer.'

'What?' The old man sounded alarmed.

'That's what he said; everything's on hold until the peeler's found.'

Gerrard's face seemed to fold in on itself. 'Such concern all of a sudden.'

'He said more officers are being sent from nearby stations,' Darragh added. 'Orders from way up the chain, apparently. The English police are suddenly very keen to have him back.'

'I bet they are,' the old man murmured. 'So he always was out here on his own private mission. '

'As we thought.'

Gerrard looked wistfully at the ocean outside. 'They had their chance to get him home and they didn't take it.'

Devlan shovelled more scrambled egg into his mouth. 'Cunts.'

Gerrard looked momentarily irritated. 'Had that man with the kitchen-fitting business – Ryan is it? Had he rung the Guards?'

'There's been no report of any incident,' Darragh replied. 'The man was bullshitting.'

'Lucky for him.' Gerrard brought his hands together to form a misshapen club of flesh. 'We need to find him first, simple as that. If he's lifted back to England, he goes home with a load of information about us – including those bloody tapes. And the name of whoever's been feeding him everything.'

Darragh nodded. 'Good thing is, they haven't the first clue where he is. Patrick said to get ready; they'll be knocking on all our properties in the area.'

'Here?'

'I guess so.'

'Lough Nakilla?'

'Yup. I'll phone Mum and let her know.'

'Golden Fields?'

'He said that wasn't on the list he saw.'

Gerrard's eyes twinkled as he glanced at Devlan. 'Buffoons that they are, I knew they wouldn't think to check back there. OK – get on the phone. I want every man on this. Asking their family, their friends, their fucking priest.' He clicked a finger. 'In fact, have the churches checked, too. He's hiding somewhere. Also bed-and-breakfast places, hotels, all that.'

Siobhain refilled the teapot and turned to Devlan. 'Can you give me some money, Dev?'

He regarded her, a fork full of white pudding inches from his mouth. 'What for?'

She looked pointedly at his plate. 'More bacon, sausage, bread, tea bags. The fridge is near-empty.'

He pulled a few notes from his pocket and counted them out. 'Forty-five euro. And get me some more smokes too.'

'OK.' She crossed the room and lifted her coat from the row of pegs by the front door. 'I'll take the Honda.'

Devlan was sawing at a piece of bacon. 'The Honda? To get to the shop?'

'It's a Sunday. I'll need to find a supermarket that's open.'

He grunted in response as she disappeared out the door. Gerrard stared after her. 'Have her followed.'

Devlan looked up, jaw motionless, eyebrows arched.

'We know nothing of that girl, other than you're riding her,' Gerrard growled. 'Have the lass followed.'

'Da, she wouldn't dare breathe a word about us.'

In the corner, Darragh turned in his seat, head cocked to the side. 'When you were with her in the sack. Did she have a rag in?'

'What?' His brother coughed out a lump of chewed bacon. 'You dirty wee fuck.'

Darragh sat forward. 'Before we closed the club, she was up to something. She'd locked herself in the toilets, I thought she was pocketing tips. Said to me she was in there changing her tampon.'

Devlan picked at his teeth with a thumbnail. 'Did she? Well, she wasn't on the curse when I was doing her just now.'

'Alice, it's Rick.'

'Have you found him?'

He winced at the question. 'Not yet. But there are a lot of officers looking.' His thoughts turned to the previous evening. Parks had taken him up to the office of Chief Superintendent Gower, where he'd had to go through everything he knew about Jon's movements. Gower had listened in silence.

A call had gone into Nick Hutcher in the RSPCA, who'd provided them with a number for Martin O'Donagh, the inspector in the ISPCA who'd led the raid on the de Avila's pet-food factory.

O'Donagh had confirmed Jon had showed up there, but on realising the dog fight had been called off, had driven back to Clifden saying he needed to speak with the de Avilas face-to-face.

That was at eleven in the morning and after that, nothing. The hospital had been checked, as had the town's hotels. No one had anything of use to report.

Rick considered the list his contact in the NCA had been sent by his Irish colleagues. Topping it was the commercial properties they already knew the de Avila family owned. After that, there were dozens of residential properties spread throughout the Connemara region. Most were holiday homes, standing empty in readiness for the tourist season. The possible locations where Jon could be being held was frightening.

'Rick.' Alice's voice was wobbling. 'I rang his mum and dad earlier. They haven't heard from him either. What's happened?'

'It'll be fine, Alice.' Rick made sure he sounded confident. 'Bloody hell,' he tried to laugh. 'For all we know, he stayed over to watch a rugby match in Dublin or something. Got drinking with a load of Irish and is sleeping it off in a hotel room.'

'No. He'd have rung me.' She started to cry. 'God, it's my fault – I pressurised him. Told him to do whatever he had to do. He was about to fly home.'

'Alice, it's not your fault. We don't even know if he found the brothers.'

She didn't respond.

'Alice, we don't know that, do we?'

'No,' she sniffed.

'OK.'

'I'm so scared, Rick.'

'Don't be. This will work out fine. Last thing, Alice.' He checked his voice, aware too much urgency was creeping in. 'We're following up leads and, chances are, we'll locate him very soon. But did he mention any specific place to you? Doesn't he have relatives in the area?' He waited with his eyes closed. Please, Alice, he thought. Give us something we can use.

'Roundstone,' she replied hesitantly. 'Didn't he mention that to you?'

'No. What is it?'

'The little fishing village where his mum's side of the family are originally from. It's about an hour's drive from Clifden. He's been popping over to visit his grandad – he lives in a little bungalow there.'

Rick scribbled the word down. The rest of his syndicate were in a silent ring round the table. DCI Parks read the word and shot a quizzical look at Rick.

He spoke directly at his senior officer. 'OK, Alice, it's a little fishing village one hour from Clifden. His grandfather lives in a bungalow there.'

DCI Parks flapped a hand at the officer who was sitting before a computer terminal. He started to tap the name in.

Rick felt his eyes sting and wiped at the sweat now trickling off his forehead. 'Don't suppose you know his name, Alice?'

'O'Coinne. The family's called O'Coinne.'

'Is she?' Devlan's lips twisted into a caricature of a grin. 'Stay put, I'm on my way.' He cut the connection and looked at Gerrard with cold delight. 'The fucking whore isn't at the supermarket. She's driven up to Moyard.'

The old man sucked air in through his nose. 'And?'

'Denis is sitting outside the office of a Bernard Reilly. That's where she is.'

Darragh turned from the plate-glass windows. 'The solicitor.' He looked to his father. 'She's speaking to Bernard Reilly.'

Devlan still looked bewildered. 'Who is he?'

'The drunken bastard who's been irritating us all these years,' Gerrard rumbled. 'So she's our tout – feeding that washed-up fucker's obsession.'

Scratching at an armpit, Devlan still looked lost. 'What obsession?'

Gerrard sighed with frustration. 'Castlebar, 1993? When Collins's car went off the road, it ploughed into that couple?'

Devlan's hand flopped down. 'Them?'

'Yes,' Gerrard snapped. 'The man who died was called Geordan Reilly. This solicitor is his brother. Ever since he's been trying to convince anyone that'll listen that we were behind what happened. The fact he's so cracked in the head has meant no one's taken him seriously.'

Darragh took off his glasses and rubbed at his eyes. 'So, who's this Hazel? She turned up in town, what, three years ago?'

Devlan nodded. 'Came from Manchester, she did. She'd lived there, for sure. Knows all about the place.'

'Where the English policeman is from, too,' Gerrard whispered. 'Where'd she been before that? Any fucking idea?'

'County Mayo,' Devlan said uneasily. 'I think.'

'Mayo. Where the Reilly family lived. You think she's part of that family?'

Devlan was off the bar stool, fingers curling then straightening. 'We'll find out. I'll drag her here by the fucking hair.'

Darragh put his glasses back on. 'We need to know how much she's been telling this solicitor.'

Gerrard's phone started to ring. He glanced at it before looking back at Devlan. 'Get up to Moyard.' He took the call, face expressionless. 'Good lads, you'll be receiving payment for this.' He closed his phone and called out to Devlan who was now at the front door. 'Where's Sean?'

'I don't know. In his flat?'

'I want him here.'

'What you trust him again?'

'Don't take that tone with me!' Gerrard roared. 'When

it was you who let a tout into our family!'

Glowering, Devlan lowered his eyes.

Breathing heavily, Gerrard continued. 'Get me Sean. There's been word from Roundstone. A black Peugeot just set off from the bungalow opposite the site we have out there. Big guy with a swollen eye was driving.'

'It's him. Let me go.' Devlan was as taut as a wire. 'Please, Da.'

Gerrard snorted. 'And have you fuck it up? This needs someone with a cool head.'

Darragh spoke. 'Are we still going to do things the way I suggested?'

Both men nodded back.

'If we are,' Darragh responded, 'we need him to believe he's calling the shots. And that doesn't mean clubbing him over the head and dragging him into the back of a van.'

They waited for him to say more.

He looked from one to the other. 'Think about it. There's an easier way to get hold of him.' He held out a hand. 'What brought this fucker to our door in the first place?'

Gerrard grunted. 'That girl, Zoë.'

'Exactly,' Darragh replied. 'So we say we've had enough and offer to give her to him if he hands the security tapes back and goes away.'

Gerrard considered the suggestion. 'The girl for the tapes? Why do you think he'll go for that?'

'Why?' Darragh replied. 'Because he's English. Ever since getting here, the arrogant twat's been expecting us to roll over and do what he wants.'

CHAPTER 44

Siobhain hurried up the bare wooden stairs. Black lettering on the door at the top spelled the words, Bernard Reilly, solicitor.

She rapped once and turned the handle. Locked. 'Jesus, Bernard!' Turning on the spot, she pulled a cigarette from the pack in her pocket and flicked a lighter. By the time a shadow appeared at the doorway to the street, she'd smoked another three.

Peering down the stairs, she watched the man step into the hallway. Wiry grey hair created a haze on his head. He looked up at her with sorrowful eyes. 'Sorry, Siobhain – the car wouldn't start.' Laboriously, he made his way up to her, removing a set of keys from the pocket of a faded suit. 'You OK, my love?'

She nodded, getting to her feet. 'I can't stay long. I only said I was going to the shop.'

'Right.' He unlocked the door and pushed it open.

Musty air hit her as she stepped into an office littered with newspapers, magazines and files. Dead spider plants lined the windowsill, the glass above it clouded with a layer of grime. He reached behind her and flicked a switch. The naked bulb hanging from the ceiling came to life, its glow filling the room with a harsh light.

She turned her eyes to the desk in the corner. Towers of paperwork covered it. Wearily, the man slumped down in the chair behind it. His eyes were bleary and she thought how fast he was beginning to age.

'Siobhain,' he stated. 'What have you done?'

She closed the door, hand lingering in the air before she turned round. 'Something terrible, Uncle Bernard. Jesus, something really terrible.'

He stood and removed a pile of newspapers from the chair to the side of his desk. After casting a despairing glance about, he balanced them across the top of a bin half-full with discarded post. 'Sit yourself down. It can't be too late to sort things out, surely.'

'I think it is. I think I'll be the cause of a good man dying.' She fought to control her words as he put an arm round her shoulders and directed her to the chair.

'Hush now. Come on, tell me what's going on.'

She sat with her hands clutching her knees, shoulders hunched. He waited in silence as she composed herself. 'I didn't tell you the truth,' she announced quietly, eyes momentarily lifting to meet his. 'I lied.'

'Why?' he whispered.

'Because I knew you wouldn't agree. And you'd have been right. Oh, God, what have I done? It's all gone wrong…it's all…I don't know how to stop it.'

'Siobhain, hush.' He looked at the bottom drawer of his desk, a fidget in his fingers. 'First, who is this man if he isn't a journalist?'

She took a deep breath. 'He's a policeman. From Manchester.'

'You know him from your time there?'

She shook her head. 'I knew about him. What he's like.'

'I don't understand,' he replied, eyes cutting to the drawer once again.

'When I ran away from that care home in Galway and went to Manchester, I didn't know anyone. So I ended up on the streets, sleeping rough.'

He hung his head. 'I'm so sorry, Siobhain. My own niece, I should never have allowed – '

'Don't. You had enough concerns of your own, it doesn't matter.' Reaching into her coat, she removed her cigarettes and offered one to him.

He took it and, once she'd lit both, reached for a large glass ashtray already scattered with butts.

'When I was there,' she continued, blowing smoke off to the side, 'I got to know this man called Salvio. I didn't realise at first, but…but he was a pimp.' She lifted the cigarette again and it trembled with the force of her drag. 'He took me into his house then he started giving me stuff…'

'Oh Jesus.' He reached down, opened the drawer and lunged at a bottle of whiskey. She watched with a resigned expression as he sloshed liquid into a glass and took a gulp. Unable to look at her, he waved a hand. 'Sorry.'

'It's OK,' she answered. 'I met this other girl called Zoë. We got on, used to talk when we got the chance. Later, after I got out and came back here, she found me.' Siobhain smiled. 'Crazy thing just arrived in the town and started asking after me. Of course, I was using the name Hazel by then, so she wasn't doing very well at finding me. We bumped into each other eventually, though.' She took a couple of swift drags. 'She didn't even have enough clothes. I gave her a top – one I blagged from the nightclub. I even gave the photo of her wearing it to Spicer, so he'd think that she worked here…' She shut her eyes again.

Bernard placed a hand on her forearm. 'Take your time.'

'In Manchester, she was with this guy called Dave. Sweet, he was. Kind to her. He got her away from Salvio. Then Dave was killed and Salvio tried to move in on Zoë again. That's when Dave's brother – this policeman – stepped in. Zoë told me how he dealt with Salvio – and that's what gave me the idea.' She slid the glass from Bernard's fingers and took a generous sip.

'The idea to get him onto the de Avilas?'

She nodded, handing the glass back.

'Why?' His voice contained a plaintive note.

'Bernard.' She looked round. 'This thing has ruined your life. Our lives. Ever since they killed my mum and dad – your brother - you've been trying to get justice.' Her face soured. 'It's fucking futile.'

'It's not! Look at the information you've been getting me.'

'What? Sheets of paper with numbers on? Records of how much money they're making?'

'It's all helping.'

Her voice dropped to a throaty whisper. 'And look at what I've had to do to get it.'

He recoiled slightly. 'I know working for them can't be – '

'Bernard.' Her voice turned hard. 'I'm Devlan's girl. He fucks me whenever he feels like it. I'm just a whore, all over again.'

'Don't.' He screwed his eyes shut. 'Don't.'

'It's true,' she spat. 'I'm that family's slave. And it's all useless, fucking useless!'

They sat in silence, smoke from their cigarettes twisting up like two lengths of pale twine.

He licked his lips. 'There are developments. Look at Omagh – the relatives of those who died there have pursued the bombers through the civil courts. They won, Siobhain. They won!'

She groaned. 'They won with the help of proper law firms, entire legal teams working for free, newspaper appeals, sure – even bloody documentaries. And they had GCHQ's records of the bombers' mobile phones. What have we got? You're the only eyewitness to say Devlan fired the shots from that car. And one of the victims was your brother. You have a history of depression, the

Guards think you're a joke – the one's not in the de Avilas' pocket. Bernard, it's futile.'

He drained his glass, hand wobbling as it lowered back to his lap. 'I won't give up. I won't.'

'I know you won't.' Tears were in her eyes as she looked at the bottle. 'And I love you for that. But it's a battle that's slowly killing you.' She took a final drag of her cigarette and ground it out. 'I knew this policeman's surname, so I searched out his number and called him. I told him Zoë was in trouble – the de Avilas were forcing her to do deliveries for them. She was in danger.'

He frowned. 'I don't understand. What did you hope to achieve?'

She bit at a thumbnail. 'I don't know. Seeing them getting away with it and no one interested in stopping them. I just wanted to wipe the smiles off their faces. See them humiliated, hurt.' She lit another cigarette. 'I knew he'd come. What Zoë told me about him, I knew it. And I knew the de Avilas wouldn't scare him. He's like one of those huge dogs they're after breeding – when the guy starts on something, he won't back down. Zoë's family, so he'd come to help her.' She nodded to herself. 'And he did. God love him, he did.'

Bernard stared into his empty glass. 'And is this Zoë in danger?'

She shook her head.

The solicitor's body sagged. 'Jesus and Mary forgive you. You played on his loyalty. You lured him here with a lie.'

She bowed her head, shoulders beginning to shake.

'And now the de Avilas mean to get rid of him? Can you not tell him the truth, warn him away?'

She met his eyes, wiping at her cheeks with the back of her hand. 'I can't find him! He won't answer his phone!' She started to sob. 'They're planning such horrible things for him.'

'They've said this in front of you?'

She reached into her pocket and took out her mobile. 'This is them talking. They sent us all outside, but I recorded it.' She accessed the file on her phone, pressed play and held it towards her uncle. 'It's filmed from the inside of a drawer, but you can hear them talking.'

He stared at the little device as the de Avilas' voices filled the smoke-filled office.

Jon turned into the car park of Gorteen Bay and pulled up in the same spot as before. Below the jostling clouds, a patchwork of shadows shifted on the sea. He focused on the purplish island on the horizon. The view seemed false, like a recording playing out on an immense screen. He examined his hands, the individual hairs, the wrinkles scoring the skin of his knuckles. The slight movement below the skin of his inner wrist. My blood isn't Alan's blood. It's someone else's.

He opened the car door and eased himself out. The mineral-scented breeze dropped and solid sunlight broke through directly above. He felt its warmth on his scalp. Turning to the beach, he hobbled past the litter bin and down the steps on to sand so pale, the patches of snow covering it were all but invisible. He set off for the water's edge, searching for any other footprints in the pristine expanse. All he saw were faint impressions left by the feet of scavenging seabirds.

The long beach curved away in a shallow arc. A couple of hundred metres on was a glistening brown lump the size of a deflated football. As he got nearer, he could make out thick, intestine-like tubes trailing out from its main part. A jellyfish, he realised. But more like an afterbirth, left by some creature that had hauled itself from the ocean under the cover of night.

Further along, he recognised the boulder his mother and her sisters had been sitting on in the photo on the bedside table. Time, he thought. Our lives, with all their highs and lows, play out over a few short decades. And then we die. But this boulder – this landscape – endures.

The beach ended at a headland. When he reached its far side, the sea was noisier: waves surging against the splintered rock of the shoreline. He looked down at seaweed beds far beneath the surface. The tendrils gently shifted and an image of his mother's face formed in his mind. He shook his head and surveyed the craggy coast, suddenly wondering where the *Concepción* been lured to the shore. In view of where he was now?

He found a smooth rock, sat down and stretched his bad leg out before him. What the hell happens now? How do I tell Mum that I know? He considered for a second pretending that he didn't, then dismissed the thought. She was prepared to build my life on a lie, but I won't carry it on. And Alan? He's my dad, he raised me like I was his son. But he's also part of the deceit. He's been lying just as much as her.

He gazed across the bay. The clouds on the horizon had cleared to reveal the Twelve Bens, each one now a spotless white. Before him, the sea sucked and slapped at the rocks, unable to leave the land alone.

Bernard Reilly's eyes were closed as he listened to the recording coming from Siobhain's phone. He heard Gerrard state that someone was passing information to the English policeman. Then Devlan announced he had Cuchullain safe.

Bernard's head came up. 'Sounds like they're planning to set the dog on – '

'Shush!' Siobhain hissed. 'Just listen – it gets worse.'

Bernard's mouth closed and he focused on the little device as Gerrard said, 'We find this person – get the tapes back – then set the dog on him. Once Cuch' has finished, we chuck what's left in the macerator.'

The solicitor's eyes widened.

'Like that shyster who tried to cheat you that time?' Devlan's voice.

'Hammell.' Gerrard again. 'Just like him.'

Looking stunned, Bernard sat up and was about to speak when Siobhain waved a hand. 'Listen!'

A background voice, fainter than the first two. 'Do you really mean to kill him? An English policeman?'

'That's Darragh,' Siobhain whispered, staring fearfully at her uncle.

Devlan again: 'He's made us look like cunts for too long, isn't that right Da?'

'It is. He has to be dealt with, Darragh.'

There was a pause before Darragh spoke again. 'If you're going to do this, let's try and make it to our advantage.'

Gerrard: 'What have you in mind, son?'

Now Darragh's voice was much closer, words perfectly clear. 'Take him to the farm and have your fun with Cuchullain. But don't put him in the mincers. When he shows up as missing, they'll turn our premises upside down. Forensics can get DNA from anything nowadays, you know that.'

Siobhain pressed stop. 'See, Bernard? They're going to hunt him down. It's all my fault!'

The solicitor's breathing had quickened. 'We've got Gerrard de Avila admitting to Hammell, Siobhain – '

'They're going to kill him! Set that enormous thing on him, torture him...' She leaned over the arm of her chair. 'God!' she gasped. 'Oh God!'

'We can alert the Guards,' Bernard stated, placing a hand on her back. 'Siobhain – they're talking about Golden Fields. I call with an anonymous tip, saying Jon is being held there.'

'What if they find him and take him somewhere else?' Siobhain moaned. 'They've enough places to choose from.'

Bernard narrowed his eyes at the mobile. 'Is there anything more on that thing?'

'I don't know. I couldn't bear to listen any longer.'

'Play it, Siobhain, for God's sake.'

Reluctantly, she reached over and pressed a button.

Darragh continued to speak. 'Make it look like a paramilitary hit instead – hammer out his teeth, smash his knees, whatever they do. Sean'll know. Then we take his body up to bandit country. South Armagh. Somewhere on the border, anyway. Dump him there.'

Devlan: 'Surely everyone will know it was us?'

'No they won't,' Darragh replied. 'There were people in town for this fight from all over. Campbell's crew from Belfast? They were asking me in the club about the English peeler who was meant to be in town. Wanting to know if it was true. Word's been spreading. Christ, the guy's been pinning up bloody posters all over the place with his phone number on. The unionists will blame the republicans and the republicans will say nothing because they don't know their arses from their elbows nowadays. Think about that British soldier. No one has a clue who killed him. We dump Spicer's body in bandit country and the unionists will point the finger at Sinn Féin and the IRA. Off they go at each other all over again.'

Devlan: 'Just like when we did Francis Collins.'

'Just like when we did Francis Collins,' Gerrard echoed. 'And while they're busy killing each other, we get stronger.'

Bernard stood, mouth gaping as his glass thudded to the floor. 'He just said…' He sat back down, eyes locked on Siobhain's mobile.

Gerrard continued. 'He's good. The boy is good!'

Movement, then Devlan's voice: 'Aye, the brain on him! It's just too fucking big, is what it is!'

The recording cut and Siobhain stared at her uncle, white-faced.

'Again,' he said. 'I want to hear it again.'

When it had finished for a second time, Bernard retrieved his glass and tried to fill it. Splashes of liquid landed on his desk. He took a mouthful, swallowed, took another and breathed out. 'Siobhain, do you know what this means?'

She turned her head slowly from side to side.

'If I get this to someone in Sinn Féin – and I have names and contact numbers – then it's all over.'

Fingers shaking, Siobhain put another cigarette in her mouth, mumbling as she lit it. 'What do you mean?'

'There'll be no court case, none of that. Francis Collins was on the IRA's army council. If they find out it was the de Avilas…' He sat forward. 'It's written in the Green Book; their rules. An internal security unit will be sent here. People trained to deal with traitors.'

'How quick?'

'They won't hang around. They never do.'

'Quick enough to save Jon?'

He shrugged.

Siobhain sucked back smoke, looked at her uncle then at her mobile then back at him. 'Do it.'

Bernard's feet shifted on the floor. 'You know what you're saying?'

She nodded. 'It's what they deserve. They killed Mum and Dad, ruined our lives. If we took it to the Guards or a newspaper, what? Years of wrangling – and no guarantees at the end. And before any of that starts, the de Avilas will kill a good man because of me. How soon can you get it to the Shinners? Someone high up in the party. Someone with clout. How long?'

He thought for a moment. 'By motorbike courier? Four hours.'

'That's not quick enough. They've got people out looking for him now.'

'There's no other way.'

'Christ!' She brushed a strand of hair back. 'Do it.'

'You'll have to leave Clifden. Now, today – never to return.'

'That's what I've been dreaming about for years.' She took another drag, stubbed the cigarette out and stood. 'I have to get back. They'll be wondering where I am.'

'I said you should leave now.'

She nodded. 'I will. I'll nip back, get my things and be off.'

'Too risky. Just keep going from here – keep going north.'

'Bernard, I've got money stashed away in Clifden. And my clothes. It'll be OK.'

He put his glass down and picked up her mobile, cradling it like a thing of wonder. 'Just be quick.'

'I will.'

'And don't worry about the policeman. I'll make the call – say that I saw him being dragged out of a van at the farm.' He held his arms out and they clung to each other for a few seconds. 'Sure about this?' he whispered in her ear.

'About what?' she answered, gripping him tight.

'Sending your phone to the Shinners?'

Her smile was lopsided with nerves. 'Yes.'

'Da? I'm here. Denis says the solicitor went in about quarter of an hour ago. A light's on in his office. They're up there together. Shall we go in and start breaking knees?'

'No,' Gerrard replied. 'We need this done quietly – no big scene. Let me think. Is it just the two of them in there?'

Devlan turned in the passenger seat to address the other man. 'Anyone else inside?'

Denis shook his head.

'Just them, Da…hang on. She's coming out! She's getting into the car.'

'Where's the solicitor?'

'Inside still.'

'What's she doing?'

'Turning the car round. Hang on…she's…she's just driven past us, heading back to you, I reckon.'

'Let her come. We'll deal with her when we're good and ready. I want you to find out what she's been telling that solicitor.'

Devlan grinned. 'Got you.' He ended the call and

turned to Denis, opening the car door as he did so. 'Wait here.'

'What are you doing?'

Devlan climbed out, held both arms to the sky and stretched. 'Enjoying myself, Denis. That's what I'm doing.'

As he made his way back to the beach, Jon's view was dominated by Errisbeg Hill. He found himself studying its craggy rough peak. High up there, he thought, would be so peaceful, so detached from the world.

The trail forked – one path curving off towards the graveyard and car park, the other continuing directly inland towards Errisbeg. Jon hesitated. The looming hill and promise of quiet solitude at the top seemed to pull at him. He reflected on how often, when faced with turmoil or upheaval in his life, he sought out the comfort of such places. Malachy used to go up and down it how many times each day? Four? He tested his knee; it felt numb but well supported by the tight bandaging. It can't take too long, surely.

The path traversed several fields; narrow gaps allowed him to squeeze sideways through the dry-stone walls separating them. Apart from the sodden earth, the gentle lower slopes were relatively easy to negotiate.

After quarter of an hour, he looked up; his guess at an hour's climb had been optimistic. He found himself trying to judge distances with his good eye, stepping onto hummocks of grass or low-lying patches of heather in an attempt to keep his feet dry. It was no use. The water that found its way into his shoes was icy and black.

As the incline grew steeper, he used his hands to clamber up sections of rock. All around him was the hard clatter of water hitting stone. Little streams tumbling in a wild downward rush as if fleeing a threat from higher up. Mosses and lichens clung in crevices and cracks, some with stalks beaded by a honey-like liquid at their top.

Rock now formed a continuous layer underfoot and he

was able to move more swiftly, limping from slab to slab, aware he was rapidly gaining height. The wind grew steadily in strength. From the beach, he thought, it looked as still as anything up here. Straightening his back, he saw he was now about a hundred metres from the summit. With every step, the speed of the wind increased. By the time he was at the stone cairn at the top, his clothes were pressed into his back.

He looked down at the beach: the car park and his Peugeot were completely hidden from view. The relentless wind had started to rob his fingers of their feeling, so he moved round the cairn to try and escape it. Now he was overlooking the vast bog. Sunlight was catching on the mass of lakes, turning their jagged shapes silver against the dark land. A colossal jigsaw, Jon thought, every piece narrowly separated from its neighbours. And somewhere, threading its way through the shimmering labyrinth, was the single-track road to Clifden.

He sank into a sitting position. All my life, they've lied to me. Every time I called Alan Dad, they knew it wasn't true. Did it set off a little pang when they heard me say that word? Occasions, like my birthday or at Christmas, presents to open on the carpet, me looking up. He heard his childhood self speaking. Thanks, Dad. It's brilliant. You're the best, Dad. Did they share small glances of guilt?

He ran his fingers across the hard stone. Cold, unforgiving. Who was he? Who was my real father? Did mum know him? Were they a couple, or was it something else? Was she raped? If she was, would Malachy and Orla have forbidden her to have an abortion? Were abortions even legal back then? What had Malachy said in the bedroom? That man who made her pregnant. Made her pregnant. Did his words hint at coercion? Like she had no choice in the process. He leaned his head back and closed his eyes. You're reading too much into his comment, he told himself. He could have meant anything.

Looking to his right, he saw down on to the little

village. There was the high street, and the harbour pier. His eyes travelled inland, trying to make out his grandad's bungalow. A white car with markings was now parked in front of the property. The speeding air was making his eyes water, so Jon cupped one hand to the side of his face. He watched as two antlike officers emerged from the bungalow and walked back to their car. What the fuck were they doing? More spies for the de Avila family? If I stood up now and waved my arms, they may well see me. He kept still as the car turned round and drove back towards the high street. The vehicle disappeared from view, re-emerging on the coast road. Jon peered round the cairn as it passed the turn-off for Gorteen Bay and continued towards Clifden.

What the hell did they want? Alarm sparked in his head. Oh my God, if they know I was there, do the de Avilas, too? I have to get back.

CHAPTER 45

Devlan eased open the door to the solicitor's office and looked in. The bloke was on his feet, facing away from him as he fiddled with something on the desk. Next to him was a bottle of whiskey, an inch or so left. Brown gaffer tape rasped as the man pulled at a roll.

The door shut with a click and the solicitor stiffened.

'Bit whiffy in here,' Devlan stated. 'Though we won't be opening a window.'

The solicitor seemed to shrink slightly before glancing over his shoulder. 'Can I help you?'

As he turned round, Devlan saw him try to slide a newspaper over whatever it was he'd been busy with. He nodded at the shiny length of tape hanging from the other man's fingers. 'You carry on there. Don't mind me, like.'

Casually, the solicitor scrunched it up. 'Bundling up old paperwork for the tip. It's amazing how fast it builds up.' There was a flush of red in his cheeks as he smiled. 'Sorry, do you have an appointment?'

'Do I need one?'

'Well, it's a Sunday. I'm not really open for business. Tomorrow, I could see you then.'

'But you saw that lass just now. I know her as Hazel,

you might call her something different.'

The skin round his mouth and eyes slipped. 'She…she didn't give a name.'

Devlan shrugged. 'Now, I dare say we could carry on like this for a fair while. You being a solicitor – even the drunken old cunt of one that you are – would probably run rings round me. I'm not so good at the talk, you know?' He crossed the room and picked up the bottle of whiskey. 'Do you mind?'

Bernard Reilly backed round to his chair and sat down. 'What do you want?'

Keeping his eyes on the other man, Devlan tilted the bottle to his lips and drained it. 'Aah,' he licked his lips. 'Good stuff that, thanks.' He sat on the corner of the desk, the empty bottle swinging between his knees. 'What's she been saying to you?'

Bernard placed a hand over each arm of his chair, the skin of his face now pale and clammy. 'Go to hell, Devlan.'

'Devlan?' He spoke softly. 'So you know who I am. Good, we're dropping the crap. That's good. What's she been telling you?'

'Fuck you.'

'Fuck me?' As Devlan began to look down, his arm shot out and the bottle connected with Bernard's face. Glass flew in all directions and his head jerked to the side. Instants later an intricate pattern of dots and lines sprang up across his forehead, nose and cheeks. The redness swelled for a second then the entire side of his face was slick with blood. He began to topple forward, chin touching his chest.

Moving quickly, Devlan shoved him back, grabbed the roll of tape and passed it round and round the armrests of the chair, fastening the solicitor's wrists to the wood. He started to groan. Devlan tore another length of tape free and stuck it over the man's eyes. Retaking his position on the edge of the desk, he picked up the broken bottle neck and waited.

The other man's head lifted.

'There he is again,' Devlan cheerfully announced, watching the solicitor try to lift a hand. Both arms began to strain at the tape. 'Now, what's she been telling you?'

He raised his chin and spoke at a point just to Devlan's side. 'Fuck you.'

Devlan reached across the desk, using the broken bottle to flip the newspaper off the object the solicitor had tried to conceal. It was a padded brown envelope. Devlan scanned the large black lettering across its front. 'Rory Duggan of Sinn Féin? I've seen him on the telly. Know the man, do you?'

The solicitor's head didn't move, breath passing rapidly in and out of his nostrils. The front of his shirt was now soaked with blood.

Devlan reached into the envelope. 'What's so urgent that you're sending it to his nice big offices in Stormont by courier?' His eyebrows lowered. 'Hazel's phone. What are you pair of fucks up to?'

The solicitor began thrashing about in his chair, legs kicking wildly. 'Bastard! You bloody bastard, you bloody –'

Devlan raised a foot and stamped down into the other man's groin.

Bernard doubled over in his chair, coughing and choking. One thought stayed clear in his head. I didn't ring the Guards. Didn't warn them Spicer is at the de Avila's farm.

By the time Jon reached the fields above the village, he guessed it was around lunchtime. Alice, he thought. I still haven't rung her. She has no idea where I am.

The path snaked across to a makeshift gate beyond which was the narrow lane leading to Malachy's place. In the hedge to his side he found a stout length of branch. After stripping off a few twigs, he used it as a walking stick to take some of the pressure off his throbbing knee. When the bungalow came into view he could see Eileen's old

Nissan parked outside. He noticed the workmen who'd been dropping off materials on the building site earlier had gone. The front door to Malachy's was ajar. 'Hello?' he called quietly, wondering whether to keep the wooden staff with him. 'Anyone home?'

Noise from further inside. He moved down the corridor, staff grasped in his right hand. 'Eileen, is that you?' He looked into the kitchen. Her back was to him and he watched as she passed an iron over one of Malachy's shirts, the kitchen table doubling as a board. 'Hi there.'

'Hello.' Her reply was clipped and cold and he immediately knew.

He lowered himself into a chair, injured leg straight out. 'Malachy asleep?'

She gave a nod.

'Thanks for patching me up.'

Placing the iron on the stove's hotplate to reheat, she turned round, eyes settling for a moment on the length of stick in his hand. 'Where've you been?'

He pointed a finger back over his shoulder. 'For a walk. I ended up at the top of Errisbeg.'

'With your leg in that state?'

He glanced down. The blood pulsing through the joint was so strong, he expected to see his trouser leg quivering. 'I wasn't really thinking.'

'What possessed you to go up there?'

He looked at her. It's obvious, he thought, that you know the answer to that. 'I needed to clear my head.'

'So you did speak to Malachy.'

He leaned the staff against his chair. 'Yes.'

Her face clouded. 'Shame on you, Jon. You played on his confusion, didn't you?'

He dropped his eyes.

'I knew it! He was so unsettled, not certain if he'd said something to the wrong person. You pretended to be Joseph, didn't you?'

He watched the pad of his thumb as it scribed circles in

his palm. 'I didn't…I just didn't point it out to him, when I realised he'd got me mixed up…'

'Well, isn't that a fine excuse!'

'I'm sorry.'

She hesitated a moment. 'So, what did he say?'

'I think you know what he said.'

She stared at him with a mixture of anger and sadness. 'Now you know.'

'Yes.'

She crossed her arms. 'I hope you're happy, finding out the way you did.'

'No,' he whispered. 'I'm not.'

When she eventually spoke, her voice was softer. 'Well, now it's done. But I don't want Malachy to know. When he wakes, I'll tell him it's OK, he let nothing slip.'

'But…I don't know if I can pretend – '

'Then go now. I'll say you called in and said goodbye.' Her jaw was tight. 'Which will it be?'

More secrets, Jon thought. More bloody secrets to keep. Lies laid over lies. 'OK, I'll do it. I'll pretend.' He swallowed. 'Who was he, Eileen? The man who…do you know who he was?'

She smoothed her apron. 'That is a talk to have with Mary and Alan, not me. And not Malachy either.'

'Of course. Sorry I asked.'

'And don't ask again.'

'OK.'

She picked a card off the counter. 'Malachy said the Guards were here.'

'I know – I saw their car from the top. What did they want?'

'They're trying to find you. It's very urgent, so they said.'

'What did Malachy tell them?'

'I'm not sure he made much sense. After you rushed off he had a try of the whiskey. I saw the glass in the sink. He sent them back to Clifden, saying you'd been staying in a hotel there. They left behind their number.' She held the card out.

Jon glanced at the name. Some officer working out of the station at Clifden. He dropped it on the table. 'Good.'

'What's good?'

'That Malachy sent them back to Clifden.'

'Why? They're the police, same as you.'

'I can't trust them, Eileen. Some of them are working for the de Avila family. The people who were behind this.' He waved a hand at his face. 'It's worrying enough they've been here.'

She frowned. 'They attacked you because you're for finding that girl, Zoë? Why is she so important?'

Jon sighed. 'It's gone beyond that now. Way beyond that. I've been looking into their business interests, too. How they make their money.'

'Convila.' She nodded to her side. 'The building firm behind that thing out there.'

'That and more. I don't know what kind of things they've done to build up the family business.'

'You'd have to ask Kieron. He knows all the gossip, not me.'

Jon rubbed his hands together. 'Eileen, I really need to ring my wife. She was expecting me back last night.' He looked at the clock. Almost three. 'My mobile's broken. Can I borrow yours?'

'You're welcome to, but it's in my house. Or you can use Kieron's, he'll be here soon.'

'I'd prefer not to wait, I should have rung hours ago.'

'Fine. My back door's always open. I think the phone's just inside, in my handbag on the windowsill. When can I check your dressings? That tear to your ear should have been stitched yesterday. I hate to think how it's mending.'

Jon tapped at the bandages. 'Feels OK – don't worry about it. Your house is by the church isn't it?'

'Yes, it's the one with the circular window at the – '

A knock sounded on the front door. Eileen turned

towards the corridor and was about to open her mouth.

Jon held up a hand. 'Don't!' he whispered. 'Don't say come in. See who it is, first.'

Clutching the crucifix at her neck, she stepped out of the kitchen and peered down the dim corridor. 'One moment!' She looked back at Jon. 'It's a man.'

'Alone?'

She nodded.

'What does he look like?'

'Your age? A bit younger? He's wearing a black leather jacket.'

'What's his hair like?'

'Straggly.'

'A bit ginger?'

'Yes.'

They've found me, he thought, struggling to his feet. Jesus Christ, they know where my grandad lives. What sort of trouble have I brought down on this family?

'Alice, it's Rick. We've got some positive news.'

'Is he in Roundstone at his grandad's?'

'We think he was. A patrol car called by earlier and the officers spoke to an old man – is it Malachy, the grandfather's name?'

'Yes.'

'OK, there's a bit of confusion but we believe Jon slept there last night. The old man said he'd got into a bit of a scrape. Black eye and some other stuff.'

'Oh my God.'

'Alice, come on. That's nothing worse than what he used to get on the rugby pitch most weekends. He's a big boy, can take care of himself.'

'Where is he now?'

'We're not sure. Back to Clifden, according to the grandfather.'

'He'll be still trying to find Zoë.'

'Sounds like Jon: refusing to give up. We've got more

information from the airport, too. He hired another car from there, a black Peugeot this time. We've got its registration. Officers are combing the town for it now. In fact, the whole place is crawling with police. Door-to-doors, road side checks. We'll find him soon, OK?'

'OK.'

'Keep your mobile on so I can get hold of you as soon as we know he's safe. And if he rings you, tell him it's vital he calls me.'

'Will do.'

'Holly OK?'

'Yeah, a bit subdued. She thought he was going to arrive this morning. But she's used to him missing stuff because of work. Rick, he'll lose his job over this, won't he?'

'Alice, you think there's been time to even think about that? Let's get him home in one piece first – then he can worry about the bollocking heading his way.'

Jon made an effort to walk normally as he approached the front door of the bungalow. The man waiting in the porch saw him and moved back out on to the drive. It's him, Jon thought. The one who helped kill Punch. The one probably with Devlan at Center Parcs, too.

Analysing the situation he was now in almost caused a bitter laugh to break from his lips. To think I originally came out here hoping to have a quiet chat with Darragh to sort things out. How wrong you were, Spicer. How bloody wrong you were. He tightened his grip on the knife's handle, its nine-inch blade hidden inside his sleeve.

After opening the inner door, he checked to his left then craned his head to the right in order to check that side with his good eye. Clear. There was a car parked on the track and Jon could make out someone in the passenger seat. He stepped into the porch and examined the man standing outside. 'Got a name?'

He clasped his hands in front of him, legs slightly apart.

'Sean.'

Jon felt a jolt in his chest. The voice – it's the same one from the pony auction place. This bastard ripped the top of my ear off. Calm, he told himself. Take it calmly now. Without turning his back, he pulled the front door closed behind him. 'Well, Sean, where are things at now?'

He held his hands out. 'Just delivering a message. I'm not carrying anything.' His eyes went to the arm Jon was keeping close to his side.

Jon drew out the carving knife. 'What message?'

'First, Gerrard de Avila wants to say whatever happened at Center Parcs was not authorised by him. It shouldn't have happened and he regrets any distress caused.'

Jon felt his teeth clamp tight. So it was the son, then. That bastard will fucking pay. He regarded the other man. The bloke obviously had more brains than Devlan. 'And what was your part in that? Was Devlan on his own or were you trailing after him like the poodle you are?' For a moment he thought the other man was going to rush at him. The knife came up. 'Go on, try.'

He stayed where he was and said, 'Gerrard wants to meet you – alone. Give you Zoë and put an end to all this.'

Jon wasn't sure he'd heard correctly. 'You what?'

'He'll give you Zoë to put an end to all this.'

My God, Jon thought. She really is here. He tried to not let his surprise show. 'Gerrard wants to meet me, does he?'

'You take Zoë and leave. No more acting the maggot.'

'Acting the…?'

'Being a general pain in the fucking arse.'

Jon examined the angles. It seemed too good to be true. 'That's the deal? They'll just hand over Zoë?'

'In return for something of theirs you took.'

Jon tilted his head. 'Something of theirs?'

'That you took from the nightclub…'

His jaw fell open. 'The tapes?'

'Give the boy a gold fucking star.'

'They want the security tapes for Zoë?' The signs his hotel room had been searched now made sense.

'Give them the tapes and forget whatever you know about their business. If they get a visit from the Guards, the Bureau, whoever, they'll take action over the fact you entered their premises illegally, broke the doorman's nose and assaulted the owner.'

Right, Jon thought. As if that it matters now. My career's finished. But, he realised, this could be a way to end the nightmare – and make sure Zoë's safe. He cast his mind back to dumping the tapes in the bin at Gorteen beach. Christ, how long ago was that? An entire week? Will they even still be there? 'I can do that.'

'I need to see them first. Those are my instructions.'

'Are they? Tell the de Avilas I need to see Zoë first. Those are my instructions.' He stared at the other man.

'OK.'

'When do they want to meet?'

'Soon as you're ready.'

'Where?'

'The farm – where the pet food is made.'

'And if I don't go?'

Sean glanced quickly back at the vehicle beyond the drive then looked down at his feet. 'Why the fuck didn't you leave before?' His voice was barely a murmur.

Jon frowned. 'What do you mean?'

'In the yard by the pony auction place.'

A partial memory came back. The bloke had whispered something as he lifted his knee from my neck. What was it? Something about giving up and going home. 'Why did you try and get me to leave?'

He checked over his shoulder another time. 'Must have been feeling generous,' he said quietly. 'Or sorry for you.'

Jon looked at the car before focusing on Sean once again. You don't want your mate to hear any of this, do you? His gaze shifted to the line of distant mountains. The clouds had thinned again and their snowy peaks were lit by an amber glow. The sun was beginning to set. 'You didn't answer: what if I don't want to meet them at their farm?'

The man made a show of looking at the bungalow's roof, then its windows, then its porch.

Jon took a step towards him. 'If anything happens to the people who live...' His words petered out. He couldn't protect them, not forever. 'OK – if I come, they have to all be there.'

'Who?'

'The family. Devlan, Darragh and Gerrard. If we're going to settle this, it has to be agreed by all of them. And if Devlan changes his mind and tries to touch any of my family – here or in England – I won't stop. I'll find him and I'll rip him limb from limb. Tell him that.'

Sean gave a knowing smile. 'Fair enough.'

'And tell them to bring my rucksack – it's got my passport and other stuff in.'

'OK.' He took a piece of paper from his pocket, stepped to within reaching distance and held it out. 'My number. Call me when you're coming. It has to be today.'

Jon didn't lift his hand.

The man waved the scrap of paper.

Jon cocked his head. 'What was it like?'

Their eyes met and the other man's eyebrows lifted.

'What was it like,' Jon continued, 'locking all the doors and windows then turning the gas on, knowing a pregnant woman and a six-year-old girl were inside?'

The piece of paper dropped slightly and the man blinked. 'What?'

'You heard me. The gas was on full and the place sealed tight. Did it make you feel like a man?'

Sean's eyes crept to the side and he murmured, 'The son of a bitch.'

Jon jutted his chin forward. 'What was it like?'

He looked up. 'Were they...did they...?'

'Get out? Yeah, they did.'

The car horn tooted and the man snapped back to the present. He looked coldly at Jon. 'What's it like to know how your country has brought such misery to mine? Shall we start with the potato famine? How about the Black and Tans, the RUC, the beatings, the killings, the torching of entire towns. The executions in Croke Park? Innocent people just there to watch football. Bloody Sunday? Paratroopers opening fire on unarmed marchers? Don't fucking lecture me, you English piece of shit.' He balled up the scrap of paper and threw it at Jon's chest.

CHAPTER 46

Devlan walked towards his father, face and clothes spattered with blood. Gerrard looked up from his newspaper. With every step his son took, his face grew darker.

'Da,' Devlan started to say. 'Before you go off on one–'

'What did you do?' The old man's fingertips were pressing into the newspaper, threatening to break through.

'Listen, Da – you have to – '

'Did you kill him?' Gerrard's voice was menacingly low.

On the far side of the room, Denis slunk behind the breakfast bar and reached down a glass.

'It had to be done,' Devlan replied.

'In his office? You did it there?'

'Don't worry. I set fire to the place. There'll be no evidence.'

'Oh, Jesus.' Darragh took off his glasses and placed them on the desk. 'Shit.'

Devlan raised a bloody hand to his face and scratched at an eyebrow with the nail of his thumb. Tiny flakes of dried blood drifted down. 'He was trying to arrange bullets for all of us.'

Gerrard glanced to the kitchen area. 'Out.'

Denis lowered the half-finished glass of water and headed straight for the door. Once the three of them were alone, Gerrard turned to Devlan. 'Clean your hands and face, for fuck's sake. You're covered.'

Devlan removed the mobile phone from his pocket and handed it to Darragh. 'Play the video. The most recent one. That's Hazel's phone.' He walked across the room to the kitchen sink.

Looking with distaste at the rust-coloured smears on the casing, Darragh started pressing keys. 'Most recent one, you say?'

Devlan nodded as he worked at his face with the washing-up cloth.

The recording began to play and when Darragh and Gerrard heard themselves speaking, they both stood absolutely still. When the recording finally came to a stop, neither spoke.

'Now you see?' Devlan asked, a damp tea towel and small vegetable knife in his hand. He sat down by the wood burner and began to scrape the blood from beneath his nails.

'What was he going to do with it?' Gerrard asked.

'Sending it to Sinn Féin. The offices of Rory Duggan in Stormont,' Devlan replied. 'It was already in a padded envelope, ready to go.'

Darragh's hand was shaking as he put the mobile down. 'They'd have killed us.'

'They'd have to get into Clifden, first,' Devlan retorted. 'We control these roads. This area belongs to us.'

A look of irritation appeared on Darragh's face. 'You think we could stop them? Us? Sean, Liam, Denis and Conor Barry. A few cousins as back up?'

Devlan wiped the tip of the blade on his trouser leg. 'We've survived in this country for hundreds of years. You reckon when Francisco swam ashore from the Concepción, he looked at the O'Flaherty's butchering his mates and thought, I'm fucked? No he kept Pio by his side and he began to fight.' He thrust the tiny knife at his brother. 'He didn't start fucking snivelling, like. And you can have that for nothing.'

'So it's one man and his dog again is it?' Darragh laughed incredulously. He turned to his father. When he saw the gleam of pride in the old man's eyes his smile vanished. 'Dad?'

'Enough,' the old man eventually said, pressing a forefinger on the mobile phone. 'This is why we never speak about that thing. Not to anyone, ever.' He looked at Devlan. 'Did you say anything to Denis?'

'Nah, did I fuck. Told him the guy came at me with a bottle, that's all.'

'Good.' Gerrard took his finger off the phone. 'Get rid of it, now.'

Devlan slid the phone's back cover off, popped the battery out and then stepped over to the stove. Using the damp tea towel to protect his fingers, he swung the door open and threw the handset onto the glowing embers. The door shut with a clang. 'Where is the fucking slag?'

'She called in with the shopping,' Gerrard answered. 'Then went back to your flat to get some sleep, she said.'

Grinning, Devlan walked over to the breakfast bar and put the knife on it. 'I'll pop over and wake her up.'

'Who is she?' Darragh asked. 'Did the solicitor say?'

Devlan shook his head. 'I did everything to that man. Worked him for I don't know how long. I think it was his heart eventually, just gave out on him.'

'Did he say anything at all?' Gerrard demanded uneasily, eyes on the phone as it began to give off curls of smoke.

'Yeah, bits. Told me he'd passed a load of stuff to the peeler.' He glanced at Darragh. 'Spreadsheets, are they called? Any documents she could grab that were left lying around.'

Darragh sat back. 'None of that is incriminating in itself. More inconvenient. We might have to get on to

Julian at Blackman and May, shift some funds around. What about the thing?' He nodded at the phone. 'Does Spicer know?'

'He didn't say.'

Gerrard brought his hands together, as if in prayer. 'I don't like this. We need Spicer. And we need to get hold of Hazel, too.'

'She can't be working with the Guards anyhow,' Devlan stated. 'She wouldn't be taking that phone to the solicitor if she was.'

'True,' Darragh answered. 'But what's the link with this Spicer person? If she's been feeding information to him via the solicitor, she must know him somehow.'

'From when she lived in Manchester,' Gerrard replied.

The corners of Darragh's mouth turned down. 'Can't see her being mates with a peeler. Maybe it's to do with the girl Spicer's been after.'

Devlan turned to the wood burner. Greenish flames were now shooting from the buckled remains of the mobile. 'She'll tell us. When we hang her over the edge of the pit and make her watch Cuchallain with Spicer, she'll tell us.' The thought seemed to mesmerise him for a second. 'Has Sean rung?'

'Just before you got back,' Gerrard replied. 'He delivered the message. Now we wait for the peeler's call.'

It was another six miles to Clifden when Liam tapped a finger on the dashboard. 'Pull over, would you. I've got to shit.'

'What, right now?'

'I'm touching cloth here, pull over.'

Sean eased the car onto the verge. 'If you'd let me take the bog road, we'd be back by now.'

'Probably,' the other man grunted. 'But that thing gives me the willies, so it does. Got any tissues?'

Sean gave him a look.

He hauled himself out and walked stiffly towards a gate

set back into the dry-stone wall.

The ring of Sean's mobile started up and he looked down at the screen. A number he didn't recognise. The peeler? 'Sean here.'

'Sean, it's Brendan Molloy, can you talk?'

The Sinn Féin official. Sean's eyes immediately went to his rear-view mirror. Liam was testing the gate, readying himself to climb over it. 'Yeah, but be quick. Did you get my message about what the de Avilas are planning?'

'Yes. There's been a lot happening this end. Sean, I'm with a colleague. You're on loudspeaker.'

'Who?'

'Rory Duggan.'

Sean Doyle licked his lips. Duggan had been with the party donkey's years. A regular face flanking McGuiness or Adams when they appeared on the telly.

'Hello Sean, it's Rory. We've not met, but I've heard a lot about you. We appreciate you getting in contact.'

Sean checked his mirror again. Liam was about to start climbing over. 'No problem.'

'Sean, I want to be clear about something,' Duggan said. 'Why are you doing this?'

'What?'

'Betraying the people who pay you – and just to protect a British policeman.'

Sean thought about Devlan. It was now obvious the man was a borderline psychopath, with all the risks and unpredictability that involved. When Cuchullain fell ill, the tour they'd arranged over in England should have been cancelled, end of story. But Devlan had insisted on taking Queenie instead, a dog they'd acquired to breed from. That was unforgivable. Then to use that dog – the result of such careful nurturing – to attack a family in a park. The fucking idiot. Then to lie about opening a window in that holiday bungalow. If the de Avila family was about to fall, Clochán kennels would be no more and the plan to establish a new, Irish, line of Alanos would come to nothing. Sean wanted to slam a hand on the dashboard. To cap it all, the family were now planning to kill a Tan policeman – jeopardising the entire quest for independence as a result. 'I said to Brendan, I've no desire to protect that peeler. But I know how things are balanced with you boys. All you've struggled to achieve these last years. The ceasefire. I didn't believe it could work. But fair play to you, it has. And now this family – this bunch of dago-descended pricks – will happily fuck it all up. Clear enough?'

He heard a quiet murmuring before Brendan spoke again. 'Sean, this situation in Clifden with the de Avila family. What's happening now?'

'I've just delivered a message to Spicer. They want him out at that pet-food place on the Letterfrack road. They intend to kill him.'

'Golden Fields farm?'

'Yes.'

'That's what we gather from someone else.'

'Who?'

'We got a call a wee bit earlier. The person played us a conversation recorded on a mobile phone. Our copy isn't the best. We're expecting the actual phone very soon. In the meantime, we'd like your opinion.'

'Opinion?'

'We think it's the de Avilas speaking, but you'll know better than us.'

Sean checked his mirror again. No sign of Liam. 'OK, let's hear it.' The recording started and he had to press the phone to his ear in order to make out what was being said. When it had finished, Sean realised he was staring down at his knees. I don't believe it. They did Collins in Castlebar. The de Avilas did Francis Collins. Brendan's voice came down the line. 'Sean?'

He drew in breath and checked the mirror again. 'I thought the security forces got to him.'

'So did we.'

'Fuck.'

'Is that Gerrard de Avila and his two sons speaking?'

'Yes.' Eyes to the mirror. Liam was now climbing back over.

'We thought so.'

Sean's mind was reeling. They were dead. The de Avilas were dead men. 'How…where did that come from?'

'A man who's been trying to convince us of it for years.'

'So…' Liam was climbing down the other side. 'I can't stay long. How will it be done? I mean, you can't get within a half hour of Clifden without them knowing.'

'Let us worry about that. We need to know when this meeting is taking place between them and Spicer.'

Liam was now on the grass verge. He paused to examine the orange twine that fastened the gate shut.

Sean said, 'As soon as possible. The de Avilas want it to happen later today. I guess that will let them dump the body in South Armagh and be back before morning.'

'We've a unit en route, but they're still some way off. Get it delayed, Sean. I don't care how, we need more time.'

'How will I – ' He looked at his mobile. The Sinn Féin official had hung up. He bit at his lip. I don't have a number for the peeler. Christ, I don't have his number! He returned the phone to his pocket and looked at his watch. Twenty to four. I can't drive back to Roundstone to warn him off. Not with Liam in the car, he'll know something's up. Shit, what the hell do I do?

The door opened. 'Did you hear me?' Liam asked.

Sean shook his head.

'No? Jesus, I ate in that Chinaman's restaurant last night. Now? My arse is like the exhaust of batman's car.'

Jon sat at the kitchen table facing Kieron. In the corner, Eileen poured boiling water into a teapot. 'I'm so sorry,' he said again.

Kieron waved a hand. 'I said not to worry. They won't bother us.'

You're wrong, Jon wanted to say. You don't know what they tried over in England. Christ, he thought, looking at the two of them. You're yet another reason why I've got to settle this thing. 'How often does the council come by emptying bins and stuff?'

'Pardon?' Eileen frowned.

Jon looked briefly to the window. 'Say at Gorteen beach. How often would the bin there be emptied?'

'Gorteen?' Eileen had arched her eyebrows. 'This time of year? Practically never.'

'In the last week or so?'

'No – we haven't had a bin lorry come by for weeks.'

Thank God for that, Jon thought. He pictured the two cassettes. They'd been lying in an open-topped bin for a week. During that time, there'd been sleet, snow and rain. The things were probably ruined. 'Gerrard de Avila wants a couple of security tapes I took from the club. He's prepared to exchange them for Zoë.'

'And you have these tapes?' Kieron asked.

'I know where they are.'

'That was the message the man relayed?' Eileen asked.

'Yes. They want to meet me at the place where they make the pet food. Golden Fields Farm.'

Kieron looked uncomfortable. 'Who does? Both brothers and the dad?'

'Yes. You don't seem happy.'

'There's a rumour. More pub talk really, but it's been doing the rounds for years now.'

Jon dipped his head. 'Go on.'

Kieron glanced uneasily at Eileen's back. 'Some people say the de Avilas used the place to get rid of someone.'

'That story?' Eileen tutted. 'Talk in the air is what that story is.'

Kieron looked over. 'Maybe.'

'Who was this person?' Jon asked.

Kieron lowered his voice. 'I don't know. A con-artist from Dublin is what I heard. He tried to take the de Avilas for a load of cash.'

Jon tapped a finger on the edge of the table. 'It wasn't Hammell, was it? Tommy Hammell?'

'I don't know.' Kieron responded. 'Who's he?'

Jon went to scratch his ear, only remembering it was covered in bandages when his fingertips connected with soft material. He lowered his hand. 'Just a name in a file that was handed to me.'

Kieron sat forward. 'Who by?'

Jon shook his head. 'I don't know. This dishevelled-looking bloke. He seemed like a bit of a tramp, to be honest.'

'Well, the story goes that this person ended up as pet food.'

The sheepdog's ears went up and a moment later they heard a door opening. The click of Malachy's walking stick got closer. Jon turned to Eileen who caught his eye and made a placating movement with her hand. The old man appeared in the doorway and looked in uncertainly.

'Dad,' Eileen said. 'You're up. Tea?'

He shuffled in, stopping for a second when he saw Jon. 'Thank you, I will.'

Eileen placed a hand on his arm and Jon listened anxiously as she spoke in Irish. The old man paused to take in her words, shoulders relaxing before he replied in the same language.

Eileen helped him to his chair by the stove. 'Jon went for a walk, Dad. Up Errisbeg of all places.'

Malachy turned to Jon. 'You went up the mountain? You must be careful, boy. The mists can close in and there's many a drop you won't know about until you're stepping off it.'

Jon sat back. 'It was a lot harder than it looks. I wouldn't want to try and do it twice a day like you did.'

'Ach, well.' His fingers went to the sheepdog, who had placed its muzzle on his knee. 'Hello, dog. Hello to you.'

Kieron gave a cough. 'Grandad, the de Avila family

want to meet with Jon. This business with the girl he's trying to find.'

'Oh,' Malachy's head swung back in Jon's direction. 'Did Eileen say? The Guards were here looking for you. I said you were in Clifden again.'

'That's fine, thanks,' Jon smiled.

'They say,' Kieron continued. 'That Jon can take her – '

'Gerald?' Malachy asked.

'No – the son, Gerrard. And his two boys, Darragh and Devlan.'

'I don't know them,' Malachy replied, cupping the end of his walking stick with both hands. 'But I wouldn't trust them. That's a family who've never been shy if there was lying or stealing to be had.'

'I was thinking Jon should meet them somewhere nearer here,' Kieron said.

Jon leaned an elbow on the table. 'Kieron, they're not going to try anything. They know I can create havoc with their business.'

'The last person who tried to do that vanished,' Kieron answered.

Jon forced his mouth into a smile. 'Yes – but at the end of the day, I'm a policeman. They know that.'

'Right.' The pitch of Kieron's voice had lifted. 'Like that stopped them from beating the living shit out of you.'

Jon couldn't help touch his swollen eye. 'That was just payback. The person who did this? I broke his nose last week. We're even, now. But if you really think I shouldn't go to that farm, then where?'

Kieron looked at Malachy. 'I'm thinking the bog road. There's no way they can spring any surprises there.'

A glint appeared in the old man's eyes. 'The halfway house.'

Jon looked from one man to the other. 'I don't follow.'

Kieron turned to him. 'Tell them you'll meet them at the halfway house. Just the three of them and this Zoë.'

Jon considered it. As a rendezvous point, it was good.

It could only be accessed by the single-lane road and everything was out in the open. 'OK, that could work.'

'And I'll be there,' Kieron said, 'to watch your back.'

Jon wagged his forefinger. 'Thanks for the offer, but no way. I go there alone. I won't involve you any more than I already have.'

His cousin crossed his arms. 'Two of their thugs were parked out front earlier. We're already involved. And they are not people you can trust.'

'Kieron, even if I wanted to take you along, they won't just bimble out there without checking it first. In fact, they'll probably have men at each end of the road. They'll check me and my car to make sure I'm alone.'

'And you will be,' Kieron grinned. 'I'll go on foot. Setting off from here, it'll take me about an hour.'

Jon glanced at Malachy who smiled right back. 'He's right.'

'How's that possible?' Jon asked.

'If you know the bog like I do, it's easy. I set off now, I'll get there first. Tuck myself in behind a rock with the shotgun – '

Jon raised his hands. 'Wait, wait, wait, wait. A shotgun?'

Eileen spoke up. 'This is talk without sense! Kieron, your father will not allow you out there with that gun.'

'It'll be fine,' her son retorted. 'I'll not use it. A precaution is all it is.'

'It's a fine idea,' Malachy said, banging his stick down.

Eileen whirled on him. 'Dad! You should know better. Jon – tell them.'

'She's right,' he nodded. 'It's really not a good idea.'

Kieron waved a hand. 'Sure it won't be loaded. But if they try to play a trick on you, I pop up from nowhere with both barrels trained on them. They'll soon think again.'

Jon shook his head. 'Kieron, I appreciate the offer. But this is something I need to do alone. I'll meet them on the bog road by that halfway house, but it'll be just me.'

'Well,' Malachy was looking towards the window. 'You'll need to telephone to them now – if you want this meeting while you still have the day.'

Jon realised the light was starting to fade. He pulled out the piece of paper Sean had thrown at him. 'Kieron, can I borrow your mobile?'

CHAPTER 47

Sean Doyle walked slowly before the plate-glass windows, phone pressed to his ear. 'Your rucksack, yeah. And all three, yeah, I heard you first time. I know the halfway house, but I'll need to check that with – ' He stopped speaking. Lowering the phone, he turned to the watching de Avilas. 'He wants to meet the three of you on the bog road. The halfway house.'

'Halfway house?' Devlan scowled, thrusting a hand out. 'Give him here. Since when does he tell us what to do?'

'He's hung up,' Sean replied, returning the phone to his pocket. 'That's what he said. The halfway house on the bog road, one hour's time. He wasn't up for discussing it.'

'Why all three of us?' Darragh asked suspiciously.

'That's what he said – so there could be no misunderstanding about settling everything.'

'Fuck him.' Devlan kicked his legs out. 'Phone him back – '

'Hang on,' Darragh cut in, a forefinger stroking his chin.

Gerrard turned to him with a questioning expression. 'Let's hear it, son.'

'Well…I'm thinking it might not be such a bad idea.'

'The bog road?' Devlan scoffed. 'Why would we want to go out there?'

'The Guards are all over town – checking all our properties, stopping cars, asking questions,' Darragh continued. 'To get to Golden Fields we have to drive through the centre of Clifden. That bog road? We can skirt round the edge of town to get to it. No one can follow without us knowing. It's the perfect place when you think about it. Middle of bloody nowhere.'

Gerrard made a clicking sound with his tongue as he weighed the suggestion up. 'You're right about it not being near anything else.' Something sparked in his eyes. 'And if we grab him there, he can be taken straight on up to South Armagh. Get's the whole thing done nice and quick.'

Devlan sat up. 'Hang on, what about Cuchullain? We're going to set him on the peeler, aren't we?'

'No,' Gerrard replied. 'It'll be simpler this way. Sean? Take Liam and Denis, check there's no one parked anywhere on that godforsaken stretch. When you get to the far end, block it. Nobody is allowed past – apart from the peeler. We'll have Conor and a couple of others watching things this end.'

'What about Hazel?' Devlan asked moodily, thinking about how the bed had been empty when he'd burst into his flat earlier on. 'Conor's still looking for her round town.'

'She'll show, don't you worry,' Gerrard replied. 'Sean? Liam? Out to Denis's place, fetch him and the three of you get going.'

They were opening the front door when Devlan called out. 'Sean? Get Denis to bring his shotgun and that toolbox.'

'OK.' The door banged shut.

Gerrard placed his hands on his knees. 'Right, how best shall we do this?'

'I'll take a van,' Devlan immediately replied.

Darragh sighed. 'Why?'

'Because I'm bringing Cuchullain.'

'I said no,' Gerrard replied.

Darragh nodded. 'We don't need that bloody great thing.'

'We do,' Devlan said triumphantly. 'Think about it. When Spicer realises it's a set-up, he's going to try and get away.'

'We have the road blocked at each end.'

'What if he just runs into the bog and fucking sinks? We want the tapes, we need to find out exactly what he knows and you want his body, remember? To make it look like some republican headers did it.'

Gerrard nodded reluctantly.

'You're going to like this,' Devlan said, eyes gleaming as he reached into his army jacket. He removed the clear plastic bag with the mangy old tennis ball inside.

'What the hell is that?' Darragh asked.

Devlan smirked. 'The peeler wants his rucksack, doesn't he? This ball is what his dog liked to chew on. I wipe it all over the rucksack and it'll give Cuchullain a target – so he knows what to attack. Da, it'll be a sight. Cuchullain will bring him down in two seconds and hold him still. We then tie the bastard up and hood him.'

Gerrard grunted in agreement. 'He's right. The dog's trained for that.'

They looked to Darragh, who threw out his hands. 'Fine.'

'OK,' Gerrard said.' We find out exactly what he knows, then we gag him before driving him to where Sean and the others'll be waiting. That way, he can't say another word in front of them.'

Devlan was banging his hands against his knees. 'There's plenty of room in the back of the van! We can let Cuchullain have a chew, then use Denis' toolkit on him. When we reach South Armagh, we just roll him out, turn round and come home.'

Darragh looked queasy. 'Who's we?'

Devlan grinned. 'Don't worry. Me and Sean'll do it. Unless you want to come for the ride, like?'

Darragh looked away. 'No thanks.'

'OK.' The old man hauled himself to his feet. 'I'll take the Mitsubishi. Darragh, you jump in with me. Devlan, fetch Cuchullain.' He glanced at his watch. 'Meet at the bog road turn-off in half an hour.'

Devlan jumped up. 'Can't wait to see his face when Cuch' jumps out of the van.'

Jon hung up. 'Right, that's it. Meeting in an hour.'

Kieron shook his head. 'They'll try something.'

Jon reached into his jacket, removed his warrant card and laid it on the table. 'Surely you agree this counts for something?'

'You think that badge will protect you from someone like Devlan? He's not right in his head, Jon.'

'Well, it's a risk I have to take.' He slipped his warrant card back in his jacket. 'Mind if I use your mobile to call my wife? I really need to speak with her.'

'Help yourself.'

Eileen gestured at the door. 'Ring from the other room, Jon. It'll be quieter for you in there.'

Once inside, he went to access the address book. It dawned on him that his wife's number wouldn't be inside. He stared at his reflection in the window, registering the nonplussed expression on his face. Christ, what's her number? I've never needed to remember it before. He tapped the phone against his palm in confusion. Shit. This is ridiculous, I don't have the faintest idea of what her mobile is. In fact, there's only one number I do know off by heart. Mum and Dad's. He peered across at the Twelve Bens. The bottom half of the range was now completely in shadow. Please don't pick up, he thought as their number started to ring. I don't have time for this. Just let me leave a message for you to pass to Alice.

'Alan Spicer speaking.'

Jon felt his breath catch in his throat. 'Alan, it's me.'

'Jon! About bloody time. Do you know how worried everyone is? They found your luggage at Manchester airport.'

'Who did?'

'Rick.'

'He's got it?'

'Yes. Alice is beside herself.' His voice grew hoarse as his voice dropped. 'To be honest son, I've been, too. Alice said you've taken a knock or two. Are you…how bad are you, Jon?'

Guilt suddenly bloomed as memories came back. Riding on Alan's shoulders, my hands fiddling in his hair. Cricket on the beach at Prestatyn – him tirelessly going to fetch the ball. The hours he spent on the touchline, cheering me on during my junior rugby days. He had to clear the lump in his throat. 'I'm all right, Dad, honestly. Listen, I've been trying to ring Ali but my mobile's bust. Can you get me her number?'

'Hang on, your mother will know where it is. I'll put her on – '

'No! Don't…don't bother her. Can't you dig it out?'

'Me? I don't know where she'll keep it.' He spoke away from the phone. 'Mary? It's Jon. He wants Alice's number, here you speak to him. Get yourself home, son.'

His mum came on the line. 'Jon! Thank goodness for that. Alice is worried sick, we all are. Where are you?'

'I'm in Roundstone, Mum. At Grandad's.'

Silence.

'Mum – I'm in a real hurry. Can you just pass Alice a message? Tell her I'm fine. I'm just about to collect Zoë and sort things out with the de Avilas. I'm not sure about Sunday evening flights, but hopefully I'll be back late tonight.'

'With Zoë?'

'Maybe. I haven't even spoken to her yet.'

She was quiet for a second. 'Alice said you'd stayed in

Roundstone last night.'

'I did. Malachy's very well, Mum. A bit shaky on his feet, but otherwise seems healthy. Mum? They've all been asking after you. Eileen, Malachy – '

'I'll pass your message on to Alice.'

Here we go again, Jon thought. She's raising the barriers. Well, it's too late for that. 'I've also met Eileen's son, Kieron. He's thirty-one, got three kids of his own already. I don't think Malachy can keep count of his grandkids, what with Holly and our second on the – '

'I'll let Alice know.'

Jon ran a palm over his face. 'Mum,' he whispered, 'I know, OK? I know the score about me. Whatever happened all those years ago, they're so sad to not still know you. Malachy especially. He misses you so much.' He paused. 'Mum? Don't cry. There's no need. There's no need to be upset.' He could feel tears running down his own cheeks. 'Alan's my dad. Not...not anyone else. Nothing can change that. Mum?'

He listened as she quietly wept.

Eventually, her sobbing slowed. 'I...I need to speak...' she sniffed. 'Alan.'

Jon nodded. 'You two talk. But tell him, won't you? He's my dad and I love you both.'

Sean pulled up and beeped his horn. Dogs started barking from inside the ramshackle cottage. On the front gate was a small plaque. Below an image of a snarling pit bull was the word, Beware. A downstairs light was on and they waited a minute. 'Give him a knock, will you?'

Liam grimaced. 'Can't you just beep again? I hate those bloody animals. Scare the shite out of me, so they do.'

'Just go round the back. He'll be in his workshop.'

'Bollocks,' Liam hissed, opening the car door and getting out.

As soon as the other man set off, Sean whipped his phone out. 'It's me. Halfway house on the bog road, about forty minutes' time. Gerrard, Darragh and Devlan. You'll not get the three of them together outside Clifden again.' He listened for a moment. 'The bog road – goes from the outskirts of town across to Roundstone. They're meeting at its mid-point. Where are your lot? OK. One problem – they'll see you coming from a way off.' He listened for a few seconds. 'I'll be at the Roundstone end of it. Me and two others.' He shoved the phone in his pocket and started tapping nervously on the steering wheel.

'Alice, it's Mary. Jon just called.'

'He did? When?'

'He said to tell you he's fine. He's going to fetch Zoë and he hopes to be back home later tonight.'

'When? When was this?'

'When did he call?'

'Yes.'

'About half an hour ago, I think.'

'Half an hour?'

'Sorry, Alice. I needed to speak with Alan, I'm sorry – '

'Where was he calling from?'

'Roundstone. He was at his grandfather's.'

'Did he leave a number?'

'No – he said there isn't a phone in the house. But I did that last-number thing. That function, you know, where you call and they tell you – '

'What is it, Mary? What number did he call on? I need to let his work colleagues know.'

Kieron looked to the west. The tops of the Twelve Bens were now in darkness. Above them, a few streaks of pink cloud fought to keep ahead of the slab of grey cloud closing off the sky. The temperature had dropped.

He adjusted the shotgun strapped across his back and examined the terrain before him. The bog was silent, a silvery maze of water stretching away into the distance.

As he picked his way forward once more, the saturated

land sucked and squelched at his feet. The tips of the trees in the middle of Cormorant Lake were now just visible. Fifteen minutes, he thought, and I'll be there.

The phone in his pocket started to ring and he jumped at the sudden intrusion of sound. Jesus, he thought, reaching into his jacket and turning it off. The last thing I need is for that thing to give me away.

Devlan came to a halt at the end of the track and looked at the half-built property before him. The roof tiles were on and the front door in, but the walls were exposed breezeblocks, awaiting a layer of render and coating of weatherproof paint. Sheets of chipboard filled all the window frames to keep the rain from blowing in.

He got out of the vehicle. The sound of waves breaking on the nearby beach filled the air. After picking a large torch off the seat, he turned on the fluorescent tube running down its side. The light flickered into life as he lifted a hand-axe and inserted the handle in the waistband of his trousers. Last, he picked up Jon's rucksack. He took another look at the deserted house. The dog would be starving.

At the front door he made a point of jangling the keys before inserting one in the lock. 'Cuch,' he called softly. 'Cuch, it's me, Devlan. You there, boy?' He listened at the door. Not a sound. Jesus, he thought, nervously licking his lips. At least Queenie would make a noise, even if it was just a welcoming growl. Tentatively, he opened the door a few inches. 'Cuch? Hey boy, it's me.'

Nothing was waiting on the other side. Torch and rucksack in one hand, he used his shoulder to push the door fully open, his other hand hovering at his side, ready to grab the axe. 'Cuch, you there?'

The soft light from the torch lit the first few feet before him, but not much more than that. He knew there was a wall about twelve feet in front – the main load-bearing one for the property. All the internal walls had yet to be put in, along with the plumbing and wiring. Swivelling the torch one way then the other, he examined the thick shadows at either end of the bare room. Was Cuchullain lurking there? A neat pile of planks, left by the builders, had been reduced to a scattering of shards and splinters. Shit, Devlan thought, those things were two inches thick. 'Cuch?' Nothing moved. He held the torch as far before him as he could and was able to make out the empty doorway leading into the other half of the house.

The lower part of the frame was missing large chunks. He wondered whether to just switch to the torch's main beam. At least it would let me fucking see properly, he thought. But he also knew how much the dog disliked having bright lights shone directly at it. Heart thudding, he called more loudly. 'Cuch, you in here?'

Above him, a floorboard creaked. His eyes shot to the ceiling then across to the stairway. Enormous pawprints showed in the dust. Something was moving above him. A slow pad, approaching the stairs. 'Cuch?' His chuckle was forced and dry. 'You been up in the bedrooms, have you?'

A dark mass detached itself from the blackness at the top step. Devlan lifted the torch and two discs briefly shone. Those eyes, he thought. Dead, like a shark's.

The animal began to descend, muscles bunching on one shoulder then the other as it took each step. All the while, its gaze stayed on Devlan. By the time it was halfway down he could make out the tigerish markings covering it. He kept his hand at his side, ready to grab his weapon. Only when the animal reached the bottom step could he see its sharp little ears weren't laid back in readiness to attack.

'Cuch, good to see you boy!' He held out his hand, breath frozen in his throat. The dog walked over and allowed its head to be stroked. Devlan breathed out. 'Jesus, Cuch. I wish you'd wag your tail or something. Just to let me know we're friends.'

The dog's shoulders pushed against Devlan's thighs as

it brought its huge muzzle close to the rucksack.

Devlan removed the tennis ball and started smearing it across the surface of the rucksack. 'Take a good sniff, boy,' he murmured. 'That smell? It's your next meal.'

CHAPTER 48

Jon left the passenger door of Eileen's old Nissan open as he walked over to the litter bin. A layer of little green sacks full of dog excrement nestled on a few empty bottles, cans and snack wrappers.

Gingerly, he pushed it all to the side and reached down to the bottom. His fingers made contact with a hard, sharp corner. Thank fuck for that, he thought, pulling the cassettes out. He held both up by a finger and thumb. Brown water trickled from each case.

'Is that them?' Eileen called over.

'Yup.'

'Surely they'll never play?'

He walked back to her car. 'I doubt that matters. They just want them back.'

She nodded at a packet of tissues on the dashboard. 'You'll need them. And you be careful now.'

'Thanks. I'll see you in a little bit.' He took his wooden staff along with the tissues and pushed the door shut.

The car pulled away. He walked over to the black Peugeot, put the cassettes on the roof and started to wipe his fingers clean. From the direction of the village came the lonely sound of a single tolling bell. Sunday evening mass, Jon thought. Why Eileen was in a hurry. He studied the fields at the foot of Errisbeg. Did farmers normally go to check their sheep at dusk? It seemed a strange time for Kieron to be doing it.

He opened the car door, slid the wooden staff across the back seat and placed the cassettes on the floor. After making sure his warrant card was in his jacket, he got in. Right. Let's get this thing over with. He allowed a brief picture of himself on the plane later on, sinking into a soft seat, a drink before him. Maybe Alice and Holly will meet me at the airport. He felt his fingers twitch as he imagined sweeping his daughter up in a giant hug, then kissing Alice. That's if they don't run a mile at the sight of my face, he smiled, starting the engine.

Ten minutes later, his headlights lit up the sign for the N59. He cut his speed in readiness to turn left onto the bog road. A car was parked across the junction. No surprise, he thought, pulling to a stop. Three men got out. He recognised them all – Sean, the one from the factory and the massive fucker who'd smashed his knee with that crowbar. He lowered his window as Sean neared the driver's door.

'Pop the boot.'

Jon did as he was asked as the big bastard peered into the back of the car. 'He's got a fucking great stick here.'

The vehicle rocked slightly as Sean slammed the boot closed. Then the rear door opened. Sean reached in and removed the length of wood. There goes my walking stick, Jon thought. His eyes went to the side mirror and Sean held up a hand. The ginger-haired one got into the car and reversed it out the way. As Jon inched past, he saw the driver staring at him with something that resembled a gloating look. What, Jon thought, are you so frigging pleased about? It's your boss who's rolling over, not me.

He smiled back, then increased his speed, following the narrow road as it entered the waterlogged terrain. Smokelike mist seemed to be rising up out of the thick grass, wisps of it trailing across the road. At one point he had to hit the brakes as a creature lolloped out of the haze. Is that, Jon thought, a rabbit? The animal went up on its hind legs and regarded Jon in a way that indicated a keen intelligence. A hare, Jon realised. He edged forward and the creature only hopped out of the way when the front bumper was almost touching it.

He carried on, the feeling of leaving civilization behind growing stronger. A gnarled tree ghosted past to his right and the road began to rise towards twin outcrops of rock. Nearly there.

The road passed between the two large rock formations and then began to level out on to the rough plateau. In the gathering night, he could make out Cormorant Lake and its tree-covered island away to his left. On the trees' bare branches, roosting seabirds were lined up like black vultures.

Two vehicles were up ahead. A dark-coloured four-wheel drive and a white van. He came to a stop, put his car in reverse and swung it back onto the swathe of grass that bordered the road. Then he sat back and watched the vehicles through his side window.

For a second, he thought something shifted in the ruins of the halfway house about twenty metres in front of him. Probably a sheep, he thought, looking back at the two vehicles. You can make the first move. There are more of you.

After a few more seconds, the doors of the van opened and three male figures got out. Where, he wondered, is Zoë? It had now grown too dark to make out if anyone else was in the cab of the van. One of the figures raised an arm and beckoned. Jon clicked open his door. Chill air hit him and he immediately reached for his jacket's zip. Shit, he said to himself. I wish I had that bloody riot gear. Or just the pepper spray. I'd settle for that. Fingers brushing over the bulge of his warrant card for reassurance, he retrieved the two tapes, hobbled a few metres forward and stopped. 'Where's Zoë?'

Two of the figures continued toward him. As they got closer, he could make out their faces. Darragh de Avila and an older man who had a passing resemblance to the nightclub owner. So that's Gerrard, he thought. They came to a halt adjacent to the halfway house and Darragh slung something towards Jon's feet.

He looked down. My rucksack.

'Everything's in it,' Darragh announced, a slight squeak in his voice.

Jon looked at him. You, he thought, like to slap women around, do you? Wait for prison. With your feminine looks, you'll soon find out what it's like to be someone's bitch.

The older man smiled. 'A token of goodwill.'

Keeping his eyes on the pair, he bent his good knee and hooked the rucksack up. Something shiny had dried across the front and down both straps. He checked the front pocket: passport, wallet and plane tickets. My God, they really do want to settle this. He hung the bag from his shoulder. 'I said, where's Zoë?'

The old man gestured behind him. 'Back of the van. Now, hand the tapes over, would you?'

Jon's gaze shifted to the two vehicles. The figure lurking near them must be Devlan. If that crazy bastard has hurt her... 'Bring her over. I want to see her.'

Devlan stood at the rear corner of the vehicle, watching as Jon lifted the rucksack. Yes, you put it on, he smiled. Now, come just a bit closer. Da, get him a bit closer and I'll unlock these doors. He felt in his trouser pockets for the van's keys and realised they weren't there. His hands went to his jacket and started feeling round. Pockets were empty. Are they still in the ignition? No – I remember placing them on the dashboard before Dad and Darragh came over to join me. The memory hit him and he wanted to shout with frustration. As they'd all climbed out of the vehicle, he'd heard a jangle in his father's hand. Da. He fucking pocketed them.

'We will,' Gerrard replied a little breathlessly. 'But first we need to talk. Will you not come closer? I can't be raising my voice like this.'

Jon measured the distances in his head. They were still a good fifteen metres away and neither man posed a physical threat. It's Devlan I need to keep an eye on. He moved forward again, halting around ten metres short of them. Glancing over his shoulder, he weighed up how far it now was back to the Peugeot. A dozen or so metres? Not that my knee will allow me to sprint. If it comes to that.

The old man held his coat open. Beneath it Jon could see the man's shirt tucked into his trousers. 'Look,' he said. 'Nothing hidden. No need to worry.' He beckoned once more. 'Come on. We won't bite.'

Liam, perched on the front corner of the car, blew into his hands. 'I hope they don't take too long. I'm freezing my nuts off here.'

Whingeing bloody twat, Sean thought.

The driver's door swung open and Denis got out. 'They won't. It'll be in the back of the van with him and off. How long to the border from here? Plenty of time to amuse themselves with him.'

Sean kept his head slightly turned, straining for the sound of any vehicle approaching from the direction of the Galway road.

Liam spat into the grass. 'Sure, that guy's going to suffer.'

'And so will the tout-girl when Devlan finds her,' Denis added. His eyes lit up. 'Maybe he'll let me have a go on her first. I've always fancied a ride on that one.'

Sean turned his head. A vehicle! The other two caught its low tone and looked up the road connecting to the

N59. Seconds later, it appeared.

Some kind of off-roader, Sean guessed, judging from the height of its headlights. It reached the junction, slowed down and started to indicate right. Range Rover, Sean thought, looking at the two letters in the registration. YZ. Londonderry. He felt the saliva vanish from his mouth. It's them.

'Shall I fetch the shotgun?' Liam murmured.

'Don't be stupid,' Sean replied. 'It'll be holidaymakers, lost their way.'

Denis stepped forwards, hands raised. 'Road's closed.'

The vehicle stopped and a slight man with short black hair and a bony face got out of the passenger side. Walking quickly towards them, he asked, 'Which of you is Sean Doyle?'

Liam and Denis turned to Sean, a look of bafflement on their faces. Sean's hand shot up like he was in class. 'Me.'

The man swung a pistol up at Denis's chest. It gave a muted phut. Denis sat down on the road, lips still parted in surprise. The man swung the weapon round. Liam just had time to begin standing, palms raised, when the noise sounded again. The tip of the ring finger on his right hand vanished and he sat back down on the car's bonnet. A hole had appeared in the chest of his jacket. The man closed the remainder of the gap, held the gun to Denis's head and fired once more. He fell back, the rear of his skull thudding against the road. Blood welling from the stump of his finger, Liam's mouth was opening and closing. The man stepped sideways, pointed the gun to Liam's temple and pulled the trigger a fourth time. Liam's head flinched as if he'd been slapped and he toppled from the vehicle.

No exit wound, Sean thought. Hollow-point rounds, ricocheting round inside the skull.

The Range Rover's doors opened and another two men got out. Sean stared at them, hand still in the air.

'Help us get them out of sight,' the first man ordered,

sliding the weapon into a shoulder holster.

No one spoke as the two corpses were dragged into the long grass of the verge.

'Right,' the man who'd done the firing said, looking off down the bog road. 'How many out there?'

Sean peeled his lips apart. 'Three.' Then, clearing his throat, added, 'Plus the Englishman.'

The man reached into his side pocket and pulled out a sheet of paper. On it was a passport-sized photo of Jon Spicer. Sean could see a series of numbers below the image, alongside a stamp for Greater Manchester Police. Must be from his personnel file, Sean thought. Jesus, they have people everywhere.

'Him?' the man asked.

'That's the one.'

The shooter turned and walked back to the Range Rover. Sean trailed uncertainly behind.

The man stopped at the open rear door and looked into the vehicle. 'It's three. You OK with that in this light?'

Sean stole a glance through to the back seat. A man was sitting there, adjusting the telescopic sights of a rifle. Holy shit, thought Sean. That's a G3-SG1, sniper's version. Telescopic sights and under-barrel bipod. So it's true; they did hang on to some of the heavier stuff.

The man with the rifle continued to prepare his weapon. 'Not sure. Get me within one fifty metres and I'll tell you. Might need the headlights on full.'

The man nodded. 'Right you are.' He turned to Sean. 'You? Why you ever ran with this shower of shit. Keep this end of the road secure until we come back. Then get yourself up to Lurgan and report to McGuire. He has work for you.'

Jon hobbled a couple of metres closer. What was Devlan up to back there? Now he seemed to be searching around in the vehicle's glove compartment.

Darragh's eyes moved from Jon to somewhere way off

behind him. 'Did you see that?' he said quietly.

Gerrard's brow buckled. 'No. What?'

'Thought I saw lights, out in the bog.'

'Car lights?'

'I don't know.' His eyes narrowed. 'Doesn't matter.'

'I want your other son here, too,' Jon said. 'What gets said now has to be agreed by all of us.'

'Devlan does as I say,' the old man stated.

Jon looked at him. 'Like trying to gas my wife and daughter?'

A muscle went off at the corner of the old man's eye. It made him look like he was trying not to wink.

Jon hitched the rucksack higher on his shoulder. 'Just get him over.'

Gerrard shrugged. 'So you give the orders now?' He dropped his chin to his shoulder. 'Devlan? Go ahead!'

The figure had got back out of the van. He hesitated then set off towards them, his footsteps the only sound. Looking confused, Gerrard glanced over his shoulder.

Gradually, Devlan's shape took form and Jon felt the muscles in his throat start to contract. Here he is. The man who released a fighting dog at my daughter, cost me Punch and almost killed my entire family. He studied the other man's face, wanting so much to see it contorted with pain. Stay in control, he said to himself. Do not lose it now.

Devlan came to a halt beside Gerrard. 'Da, you took the keys to the fucking van.'

That same high voice, Jon thought. Both brothers sounded like their balls never dropped.

A look of dismay passed across the old man's face. 'I did?' He started patting the pockets of his coat.

Devlan's eyes locked with Jon's. 'The fuck are you staring at?'

Jon kept looking. I can feel the hatred coming off him, he thought. Like needles in the air. Play it nice and easy. You're nearly out of here. Don't do anything to provoke things. The words were out of his mouth before he even knew he was about to say them. 'You, my friend, need bringing down.'

The skin below Devlan's eyes flinched as if specks of dust had blown into them. Then his lip curled back to expose his crooked teeth. 'Me? I need bringing down?'

Jon nodded.

'Yeah?' Devlan gloated, like he knew some kind of secret.

In the silence that followed, Jon thought he heard the faint rumble of a car's engine.

Not taking his eyes off Jon, Devlan half-turned towards Gerrard. 'Can you believe this cunt?'

'No,' the old man murmured. 'I can't.' He removed a set of keys and handed them to his son.

'Let's see about bringing things down,' Devlan snapped, moving back a step.

His words caused the other brother to shift nervously to the side. Jon registered the movement and a sense of unease swamped the pit of his stomach. That wasn't about handing Zoë over. *Are they planning something else?* Curling his fingers more tightly round the strap of his rucksack, he looked past them towards the van. *Is Zoë even in there? Jesus, is this a trap after all? What are they up to?* His heart suddenly started pounding. *I might have to run. Whether my fucked-up knee wants to or not.*

The old man's eyes shrank to slits as the unmistakable sound of a car engine drifted to them from across the bog. 'That Sean?'

Jon risked a quick glance behind him. Headlights flashed momentarily in the vast expanse of darkness. They vanished as the road dipped, only to reappear again slightly closer. *Whoever's driving that,* he thought, *is in one hell of a hurry.*

'That Sean?' The old man repeated more loudly. 'Devlan? Ring his number.'

Cursing, the son took out his mobile, pressed a few buttons and held it to his ear. A few seconds passed as the sound of the approaching vehicle grew in strength. 'He's not answering.'

Darragh's eyes bounced from his father to his twin and back again. 'Dad?'

Gerrard tilted his head to the side to look past Jon. 'What's he playing at?'

'Da, I'm opening the van,' Devlan said, backing off another couple of steps, phone still held to his ear.

This isn't right, Jon said to himself, beginning to move away from the group.

'You want Zoë?' Gerrard barked, thrusting a forefinger at Jon. 'Then don't you take another step.' He glanced back at Devlan. 'Try Liam's phone.'

Jon felt light-headed with the adrenaline coursing through him. He looked down at the tapes in his hand. This is not fucking right.

'Fuck!' Devlan started keying in another number.

Jon lifted his chin. 'Zoë!' he shouted down the road. 'Zoë, are you there?'

Gerrard's fists were clenched at his sides. 'Is he answering!'

'No – it's just bloody ringing.' Devlan took another step closer to the van.

Then the road at Jon's feet lit up, individual stones suddenly visible in the wash of light. He glanced over his shoulder. What was going on? Behind the headlight's glare was the dark outline of a vehicle. It filled the space between the twin outcrops of rock some hundred metres away. Jon wasn't sure if he heard one of its doors close softly before it began to advance slowly once more.

Darragh squinted. 'Is it the Guards? That's too big to be Sean's car.'

'Not the Guards,' Gerrard murmured. 'Devlan?'

'No fucker's answering!' Devlan replied, still edging away.

I'm caught in the middle, Jon thought, keeping his eyes on the de Avilas. A rabbit in the bloody headlights. The low throb drew closer and now Jon could hear bits of gravel making a popping sound beneath the vehicle's oversized tyres. The noise of the engine dropped abruptly.

No one moved and Jon thought for a second that whoever was driving the vehicle was awaiting instructions.

'Da?' Devlan whined. 'I'm letting him out.'

Him? Jon thought. Who is him? Oh fuck, does he mean the other Alano? That's what they've got back there, not Zoë. Dizzying nausea caused him to take a shuffling step sideways as he slung the tapes into the long grass of the verge. They're going to let that thing loose on me.

Whiteness was suddenly all around them as the vehicle's lights went on full beam. Jon saw the shadow of his legs stretching across the tarmac towards the de Avilas. Gerrard and Darragh immediately raised their hands in an attempt to shield their eyes. Behind them, Devlan turned and started to run.

The air at the side of Jon's head seemed to come apart: thin whips followed a nanosecond later by two sharp retorts from back down the road. First Gerrard then Darragh flew backwards as if yanked by invisible wires. Jon dropped to the ground as the air hissed again.

Devlan was a handful of metres from the van when his shoulder jolted. The phone flew from his grip. Jon wrapped his arms over his head as another retort rang out. Something sparked off the front of the van then shrieked away into the night. A flapping of wings broke out from the nearby lake as the cormorants took flight. Devlan regained his stride. Now roaring at the top of his voice, he was almost within touching distance of the van. A series of deep and savage barks started up from within the vehicle, followed by a thudding noise. The entire thing began to rock on its tyres.

Another retort and Devlan's torso was driven suddenly forward, as if he was a sprinter dipping to cross the line first. His head cracked into the van's front grille and his legs buckled. Jon brought his own knees up into a foetal position as car doors started to slam. Footsteps rapidly approached. Jon lay still and he knew that, even if he wanted to move, his muscles wouldn't respond. The footsteps passed him and three pairs of legs came into view.

'Make sure of them.'

Two of the people split off to where Gerrard and Darragh lay motionless, arms thrown out at their sides. Jon lifted his elbow a fraction and watched as the two striding men produced handguns. They fired directly into the father and son's heads. Oh no. Oh shit. Oh, oh fucking shit.

The third man calmly approached Devlan, who was now on his back, groaning. The hand holding the van's keys flapped lazily in the air. The man positioned his pistol inches from Devlan's forehead and pulled the trigger. Devlan's hand fell to the road with a slap and both legs went into spasm.

The man straightened up, frowning with irritation. The booming succession of barks continued. 'What?' he said, seemingly to himself. Turning his back on the van, he raised a hand and pressed two fingers against his ear. 'Say that again.' He listened to the earpiece for a moment then lowered his hand and gestured at the halfway house to the other men. They brought their weapons up and moved off to each side.

'Break open that shotgun,' the leader called, gun also directed at the ruins. 'Toss it on to the grass and come out.'

A second later a shotgun was thrown from behind the remains of the foremost wall. 'It's not loaded.' Two pale hands appeared, followed by Kieron's face.

No, Jon thought. Oh Jesus Christ, no. 'I'm a policeman,' he said, raising himself onto his knees. 'With the – '

'We know what you fucking are,' the leader snarled, still looking at the halfway house.

'He's not part of this,' Jon continued hesitantly, raising his hands. 'For God's sake, he shouldn't even be here.'

The leader glanced to Jon. 'Who is he?'

'Just a sheep farmer. My cousin. Nothing to do with the de Avilas. Or me.'

The man considered Jon's response before turning back to Kieron. 'Stand up.'

Kieron slowly raised himself to his feet. He was breathing so fast he seemed about to choke.

'Cousin, are you?'

Kieron managed a single nod, face a deathly white.

The man took a few steps closer, gun still raised. 'Name?'

'Kieron.'

'Kieron what?'

'Kieron O'Coinne.'

'From?'

'Roundstone.'

'So Kieron O'Coinne from Roundstone, you'll know never to speak of this.'

His lips bobbled for an instant. 'Never.'

'Fuck off out of here.'

With a helpless glance at Jon, Kieron turned round and vanished into the darkness. Moments later they heard a sloshing sound as his footsteps rapidly receded.

The leader lifted a little mouthpiece on the wire hanging down the side of his neck. 'All clear? OK. The noise? A dog. In the back of the van. Open it? You're joking. Thing sounds fucking huge.'

He lowered his weapon and held a hand out to Jon. The tips of his fingers flexed a couple of times. 'On your feet.'

Feeling sick, Jon raised himself up.

'What's in the rucksack?'

Jon realised it was still hanging from his shoulder. 'Erm…hand luggage, for the airport.'

'Passport?'

'Yes.'

The leader turned to the other two men. 'Get rid of him.'

CHAPTER 49

Jon was marched back to the Peugeot and shoved into the front passenger seat. He stared into the blackness beyond the windscreen. They just executed the entire family, he thought. All three. Just bent down and shot them. And the other gunshots. Where were they coming from? Who else is out there? He glanced fearfully in the direction of the rocky outcrop.

The driver's door opened. 'Keys.'

Jon pointed. 'Still in the ignition.'

The man started the engine, palming the wheel as he pulled onto the single-lane road. As they passed between the two formations of rock, the car's headlights picked out a young man perched on a ledge to their left. Balanced across his lap was rifle with an enormous telescopic sight.

The car slowed and the driver partly lowered the window. 'Thought the last one was going to make it to the van there.'

The sniper's voice was calm and businesslike. 'Never.'

The car carried on, dropping down back into the wreaths of mist. A short while later they emerged at the junction with the R341.

Jon saw Sean standing by the side of the road, no sign

of his two companions. The man's face looked strained with nerves. Were you, Jon wondered, part of this? The driver slowed once more and Sean walked round the vehicle.

'It's done,' the man at the wheel stated. 'Wait here until they come back.'

He knew, then, Jon thought. They're all working together.

The driver started forward then touched the brakes once again. 'There's some kind of a dog back there.'

Sean's eyes went to Jon for a second. 'Is it alive?'

'Was when we left.'

'Right.' Sean started towards the car parked on the verge. 'I'll take care of him.'

Within minutes they were on the wider expanse of the N59. A sign stating they were seventy-six kilometres from Galway went past. Is that, Jon thought, where we're going? Nothing was said by either man as they sped through the night.

The dashboard clock read 6.37 when they crossed the River Corrib. An airport sign appeared and the driver took it. Jon didn't stop praying until he could see the bright lights bathing the terminal. They stopped in the drop-off zone and the man in the back got out. The door at Jon's side opened.

They trooped into the terminal building. The TV above the Avis desk was blaring away as the two men studied the departures board. There were only two flights left on it, a 6.55 to Glasgow and a 7.20 to Southampton.

'You're going to Scotland,' the man to his right announced, directing Jon towards the information desk.

Jon fumbled with the zip on his rucksack and took his wallet out. Once the flight was paid for, the woman handed him his tickets, eyes not straying to the pair of men hovering just behind. 'Head straight through,' she said with a rigid smile. 'Boarding's started.'

Jon felt a tug on his sleeve and he started towards the

entrance into the departure lounge. As he approached the gate he saw a thin woman in the seating area of the café talking on a mobile phone. Seeing him, she started getting to her feet, the rims of her eyes looking red and sore.

The barmaid from Darragh's. I wonder where she's going, he thought matter-of-factly before beginning to look away. She's got one of my missing posters for Zoë in her hand. Something in his head clicked. He looked back at her. You're Siobhain.

Phone half-lowered, she was now standing, tears filling her eyes. She mouthed two words. I'm sorry.

Jon felt his pace slow.

She wiped at her eyes. 'I'm so sorry.'

'Siobhain?'

She nodded.

He felt a hand on his shoulder and shrugged it away. 'Two seconds. Two fucking seconds. Please.'

The man who'd driven the Peugeot looked at the departure gate. The security guard stationed there was watching. 'You're on that plane, whatever,' the man murmured.

Jon turned to the girl. 'Where's Zoë? Is she still in Clifden?'

'I knew you'd come. If I called you, I knew you'd come.' Fresh tears started down her cheeks as she raised the ancient-looking mobile. 'She's here.'

Jon looked at her hand. 'What?'

'She's here.' The phone was held out.

Tentatively, Jon took it. 'Hello?'

'Jon, is that you?'

Zoë's voice, Manchester accent unmistakable. 'Where are you?'

'Dingle.' There was alarm and confusion in her voice.

'Dingle?'

'A few hours' south of Clifden.'

'Are you all right?'

'What's going on? Why are you there with Siobhain?

She wasn't making much sense.'

He looked at Siobhain for a moment. I don't understand this. 'Are you safe?'

'Yes, I'm fine...I live with someone now. He treats me well. Jon, is Jake OK?'

'What? Yes.'

'Thank God. I thought maybe that's why you'd come over. Jon, I'm clean. I've not touched drugs for months. I know I've not been there for him, but I feel stronger now. I think, maybe – '

The phone was yanked from his fingers. Jon looked to the side. One of the men was thrusting it back to Siobhain as the Tannoy came to life.

'Final call for flight AR153 to Glasgow. Would all remaining passengers proceed immediately to gate one.'

A hand pushed him. 'On that fucking plane.'

Siobhain's shoulders rose and fell as she swallowed back tears. 'They killed my parents. I used you. I'm so sorry. I used you to get back at them. No one else would help.'

'Who?' Jon asked, as he was shoved toward the gate.

'The de Avilas.'

Jon tried to stop himself from being forced forward again. 'The de Avilas killed your parents?'

'Yes,' she replied, shadowing him on the other side of the partition. 'My name is Siobhain Reilly and the de Avilas killed my mum and dad. Castlebar, 1993.'

At the periphery of his vision, Jon saw the car driver's head turn. 'You're Siobhain Reilly?'

'Yes,' she whispered.

Jon felt the hand gripping his upper arm fall away. The other man had stepped back, too. What's going on here? He looked back at Siobhain. 'Was she...did Zoë ever work at Darragh's?'

'No.' The word caught in her throat. 'It was the only way I could get at the de Avilas. Bernard had tried going to the Guards, the politicians – no one would believe him.

They weren't interested.' Something said on the nearby television caused her to look abruptly up at the screen mounted on the wall. 'See? They killed him. Oh God, they killed Uncle Bernard.'

Jon's eyes lifted. Garda officers and firefighters were gathered on a little high street, hosepipes running through the doorway to their side. The photo of a man was filling the corner of the screen. The tramp from the pony auction. But looking younger and in a suit, tie slightly askew. The reporter was talking about a fire in the offices of a solicitor called Bernard Reilly.

'Final call for flight AR153 to Glasgow. Would passenger Jon Spicer please proceed immediately to gate one.'

'Go,' Siobhain waved a hand, unable to take her eyes from the screen. 'Go home.'

Feeling like someone else was controlling his movements, Jon started towards the entrance into the departure lounge. 'Call the number,' he said over his shoulder, nodding at the poster clutched in her hand. 'Tell whoever answers to get word to my wife. Let her know that I'm all right.' A conveyor belt was in front, a stack of black plastic trays to the side. The de Avilas killed Siobhain's parents. Castlebar. A woman in a white shirt was asking him something as he walked through the archway of the metal detector. Zoë's OK, living somewhere else. She never was at Darragh's. The security guard on the other side was waving him to the right with short, urgent movements of his hand. Glass doors, a woman in day-glo orange tabard signalling to him.

He walked across, mind reeling as the meaning of what Siobhain had said began to stick. It was all a set-up. None of it was true. The woman reached out and plucked the boarding pass from his hand. She tore the stub off and gave it back.

Cold air, damp tarmac underfoot. The metal steps into the plane were steep and he had to clutch the handrail as he hauled himself up. A stewardess was waiting. Her mouth was moving as she nodded to her side, empty seats ahead, row after row. He slumped down and leaned his forehead against the little window.

The men in the Range Rover, their accents were like Sean's, Northern Irish. Retribution, surely. But for what? Something to do with Siobhain's parents' death? They'd stepped back when she'd said her name. The man with the rifle, that was proper military hardware: they had to be IRA. What had Rick said? There was no way they'd ever handed their entire arsenal in. He saw once again the way Gerrard and Darragh had been knocked clean off their feet. A hand touched his shoulder and he had to exaggerate the turn of his head to see her with his good eye.

'Could you fasten your seat belt, sir?'

He realised the plane was already taxiing along the runway. He clicked the belt into place. Seconds later, he was pressed back into his seat as the engines roared. The floor tilted soon afterwards and he felt the plane rising up, his ears creaking and popping. As they gained height he could see more and more dots of light sprinkled across the dark land below. He was reminded of the night sky above Roundstone and then the plane passed into cloud and the view below was gone.

EPILOGUE

Jon ran a finger along the top of his disfigured ear. The ripped tissue had healed well, but the missing part gave his head a slightly unbalanced appearance. He lowered his hand and smoothed down the stray thread sticking up from his threadbare armchair. 'I always said you'd sail those exams. I bloody managed to.'

On the sofa to his side, Rick nodded. 'Yeah, but it still reminds me of being at school. The nerves. I bloody hate them.'

'Nerves?' Jon scoffed. 'You're able to handle a lot worse than exams, mate. So he's OK, is he? Your new partner.'

Rick took a sip from his bottle of lager. 'Yeah. He'll be fine. Keen as mustard to learn.'

'Just like you were when you first joined the MIT.'

Smiling, Rick swilled the liquid in the bottle round. 'Suppose I was.'

'But now you're a DI...' Jon took a swig from his own drink. 'Old hand that you are.'

Rick glanced across. 'So what about you? Will you take it?'

Jon thought about the last three months. Once he'd got

back from Ireland, he'd been summoned to Longsight station and told by Gower he was out of the MIT: permanently. The Chief Super had seemed a touch sad explaining that he'd simply run out of DCIs willing to have Jon in their syndicate.

He'd also stated that Jon was suspended while the powers-that-be debated exactly what to do with him.

Then, a few weeks ago, came the call from a senior officer in Manchester's Counter-Terrorism Unit.

Word had spread to it of Jon's exploits in Connemara; how he'd pursued the de Avilas with a relentless determination. The ear-ripping story, and how Jon had managed to drive himself away from it, had already become a favourite tale. The senior officer who'd rung was aware Jon was suspended from duty. He wanted to let Jon know the Unit were about to start recruiting officers. If Jon were to apply, he hinted, a position would be his.

'Not sure,' Jon shrugged, looking at Rick. 'It's an odd one. There'll be all the training to get through, for a start. Tests.'

Rick mimicked Jon's gruff tones. 'You're able to handle a lot worse than tests, mate.'

Jon suppressed a grin before holding his bottle up in salute. 'Got me. Their command structures aren't the same as in the MIT, either. Often, there's no set working day. You get a call about an operation and you're off.' He raised his eyes to the ceiling. 'Anyway, it's not just down to me, is it?'

Muffled footsteps moved around above them.

A shrill bark came from outside. Jon glanced out at the backyard. Holly was with Zak, both of them giggling as the Boxer puppy bounded after a tennis ball, all gangly legs and clumsy paws. Still can't get used to the long tail, he thought, thinking how Punch's had been docked at birth.

When the vet, Valerie Ackford, had rung, Jon didn't think her proposal was a good idea. But Alice had asked that he consider it for a day or two before deciding. In that time she'd slowly persuaded him to at least visit the house where the owner of the donor dogs who'd provided Punch's blood transfusion lived. Her third Boxer, Bertha, had given birth to a litter of five pups. Four had been taken, but – she'd wondered – did the owner of Punch want the last one? A little female with a chestnut coat and white bib. Jon knew, as he'd set off for the lady's house, that he wouldn't be returning home empty-handed. And sure enough he'd come back with the small dog.

Holly had wanted to call her Punch, but Jon had gently encouraged his daughter to try and think of another name. Maybe Judy? She'd asked why the puppy had a long tail, whereas Punch didn't. Jon explained that it was now considered cruel – and against the law – to snip them down to a little stump.

She'd played with the young dog for a while before looking up at Jon and saying, 'Wiper.'

'Sorry, sweetie,' he'd replied. 'Say that again?'

'Wiper.'

'Wiper?' He'd frowned. 'You want to call it Wiper. Why?'

She'd pointed to its spindly tail sweeping from side to side. 'Because that's what it looks like.'

Jon nodded as his mind went back to the handful of days he'd been permitted to remain in Longsight station. The report about what had taken place in Connemara had taken him two entire days to complete. But Jon knew perfectly well, even before he'd handed it in, there'd be no follow-up.

While he'd been compiling it, internet searches he'd been making on Irish news sites had revealed that the de Avilas were believed to have fled abroad to avoid the attention of a major investigation by the Criminal Assets Bureau into their business empire. Since then, the investigation had unearthed a sprawling network of properties and other assets: funded, it was believed, by tax evasion, intimidation and bribery. In addition, Devlan de

Avila was a suspect in the murder of a solicitor called Bernard Reilly. Motive remained unknown.

There had been no mention of the bog road. Jon found that he now couldn't think of that silent collection of lakes without seeing the de Avila family entombed in black mud, a layer of cold, dark water pressing down upon their corpses.

Four days after his plane had landed in Scotland, the Police Service of Northern Ireland had announced that the killer of the British soldier had been helped into the foyer of a station in Lurgan, County Armagh, where he'd confessed to the crime. His name was Kevin Mulgrew. In July 2000, under the terms of the Good Friday Agreement, he'd been released fourteen years early from the Maze prison, originally locked up for his part in planting a bomb that had gone off on the Shankill Road, killing seven people. The man had insisted that, although a member of the IRA when he'd helped plant the bomb, he'd defected since his release to the Continuity IRA – though that organisation flatly denied it. Following his arrest, the furore at Stormont had gradually died down.

The puppy barked again. 'So, I bet the guy in Spain was pleased about getting his dog back,' Rick said.

'Yeah – I gather it's rounding up cattle again where it should be – hundreds of bloody miles away.'

'Feel sorry for the poor cows.' Rick lowered his voice. 'Still reckon that head case was going to set the thing on you?'

Jon gave a single nod. 'The more I think about it, the surer I am. They really meant to kill me.' He looked at his old work colleague for a second before breaking eye contact by sipping at his beer.

'I can't believe they took out that man on the IRA's council – if they ever did.'

'Come on,' Jon protested. 'It all fits – the names in the file that solicitor handed me, the fact they bought the pet-food factory he owned. Those blokes who showed up on that bog road, they were IRA. Had to be. Your mate in the NCA is bang on with his theory.'

'Well,' Rick whispered. 'I'm so glad the de Avilas chose to become tax exiles.' He flashed Jon a loaded look.

'You know what? I never read the rest of that document – the account of the ancestor who was shipwrecked.' Jon took another sip. 'What happened?'

'That chieftain O'Rourke? He was eventually captured in a skirmish with the Governor's forces. Taken to London and hanged for offering succour to survivors of the Armada.'

'Where was his castle?'

'Possibly County Leitrim, though no one's really sure.'

'Francisco de Avila?'

'Headed back to Carna with the remains of O'Rourke's private army. Saw off a much-weakened force of O'Flahertys and carved out his own little domain.'

'Which the family held on to ever since,' Jon replied.

'Yup. Four hundred-odd years. Quite a little dynasty.'

'The dog, Pio?'

'Buried near Carna. No one's sure where; there are so many tombs and burial stones dotted about.'

The sheer rawness of the region hit Jon once more – its stormy weather and hostile terrain. As a small tremor gripped his shoulders the phone began to ring. He grabbed it and looked at the screen. 'This might be Eileen. She said she'd try and ring before lunch. Hello?'

'Jon, it's your Aunty Eileen!'

'Hi there, Eileen. How's it all going?'

'Grand, just grand. We're all a little tired – away to our beds late again last night. A lot of catching up, as you can imagine.'

'How're Malachy and Kieron?'

'They're both fine. Kieron took your father to a Gaelic football match yesterday in Clifden.'

My father, Jon thought. He realised how easily the term sat with him. And so it should do, he scolded himself –

that's exactly what he is.

'He loved it,' Eileen continued. 'Said he wished he'd played it, and not rugby league, in his youth.'

Really? Jon thought. He must have been impressed. 'And Mum?'

'She's sitting out in the porch with Malachy. It's so nice to see them together again. They took Jake out to Gorteen earlier and put flowers on Orla's grave.'

An image of the little cemetery overlooking the beautiful bay pinged up in Jon's head. I can't wait to go back one day, he thought. See Holly's face when she spots that expanse of white sand.

'And, of course, Malachy has his view,' she added.

'All the building work has stopped, then?' Jon asked, picturing the site on the other side of the little road.

'Not just stopped. They've looked at planning permission for all manner of their properties. A few in the local government have lost their jobs – that Convila company should never have been granted permission to start building them.'

Jon smiled. 'That's great news. Did you manage to find out anything more about the girl – Siobhain?'

'Kieron's been asking for you. That poor uncle left her some money, along with a house. We're not sure where she is, though the property is now up for sale.'

Off the radar, Jon thought. Or somewhere in Dingle, with Zoë. The words Zoë had spoken over Siobhain's phone when he was in the airport came back. Something about being clean, feeling sorted, ready to…what? Come for Jake? The phone had been snatched from his grasp before she could finish the sentence.

Movement in the doorway caused Jon to turn his head. He felt a smile appearing; Alice was standing there, a little lump in the crook of her arm.

'Here he is, all clean and fed.'

He gazed at his wife's face, the clean glow of her skin.

Rick sprang to his feet. 'I'll have a cuddle.'

She handed the infant over, catching Jon's eye. 'Is that Eileen?' she whispered.

He nodded as Rick held the baby up. 'Hello, little Doug. You're going to be a bruiser, aren't you? Just like your daddy.'

'Eileen? I'd better go,' said Jon. 'Maybe call you tomorrow?'

'Please do – and visit soon, won't you?'

'We will,' Jon replied, memories of Connemara's savage beauty sweeping through his mind.

THE END

ACKNOWLEDGEMENTS

As usual, the expertise of others played a vital part in writing this book.

All my thanks to –

Nicola Crooks, RVN, for her insights into treating dogs.

Mike Butcher, RSPCA, for his insights into fighting with dogs.

An anonymous ex-member of SOCA, for his insights into all sorts of murky stuff.

PECKING ORDER

Rubble lives alone in a caravan and works on a battery farm. There, he spends his days disposing of sick and injured chickens. But all the while, he dreams of another life. A life of adventure in the army.

One day, a mysterious visitor arrives and witnesses the child-like relish Rubble takes in killing. Soon, Rubble is employed on a secret – and very sinister – project.

But Rubble is being cruelly used. And the only way he'll realise it is with the help of the only person he confides in: a fortune-teller working on a premium-rate telephone line.

In this chilling thriller, one thing quickly becomes clear. Life can be brutal.

PECKING ORDER - CHAPTER 1

With a sound of two twigs snapping, the chicken's legs broke in his hand. The bird transformed from a hanging bundle of limp feathers to a screeching mess and his fingers instantly uncurled. It dropped fifteen feet to the sand-covered ground where it began flapping round in tight circles like a clockwork toy gone wrong.

'Grab them when I lift them upwards!' shouted the man in shit-splattered overalls, standing on a narrow ledge on the lorry's side. 'If you don't,' he carried on with a note of triumph, 'they swing back and that happens.' He nodded towards the ground but his eyes remained locked on the younger worker.

'Yeah, sorry,' the teenager replied, disgustedly peeling silver scales of chicken skin from the palms of his hands.

Despite his heavy build, the man clambered nimbly along the stack of cages welded to the lorry's rear until he was directly above the stricken bird. With its ruined legs splayed uselessly off to one side, it continued its futile revolutions, the repeated cries from its open beak merging into something that resembled a scream.

He dropped from the side of the vehicle and landed with both boots on the bird's outstretched head and neck.

SLEEPING DOGS

A thick squirt of blood shot out from under one heel and all movement immediately stopped. The only thing to disturb the silence that followed was a pigeon cooing gently from amongst a copse of beech trees nearby. The man stepped back, revealing a pulp of bone mashed into the loose sand. Then, relishing the appalled attention of the audience watching from the shed above, he swung back a stubby leg and booted the carcass high into the air. A handful of reddish coloured feathers detached themselves, one catching in the current of air blowing from the extractor fan mounted on the shed's side. The feather tumbled away, up into the clear blue sky.

With arms that seemed a little too long for his body, he climbed back up the wall of cages, each one bristling with beady eyes, jagged beaks and shivering combs.

'It's simple - keep them hanging upside down and they don't move,' said the man, reaching into another cage and dragging two squawking birds out by the legs. Once their heads were hanging downwards in the open air they immediately went still and he lifted their passive forms to the open door. This time the youth successfully grabbed the legs, and before they could start swinging back, he whipped them inside the shed.

'You'll be doing four in each hand by lunch - now out the way,' said the man perched on the lorry's ledge, another brace of birds already dangling from his arm. Though no one said anything, something about the over-enthusiastic way the older man gave out directions reminded everyone of the playground: a schoolboy, prematurely invested with authority by his teacher.

The youth got off his knees and, with a bird in each hand, turned round. Immediately in front of him inside the shed was a tier of empty cages, six high. It stretched away in both directions, the dimness inside making it impossible to see right to either end. The walkway he was standing on was made of rippled concrete and barely wider than his shoulders.

Coating it was a mishmash of shell fragments, feathers and dried yolk. He had to struggle round the person next to him, banging one of the chickens against the wall. Once past, he set off into the shed's depths.

Away from the fresh air at the open door the temperature suddenly picked up and the sharp smell of ammonia dramatically increased. His way was lit by a string of naked bulbs dangling at ten metre intervals from a black cable running just above his head. A thick sandy coloured dust clung to everything. Even the top of the cable was covered in it like powdery snow on a telephone line. The bulbs themselves were almost completely obscured - only the bottom third of each was exposed, and the yellowish light they gave out made him squint. In the gloom above, the residue had formed into web-like loops, which curled from the roof, the occasional strand brushing the top of his head. It seemed like a living thing, a kind of airborne mould that made the very air thick and heavy. He imagined that, if he stood still long enough, the spores would settle on him, and eventually he too would become wrapped in its cloying shroud.

To his right the small conveyor belts running along in front of each cage clanked and whined, the moving surface transporting pellets to scores of cages that would soon be stuffed full of birds. Set into the ceiling above him was the occasional fan, blades lazily revolving. Their motion served only to circulate the warm air, carrying the dust into every crevice and onto every available surface.

He walked to the first gap in the steep row of cages, turned right and then immediately left into one of the central aisles. In the gloom ahead of him a dark form crouched. As he walked up to the person he had to step over a lump on the ground. Looking down he saw the tips of feathers and was shocked to realise it was a dead bird. From the layer of powder almost engulfing it he guessed it had been lying there for quite some time. Now in front of the person, he held the two birds out.

'Cheers,' said the woman emotionlessly, taking them from him and shoving them upside down into the open doorway of the nearest cage. The birds began clucking in protest, and one started flapping its wings. 'Get in,' she said aggressively through clenched teeth, forcing them forward with the flat of her hand. Inside what was little more than a hamster's cage, two other birds were already jostling for a firm footing on the wire mesh floor. He watched as one wing fluttered at the side of the door. With a final shove she got them inside, breaking several feathers in the process.

Swinging the wire door shut she announced, 'Home sweet home.'

PECKING ORDER - CHAPTER 2

Out in the bright sunlight the rust-coloured feather rose upward through the air, carried on the light breeze blowing between the two elongated buildings. It drifted along for a while and then gradually began to lose height. Finally it settled on the ground, just in front of a weathered pair of brogues. The leather creaked slightly and a thin, angular hand picked it up.

'Who,' said the man, gently rolling the shaft of the feather between a skeletal finger and thumb, 'is the man giving instructions?'

'That's Rubble,' replied the farm owner. 'I don't need guard dogs or anything with Rubble living here. He's my walking, talking Rottweiler.' He spoke a little too fast, trying to impress.

'Where did he get a name like that?' Other hand running through a wiry beard that was shot through with flecks of grey.

'Oh, it's short for Roy Bull. Rubble just seems to fit him better somehow.'

'And he lives here, on the farm?'

'Yeah, in a caravan at the bottom of the lane down there.' He pointed to the copse of beech trees, where an occasional glimpse of white showed between the gently shifting leaves. 'He's just a child really - in terms of IQ. But he certainly likes killing things - chickens, foxes, rats, mink. Even cats, some villagers believe. And if I hadn't pulled him off the animal liberation woman last year, he'd have probably done her too.'

Made in the USA
Charleston, SC
30 November 2014